Sharon Kendrick once won a national writing competition by describing her ideal date: being flown to an exotic island by a gorgeous and powerful man. Little did she realise that she'd just wandered into her dream job! Today she writes for Mills & Boon, featuring often stubborn but always *to die for* heroes and the women who bring them to their knees. She believes that the best books are those you never want to end. Just like life…

Melanie Milburne read her first Mills & Boon novel at the age of seventeen, in between studies for her final exams. After completing a master's degree in education she decided to write a novel, and thus her career as a romance author was born. Melanie is an ambassador for the Australian Childhood Foundation and a keen dog-lover and trainer. She enjoys long walks in the Tasmanian bush. In 2015 Melanie won the Holt Medallion—a prestigious award honouring outstanding literary talent.

D1347736

CROWNED FOR THE SHEIKH'S BABY

SHARON KENDRICK

TYCOON'S FORBIDDEN CINDERELLA

MELANIE MILBURNE

MILLS & BOON

First Published in Great Britain 2018
by Mills & Boon, an imprint of HarperCollins*Publishers*
1 London Bridge Street, London, SE1 9GF

Crowned for the Sheikh's Baby © 2018 by Sharon Kendrick

Tycoon's Forbidden Cinderella © 2018 by Melanie Milburne

ISBN: 978-0-263-93538-7

MIX
Paper from
responsible sources
FSC® C007454

This book is produced from independently certified FSC™ paper
to ensure responsible forest management.
For more information visit www.harpercollins.co.uk/green.

Printed and bound in Spain
by CPI, Barcelona

CROWNED FOR THE SHEIKH'S BABY

SHARON KENDRICK

This book is dedicated to the urbane
and dashingly handsome Matt Newman,
with thanks and gratitude for his generous donation
to the amazing charity The Back-Up Trust.

PROLOGUE

We trust you will find everything to your satisfaction.

KULAL'S MOUTH HARDENED into a cynical smile. As if. When did anything in life ever *truly* satisfy?

Crushing the handwritten note—one of the many personal touches which made this Sardinian hotel complex so achingly luxurious—he threw it into the bin in a perfect arcing shot and walked over to the balcony.

Restlessly, his eyes skated over the horizon. He wondered why he could feel no joy in his heart or why the warmth of the sun left him feeling cold. He had just achieved a life's ambition by bringing together some of the world's biggest oil moguls. They'd told him it was impossible. That masterminding the diaries of so many powerful men simply couldn't be done. But Kulal had proved them wrong. He liked proving people wrong, just as he enjoyed defying the expectations which had been heaped on him since the day his older brother had turned his back on his heritage and left him to rule.

He had worked day and night to make this conference happen. To convince attendees with his famously seductive tongue that it was time to look at renewable energy sources, rather than relying on the fossil fuels of old. Kings and sheikhs had agreed with him and pledges had been made. The cheers following his opening speech had echoed long into the night. There were now but a few days left for him to hammer out the fine details of the deal—and he was able to do it in a place which many people considered close to paradise. Yet he felt...

He gave a heavy sigh which mingled with the warm Sardinian breeze.

Certainly not drunk with glory, as other men in his position might be, and he couldn't work out why. At thirty-four, he was considered by many to be at his intellectual and physical peak. He was known as a fair, if sometimes autocratic ruler and he ruled a prosperous land. And yes, he had a few enemies at court—men who would have preferred his twin brother to have been King because they considered him more malleable. But all rulers had to deal with insurrection. It came with the job—it was certainly nothing *new*.

So why wasn't he punching the air with glee? Kulal contemplated the horizon without really seeing it. Perhaps he had been working so hard that he'd neglected the more basic needs of his body. Not to put too fine a point on it—his legendary libido, which had been sidelined ever since he had finished with his long-term mistress a few months back. It didn't help that she had made the break-up official with a tearful interview in one of those glossy magazines that filled women's heads with meaningless froth. And that as a consequence, his name had zoomed back to the top of one of those tedious 'most eligible' lists—and he now seemed to be on some kind of matrimonial hit list. Rather ironic since he had always avoided marriage like the plague, no matter how determined the woman.

He yawned. His relationship with the international supermodel had lasted almost a year—a record for him. He had chosen her not just because she was blonde and leggy and could work wonders with her tongue, but because she seemed to accept what he would and wouldn't tolerate in a relationship. But in the end, she had sabotaged it with her neediness. He'd stated at the start that he wouldn't put a ring on her finger. That he had no desire for family or long-term commitment. Because didn't domesticity forge cold chains, which could suffocate? He had promised sex, diamonds and a fancy apartment—and had honoured those pledges in full. But she had wanted more. Women always did. They wanted to bleed you dry until there was nothing left.

Dark and bitter memories washed over him, but he forced himself to block them out as he leaned against the rail of the balcony, looking out at boats bobbing around on the Mediterranean. He thought how different this busy stretch of water was from the peace of the Murjaan Sea, which lapped on the eastern shores of his desert homeland. But then, everything about this place was different. The sights. The scents. The sounds. The women who lay on sun-loungers in their minuscule bikinis. One of his aides had told him that the loungers directly beneath his penthouse suite were always the first to go—presumably occupied by those hoping to catch the eye of Zahristan's Desert King. Kulal's lips curved in disdain. Did they, like so many others, imagine themselves in the role of Queen? That they would succeed where so many had failed?

Surveying the women directly beneath him, he felt

not a flicker of excitement as he glanced at their half-naked bodies, which glistened in the sun. He thought they looked like oiled pieces of chicken about to be thrown onto the barbecue, their half-open mouths thick with lipstick and tilted straw hats protecting their hair extensions.

And then he saw her.

Kulal tensed, his eyes narrowing and his heart beginning to pound.

Did she capture his focus and keep it captured because she was wearing more than anyone else, as she hurried across the terrace with an anxious look on her face? In fact, she was wearing the standard hotel uniform—a plain yellow dress, which was straining over her voluminous breasts and clinging to the swell of her curvy buttocks. He though how *fresh* she looked with that shiny ponytail swishing against her back as she walked. Certainly, when contrasted with all the flesh on show, the brunette seemed positively *wholesome* and, although such women were rare in Kulal's world, he reminded himself that she was a member of the hotel staff. And sleeping with staff was never a good idea.

But a small sigh escaped his lips as he turned away. Pity.

CHAPTER ONE

'HANNAH, DO NOT look so nervous. I merely said I wished to speak to you about the Sheikh.'

Hannah tried to smile as she looked up at Madame Martin—fixing her face into the kind of expression which would be expected of a highly experienced chambermaid. She must look eager—and at all times, because this job was the opportunity of a lifetime and breaks like this didn't come along very often. Wasn't it true that every other chambermaid at the Granchester in London had been green with envy when Hannah had been picked to work in the fancy Sardinian branch of the hotel group because they were short-staffed? She suspected they would have been even more envious if they'd realised that Sheikh Kulal Al Diya was a guest here—a billionaire desert king who everyone on this Mediterranean island seemed to think was some kind of walking sex god.

But not her.

No, definitely not her. She'd only seen him a couple of times, but each time he'd terrified her with all that dark brooding stuff going on and that way he had of slanting his black eyes in a way which had made her feel most peculiar. Hadn't her breasts sprung into alarming life the first time she'd seen him, causing her nipples to feel as if they were about to burst right through her bra? And hadn't she wanted to squirm with a strange and unfamiliar hunger as that ebony gaze had swept over her? For once, she hadn't felt in control and that had made her feel extremely uncomfortable, because Hannah liked to feel in control.

She brushed her clammy palms down over her lemon-coloured uniform—a bad idea since it drew the attention of Madame Martin to her hips and instantly the Frenchwoman frowned.

'Tiens!' she exclaimed. 'Your dress is a little tight, *n'est ce pas*?'

'It's the only one they had which fitted, Madame Martin,' said Hannah apologetically.

The elegant woman who was in charge of all the domestic staff at Hotel L'Idylle raised her perfectly plucked eyebrows. *'C'est vrai.'* She gave a resigned sigh. 'You Englishwomen are... 'Ow you say? Big girls!'

Hannah's smile didn't slip because who was she to deny the truth behind Madame Martin's words? She certainly wasn't as slim as her continental peers. She liked her food, had a healthy appetite and wasn't going to make any apology for it. Like much else, mealtimes had been unpredictable when she'd been growing up and you never forgot something like that. She'd never forget the dull gnaw of hunger, or how eagerly she'd seized on any scraps she'd managed to salvage to put together something resembling a meal. She didn't spend her life picking at her food, that was for sure—unlike her sister, who seemed to think that eating was an un-necessary waste of time.

But she wasn't going to worry about her sister, or

dwell on the troubled times of their growing-up years. Hadn't that been one of the reasons for leaping on this job so eagerly—even though she'd never even been out of England before? She had decided she was going to start living her life differently from now on and the first part of that plan was to stop worrying about her baby sister. Because Tamsyn wasn't a baby any more; she was only two years younger and perfectly able to stand on her own two feet—except that was never going to happen if Hannah kept bailing her out every time she got herself into trouble.

So think about yourself for once, she reminded herself—and concentrate on the unbelievable bonus you've been offered for a few months of working in this Sardinian paradise.

'What exactly did you wish to talk to me about, Madame Martin?' she enquired eagerly.

The Frenchwoman smiled. 'You are very good at your job, Hannah. It is why you were sent here by our London branch, but I have observed you myself and thoroughly approve of their choice. The way you fold a bedsheet is a joy to watch.'

Hannah inclined her head to accept the compliment. 'Thank you.'

'You are quiet and unobtrusive. You move *comme une souris*—like a mouse,' Madame Martin translated in reply to Hannah's confused look. 'Put it this way—nobody would ever notice you in a room.'

'Thank you,' said Hannah again, rather more cautiously this time because she wasn't sure if that really sounded like a compliment.

'Which is why the management have decided to give you some extra responsibility.'

Hannah nodded, because this was something she was good at. Throw responsibility at her and she would soak it up like a sponge with water. 'Yes, *madame*?' she said and waited.

'What do you know about Sheikh Kulal Al Diya?'

Hannah tried to smile, but it was difficult when an unwanted shiver was rippling its way down her spine. 'He is the ruler of Zahristan, one of the biggest oil-producing countries in the world, but he's a leading exponent of alternative energy. All the staff were briefed about him before he arrived,' she added hastily, in response to Madame Martin's look of surprise.

'*Bien,*' said the Frenchwoman approvingly. 'It was he who organised this international meeting, which has brought so many prestigious leaders to the hotel and has done much to elevate the profile of our new conference centre.'

'Yes, Madame Martin,' said Hannah, still not quite sure where this was heading.

'And you are perhaps aware that many people have been trying to seek out the Sheikh's company,' said Madame Martin slowly. 'Since he is a man of great influence.'

'I'm sure they do.' Hannah noted the pause which followed and which she somehow got the idea she was expected to fill. 'It was exactly the same in the London branch of the Granchester—the more powerful the guest, the more people want to get to know them.'

'Especially if the man happens to be newly single and extremely good-looking,' said Madame Martin, with a busy wiggle of her manicured fingers. 'But His Royal Highness has no wish to be the focus of the attentions which someone in his position always attracts.

It is why he occasionally chooses to travel with only a very modest entourage, but unfortunately that only makes him more accessible to the general public. Why, only last night, a well-known heiress managed to bribe her way past security and make her way to his table.'

Hannah winced. 'Was there a scene, *madame*?'

'I'm afraid there was, and we do not tolerate "scenes" here at L'Idylle. Which is why, for the remainder of his stay, Sheikh Al Diya intends to finish the rest of his business in the sanctuary of his suite, which is certainly big enough to accommodate his needs.' There was a pause. 'And why you are being assigned to work exclusively for him.'

Hannah screwed up her face in confusion. 'You mean, I'm to make his bed and change his towels?'

'Of course. But you will also serve His Royal Highness any meals he orders and make sure there are drinks and snacks for his guests. Keep the water in the flowers topped up. Tidy up after him and make sure that nobody unauthorised tries to gain entry to his rooms. Security here is tight, but there is no such thing as completely reliable security. Why, even in your famous Buckingham Palace, intruders have successfully gained access, is that not so?' The Frenchwoman's face grew stern. 'Do you think you are capable of what I am asking of you, Hannah?'

Hannah's first instinct was to say no. To protest that she was a chambermaid and nothing more. Someone who silently serviced the hotel bedrooms and learnt more about the guests than they would probably be comfortable with, if they only realised how many clues about themselves they left laying around the place. She wasn't really confident enough to wait on a desert king, or to swish around topping up the water in expensive vases of flowers. She wasn't really a *maid*.

'Isn't there someone else who would rather do it, Madame Martin?' she questioned doubtfully. 'Someone with a bit more experience of that kind of thing?'

'Indeed there is.' Madame Martin pursed her lips. 'I am sure I could have the female staff queuing from here to our capital city of Cagliari, but none of them have your characteristics, Hannah. You are a young woman whose head is planted firmly on her shoulders, as you English say. You will not be seduced by a pair of flashing black eyes and a body which makes grown women shiver.' Madame Martin seemed suddenly to realise what she was saying, and as she pulled herself together, she fixed Hannah with another stern look. 'Can I rely on you to accept this task, so that I can report back favourably to your superiors in London?'

Hannah swallowed as she recognised it was going to be impossible to refuse—and why would anyone in their right mind want to? Surely a temporary promotion was a good thing. A chance to get the pay-rise she'd been hoping for. A pay-rise which might make it possible for her to one day buy a tiny place of her own.

A home of her own.

The chance to put down roots at last.

'Will you do that, my dear?' prompted the Frenchwoman kindly.

Hannah swallowed down the sudden lump which seemed to be clogging up her throat, wondering why she still reacted so stupidly to someone speaking to her with affection.

Because she wasn't used to it?

Or because she mistrusted it?

Nodding her head, she produced a tentative smile. 'I would be honoured, Madame Martin,' she said.

'Bien.' Madame Martin gave a brisk nod. 'Then come with me and I will show you around the suite of His Royal Highness.'

Hannah followed her superior along wide and airy corridors, which overlooked the small, natural harbour outside. Purple bougainvillea rippled softly in the breeze and the sky was the bluest she had ever seen. Every day was the same—picture-book perfect. Or at least, that was how it seemed. It hadn't rained in paradise for as long as she'd been there and sometimes she could hardly believe she was.

Who would have thought it? Humble Hannah Wilson experiencing life in one of the fanciest resorts in Europe. The rootless orphan who'd never really known anything except making do was now working in a hotel which redefined the word luxury. A place which regularly entertained princes and tycoons, heiresses and film stars. And now a sheikh.

A sheikh for whom she was to work exclusively!

'You must continue to be unobtrusive,' Madame Martin was saying. 'When the Sheikh arrives in his suite, you will quietly enquire what he requires and make sure he gets it. Immediately.'

'And if he doesn't actually want...*anything*?' Hannah questioned cautiously.

'Then you will vacate the premises as quickly as possible and await further instruction. You are being moved to a small staff room just along the corridor from his suite. Can I rely on you, Hannah?'

Hannah nodded in agreement because what else could she do? 'Yes, Madame Martin.'

'One last thing.' The Frenchwoman's voice lowered into a conspiratorial whisper. 'The Sheikh is known as a man of great, shall we say—*appetite.*'

'You mean he likes his food?' questioned Hannah cautiously.

'No, I do not mean that.' An impatient shake of her head barely displaced an immaculate strand of Madame Martin's hair. 'I mean that he may have female guests visiting him and, should you find yourself dealing with them, you will treat them as if they were princesses. Which is probably their ambition,' she finished, with a dry laugh. 'Is that clear, Hannah?'

'Yes, *madame,*' answered Hannah as they entered the elevator, slotting in the special card which gave access to the exclusive penthouse suite, a journey which took mere seconds before the doors slid open. Hannah saw two bulky men in dark suits standing poker-faced on either side of a large door and she blinked. Could those bulges she could see in their pockets possibly be *guns*? She guessed they could. Of *course* the Sheikh would have bodyguards who looked as if they were made of steel and iron, rather than flesh and blood. Whose eyes didn't even flicker as she stared up at them. A sudden realisation of what she had let herself in for made her spine tingle with apprehension.

'*Voilà!* We are here,' said Madame Martin. 'Come.'

After a cursory knock, which went unanswered, the door was unlocked and Madame Martin walked straight in. Hannah thought she was prepared for any eventuality...for dancing girls, or some kind of harem. Or maybe a smoke-filled room where some kind of high-stakes card game was taking place.

What she had not been prepared for was the sight

which greeted her—of the Sheikh himself. Her eyes nearly bulged out of their sockets and her throat dried to dust. After the kind of build-up she'd been given, Hannah wouldn't have been surprised to see him lying half-naked on one of the sumptuous velvet sofas, while some gorgeous nubile woman administered to him with warm oils. Or wearing something lavish and ceremonial—golden robes, perhaps—which swished as he walked.

In fact, he was seated at a desk which overlooked one of the resort's many swimming pools and there wasn't a golden robe in sight. He was wearing dark trousers and a blue shirt so pale that it was almost white. The shirt had two top buttons undone and the sleeves had been rolled up to reveal his hair-darkened forearms. Hannah noted these things almost automatically—perhaps as a kind of defensive mechanism. As if labelling the most commonplace things about him could protect her from the impact his sudden searing black gaze was having on her.

Because there was nothing commonplace about his face. It was a face in a million, no question about that. An unforgettable face—with those imperiously high cheekbones and his hair which gleamed like sunlit tar. The olive skin of his hawk-like features glowed with health and vitality, and there was an unmistakably arrogant tilt to his proud jaw. But it was the eyes which did it. She'd seen them from a distance, but up close they were unsettling. More than unsettling. Hannah swallowed. Hard and unflickering and blacker than any eyes had the right to be. And they were staring at her. Staring as if she had some smut on her nose, or the dark stain of sweat at her armpits. Hannah shifted uncomfortably beneath the intensity of that gaze, her hands nervously fluttering to brush away imagined dust from her slightly too small dress until she remembered that she wasn't supposed to be drawing attention to her hips like that.

'I am extremely sorry to disturb you, Sheikh Al Diya,' Madame Martin was saying smoothly. 'But since no one answered my knock, I assumed nobody was here.'

'I did not hear you knock otherwise I should have sent you away,' said the Sheikh, an impatient wave of his hand indicating the mountain of paperwork piled in front of him. 'As you see, I am busy.'

'Of course, Your Royal Highness. Perhaps you would prefer us to come back at a more suitable time?'

Kulal put his pen down and studied the two women who were standing before him—the too thin French matron and the curvy chambermaid he'd seen hurrying across the patio a couple of days earlier, with an anxious look on her face. What he would *prefer* was not to have been interrupted in the first place because he was at a very delicate stage of negotiation. But suddenly, the ever-engrossing topic of solar power melted away as he stared at the ponytailed brunette whose fingers were smoothing down her unsightly uniform dress.

Was that an unconscious gesture to draw his attention to the fecundity of her hips and breasts? he wondered. Or was it deliberate? Either way, she had hit the jackpot. No doubt she was aware that her ripe body was designed to send his hormones shooting into disarray and, inconveniently, they were doing just that. He felt his groin tightening as he imagined his tongue trailing a slow path over those magnificent breasts, and for a moment, he cursed the insidious power of Mother Nature— for were they not all puppets in her need to continue the human race? And *that* was the reason behind his instinct to get the chambermaid horizontal as quickly as possible, before impaling her with his hardness.

He expected her to meet his gaze with a knowing look of challenge, for he had never met a woman who wouldn't put out for him within the first minutes of meeting. But the humble chambermaid had dropped her gaze to the ground, her cheeks blooming like roses as she studied the Persian rug at her feet with a fierce intensity.

Unusual, conceded Kulal as he leaned back in his chair. Very unusual. 'Now that you have managed to successfully interrupt my train of thought,' he said acidly, 'you might as well tell me why you are here.'

'I was showing Hannah around your suite, Your Royal Highness.'

Hannah. Kulal ran a slow finger around the circumference of his mouth. An ordinary name yet somehow it pleased him.

'Because?' he interrogated.

'In view of the enormous interest your presence has generated, and after the unfortunate scene in the main restaurant last night, we decided it would be preferable for you to have your own private maid for the duration of your stay,' said Madame Martin. 'Especially since His Royal Highness has brought with him only a skeleton staff.'

'Because I have no wish to burden myself with the cumbersome accruements of the royal court!' snapped Kulal. 'You try travelling with an entourage of a thousand and five hundred tons of luggage, like some of my desert neighbours! If I fill the entire hotel complex with my staff, then how the hell is there going to be room for anyone else?'

'Quite so. And I can only imagine your aversion to such a logistical nightmare, Your Royal Highness,' replied Madame Martin diplomatically. 'Which is why one of your aides made the request earlier and why we are assigning you Hannah, who from now on will be exclusively under your command.'

This was language Kulal was used to.

Command.

Exclusivity.

Words of possession and control, which went hand in hand with being a sheikh. But somehow the words had taken on an unexpectedly erotic flavour when applied to the curvy little servant who stood in front of him. He felt his heart miss a beat as he looked at her still-bent head, the straightness of her parting cutting a stark white line through her shiny brown hair. But her shoulders were stiff and if her body language was anything to go by, she certainly wasn't as honoured by her sudden promotion as perhaps she should have been. And despite the knowledge that fraternising with the staff was a very bad idea, Kulal couldn't deny that he found such an unusual response curiously *exciting*.

'So how do you feel about working for me, Hannah?' he questioned softly.

She looked up then and he was surprised by eyes of a startling hue—blue eyes which resembled the colour of the aquamarines his mother used to wear around her throat. Expensive jewels bought by his father in an attempt to compensate for his frequent absences. As if pieces of glass could ever compensate. But his mother had been weak. Weak and manipulative. Prepared to put her own desperate needs above those of her children. Kulal's mouth hardened as he obliterated the harsh memories and listened to the chambermaid's response.

'I am happy to serve you in any way I can, Your Royal Highness,' she said.

She delivered the words as if she had been coached and maybe she had, for they were dutiful rather than meaningful. A rare flicker of humour lifted Kulal's lips, but it was gone as quickly as it had arrived. He gave a dismissive nod and picked up his pen. 'Very well,' he said as he pulled one of the documents towards him. 'Just make sure you don't disturb me. Not in any way. Do you understand?'

'Yes, Your Royal Highness,' she said, still in that same dutiful voice, and Kulal found himself almost disappointed when she bobbed a clumsy kind of curtsey before backing out of the room as if she couldn't wait to get away from him.

CHAPTER TWO

DON'T DISTURB ME. That had been the Sheikh's only instruction when she'd first started working for him, but Hannah wondered how the powerful Kulal Al Diya would react if he knew how much he was disturbing *her*.

She wished he wouldn't look at her that way.

She wished he wouldn't make her *feel* this way.

Or was it all a figment of her imagination? Was his searing ebony gaze *really* lingering on her for longer than was necessary, or was that simply wishful thinking on her part? One thing she certainly wasn't imagining was the aching of her body in response to that look. Whenever he walked into the room, her senses felt as if they'd been brought to life—yet was she really misguided enough to think the sexy desert King would give a second glance at her—plain and inexperienced Hannah Wilson?

Her heart was pounding as she prepared his coffee. After his short-tempered response at their initial meeting she had expected him to be difficult to work for. She'd thought he would be all distant and haughty, as befitted a man of his status. Yet it was funny how sustained contact with someone could make them seem more human—even someone as exulted as a desert king.

She tipped extra sugar cubes into a porcelain bowl because the Sheikh was rather partial to sugar. In fact, as far as she could make out, sweetening his coffee was the closest he got to indulgence. He didn't drink alcohol, nor smoke those pungent cigars which some of the richer clients puffed on when they were out on the smoking terrace. He even seemed able to go without food for long periods of time—as if fasting came naturally to him. Which might explain the magnificence of his iron-hard body which she had once seen—inadvertently—when he had emerged unexpectedly from the shower.

Even now it made her breathless to remember it. Diamond droplets of water had glittered against his dark skin and Hannah had found herself mesmerised by endlessly muscular legs and narrow hips against which the white towel slung round them had looked woefully inadequate. For a moment, she had been completely flummoxed, unprepared for the sudden rush of heat which had made tiny beads of sweat appear on her heated brow.

'Oh!' she remembered exclaiming weakly, clutching onto her feather duster as if it were a life-raft, yet unable to drag her gaze away from his spectacular body.

To his credit, he had seemed as surprised to see her as she was him, a deep frown making his jet-black eyes appear even more laser-like in their intensity than usual. 'What the hell are you doing here?' he had demanded.

'I work here, Your Royal Highness.'

'You told me you'd finished for the day.'

Hannah had been so startled by the realisation that he'd actually been listening to her that she'd begun to recount the boringly domestic reason why she'd still been on the premises. 'I had,' she'd said quickly. 'Only I spotted a cobweb, high up on one of the ceilings, and since I thought you'd already left for your helicopter flight—'

'You decided to destroy the poor spider's home?' he'd drawled, his eyes gleaming with what had appeared to be mischief. 'My, my, what a heartless woman you can be, Hannah.'

And Hannah had blushed even more. She had gone the colour of a beetroot or one of those dark 'heritage' tomatoes which room service kept always sending up whenever the Sheikh asked for a salad. Because she wasn't used to being teased—and she certainly wasn't used to being teased by a half-naked man, with an implied level of intimacy which was completely outside her comfort zone. Maybe that was why she'd blurted out the first stupid thing which had come into her head and said it with a fierceness which had seemed to take him by surprise.

'I would *never* kill a spider. They have just as much right to be here as we do.'

There had been a pause. 'Then I must be careful what I accuse you of in the future,' had been the Sheikh's slow and thoughtful response.

Even now Hannah's cheeks went pink when she remembered it. Did he say things like that just to get a rise out of her? Sometimes she suspected he did—until she forced herself to remember the reality of her situation. As if someone like Kulal Al Diya would have the inclination to tease the lowliest of hotel workers when she knew for a fact that a famous American singer with an instantly recognisable name had called him yesterday afternoon. Hannah had almost dropped the phone when she'd answered it. Briefly, she'd thought about how much this particular woman's autograph would raise if you auctioned it on the Internet—before handing the phone over to the black-eyed desert King. The Sheikh had shut the door of his bedroom to take the call in private…and Hannah had been unprepared for the sudden rush of envy she had experienced.

And that was when she'd started wondering what it would be like to have a man like Kulal Al Diya as your lover. Imagining what it would be like to wake up in those powerful arms while his black eyes raked over you. Or how it would feel to have those long fingers slowly stroking skin which was growing heated even as she thought about it.

Just *stop* it, Hannah. Had that cheesy film she'd watched on her day off kick-started such crazy fantasies? Or was it because she'd been sitting there with nothing but a bumper carton of popcorn for company, surrounded by couples who were making out? With an impatient click of her lips, Hannah straightened an embroidered silk cushion. For some people, this would have been the job from heaven but it was rapidly turning into the job from hell—and all because she couldn't stop obsessing about a hotel guest in a totally unprofessional way. Had she chosen someone completely out of reach because that was *safe*?

Or was it talking to her sister the other night which had made Hannah feel more of a loser in love than usual? Tamsyn had sent a photo of herself about to go out for the evening, her red hair cascading down her back like a fiery waterfall, her big green eyes fringed with spectacular black lashes. And hadn't Hannah felt a little *resentful*—wondering how it was that, despite Tamsyn's dire financial situation and lack of regular employment, she could still manage to look like a film star and go out and have a good time?

'Are you ever going to serve that coffee, Hannah? Or are you just going to stand there muttering to yourself all morning?'

The richly accented voice breaking into her thoughts made Hannah jump and she turned to see the Sheikh sauntering into the room, with all the unleashed power of a hand-reared leopard. She watched as he sat down. It had taken a bit of adjustment to get used to his western taste in clothing because she hadn't realised that sheikhs wore *jeans*...especially not spray-on faded ones which made him look like a poster star for the brand. Her fingers tightened around the coffee cup, but not nearly as much as her breasts were tightening beneath the snug fit of her uniform dress. *Had* she been talking out loud?

Was he aware she'd been having stupid fantasies about him?

Of course he wasn't—he might be a famously good negotiator, but he wasn't that clever!

'Certainly, Your Royal Highness,' she said efficiently as she carried the cup over to his desk, where he was looking at some exotic-looking map. He liked looking at maps, and on one memorable occasion had pointed out a mountain range on the north-eastern side of his country, describing the snowy peaks in a way which had made Hannah feel all dreamy. He'd told her about Mount Taljan, which was the highest and most beautiful mountain in all of Zahristan, casually mentioning that he'd scaled it when he was just seventeen years old.

He looked up as she put the cup down in front of him, his black eyes raking over her like glowing coals and, as usual, she was momentarily flustered by the intensity of that gaze.

'Is…is there anything else I can get you, Your Royal Highness?' she questioned politely.

Kulal leaned back in his chair to study her, knowing if he did so for long enough then her cheeks would inevitably take on that rosy hue he found so entrancing. And then she would squirm with embarrassment until he put her out of her misery and dismissed her. His lips curved into a reflective smile. He knew she was attracted to him—which came as no great surprise; what *was* surprising was her total lack of attempt to capture his interest, especially given her rare proximity to his royal presence. In his own country, the majority of his personal servants were male and, in the west, few women would have been given the unfettered access which Hannah had been granted.

Yet there had been no change to her outward appearance, which would have been usual. No subtle lick of lipstick, or an application of mascara to make those extraordinary aquamarine eyes look even bigger. Nor copious amounts of perfume applied to wrist or cleavage, intended to beguile his nostrils with the scent of her femininity. His eyes narrowed. And wasn't her lack of artifice refreshing—coupled with a naivety which was rarely found in the world he inhabited?

He dropped a sugar cube into his coffee, and then a second before taking a sip. 'Excellent,' he murmured.

Hannah beamed with satisfaction. 'I trust everything else is to your satisfaction, Your Royal Highness?'

He glowered. 'Why do the staff here keep saying that same thing over and over again?'

She wriggled her shoulders a little awkwardly. 'It's

the Granchester's promise, Your Royal Highness. They like us to reinforce the group's core message.'

'Well, I've got the *core message* loud and clear so don't bother saying it to me again, understand?'

She pursed her lips together. 'Yes, Your Royal Highness.'

Kulal took another sip of coffee. He'd been awake until the early hours, fine-tuning the announcement which he planned to make to the world very soon—a dramatic development about cheaper solar power, which would inevitably stir up envy among his competitors. His time here on Sardinia was almost over and tomorrow he would return to Zahristan and the inevitable affairs of state which had been piling up in his absence. But before that happened, there was the little matter of an invitation to a party on the other side of the island, a party he could have easily given a miss, were it not being thrown by one of his oldest friends.

He stifled a sigh because he was in no mood for entertainment and not just because he could do with a good night's sleep. Parties were predictable and tedious. The same boring small-talk and disingenuous asides. And the more elevated your status, the more predictable they became. He scowled, for his recent break-up would only exacerbate the rush to pair him off with someone new. People spent far too much time contemplating his marital status and it was none of their damned business. Sometimes he thought he should put the world straight by openly stating his intention to defer marriage for as long as possible, but why fuel speculation?

He thought about the women who would doubtless be in attendance because his friend Salvatore believed that a vacancy in a man's bed should be filled as quickly as possible. And Salvatore had connections to some of the most desirable women in the world. The kind of women most men drooled about, with their gym-honed bodies and diamonds which some adoring daddy had probably bestowed on them for their eighteenth birthday. Women who would slip him little pieces of paper with their cell phone number written above a line of kisses.

Kulal yawned, because the idea of being hit on was failing to heat his blood and he allowed his gaze to return to the chambermaid who was self-consciously straightening cushions. As she straightened up, her cheeks automatically flared when she noticed her gaze on him and he could not resist a slow smile. When was the last time he'd seen a woman *blush* like that?

'You don't say very much, do you?' he observed.

'My role here is to attend to your needs, Your Royal Highness, not to converse,' she said primly.

'You're English?'

She surveyed him with a suspicious blinking of her eyes. 'I am, Your Royal Highness.'

'So what brings you to Sardinia?'

She hesitated, as if she was surprised he was asking. She should be, he thought wryly—because he was pretty surprised himself.

'I usually work for the Granchester in London,' she explained falteringly. 'Which is one of the finest hotels—'

'Yes. There's no need for any more corporate-speak,' he said sardonically. 'I know the chain well. And the owner, as it happens.'

Her eyes widened. 'You know Zac Constantinides?' she questioned breathlessly.

'I do. I'm currently doing some business with his

cousin—Xan. He was here at the conference earlier in the week. You didn't realise? No. You probably didn't. He likes to keep a low profile.' His mouth twisted into a wry smile. 'He's lucky he's able to.'

Hannah frowned. Xan Constantinides. The name rang a bell. Had her sister mentioned it, or had she imagined that? 'Yes, Your Royal Highness,' she said, which was her default answer when she couldn't think of anything else to say.

'Continue with your story,' he instructed. 'About how you came to be working here.'

Hannah hesitated, because she didn't realise she was actually telling him a *story*. And why was he so interested in *her* all of a sudden? Was he planning to make a complaint—telling Madame Martin she'd been muttering to herself and flinging her duster at imaginary cobwebs? Or that she'd been stalking him, hanging around the place when she was supposed to have gone home in order to see him emerging half-naked from the shower? Hannah bit back a smile. No. Nobody would believe *that*. She strongly suspected that another reason why she'd been chosen for this job was because she was exactly the kind of person who *wouldn't* ogle the royal guest, despite the fact that nobody could deny his drop-dead gorgeousness.

She realised he was still fixing her with that carelessly questioning look and so she shrugged. 'They've been short-staffed here,' she explained. 'I'm not quite sure why. They needed someone to fly out here and join the chambermaid staff, and I was the one they picked.'

'Because?'

She shrugged. 'I suppose because I'm considered very reliable.'

His mouth curved into a smile. 'Reliable?'

'That's right.'

'You don't sound too happy about it.'

Hannah never knew what made her come out with it. What made her blurt out the truth to *him*, of all people—but she did. 'I'm not,' she admitted, with a slight rush of heat. 'Especially as I'm also known as steady and sensible.' She thought about the things people always said about her.

'Good old Hannah.'

'You want someone to fill in on New Year's Eve? Ask Hannah. She'll have nothing better to do.'

'But surely these are positive things?' the Sheikh was saying.

'I'm sure they are,' she answered stiffly. 'But they're not really what someone my age wants to be known for, are they? They're the sort of traits which are better suited to a woman of middle age.'

'And how old are you, Hannah?' Kulal questioned kindly, finding himself suddenly engrossed in the kind of conversation he could never remember having before.

She lowered her lashes to shade her magnificent eyes. 'Twenty-five.'

Twenty-five.

He had thought she was older. Or younger. Actually, when he stopped to think about it—and why would he have done that until a few moments ago?—she was of an indeterminate age. Her plain uniform dress was timeless and the high ponytail was like a flashback to those nineteen-fifties rock 'n' roll films one of his tutors had once smuggled into the palace before being sacked for his libertarian attitude. It was only after the tutor had left that Kulal had realised how much he had protected him and his twin brother against the realities of life in the royal residence—and once he had gone, how the scales had fallen from their eyes. Suddenly, there had been no filter between them and their warring parents, who had turned the gleaming citadel of the palace into a gilded battlefield.

Was that why Kulal was overcome by a feeling of benevolence towards this humble soul, who stood before him? By a sudden curiosity to see what the chambermaid looked like as a real woman, rather than a drab servant who was old before her time? She had spoken with a certain resignation—as if her life up until then had been short of fun, and something about the submissive set of her shoulders told him his assessment was probably accurate. Kulal had never experienced poverty, but his powers of observation had been well honed and he noticed that her ugly black shoes—although carefully polished—were decidedly thin and worn.

So couldn't he show her a little kindness? Wave a magic wand and introduce some glamour into her life? What if he took her as his guest to Salvatore's party? His eyes narrowed in silent calculation. Such an action would ward off the attentions of hungry women who might have heard he was single again. And wouldn't having a woman by his side free him up from having to spend any longer there than necessary? It wasn't as if his intentions towards the chambermaid were questionable—and not just because she was a member of staff. Because he knew what women were like. He was soon to leave the island and the last thing he needed was her plaintive sobs because he had bedded her and she'd fallen 'in love' with him. He gave a silent nod of satisfaction. He was being benevolent, nothing more—

and there was no doubt that the mischievous subterfuge of his proposal would add a certain *spice* to the party.

'Are you busy tomorrow night?' he questioned slowly.

Quickly, she looked up. 'You mean, am I on duty? No, not officially, but if there's something special you need me to do—it will be very welcome overtime, Your Royal Highness. I'll just fill it in on my timesheet and submit it to Madame Martin.'

For a moment Kulal was irritated. So she thought of spending extra time with him in terms of the overtime, did she? Didn't she realise the great honour he was about to offer her? It was an outrageous response yet, curiously, it spurred him on and not simply because he'd never been side-lined in such a way before. Because surely a young woman of twenty-five should be thinking about more than her *salary*—especially when she was living on this stunning Mediterranean island. Idly he wondered if she had ever worn silk next to that creamy skin which blushed so easily, or whether she had ever danced beneath the stars. Wasn't it about time she did?

'I'd like you to come to a party with me,' he said.

Her face assumed a wary expression. 'You mean, to work?'

'No, not to work,' he negated, a flick of his hand indicating his impatience. 'As my guest.'

Her head jerked back. 'Your guest?'

'That's right.'

Unvarnished nails on show, she splayed her fingers over her breastbone and let out an odd kind of squeak. *'Me?'*

'Why not?' he drawled. 'You don't strike me as

someone who goes to many parties and I thought that all women liked parties, and the chance to dress up. Wouldn't it be fun to do something different for a change?'

'You're inviting me to a party because you feel sorry for me?' she said in a small voice.

'Partially, yes,' he agreed, surprised enough by the honesty of her question to give her an equally honest reply. 'But your presence at my side will be advantageous to me.'

She screwed up her face. 'I'm not sure why.'

'It will deter other women from hitting on me. Because I'm not in the mood for predatory.' His eyes glittered. 'Frankly, I am bored with predatory.'

Her cheeks went very pink when he said that and she shifted awkwardly from one flat and clumpy black shoe to the other before shaking her head. 'It's very kind of you to ask me, Your Royal Highness, but I'm afraid I can't do it.'

'Can't?' Kulal frowned, because hesitation was one thing but refusal was something else. Something he wasn't used to and would not tolerate. 'Why not?'

'Because members of staff aren't allowed to fraternise with the guests. It's a hotel rule and grounds for instant dismissal.'

His smile grew wolfish. 'Only if they get to know about it.'

'Everyone will know about it!'

'How? This is a very exclusive party and it's on the other side of the island. I doubt whether anyone else from the hotel will even be invited and even if they are, they aren't going to recognise you.'

Again that suspicious look. 'Why not?'

Kulal slanted her a smile, her genuine reluctance fuelling his determination. 'Because you won't be in uniform.'

She stared at him uncomprehendingly.

'Wouldn't you like to put on something pretty for a change?' he continued. 'To dress like a princess, even if it's only for one night?'

'I don't have anything remotely princess-like in my wardrobe,' she said woodenly.

'Then let me fix it so that you do.'

Again, those aquamarine eyes narrowed with suspicion rather than the gratitude he would have expected.

'How would you do that?'

'Easy.' Kulal shrugged. 'All I have to do is pick up the phone and have one of my staff find you someone who deals with such matters. Someone discreet who can transform you into someone even you won't recognise.'

'You mean like Cinderella?' she said slowly.

His lips curved, for his tutor had also taught him about the English obsession with fairy tales and their need to transpose them onto real life. 'If you like.'

She tilted her chin upwards and, for the first time, he saw a flash of spirit in her aquamarine eyes. 'Does that mean my clothes will turn back into rags at midnight?'

'You can keep the dress, if that's what you're angling for.'

'I wasn't!' she said, before shaking her head. 'Look, it's very nice of you to offer but it's…it's a crazy idea and I can't do it. It's too risky.'

'Haven't you ever taken a risk, Hannah?' he questioned softly. 'Haven't you ever done something you shouldn't?'

And *that* was what got to Hannah—the definite challenge in his voice, which was laced with slight contempt. She looked into the gleam of his hard eyes and thought about it. Of *course* she'd never done anything dangerous, because keeping to the straight and narrow had been the only way she and her sister had been able to survive. And that way of living had stuck to her like glue. She'd got the first job she'd applied for and kept her head down. She'd been cautious and careful and saved what little money she could and used her leisure time trying to make up for her woeful lack of education by studying.

Just as she kept fit by taking scenic hikes through the English countryside, which were beautiful as well as free. But she'd never done anything impetuous or stepped outside her comfort zone, and maybe it was starting to show. Was her attitude making her old before her time? Was that why she was considered a no-risk temptation for the sexy Sheikh? Frumpy Hannah Wilson who would one day look in the mirror and discover she'd become the lonely middle-aged woman she'd been channelling all these years.

She met the desert King's mocking gaze, trying to ignore the sudden thrill of possibility which had started bubbling up inside her. Trying to dampen it down with her habitual sensible attitude, but suddenly the temptation was too strong for her to resist and she licked her lips.

Could she do it?

Should she do it?

And then she looked at him and her heart gave a dangerous leap. How could he manage to look so *edgy* even when he was doing something as benign as sitting in a chair, drinking coffee? With his black eyes and faintly mocking smile, he was the most gorgeous man she'd ever set eyes on and nobody like him was ever likely to make such a proposition to her again. So what if she *was* just there to protect him from predatory women, or if he was insisting on giving her some kind of makeover in case she disgraced him? Wouldn't this be something to tell the grandchildren, if she ever found a man she wanted to marry and vice versa? Something to mention casually to Tamsyn next time her sister nagged her about leading such a boring life?

'Very well, I'll do it,' she said, and, because he seemed to be waiting for something else, she stumbled out her thanks. 'Th-thank you very much indeed, Your Royal Highness.'

'You're welcome,' he drawled, eyes gleaming. 'But if you're going to do a convincing impression of being my date, you're going to have to stop using my title—especially in that deferential way. Call me Kulal. Try to talk to me as if I was a normal date.'

As colour flooded into her cheeks Hannah wondered what he'd say if he knew she wasn't really the kind of person who had normal dates. Nor any kind of date, really. 'I'll try.'

'Go on, then. Say my name.'

He was gazing at her expectantly and Hannah found herself complying. 'Kulal...' she whispered, thinking how strange it felt to use his first name. More than strange. Just the sound of it coming from her lips felt... *sexy*.

'Very good,' he said, and smiled. 'That wasn't *too* difficult, was it?'

A look of complicity flowed from his black eyes and Hannah was aware that, with that simple exchange, something had been forged between them. A secret which separated them from the rest of the world. Wasn't that called *collusion*?

The enormity of what she was about to do washed over her. 'Nobody must…' She looked at him and swallowed.

He raised his dark brows. 'Nobody must what, Hannah?' he prompted silkily.

'Nobody must find out,' she finished quickly. 'Or I'll lose my job.'

CHAPTER THREE

At a rare loss for words, Kulal stared at the woman who stood before him.

The little chambermaid…transformed!

He studied her for a long moment and felt a flicker of apprehension whisper over his skin. Would he so willingly have offered to have a stylist dress her if he'd realised that the end result was going to be quite so… *tantalising*? That the bodice of her silk dress would cling so entrancingly to her breasts—emphasising their lush weight in a way which the lemon uniform had only hinted at?

He swallowed. The long, floaty dress outlined her shapely legs and gave a glimpse of the bare toes which peeped from glittering sandals as she walked towards him. The functional ponytail was now a distant memory, and her hair tumbled in a dark and silky profusion around her shoulders and, dazedly, Kulal shook his head. Had he been completely naïve? he wondered impatiently. Had he played Pygmalion by bringing the curvy little statue to life, without even stopping to consider that her resulting sensuality was something he would now have to spend the rest of the evening resisting? Had he *really* thought he would be nothing but a cool onlooker, curiously observing the results of her expensive makeover? *Yes, he had.* He said something low and fervent in his native tongue and immediately she fixed him with a look of uncertainty.

'You don't like it?' she said tentatively.

He didn't quite trust himself to reply immediately. Instead, he turned the question round. 'Do you?'

She shrugged and the movement drew his attention to the creamy swell of her breasts—as if any extra encouragement were needed!

'I'm not sure,' she said, her hands skating over the wide beam of her hips against which floated layers of ice-blue silk. 'You don't think it's too much?'

'Too much for what?' he questioned roughly. 'You certainly won't be overdressed, if that's what you're worried about.'

It wasn't. Hannah swayed a little on her skyscraper sandals. Her main worry was that she wouldn't be able to live up to the image of what these clothes represented. Because she'd stared into the mirror and seen someone she didn't recognise staring back. A polished woman exuding a sophistication which was fake. She felt like a fraud—which was exactly what she was. A hotel employee dressed up to look like one of the guests. What if someone started talking to her and realised that she hadn't got much to say for herself—and that all the glossy potential of her appearance was false? What if someone sussed her out and *reported* her?

'I'm worried how we're going to get out of the hotel without me being noticed.'

He smiled suddenly as if he had decided to enjoy the subterfuge. 'Oh, don't worry about that,' he said airily. 'It's all taken care of.'

Hannah soon realised that Kulal wasn't exaggerating—and that pretty much anything was possible when you were a king. He might not have a full entourage of staff in tow, but there were enough bodyguards and heavies who seemed to appear from out of nowhere to swarm around them in a protective coterie as they were taken through the maze of back corridors to the helipad outside where a helicopter was waiting. And even if anyone *had* bothered to spare Hannah a second glance—most eyes were on the imperious strut of the Sheikh, because he was the one who commanded everyone's attention. Nobody would have guessed that the woman in the expensive dress and glittering jewels was really a humble chambermaid they'd barely noticed earlier.

She felt a little queasy as the helicopter made its swaying ascent into the sky but soon they were up amid the stars, looking down onto the twinkling lights of L'Idylle, and Hannah looked around her, breathless with wonder.

'Ever been in one of these before?' questioned Kulal above the sound of the clattering blades.

Hannah was so engrossed in the view that she spoke without thinking. 'What do you think?'

Despite her undeniable lack of protocol, Kulal smiled. How refreshing it was to be out with someone so deliciously unsophisticated! Instead of hanging onto his every word, she was sitting exclaiming about the beauty of the stars. Unless that was an attempt to convince him that she had *depth*. He felt a slight whisper of self-admonishment as he acknowledged his own cynicism, wondering when such a jaded attitude had fixed itself firmly in his heart and taken root there.

You know when, he thought, unable to prevent the rush of memory which still had the power to make his heart clench with pain. *When your mother took the ultimate revenge on your father and destroyed your faith in women for ever.*

Did she feel his eyes on her? Was that why she turned, a look of uncertainty crossing over her face, as if she'd just remembered where she was—and who she was with. 'You haven't told me anything about this party,' she said.

'Like what?'

'Well, like who's throwing it, for a start.'

He leaned forward to alleviate the need to shout above the clatter of the blades. 'An Italian property tycoon called Salvatore di Luca, who happens to be one of my oldest friends,' he said huskily, his throat growing dry as the subtle fragrance of her perfume had a predictable if unwanted effect on his senses. 'I first met him when I was studying in Norway.'

'What were you studying?'

It was a long time since anyone had asked him that, but the interest in her eyes looked genuine. 'A Master's degree in energy and natural resources.'

'Gosh. That sounds very high-powered. Did you like it?'

Kulal tensed. As much as it would have been possible to have liked anything at that time. He had used the course as an escape from the unbearable events at home, but he wouldn't tell her that. He never talked about that. Not even with his twin brother, who had found her. Who had…

He cleared his throat, but it didn't quite remove the bitter taste in his mouth. 'I liked it well enough and it has been very useful to me in my role as Sheikh. Salvatore and I were on the same course and we've stayed in touch, although our lives are very different. He lives in Rome but has a holiday place here in Sardinia.'

'So what's the party in aid of?'

'Why, me, of course,' he said softly. 'Once my old friend discovered I was working on the island, he wanted to show me some of the hospitality for which he is renowned.'

'You don't sound overjoyed about the prospect.'

He shrugged, as he spoke in a rare moment of candour. 'Sometimes it becomes rather tedious always to be the focal point of people's attention at these events.'

She chewed her lip. 'So how are you planning to explain me?'

A slow smile curved his lips. 'Oh, don't you worry about that. I never have to explain anything,' he said arrogantly. 'Nobody need know your true identity. Tonight you can be whoever you want to be, Hannah.'

Hannah's heart pounded. It felt as if he were waving another magic wand—a continuation of the spell which had made her into this glossy woman travelling by helicopter to a party. It was exciting but it was scary, too. She stole a glimpse at his hawk-like profile, knowing that she mustn't make the mistake of believing this was real. Or that the desert King in the dark dress suit really *was* her date for the night.

The helicopter dipped downwards towards a pad fringed with burning torches where an imposing man was waiting to greet them—the flames painting his face with bronze and gold. The wind plastered Hannah's dress against her legs as they emerged from the helicopter and her carefully dried hair blew wildly around her shoulders. Salvatore di Luca greeted Kulal with affection but his words to her were cursory—as if it was a waste of his time getting to know her. As if she was just one in a long line of women Kulal had brought to parties over the years.

Well, of course she was!

Taking care not to trip in her spindly sandals, Hannah followed the two men onto a terrace where the milling guests were assembled near the swimming pool. Tall trees were lit with fairy lights and flower-strewn tables were decked with candles whose flames barely flickered in the stillness of the evening air. The momentary silence which greeted their appearance was followed by a burst of excited chatter and Hannah could feel countless eyes boring into her. And suddenly she understood exactly what Kulal had meant. It *was* disconcerting to be the focus of everyone's attention and she wondered if people could tell she was wearing a borrowed dress and jewels.

The sultry sound of jazz began to drift through the air and a voluptuous singer in a silver dress began warming up. Over by the gin bar Hannah could see a Hollywood A-lister who'd recently been dating a woman half his age—and surely that was a famously tearaway European princess doing an impressive yoga pose by the side of the swimming pool?

And that was when the fun really began. Well, for everyone except her. She seemed to be the only person who didn't know anybody else and it was all too easy for Hannah to become tongue-tied. Her nerves weren't helped by the fact that she happened to be with the most important person at the party and he was the only person they wanted to talk to. Even when Kulal introduced her to people, their interest was polite rather than genuine. A couple of times, she got shoved aside as if she was an impediment to the main attraction, but she acted as if it hadn't happened, her smile as determinedly bright as the one she used at work if she happened to walk in on a couple having sex, who hadn't bothered to put the 'Do Not Disturb' sign on the door.

But when a sparky blonde came up and started chattering to Kulal in what was obviously his native tongue, Hannah gave up. Why fight it? Why bother reaching for something which could never be hers? Didn't matter how well she scrubbed up in the borrowed finery—it was all superficial. She was still the chambermaid. Still the outsider. Always had been and probably always would be.

Unnoticed, she walked across the crowded terrace and perched on the edge of a fountain so that she could people-watch and listen to the band. She saw people hovering around Kulal and couldn't deny the sudden wistful punch to her heart as she surveyed his powerful physique and jet-dark hair. But the music and the scent of jasmine were pleasures in themselves and Hannah sat sipping at her cocktail, in which floated tiny violet flowers. She watched a waitress tottering along the edge of the swimming pool carrying a tray of drinks, a deliberate sway of her curvy bottom as she passed the Sheikh only adding to her precarious posture.

She's going to drop those if she isn't careful, thought Hannah anxiously, just as the loud crash of crystal hitting marble tiles shattered the buzz of the party.

It was almost comic, the way everyone stared at the waitress scrabbling around amid the debris, as if she were an alien who'd just fallen from space. Quickly,

Hannah put her glass down and went to help, crouching down and stilling the woman's shaking fingers, terrified she was going to slice her hand open. The chatter resumed as Hannah took over the clear-up operation, becoming so engrossed in her task that it wasn't until she'd dropped the final piece of crystal onto the tray that she suddenly became aware of someone standing over her.

Looking up, she met Kulal's bemused expression and was still so caught up in what she was doing that she spoke to him almost absently. 'Do you think you could get me a dustpan and brush from somewhere?'

'A dustpan and what?' he echoed incredulously.

She realised he didn't have a clue what she was talking about and was wondering how to explain what it was—perhaps by some elaborate form of charade—when a waiter came over and started berating the waitress in a torrent of furious French.

'Come,' said Kulal firmly, pulling her to her feet. 'I think you've done quite enough. Let them sort it out among themselves. Unless you're planning to put on an apron and take over her job for the rest of the evening? Do you ever stop working, Hannah?'

In the darkness, Hannah blushed as she registered his sardonic tone. 'I couldn't just leave the poor girl to struggle by herself—and nobody else was bothering to help, were they?'

'Not everybody here has your skill-set,' he said drily.

She realised that his hand was at her elbow and he was leading her away from the curious eyes of the onlookers, towards the shadowed lawns which stretched out behind the swimming pool. It was peaceful here. And deserted, too. She could still hear the music, but it was just her and Kulal—who had a look on his face which was mid-way between irritation and amusement.

'Are you enjoying the party?' he questioned.

'It was very kind of you to bring me.'

'That wasn't what I asked, Hannah.'

Awkwardly, she shrugged. 'I'm glad I came.'

'Oh?'

She hesitated, but something in the piercing gleam of his black eyes made her answer his question truthfully. 'It made me realise that high-society parties aren't all they're cracked up to be.'

'And why might that be?'

She hesitated only for a second. 'Well, nobody really talks about anything very much, do they? All the men seemed so competitive and most of the women were all over you like a rash, which made me think that bringing me here wasn't as effective as you'd hoped. Or maybe I'm cramping your style.' She looked at him questioningly. 'In which case, I could easily make myself scarce until you're ready to go, if that's what you want.'

Kulal felt a tug of admiration. He'd heard people around him exclaiming in horror when the little chambermaid had been crouching down, careless of the way her costly dress had been rucked up around her bare thighs, yet he had admired the way she had leapt to the defence of the hapless waitress. And now, instead of plying him with saccharine words of gratitude, she was echoing his very own sentiments about these kinds of occasions.

His eyes narrowed. People rarely told him what he needed to hear—only what they thought he *wanted* to hear, and the two were rarely the same. And suddenly the desire to feel her in his arms was overwhelming. Too overwhelming to resist—and why should he? What harm would it do? 'Dance with me instead,' he said.

Hannah blinked at him. 'What, here?'

'Right here.'

Perhaps if he'd insisted on taking her to the small dance floor in front of the band, where they would have been visible to the other partygoers, Hannah might have refused. But he didn't. He just pulled her into his arms as if he danced on moonlit lawns every night of the week and every bit of apprehension drained from her body. Because what woman would have objected to being held by the Sheikh like this? Hadn't this been one of the forbidden fantasies she'd tried not to have while she'd been working for him? Only she was discovering that sometimes reality exceeded the fantasy—exceeded it in a way which was outside her understanding.

Suddenly, the dance seemed irrelevant to what was happening inside her body. Her nipples had become rock-hard and she wondered if he could feel them pushing insistently against his dress shirt. And now there was a distracting ache, low in her belly, and she knew she needed to stop this before she did something she regretted—like whispering her lips along the darkened edge of his jaw and begging him to kiss her. Her cheeks were burning as she pulled away from him and she met the hectic glitter of his dark gaze.

'I think I'd better go back now,' she said huskily. 'To the hotel, I mean.'

'Oh?' On the shadowed lawn, he raised a laconic eyebrow. 'Why?'

You know why. Because you're making me want things I have no right to want. Because I'm a virgin and you're a man of the world and I've spent my whole life being cautious.

'I'm tired,' she said.

He must have known it was an excuse, but he didn't query it. Maybe he realised that it was the right thing to do. Or the only thing to do. There was a brief silence before he nodded. 'Okay. I could use an early night myself. Let's go.'

And wasn't human nature unpredictable? Because as soon as Kulal agreed to her request, Hannah began to regret her decision. Couldn't she have danced with him a bit longer? Enjoyed what was happening without making such a big deal of it and bringing the evening to such an abrupt end?

The waiting helicopter whisked them back through the starry skies and her heart was racing as they crept through the hotel corridors. But they managed to slip into Kulal's private elevator and make it back to the penthouse suite without being seen. The usual inscrutable bodyguards lined the corridor but Hannah had become so used to seeing them that she barely gave them a second glance. She came to a halt outside the door to her room and stared up into Kulal's carved features, wondering if she ought to offer to turn down his bed for him before she retired for the night. Until she drew herself up short. Was she *crazy*? Was she planning to tiptoe into his vast bedroom and leave a chocolate on the pillowcase?

'Thank you very much for the evening, Your Royal Highness,' she said formally as she pushed the door open. 'I'll put the dress, shoes and necklace into a bag and drop it off first thing and now I'll say goodnight.'

The Sheikh didn't appear to be listening; he was too

busy looking over her shoulder into her room, his black eyes thoughtful. 'It's very small,' he observed, his gaze skating over the narrow bed and functional furniture.

'Of course it's small,' she said defensively. 'I'm staff, remember?'

But Kulal wasn't really thinking about her status right then. He wasn't really thinking about anything other than the frustration which was heating his blood and refusing to be cooled by reason. He had been very turned on during that tantalisingly brief dance and, despite all his best intentions, had been contemplating brushing his fingertips over her luscious breasts when she'd pulled away and told him she wanted to go home. He remembered feeling startled because that had never happened before—not unless it was with the expectation that they would quickly adjourn to the nearest bedroom. But not with this little chambermaid. She was primly saying goodnight to him as though that was exactly what she wanted, even though the darkening of her aquamarine eyes left him in no doubt that their desire was mutual.

If he was being sensible, he would turn away. Go to his room and kill off his ardour with an icy shower. And maybe, instead of flying straight to Zahristan tomorrow, he could take a detour via Sweden—call in on that delicious blonde actress he'd never got around to bedding a few years back. Hadn't she sent him a text the other day, disingenuously saying she was sorry to hear about his recent relationship break-up? He thought what else she had written as a postscript, making it graphically clear she wanted him as her lover.

But he didn't want that woman with her bony hips which would grind into a man's flesh like weapons. He wanted softness and voluptuousness. Lush breasts he could bury his head in and a trembling mouth he could plunder to his heart's content. For the first time in his life, he wanted someone who was outside his realm of experience—was it novelty value which made him hunger for the little chambermaid so much?

He pulled Hannah into his arms and saw her eyes widen as he began to run his fingertip down her spine.

'Kulal?' she whispered.

'Yes?' he whispered back, lowering his head so that their mouths were centimetres apart. He was close enough to kiss her, but he paused long enough to allow her to shake her head. To give her a second opportunity to pull away from him. Because that was the right thing to do, even if every atom in his hungry body rebelled against such an idea.

But she didn't pull away. Her lips parted and as lust fired in his belly, he knew he wasn't going to take her back to his own bedroom. That he had no desire to walk past the line of bodyguards stationed there, even though they had witnessed countless transgressions such as this in the past. And maybe it was better this way. Less intimidating for her—and certainly more novel for him. He pulled her a little closer and felt his erection grow even harder.

'Wh-what are you doing, Kulal?' she questioned breathlessly.

It occurred to him that women were rarely original at moments like this. What did she think he was doing—writing a research paper on solar energy? He allowed his lips to drift over the silky texture of her neck, his words muffled by the lazy indulgence of that first, slow kiss. 'I think we both know the answer to that question.

I'm going to make love to you, that's if you want me to—which I think you do.'

Hannah swallowed, trying to fight the feelings which were fluttering inside her. She should tell him to stop before this went any further. Before he started to touch her trembling breasts, which were aching to be touched. But she couldn't. She just couldn't. How could she turn her back on something which felt so wonderful? The most wonderful thing she'd ever experienced. She hadn't realised that being in a man's arms could make you feel like this—as if you could leap up into the air and just *fly*. She made a helpless little sound as his mouth brushed along her jaw and her eyelids flickered to a close. Was that his *tongue* she could feel, trailing an erotic and moist little path over her skin? She shivered as he did it again. Yes, it was.

She wasn't sure if he was waiting for some kind of response, but she guessed she gave one when she suddenly folded her arms tightly around his shoulders.

'I'm taking it that's a yes?' he said on a low growl.

'It's certainly not a no,' she said, with a boldness she hadn't known she possessed.

He laughed as he stepped inside and kicked the door shut behind them and then he was kissing her properly. Or maybe that should have been improperly. His hands were sliding over her silky dress as he murmured something in a language she didn't understand. But maybe she didn't need to. Maybe this was something which was meant to be enjoyed without commitment or expectation. And didn't they say that the language of love was universal?

She should have felt shy as he slid her zip down and peeled the delicate dress from her body, but she didn't.

Not when it seemed that her voluptuous curves pleased him. The stylist who had transformed her had insisted on matching underwear and Hannah was glad now that she had agreed. Glad she was wearing a deceptively delicate bra which disguised the fact that it had needed to do a lot of elemental support work. Deftly, he unclipped it and as her breasts came spilling out, he gave another appreciative murmur before locking his hot lips around one thrusting nipple. Hannah gasped—she couldn't help it. She felt as if she'd taken a one-way trip to heaven. As if she'd found something she hadn't believed existed. And suddenly she wanted to touch *him*. To feel the Sheikh's skin beneath her fingers.

With the nimbleness which had made her the finest chambermaid in the Granchester group, she slid free the mother-of-pearl buttons to liberate his powerful chest, her hands running greedily over the hard muscle which sheathed the silken skin. Was that what made him groan like that? What made him pick her up as if she were composed of nothing heavier than feathers, before carrying her towards the tiny single bed and depositing her on the mattress?

And still she didn't feel shy—not even as he removed the clothes from his body, his eyes not leaving her face. Nor when he was completely naked and leaning over to slither her panties all the way down her thighs and she felt cool air wash over her naked skin. There was no time to feel anything—other than a joyful recognition of the greedy hunger which was spiralling up inside her, so that when Kulal lay down on top of her—because the bed wasn't really big enough for any other kind of combination—all Hannah could do was to give a shuddering little moan of relief.

'You like that?' he said, a smile playing around the edges of his lips as he gazed down at her, his hand between her thighs.

Was he referring to the fact that she could feel his blunt hardness pushing unashamedly against her belly? Or was it one of those questions which didn't really require an answer—not when he was now discovering the molten heat between her legs with a finger which was making her writhe with pleasure?

'This is crazy!' Hannah gasped. 'I can't—'

'Oh, yes, you can,' he said, his tongue snaking over her breasts until her nipples felt as if they were going to explode.

And who was she to contradict him, when their bodies seemed to fit together as if they had been made for each other? When she was so hungry for him that she even managed to giggle as he clumsily tore open what was obviously protection and heard him give a muffled curse. She didn't stop to think, or to question why he just *happened* to be carrying a condom around with him because for the first time in her life, Hannah hadn't just stepped outside her comfort zone—she'd taken a great flying leap into unknown territory.

And she loved it.

She loved everything about it. Kissing him and touching him. Running her fingers through the tousled splendour of his thick black hair. Skating her palms over the honed planes of his spectacular body until he bit out that he couldn't take much more. Suddenly, she wasn't humble Hannah Wilson any more—but a woman who seemed to be able to drive this hawk-faced man wild with desire. Her initial shyness had been melted away by their rapidly growing intimacy, and suddenly Hannah realised he was pushing her thighs open to enter her.

The next few seconds were a bit of a blur. There was a little bit of pain—though not very much. And there was undeniable surprise on the face of the Sheikh as he stilled, mid-thrust. But then their bodies seemed to take over and everything else got forgotten when he started moving again until she was gasping out words she hadn't realised she knew. She heard herself making broken little pleas as she hovered on the edge of something which seemed tantalisingly out of reach.

But at last she found it. And it wasn't just what she had thought it might be—it was more. So much more. She gave a disbelieving cry, and as she began to convulse around the Sheikh's thrusting hardness, he gave a low and exultant shout of his own. And as Hannah felt his big body quivering with pleasure, she found herself thinking that she never wanted this night to end.

CHAPTER FOUR

'So WHEN WERE you planning to tell me?'

Swallowing down the nausea which was rising in her throat, Hannah looked at her little sister, trying not to react to the accusing stare which had accompanied her accusing words. Trying to convince herself that Tamsyn couldn't possibly *know*—not when she'd only just found out herself.

'Tell you what?' she questioned weakly.

'About your pregnancy, of course,' hissed Tamsyn. 'Or were you planning to keep it a great big secret until you were just about to pop?'

Hannah swallowed again, only this time the saltiness in her throat felt suspiciously like the taste of tears—and she'd convinced herself she wasn't going to cry. She wasn't, she thought fiercely. Because tears wouldn't solve anything. She'd learnt that the hard way.

'How did you know?' she whispered.

'Hello? Are you *serious*?' Tamsyn filled up the kettle, not appearing to notice that she was splashing water all over Hannah's carefully polished tiles. 'It must be obvious to everyone.'

'Nobody at the Granchester knows,' said Hannah quickly.

'Really? Well, maybe the other staff don't have eyes in their heads or maybe I just know you better than anyone, but it's as obvious to me as the nose on your face. Look at you, Hannah—your breasts are enormous and your complexion looks green...'

'Thanks,' said Hannah tonelessly.

'I can't believe it. You, of all people.'

'What's that supposed to mean?'

Tamsyn shrugged. 'You're the one who was always so good. Who never put a foot wrong.'

Hannah didn't answer, just stared up into her sister's bewildered face. It was true. She'd been the model child. The peacemaker. The quiet one who had learnt that saying as little as possible and pretending the bad stuff wasn't happening was the best way for things to get back to normal. Whatever normal was. But this was one situation where pretending it wasn't happening wasn't going to work.

'So who's the daddy, Hannah?' continued Tamsyn. 'I didn't even realise you were in a relationship.'

Because she wasn't in a relationship, that was why. Hannah leaned back in the armchair and closed her eyes, not wanting to betray her fear, knowing that sooner or later she was going to have to come clean. To say the words out loud. Because words would make it real. They would confirm what up until now had just been a nagging fear.

She was pregnant.

She was carrying the desert King's child beneath her thundering heart.

Her mind took her back to that crazy night when Kulal had laid her down on that narrow single bed, his black eyes full of intent as he had run a careless thumb over her thrusting nipple. What had happened next had seemed inevitable—but that wasn't really true. She could have stopped him. He'd given her every opportunity to do so, but she had just carried on regardless. She had broken every rule in the book—and she wasn't just thinking about the Granchester's strict policy of not fraternising with guests. Hadn't she clung onto her virginity as if it was something very precious? Hadn't it been a big deal for her, having seen what the fallout from casual sex could be? While most women her age seemed content to be free with their bodies, Hannah had been the opposite—as prim as a woman from a different age.

And she had surrendered all that innocence to a man who had simply taken it as his due! Who afterwards had looked at the ceiling with a reflective look on his hawk-like features.

'I've never done it in such a narrow bed before,' he had observed thoughtfully, his fingers sliding between her thighs and easing them apart. 'I think it adds a certain *something*.'

But even that arrogant boast hadn't been enough to kill her hunger for him. Instead, she had just turned to him with silent invitation in her eyes and he'd done it to her all over again. And again. She remembered the intensity of feelings which had seemed to explode inside her, like a bomb which been waiting a long time to be detonated. Was that why she had responded like someone she didn't really know—showing a side of herself she hadn't realised existed? Like a wildcat, she thought guiltily. Like…

She remembered what he'd said, just before the first time.

'You want this, Hannah?'

'Yes.'

'And so do I. But it's one night only—do you understand? Not just because I am a king and you a chambermaid, and our positions in life are so incompatible. The truth is that I've just come out of a relationship and I'm not looking for another one. If you want more than that, I cannot give it to you and I'll walk out of this room right now and leave you alone, no matter how hard I might find it.'

But Hannah had been powerless to resist him. How could she have resisted him when just looking into those gleaming black eyes had made her want to melt?

'One night is fine with me,' she had whispered back.

'So who's the daddy?' repeated Tamsyn, cutting impatiently into Hannah's uncomfortable thoughts.

And that was when Hannah realised that the tables were turned for the first time in their lives. That Tamsyn, for all her wildness, had never presented with a problem as big as this. A problem which seemed insurmountable. Which had made her thoughts spin with increasing desperation, ever since she'd first seen that blue line on the pregnancy test.

'You won't be able to keep it a secret for ever, you know.' Tamsyn poured boiling water into the teapot before looking up. 'Is it that bloke who works in the accounts department—the one you got off with at the Christmas party?'

Hannah shuddered. No way. That particular encounter had ended humiliatingly when he'd shoved his hand up her jumper and she'd jumped away and told him she didn't want sex in the stationery cupboard, and he had sneered and told her she was fat and frigid.

She certainly hadn't jumped away in horror when Kulal had touched her, had she?

But she knew Tamsyn was right. She couldn't keep it a secret. She had no right to do that. And wasn't the truth of it that if she disregarded her thoughtless and stupid behaviour… She swallowed again. If she thought about the *reality* rather than the repercussions—then she couldn't deny the unexpected sense of excitement which was bubbling away inside her. She was going to have a baby and she would love and protect that baby with all her heart, just as she'd done for her little sister—no matter what obstacles lay ahead.

'His name is Kulal.' For the first time since she'd lain in his arms she said his name out loud and even as she uttered it, she thought how bizarre it was that her very first lover should have been the influential desert King.

'Nice name,' said Tamsyn approvingly. 'What's he like?'

And here it was—in all its unvarnished and frankly unbelievable truth.

'He's…well, he's very powerful and dynamic.'

'Really?'

She heard the doubt in Tamsyn's voice which she couldn't quite disguise and, for the first time in her life, Hannah wasn't sure how to respond. Because she had always been the one who came armed with words of wisdom. Words to soothe and comfort. There hadn't been a single bad situation during their growing up which she hadn't felt equipped to deal with.

Until now.

Had she been guilty of thinking she was so clever—so *invulnerable*—that she would never find herself in a situation like this? Well, here was reality—about to teach her the hardest lesson of all.

'He's a sheikh,' she said.

Tamsyn screwed up her face. 'What are you talking about?'

Hannah swallowed. 'The father of my baby. He's a...' She cleared her throat because not only did it sound unbelievable—it also sounded slightly grandiose. 'A desert king,' she finished quietly.

She could see that Tamsyn was trying not to laugh, but then the gravity of the situation must have hit her and the smile was wiped from her sister's wide mouth. 'This is no joking matter,' she said crossly.

'I'm not joking—he *is* a desert king.'

'Hannah.' Tamsyn glared. 'You're not experienced. You don't realise what men are like. They say all kinds of things when they're trying to get a woman to—'

'He *is*!' declared Hannah, with an uncharacteristic burst of fervour because usually, she trod carefully where Tamsyn was concerned. 'He's called Sheikh Kulal Al Diya and he's the King of Zahristan.'

'Good...*grief.*' There was a pause and then, the tea-making forgotten, Tamsyn slumped against the sink, her eyes wide. 'Not...not the one in the papers who was described as—'

'One of the world's most eligible bachelors?' supplied Hannah. 'Yes, that's him.'

'But...how? I mean, *how*?'

The question was well-meant, but it hurt. Because Tamsyn's incredulity said a lot. It said: how could someone like Kulal have possibly become involved with a woman like *her*? Yet Hannah was in no position to criticise her sister's disbelief, when she felt pretty much that way herself.

'He needed a partner to take to a fancy party.'

'And he chose *you*?'

Hannah drew her shoulders back and spoke to Tamsyn with uncharacteristic coolness. 'Yes, he did. I was working for him.'

'As a chambermaid?'

'As a chambermaid,' Hannah agreed tightly. 'I was assigned to work solely for him. Sometimes we used to chat about stuff. We got on quite…well.'

Tamsyn gave a raucous laugh. 'I'll say. So you went off to a party with him and…?'

'I'm not going to spell it out for you, Tamsyn—it's pretty obvious what happened.'

Tamsyn looked momentarily surprised—as if this new and rather bolshie sister, who usually trod so carefully, was taking a little getting used to. She nodded. 'So what are you planning to do?'

Hannah hesitated before answering because this was the bit she still wasn't quite clear about. Because the moment she told him, she would lose control over the situation. Instinct told her that. Kulal wasn't just a powerful man—he was also a desert king and weren't royals notoriously possessive about their heirs? The truth was that she didn't know how he would respond because she didn't really know *him*. He might try to take control of her and the baby. He might deny all responsibility and send her packing. In many ways, it would be easier all round if she just crept away and brought up the baby on her own without bothering to tell him.

A long sigh escaped from her lips. It would be easier, yes—but deep down she knew she couldn't go through

with it. Because Hannah had grown up never knowing or meeting her father, and she knew all about the
huge emotional hole that could leave at the centre of a
child's existence. There were risks involved in letting
him know—of course there were—but these were risks
she had to take.

'I'm going to tell him, of course,' she said. 'As soon
as you've gone, I'm going to telephone him.'

The only problem being that she didn't actually have
a number for him, because he hadn't given her one.
Well, why would he, when he'd never been intending
to see her again? There had been one final, lingering
kiss and Hannah, completely exhausted after their en-
ergetic night, had fallen into a deep sleep. And when
she'd woken up, he was gone. The penthouse suite along
the corridor had been cleared of all evidence that Kulal
had stayed there. The bodyguards had disappeared and
so had the Sheikh's luggage. Even the fancy dress and
priceless necklace were gone, presumably on their way
back to the stylist. It might have all been a dream, were
it not for the pleasurable aching of her body. And yet
she had still been suffering from some kind of delu-
sion, hadn't she? There had still been a stupid part of
her which had wondered if he might have left her a note
or *something*.

But whisking her way around his suite—supposedly
giving it the most thorough cleaning of its life—had
failed to produce any kind of sentiment that Kulal Al
Diya would ever give her another thought. Hannah had
felt flat—there was no denying it. It had been the most
spectacular introduction to sex and now she was going
to have to resign herself to her usual frigid life. Yet it
had been more than that. In his arms, she had felt like

a woman who was capable of anything. He had been tender with her. And passionate. In fact, he had been everything a woman dreamt a man could be.

Maybe it was easy to be that way when you knew you were never going to see someone again. When you knew that you weren't even going to have to speak to them in the morning. She told herself she should be grateful he'd just crept away in the early hours, because the reality of waking up in that cramped staff bedroom would have been embarrassing. Would she have boiled the electric kettle which was jammed onto one of the shelves and offered to make him a mug of herb tea? Then watched as he put on his clothes and tried to make his escape as quickly as possible?

She'd tried to feel indignant that he'd beat such a hasty retreat, but she couldn't quite bring herself to be angry with him. Had she somehow been aware—on a deep, subliminal level—that the cells of his child were already multiplying rapidly inside her? Was that why she found it so difficult to stop thinking about him, with a heart that beat a little too fast and a soft yearning which made her feel uncomfortable?

But Hannah knew that feelings passed. All of them. And that eventually the intensity of what was happening to you faded with time. She'd told herself to be grateful that nobody at the Granchester had found out and her job was safe. She'd got away with it, scot-free. Or so she'd thought. She had worked for two more weeks at the Sardinian hotel before returning to London, just in time to discover that her period was late and to try to deny to herself why that might be. Until denial was no longer an option…

Hannah clicked onto the Zahristan website but, naturally, there was no handy link to the King's email account. She found the number of the Embassy in London and tried ringing, in the hope of being able to convey a subtle message through one of the diplomats. But the phone system was automated and her dilemma didn't fall into the category of someone visiting the country who was chasing up their visa. She supposed she could mail Kulal a letter and emblazon it with 'private and confidential'—but there was no guaranteeing he would receive it unopened. The embassy might think it was from a crackpot and even if they didn't, it meant that the Sheikh would discover he was going to be a father *after* his staff had found out. Hannah knew very little about royal protocol, but even she could recognise that would be a big mistake. A very big mistake.

She needed to tell him in person—but how?

There *was* a solution—to use the money she'd been squirrelling away since she'd first started work. The little sums of money which had grown, bit by bit, into a halfway decent sum which would one day become a deposit on a home of her own.

Could she break into it to buy herself an airline ticket to Zahristan?

Her heart began to pound. There was no other option—because how else was she going to get to see Kulal? But that money was sacrosanct and symbolic. She'd promised herself she would never touch it and now fear washed over her as she realised that once again she wasn't playing safe. Because this wasn't risk-averse Hannah. This was more of the same Hannah who had leapt into bed with the desert King, when deep down she'd known she shouldn't. Her hand went down to cradle her belly because she knew she had little choice. She'd protected Tamsyn when they had been growing up—just as she would protect her baby now. She didn't know how Kulal would respond, but that wasn't her problem. She needed to give their child the best possible chance—and everything else was outside her control.

And surely he would have the decency to refund her air fare?

Which was how she ended up in a plane, crossing the Murjaan Sea and heading towards the Sheikh's homeland.

She was fortunate that Zahristan had opened its borders a decade ago, after winning the war with neighbouring Quzabar, and fortunate that she had enough annual leave to book herself a last-minute break. She couldn't decide if it was good fortune or fate that her visa-acquiring trip to the Zahristan Embassy had introduced her to a helpful woman called Elissa. Elissa had informed her that visitors were allowed access to the Sheikh's palace every Tuesday and Thursday afternoon, and His Royal Highness was actively encouraging trips from foreign visitors. At this, Hannah's heart had leapt—because surely she could engineer some kind of meeting if she gained access to Kulal's home.

After consulting a weather map, she discovered that the temperature of her destination was roasting and so she used some more of her precious savings to buy some suitable clothes. Inexpensive clothes in natural fabrics in light colours which wouldn't absorb the heat. Clothes which would disguise her tender breasts which were the only outward sign of her pregnancy. But most important of all—new clothes which meant she wouldn't turn up at a fancy palace looking like a tramp.

The flight was long and her limbs felt cramped, because she hadn't wanted to squander any of her precious money upgrading her seat. She tried distracting herself by reading what was supposed to be the definitive history of Zahristan, but the clunky paragraphs didn't manage to hold her attention for long. For a long time, the book lay open on the same page as she wondered what would happen when she finally gained access to Kulal. Would she be thrown in some dark jail—forced to wait for the British consulate to come and bail her out and put her on the next flight to England, with a fierce lecture on compromising international diplomacy ringing in her ears?

But even if the worst happened and she didn't get within a hundred yards of him, at least she would have tried.

Hannah stared out of the plane window—at the seemingly endless expanse of desert. As the aircraft began to descend, she could see the welcome green of palm trees and in the distance a gleam of water, surrounded by tents. And now they were approaching a city—with turrets and gleaming spires, just like in a fairy tale. There were flashes of blue and lots of gold. This must be Ashkhazar, which she'd just read about. A rich city with a troubled history. Hadn't Kulal mentioned it briefly when she had run her fingertip over the raised scar which ran from nipple to groin and was the only blemish which marred his perfect body? But he hadn't wanted to talk about what had caused it. The truth was he hadn't wanted to talk about anything much, except how much he liked her breasts. Well, he was going to have to talk about his baby, whether he liked it or not.

And then her stomach gave a flip as the airport watchtower grew closer and she closed her eyes as the huge aircraft began to swoop towards the runway.

CHAPTER FIVE

FROM BEHIND THE tinted windows of his heavily bullet-proofed car, Kulal watched the plane land and he felt a wave of anger as the passengers began to disembark.

He saw her immediately—instantly recognisable, and not just because she was the only woman travelling solo.

Did she really think she could sneak into his homeland without him getting wind of it?

Her head was uncovered, but at least her shoulders were not bare. She was wearing a pale dress which hung almost to her ankles. It was a modest dress, even by Zahristan standards, but it failed to disguise the generous curve of her breasts or the womanly swell of her buttocks, and Kulal's jaw tightened. It would be easier all round if he simply had her brought to his car for the short drive to the city but that might amount to something resembling an official welcome and he would not countenance that. He watched as another black limousine edged onto the tarmac and one of his most trusted aides got out of the car.

Kulal spoke rapidly to his driver. 'Wait until Najib gets her into the limousine,' he bit out. 'And then tail them.'

'Yes, sire.'

He didn't say another word during the journey which followed, his eyes fixed resolutely on the car in front of them as they drove at speed through the wide roads which led into the city. When the first limousine drew to a halt, he could see the look of consternation on Hannah's face as she gazed up at the impressive gilded façade of the famous building and for a moment, he wondered if she might refuse to go inside and then what would they do? But Najib was a master at getting people to carry out his master's wishes and within minutes, she was walking up the marble steps, while yet another aide carried her single suitcase.

He waited for several minutes before discreetly entering the building, two of his bodyguards tailing him like shadows. But as the elevator ascended, Kulal found his thoughts drifting back to another similar ride—when he had been obsessed by the rise and fall of Hannah's magnificent breasts, covered in the delicate silk of the dress he had ordered for her to wear to the party. Had he been completely insane? Carried away by what he'd convinced himself was nothing but an altruistic action to give the little chambermaid a well-deserved treat, without bothering to examine the real motive of desire which was bubbling beneath the surface of his intentions? Probably. His mouth hardened into a grim mockery of a smile. Didn't they say that men were architects of their own destruction?

The elevator doors opened and as he strode along the corridor he saw Najib standing sentry outside a door, his face inscrutable.

'What did she say?' questioned Kulal as he grew close, and Najib gave a brief bow before shrugging.

'She was a little *militant* at first, sire—but then she seemed to grow resigned to her fate and offered no resistance.'

'Good. Let us hope that state of affairs continues. Stand back, Najib.'

'Should I not accompany you inside, sire?'

Briefly, Kulal's lips curved. 'You think the little Englishwoman will attack me?'

'I thought I saw fire in her eyes, sire.'

Kulal's lips hardened. 'The fire will soon be doused, Najib. Make no mistake about that.'

He pushed open the door and saw Hannah. She was standing by the window, as if she had been staring out onto the magnificent mixture of ancient and new to be found in the city streets outside. At the sound of the door closing, she whirled round and his first thought was that Najib had been right. That was definitely fire he could see in her eyes—something he had not witnessed in all the time she had serviced his penthouse suite. The blaze of aquamarine as she glared at him almost dazzled him and she must have been shaking her head because gleaming strands of mahogany hair had broken free from the confinement of their elastic band and were tumbling in glorious disarray around her shoulders. For a few distracting seconds, he felt the instant flare of lust before instinctively subduing it. Because wasn't it lust which had got him into this predicament?

'Would you mind telling me what is going on?' she demanded, her voice rising. 'Why I was bundled off the plane and into a waiting car as if I was some sort of criminal? And why I've been brought here—to this fancy hotel—when I have a room reservation at the Souk Vista Hostel?'

Kulal had been anticipating many reactions, but such a feisty question from a woman of her stature only confirmed his suspicions about the reason for her journey. His eyes narrowed, for although he had encountered determination from ex-lovers many times in the past—nobody had ever been quite as audacious as Hannah Wilson. Well, she would soon discover that coming here had been a big mistake. A very big mistake.

'I assume you wanted to see me,' he said coolly. 'So I thought I would curtail any unnecessary time-wasting by bringing you straight here.'

'When your aide said...' For a moment her confidence appeared to waver. 'When he said he was taking me to the palace...'

Kulal's lips curved into a smile he fully intended to be cruel because now he was dealing with something he'd encountered ever since he first became aware that his blood was blue, and he was in possession of connections most people could only dream of. Was that what Hannah ultimately wanted? he wondered cynically. A share of his unimaginable riches and access to his privileged life? In which case, perhaps it was necessary to teach her a small lesson—just to set the matter straight before she let her imagination run away with itself. 'And you thought they meant they were bringing you to my palace?' he queried, his gaze deliberately lingering on the golden logo of a crown which was embroidered onto one of the napkins which adorned a gleaming table. 'Rather than the Royal Palace Hotel?'

The dull flush of her cheeks told Kulal his guess had been accurate and, mockingly, he raised his eyebrows. 'I hope you aren't too disappointed, Hannah. Did you think our one night together would entitle you to enjoy some of the perks of having a royal lover? And that I would be taking you on a sightseeing tour of the fabled gardens of my palace, or dipping into the Al Diya jewellery collection to present you with a precious bauble?'

'Of course not,' she said stiffly.

'I thought you would feel more at home in a hotel,' he added carelessly. 'And of course, it carries the extra benefit of not compromising me in any way.'

It was the most patronising thing she'd ever heard and Hannah had to suck in a deep breath to stop herself from shaking, telling herself that nothing would be achieved by giving into the rage which was smouldering inside her, like a fire which refused to die. Because showing your feelings made you vulnerable—and she had the scars to prove it. Letting emotion get the better of you was a bad idea. Remaining cool and calm was the first law of survival—she knew that. But although she'd spent most of her life following that creed, she wasn't finding it so easy right now. Were her fluctuating hormones once again to blame—making her react in a way which was alien to her? Or did none of the usual rules apply now that she had an unborn child to protect?

Because things were different now and she needed to recognise that. When she'd been looking after Tamsyn, she'd been nothing but a child herself and her options had been limited. But she was an adult now. She might not have Kulal's material wealth or power, but she was resourceful as only someone in a dilemma could be and would not be treated like some docile little prisoner.

So stick to the facts.

'You don't even know why I'm here,' she said.

'Of course I do.'

She blinked at him and gulped. 'You do?'

'Oh, Hannah.' He gave a short laugh before his hawk-like features hardened into a cynical expression. 'You wouldn't need to be a genius to work it out. You've decided that you're *in love* with me, haven't you?'

For one stomach-churning second, Hannah actually thought she might be sick. But it wasn't just the Sheikh's swaggering arrogance which she found so nauseating—it was the way he had said the word *love*. As if it were some unspeakable type of illness. As if it were something beneath his contempt... Clenching and unclenching her fingers, she looked up at him, trying to keep her voice steady. 'What makes you say that?'

'You have been pining for me, I guess,' he said softly, before shrugging his broad shoulders. 'That in itself is not unusual—but the fact that I took your virginity has probably given our night together more significance than it warrants. Am I right, Hannah?'

Hannah flinched, wondering how she could ever have fallen into the arms of someone so unspeakably arrogant.

You know how, whispered the voice of her conscience. *Because he's so irresistible—even now, when he's looking down his haughty nose at you.*

Because despite the insulting reception he'd given her, she was far from immune to the attraction which had got her into all this trouble in the first place.

In Sardinia, she had only ever seen Kulal dressed in western clothes. Faded jeans and T-shirts, impeccably cut business suits or, on that fateful night, a dark dinner suit, just like those worn by all the other men at the party. But today, he was looking emphatically sheikh-like in a robe of white silk which flowed down over his muscular body. A matching headdress, held in place by a circlet of knotted gold, emphasised the stark outlines of his hawk-like features. He looked exotic and powerful. He looked like a stranger. He *was* a stranger, she reminded herself bitterly. A stranger whose child was now living beneath her breast.

'I hate to disillusion you,' she said, concentrating on trying to match his own emotionless tone. 'But I am definitely not pining for you.'

'No? So why come here?' he drawled. 'Why bother flying out here in secret?'

But it hadn't been a secret, had it? His words reminded Hannah that this whole set-up seemed premeditated and that a car had been waiting for her when the plane had touched down. She lifted her chin, the pulsing of a nerve above her jaw the only outward sign of her growing anxiety—because if *Kulal* knew she was here, then who else did? How would such an action appear to the outside world—and, more importantly, to her employers? A lowly chambermaid flying out to confront a desert king! She reflected on her many years of service at the Granchester and a ripple of fear whispered down her spine at the thought of being sacked for such unprofessional behaviour. 'How…how did you know I'd be on that flight?' she questioned croakily.

'Are you really that naïve?' He spat out the question impatiently. 'My security people run automatic checks over all the flight lists and flag up anyone of particular interest and naturally you fell into that category. A woman who needs an urgent visa to visit my country—didn't you consider that might have alerted the suspicions of the authorities?' He gave an impatient sigh. 'Especially since you were asking so many questions about access to the royal palace—and a further check threw up the fact that you work for the Granchester Group and I'd recently been staying in one of their hotels.'

Hannah stared down at her fingernails she'd spent the past few weeks forcing herself not to chew, and suddenly she knew she couldn't put it off any longer. She had to tell him. But it was with an instinctively sinking heart that she met the ebony coldness of his eyes. 'I'm pregnant, Kulal,' she said quietly.

There was a pin-drop silence as he looked at her, the expression on his hawk-like features inscrutable as he shook his head.

'You can't be. I used protection.' His voice was cold. 'I always do.'

Had he added that last bit just to hurt her? To remind her that she was nothing special? Just another women who had succumbed to all that arrogant alpha appeal…? Hannah chewed her bottom lip. Probably. But she wasn't here to protect her own feelings—she was here to do the best for her baby and reacting with anger to his inflammatory comments would serve no useful purpose. 'I'm afraid I can,' she contradicted. 'I'm carrying your baby, Kulal,' she added for extra emphasis and saw his body tense.

Kulal felt the sudden rush of blood to his head as adrenalin flooded through his system and disbelief warred with the evidence right in front of his eyes—because she was here, wasn't she? A place where she had no right to be. He observed her stillness and the unnatural calmness of her expression—as if he was waiting for her to relax and tell him she'd made the whole thing up—but he knew he was waiting in vain. Of *course* she was pregnant—why else would she have flown out here in a dramatic way he suspected was completely out of character? His heart began to pound loudly in his chest and he recognised the sensation instantly because he used to feel that way when he was about to go into battle. But war had never filled him with the uncertainty which now assailed him and which instantly put him on the offensive.

'So have you come here to bargain with me, Hannah?' he demanded. 'To see how much money you can get out of me?'

Hannah flinched. If she had been in London—if her baby's father had been a *normal* man—she would have risen from the chair, no matter how shaky her legs, and walked out of the room, telling him she would speak to him when he was prepared to be reasonable. Because surely a display of emotion would be justified in those circumstances.

But she wasn't in London and Kulal was *not* a normal man, no matter how much she wished he were. She was stuck in a fancy hotel room in *his* country, miles away from home and everything she knew. The air felt icy from the over-efficient pump of the air-conditioning and outside the huge windows she could see the golden gleam of a beautiful dome. It couldn't have been more unlike the view from her own humble little bedsit, but she mustn't let the undeniable glamour of the location stop her from dealing with practicalities.

'No, I haven't come here to bargain with you,' she said quietly. 'Nor to be spoken to as if I were someone motivated by nothing other than greed.'

'Really? Then what do you want?'

Wasn't it obvious? Wouldn't anyone with a shred of decency in their soul have done the same—or was Hannah just hypersensitive about the subject of paternity because her own start in life had been less than ideal? She looked into his eyes, but they were cold and hard. As hard as the dagger she'd suddenly noticed was hanging at his hip... 'Because I wanted to give you the opportunity to be a part of your baby's life,' she said quietly.

'In what capacity?'

He was so *cold*. So *unfeeling*. Hannah wanted to pick up a tiny golden box which sat on one of the polished tables. She wanted to hurl it against the wall or the chandelier. To make a noise and to *break* something—as a gesture of defiance as well as one of protest. But she wasn't going to act like a wronged woman—causing a scene and wringing her hands together as she begged him for help. She was going to act with a dignity which would surround her and the baby with a calm and protective aura.

'I hadn't thought that far ahead,' she said. 'I didn't get much further than figuring that you deserved to hear it from me, before anyone else. It's why I came.' She tried and failed to suppress the sudden shiver which made her skin grow all goosebumpy. 'I would have phoned if I could—but, as we both know, you didn't leave a number.'

Kulal nodded, the sudden blanching of her cheeks plucking at his conscience and making him walk towards an inlaid table on which reposed a selection of bottles and glasses. He poured her a long glass of fireberry cordial and handed it to her, and as their skin touched, the sheer enormity of the life-changing fact once again hit him like a sledgehammer.

She was pregnant.

Pregnant with *his* baby.

Didn't matter that he'd never wanted a child of his own. That he sometimes thought he would prefer his paternal cousin to inherit the kingdom, rather than condemning himself to family life—a way of life he had always carefully avoided because of the chaos and pain of his own childhood. Even his natural love of independence now took second place, because this changed everything. And he needed to think carefully about what to do next.

Very carefully.

He stared at Hannah, at the fatigue which was creasing the corners of her mouth and the untidy tumble of her hair. 'It's been a long day and you look exhausted, so why don't you go and freshen up?' he suggested.

She put down the half-drunk cordial and as the pink liquid sloshed against the sides of the glass, she regarded him with suspicious eyes. 'What exactly are you suggesting?'

He felt a flicker of irritation. Did she think he was making a pass at her? That he wanted her to go and bathe and prepare herself for him? That he would actually want to be intimate with her at a moment like this, when his whole life was about to change and she was the instrument of that change? *But that wasn't all he felt, was it?* There was something else. Something he couldn't quite put his finger on. He felt a steely clench around his heart.

Was it fear?

Yet he was known for his fearlessness—even as a teenager, when he'd run away to join the Zahristan forces during the fierce border war with Quzabar. His late father had hit the roof when Kulal returned, with the livid blade mark which travelled from nipple to navel.

He had been lucky not to die, the old King had raged—but Kulal hadn't cared about his brush with death. Even before he'd left the palace to fight, he had been given hints of the frailty of human existence. He had learnt lessons which had stayed darkly in his heart. And now it seemed there was another lesson to be learnt.

He stared at her, his lips curling. 'I am merely suggesting you might wish to change—perhaps to rest—before we have dinner.'

She gave a hollow laugh. 'You really think I want to have dinner with you, Kulal?'

'Actually, no. I don't. I think we've been forced into a position where we're going to have to do things which neither of us will find particularly palatable—'

'I'm keeping my baby!' she defended instantly.

Kulal stiffened, his nostrils narrowing as he inhaled an unsteady breath. 'How dare you imply that I should wish otherwise?' he flared. But although his anger would have filled any of his subjects with fear, it was having no effect on Hannah, for she was tilting her chin in a way which was positively *defiant*.

'I'm just letting you know the ground rules from the start, so there can be no misunderstanding,' she said. 'And I can't see the point of us having dinner.'

'Can't you?' He raised his eyebrows. 'You need to eat and we need to talk. Why not kill two birds with one stone?'

Her gaze became hooded, thick lashes shuttering her aquamarine eyes like dark feathers. 'I feel it's my duty to tell you,' she flared, 'just in case you're getting any autocratic ideas of whisking me away so I'm never heard of again—that my sister knows exactly where I am and she has the number of the police on speed-dial.'

It was such an outrageous remark that Kulal almost smiled until the gravity of the situation hit him and all levity vanished. Because humble Hannah Wilson was not as compliant as he had initially thought, was she?

'Let's say eight o'clock, shall we?' he questioned, eager to reassert his authority. 'And please don't keep me waiting.'

CHAPTER SIX

PRIMED FOR THE Sheikh's knock at precisely eight o'clock, Hannah sneaked one last glance at the mirror, then wished she hadn't. Because this was the reverse side of the fairy tale, wasn't it? This was the reality. Last time she'd spent the evening with Kulal, she had been transformed with a wave of the stylist's magic wand. With her costly jewels and a silken gown she'd looked like someone he might wish to be seen with. But not any more. She had been sick during the early weeks of her pregnancy and, as a consequence, her face had acquired a horrible gauntness. Her dress looked cheap—because it was—her breasts felt heavy, and now she was going to have to endure a stilted dinner in some fancy restaurant with a man who had never wanted to see her again and meanwhile…

Kulal hadn't said a single positive word about the baby.

He hadn't said any of the things she'd secretly been wishing for, even though she'd told herself it was madness to expect anything from such a man. He hadn't reassured her that, although becoming a father had been the last thing on his mind, he would step up to the plate and take responsibility—and he certainly hadn't cooed with pleasure or puffed his chest with pride. He had just studied her dispassionately as if she were no longer a woman, merely an inconvenience who had suddenly appeared in his life. He had installed her in a suite at the Royal Palace Hotel—admittedly the biggest suite she had ever seen. But she had felt small and insignificant within its gilded walls and, when she'd woken from her restless nap, had wandered aimlessly from room to room, wondering what on earth was going to happen next.

An authoritative rap put paid to any further introspection and Hannah opened the door to find Kulal standing there, the bronze shimmer of his robes alerting her to the fact that he too had changed. Had he rushed back to the *real* palace for a quick wash and brush-up, she wondered—just about to tell him that she wasn't sure she could endure going to a stuffy restaurant, when she noticed two hotel employees wheeling a vast trolley towards them, bearing unseen dishes topped with gleaming silver domes.

'I thought we'd eat here,' he said peremptorily, walking into the room without invitation, the waiters trundling the trolley immediately behind him.

Hannah opened her mouth to object to his cavalier attitude then shut it again. Because really, what was the point? While one waiter set the table positioned in a far alcove, she was forced to endure the tops of the silver dishes being triumphantly whipped off by the other, like a magician producing a series of rabbits at the culmination of his act. But she felt no enthusiasm for the feast which was revealed, despite the alluring display of pomegranate-peppered rice and vegetables cooked with nuts and a sweet paste she'd never heard of. She waited until she and Kulal were alone before turning to him, not caring whether her face showed her growing frustration or not.

'Why are we eating here?' she questioned baldly. 'Because you're ashamed of being seen with me?'

He didn't react to her truculent tone, adopting instead a tone of voice she suspected was meant to calm her down.

'A public appearance will serve little purpose other than to aggravate the situation,' he said. 'I don't particularly want reporters seeing us out together—not at this stage. Sit down, Hannah. You should eat something. Now. Before we have any kind of discourse. Before you keel over and faint—because that really *would* be a bore.'

His tone was crisp and authoritative and, although Hannah was still in a mood of rebellion against his high-handedness, she knew that for the sake of her baby she should heed his words. So she sat down opposite him, at a table laid with snowy linen, silver cutlery and crystal glasses—and ate some food with all the enjoyment of somebody being forced to finish a school dinner. It was only when she had put her fork down that she noticed his own plate lay barely touched.

'Yet you aren't eating yourself?' she observed.

'I'm not hungry. I have work to attend to after our meeting and food will make me sleepy.'

His answer left Hannah in no doubt that whatever he was planning, it certainly wasn't seduction—and she was unprepared for the feeling of *rejection* which washed over her. Was he regretting ever having been intimate with her? she wondered. Probably. If she had been in his shoes wouldn't she have felt the same way?

Carefully, she folded her napkin—the way she'd seen countless guests do at the Granchester—and placed it on the table. But the first proper meal she'd had in days was actually making her feel stronger—and strength was what she needed right now. Trying not to be affected by the dark glitter of his eyes, she sat back in her chair.

'So,' she said.

'So?' He raised his eyebrows at her questioningly.

Hannah's foster father had been a gambler and she knew a bit about bargaining. She knew that in a situation like this, where the stakes were high, whoever broke first would lose, and who kept their nerve would win. But she suspected that there weren't going to be any real winners or losers in this situation and, besides, she hadn't come here to make demands of him. She didn't want his money or a title, no matter what he might think. She'd come here to give him her momentous news in person and the rest was up to him. And wasn't there something else? The only positive glimmer in his attitude towards her?

'I suppose I should be grateful you haven't demanded a paternity test,' she said.

He shrugged. 'I thought about it. I spent the hours between our meeting this afternoon and coming here this evening wondering whether I should ask the palace doctor to accompany me and have him test you.'

'But you decided not to?'

His eyes glittered as he acknowledged her challenge. 'I did.'

'Might I ask why?'

He leaned back in his chair to study her. 'I realised that a woman who had waited until she was twenty-five to take her first lover would be unlikely to take two within the space of a few months.'

There was a pause as she summoned up the courage to say it. 'Yet you didn't mention it at the time.'

'Your virginity, you mean?' he probed.

For all her newly acquired bravado, Hannah found herself blushing and, as a distraction, took a sip of the delicious sweet-sharp pink drink which she'd never tasted anywhere else. 'Yes.'

'What was I supposed to do? Exclaim with delirious joy?' His lips curved into a mocking smile. 'Or perhaps you expected me to be angry? To demand why you had waited for so long to have sex, and why you hadn't told me?' He shrugged his broad shoulders and his powerful muscles rippled beneath the bronze silk of his robes. 'My ego would not have allowed me to ask such disingenuous questions and, besides, you are not the first virgin I have bedded.'

Oddly enough, that hurt—even though it infuriated Hannah that it should do. She told herself she shouldn't allow herself to be hurt by a man who had never intended their liaison to be anything other than a one-night stand—and it was certainly not a good idea to start imagining the other women who had sighed with pleasure in his arms. 'Anyway, that's beside the point...' she said, determined not to allow a dangerous wistfulness to creep into their negotiations.

His black gaze lasered into her as her words tailed off. 'Which is?'

'I need to know what kind of involvement you'd like in the baby's life. If any,' she added quickly, because she certainly wasn't going to force him into something he didn't want to do. And you can't force him, she remembered. He's a king. 'To know how we're going to deal with this situation.'

He drifted his fingertip around the rim of his crystal glass before lifting his gaze to hers and his face had assumed an almost cruel expression. 'And what would you like to happen, Hannah?' he questioned softly. 'For me to marry you in a glittering ceremony and make you my Queen—is that your secret dream?'

Hannah didn't react in the way she wanted to. In the way her seething hormones were urging her to. Years of keeping the peace were finally paying dividends so that she was able to produce a calm look in response to his arrogant statement.

'Are you making the assumption that I would say yes to such a proposal?' she questioned coolly.

It gave her an inordinate amount of pleasure to see him looking momentarily wrong-footed. And confused.

'You're trying to tell me you would refuse such an offer?' he demanded.

And suddenly all Hannah's determination to keep calm dissolved beneath his arrogant sense of *certainty*. 'Too right I would,' she said fervently. 'I don't really know you and at this moment, I'm not sure whether I even like you. We both probably want completely different things, so why would I marry you? I've had enough experience to realise that unless two people share a common goal, then marriage can be an out-and-out disaster.'

Kulal grew very still because, uncannily, she was echoing his own thoughts on the subject. He stared across the table at her. Had she guessed about his childhood? Pieced together the deliberately vague facts which were the only ones on record and somehow made sense of them? Stored that knowledge away as a point-scoring weapon to use when the time was right?

He sucked oxygen deep into his lungs. No. His parents' marriage had been a secret to the rest of the world because in those days, the press had not been at liberty to report on rumours and hearsay. And although Kulal was regarded as a modern monarch, he was grateful for those historic restrictions. Even his mother's death had been hushed up in the only way which had been acceptable at the time and if you buried something deep enough, you could guarantee it would never see the light of day. He swallowed, wanting something to distract him from the bitter memories which were darkening his mind, and so he did what for him was unthinkable. He asked Hannah about her past.

'Your parents weren't happy?'

She shook her head. 'No.'

'And where are they now?' he said. 'Are they going to make a dramatic appearance, demanding I do the right thing by you?'

Did she recognise that his questions were a tactical move to focus attention on her, not him? Was that why a shadow crossed her face and why her curvy little body suddenly tensed?

'I didn't have any parents.'

'You must have—'

'Oh, there were two people who *conceived* me,' she said, not appearing to care that she'd interrupted him. 'But I didn't know them. Or rather, I can't remember them.'

This was the point at which Kulal would normally grow bored, and wary. He'd learnt to his cost that the more you allowed a woman to talk about herself, the

more it gave a falsely inflated sense of her own impor-
tance. But he could see this was different. Hannah was
not some lover who would soon be removed from his
orbit as diplomatically as possible, once he had taken
his fill of her. If he wanted any part of his child's life,
then she was going to be around for the long-haul.

His mouth hardened. How ironic that his future was
to be inextricably linked to a woman he'd spent a single
night with. A woman who could not have been more
unsuitable for the task of bearing his heir. Yet their
child would carry the genes of both their forebears,
he reminded himself—so wasn't it his duty to gather
as much information as possible? His mouth hardened
with new resolve. Because you never knew when such
information might become *useful*.

He stared at her, aware that her defiant mask had
slipped—showing a trace of vulnerability which had
softened her face. And for some crazy reason, he was
reminded of the night he'd spent with her, when her
rosy lips had trembled whenever he had kissed her.
When she'd shivered with ecstasy as he'd brought her
to yet another breathtaking orgasm. When she'd curled
up in his arms afterwards and clung to his neck like a
little kitten. 'So what happened with your parents?' he
questioned, aware that his voice had gentled. 'Do you
want to tell me?'

Actually, no. Hannah didn't want that. Not at all. But
the only thing worse than telling him would be *not* telling him. He seemed to want to keep their liaison and
everything else a secret, but she wasn't naïve enough to
think they could do that for ever. If word got out that she
had been the Sheikh's lover, then wouldn't people start
prying into her background and rooting up all kinds of

horrible stuff? She would come over as the victim she had tried so very hard not to be.

So take control of the facts and tell him yourself.

'I was brought up in care,' she said slowly. 'With my sister.'

'Care?' he questioned blankly.

'It's when your parents can't look after you—or if they don't want to.'

'And which category did yours fall into?'

Hannah shrugged. 'I don't really know a lot about them. Only what I was told when I was old enough to understand. My mother was kicked out by her parents when she was seventeen.' There was a pause before she said it, because she didn't want to say it. If she told him, would he freak out? Worry that his baby was going to inherit some disturbing traits, like addiction? But if he freaked out, then so be it. She couldn't change facts and she mustn't start being afraid of how Kulal might choose to interpret them, just because he was in a position of power. 'She developed a drug habit.'

'Your mother was a junkie?' he exclaimed in horror.

Hannah's lips tightened. It was funny how you could still be loyal to someone who hadn't wanted you. Someone who had broken every rule in the parental handbook. 'She didn't inject,' she said defensively, as if that made everything all right, and she found herself wondering if children were conditioned never to give up hope that one day their parents would love them and cherish them. Her hand moved instinctively to lie on her belly and she saw Kulal watching her closely. 'But she took pretty much everything else which was on offer. My father was a rich student from New York, who enjoyed the same kind of...*pastimes*. The pregnancy wasn't planned—obviously.' Her mouth twisted. 'Apparently, my mother wanted to get married. But then his parents arrived from America, scooped him up and put him into rehab and gave my mother a very large cheque, making it clear that, if she cashed it, they never wanted to see her again.'

'And?' he said, into the silence which followed.

'That's exactly what she did. She took the money and ran.'

'So was that a satisfactory outcome?' he questioned softly.

Hannah shrugged. 'Satisfactory for her, I guess—until she ran out of cash. She started renting an apartment which was way too expensive for someone with limited funds and no employment. But in the circles she mixed in, she was suddenly seen as something of a catch—for as long as the money lasted. And that's when she got pregnant with my sister.'

'You mean, your father came back from America?'

'No, that's not what I mean at all,' she said, giving a hollow laugh. 'My sister and I don't share the same father.'

Thoughtfully, he nodded. 'I see. So you're not full sisters, just half-sisters?'

His words were like punches and Hannah recoiled from them. 'Not just *anything*,' she contradicted, her hand slapping against a heart which was racing like a train. 'Tamsyn and I are as close as any two sisters could be and I would do anything for her, do you understand? *Anything.*'

Again, he nodded. 'Tell me what happened to you both.'

Had he used the word *both* to mollify her—a silent

admission that he had underestimated her loyalty to her sister? Hannah didn't know, but she found herself wanting to continue with her story. Was that because she never talked about it? Why would she? Yet she was finding it cathartic to let it all out for once, to tell the father of her child all about her chequered background.

'The local council stepped in and put us in a home and tried to get us fostered out as quickly as possible.' She saw another look of non-comprehension cloud his ebony eyes and it occurred to Hannah that, for all his power and position, Kulal was ignorant about some things. Well, of course he was, she thought. He'd been protected for all his privileged life, hadn't he? He wasn't like her. Thrown to the wolves and left to fend for herself… 'They try to find you a family, who can then foster or adopt you,' she explained.

'Is that what happened to you?'

Hannah shrugged as she reached for her glass and took another sip of the sweet-sharp cordial. Yes, a foster home had been found for her and Tamsyn. All the boxes on the form had been ticked by the social worker in charge of the case and everyone had been satisfied that two neglected little girls had a stable home to go to at last. But it hadn't felt like that. How could she explain to a man like Kulal that something which appeared normal on the outside could be anything but normal when you were inside, living it?

'We had a roof over our heads and beds to sleep in,' she said.

Kulal's eyes narrowed. 'You weren't happy?'

She hesitated. 'Happiness is overrated, don't you think?' she said brightly. 'We waste so much time chasing it and, in my experience, it never lasts. My foster father spent most of his money gambling, or wining and dining whichever woman he happened to be seducing at the time.'

His big body suddenly grew tense and his eyes became so dark it was as if someone had suddenly snuffed out all the light which normally gleamed in their ebony depths. 'I think many people have experience of fathers who like sexual variety,' he ground out.

Hannah blinked. Was he saying something like that had happened to *him*? 'You mean your—?'

'This is your story,' he said roughly. 'Not mine.'

She nodded. 'My foster mother was the kind of woman who just pretended nothing was wrong, even though there was barely enough money for food sometimes. She liked to put on a bit of a show in front of all the neighbours. I was forced to resort to unsavoury methods of making sure Tamsyn and I got fed. Skips containing food thrown out by the supermarkets was my favourite.'

He recoiled in horror. 'So why didn't you tell someone in authority? Ask to be sent to a different home?'

'Because Tamsyn was mixed up and difficult!' she burst out, as all the feelings she'd been bottling up for weeks could no longer be contained. 'She'd had a terrible start in life—far worse than mine—and she acted out on it. Not many people could have coped with her and I knew that if I complained, we would be split up.' She pushed back her chair so that it scraped against the marble floor and rose shakily to her feet. 'And I couldn't bear for us to be split up!'

He rose as soon as she did—moving towards her with his bronze robes shimmering as he gestured towards the chair she had just vacated. 'Please sit down,

Hannah. I didn't mean to disturb you with my questions.'

'I don't want to sit down! I want…' Her words faded away and suddenly it was all too much. She had told him far too much. Hannah walked over to the window, blinking back the unwanted tears which had sprung to her eyes as she looked out at the turreted skyline.

'I think I know what you want, Hannah.'

She blinked away the blur of tears as his voice grew closer. She could hear the richly accented inflection which reminded her so vividly of the night she'd spent with him. That unforgettable night, when he'd whispered things in a language she hadn't understood but that hadn't seemed to matter at the time. Because Kulal had made her feel like a woman for the first time in her life. He had taken her in his arms and given her the gift of sexual pleasure. Was that why her skin was automatically reacting to the soft caress of his words, even now? Why the tips of her breasts were growing heavy and she found herself longing for him to cup them again, to circle his thumbs over their nail-hard tips and then to take them in his mouth?

With an effort, she reminded herself it was no good getting aroused at a time like this. Or sentimental. She needed to fight the sudden rush of longing which was welling up inside her. But deep down, she was praying he would pull her into his arms and comfort her. Smooth her head as you would a frightened child. Tell her that everything was going to be all right and he would do everything within his power to make that happen.

But he didn't. He just continued speaking in that same measured tone and Hannah didn't dare turn to face him because she didn't trust her own reaction.

'Do you?' she said woodenly.

'Indeed I do. A solution which could work well for everyone.'

'A solution?' she questioned doubtfully, but her question was definitely tinged with hope as she turned to face him.

'Something which would minimise the damage of this unexpected event.'

Minimise the damage. Those were not the words of someone intent on soothing a troubled heart. Those were fighting words—Hannah instinctively recognised that. Ironing every trace of emotion from her voice, she stared into his ebony eyes. 'What exactly did you have in mind, Kulal?'

Unusually, Kulal hesitated before saying his next words, aware of their impact and their power. But what *other* solution could they reach, in the circumstances? He hadn't wanted to be a father but, since the decision had now been forced upon him, he needed to take control. To do the right thing—as he had spent his whole life doing. The only thing. He met the blinking scrutiny of her gaze with a renewed feeling of resolve. 'You say that your own mother was given a cheque in order to make her life easier and that she squandered that sum by living beyond her means.'

'That's right,' she agreed steadily. 'I did.'

'What if I were to go one step further?' he mused. 'What if I were to guarantee you the kind of sum which would mean you wouldn't "run out" of cash ever again?'

'You're talking about a lot of money,' she said carefully.

'I am,' he agreed, with equal care.

'And what would I have to do in return for such a sum?' she questioned, her voice trembling a little now.

'I think we both know the answer to that, Hannah,' he said, almost gently. 'You do the only sensible thing. Give me the child to be brought up as my heir.'

'G-give you the child?' she echoed.

He nodded. 'In the absence of any other heir, this child could inherit all that I own—my lands, my crown and my kingdom. Let your baby go and I promise to do everything in my power to provide everything he or she needs. They will grow up as a Zahristan royal with all the luxury that entails, not someone who is constantly being dragged between two cultures.' He paused and suddenly his face changed, became a harsh, stark study in light and shade. 'Between two people who are little more than strangers to one another.'

Hannah felt grateful for the anger which had started to flood through her like a tidal wave, obliterating the trembling emotions which his callous words had provoked. Because anger made you strong. It didn't weaken or debilitate you in the way that pain or fear or desire did. Perhaps if she had been bigger she might have flown at him and slapped her palm against his arrogant face and hit him over and over again. But her blows would be ineffectual, and to attack him physically would be to humiliate herself.

Instead, she drew on all her reserves of inner strength as her well-honed survival mode kicked in, just as it had done so many times before. And suddenly it was easy to look at those cruel lips without remembering what it was like to kiss them. And even easier to find the right note of contempt in her voice as she stared into the fathomless gleam of his black eyes.

'I'm not going to dignify your insulting offer with an answer. I'm going back to England, where I will continue working and raising my child on my own as so many other women do. And you can go to hell, Kulal,' she added bitterly.

CHAPTER SEVEN

'HE DIDN'T SAY *THAT*? Come off it, Hannah—you're exaggerating!'

Hannah shook her head as she stared into her sister's emerald eyes. 'I wish I was, but that's the truth,' she said tiredly.

'He offered to *buy your baby*?'

'He didn't phrase it quite as brutally as that, but that's what it came down to, yes.' Hannah moved her shoulders restlessly. 'Perhaps I shouldn't have told you.'

'Too right you should have told me,' said Tamsyn fiercely. 'I feel like going to the papers and exposing him for the man he really is. It's outrageous. It's barbaric! It's—'

'And if you ever do that,' interrupted Hannah quietly, 'in fact, if you ever discuss this with anyone without my permission—I will never speak to you again.'

Tamsyn shook her head, her rich red curls shimmering all the way down her narrow back. 'I just don't get it. You're being loyal to *him*? King Callous? Someone who doesn't deserve your loyalty?'

'I'm trying to do what is best for the baby,' said Hannah as the kettle whistled out the fact that it had boiled. Reaching up, she took two mugs from the cupboard and dropped a peppermint teabag into each. 'And forming some kind of vendetta against the baby's father is not what I had in mind.'

'So he didn't try to stop you when you told him you were leaving?'

Hannah nodded. 'He did. He backtracked and apologised and told me he should never have said it, but the damage was done as far as I was concerned. I told him I had no intention of changing my mind and was flying back to England as soon as I could fix a flight. And that's when he insisted on putting me on one of his private jets.'

'But you refused, right?'

Hannah picked up the kettle and poured boiling water onto the peppermint teabags. She had *wanted* to refuse and pride had been urging her to do just that, but she'd been emotionally wrung out by everything that had happened and physically exhausted, too. She had started to worry that so much stress would be bad for the baby and the thought of being able to sleep in a proper bed on the Sheikh's plane instead of being cramped in the middle of a row of four had proved too powerful a lure to resist. But she hadn't given him her acceptance until one final streak of defiance had reared its head and she had blurted out a sarcastic question to the black-eyed Sheikh who stood before her.

'But what will people think when they see some unknown English chambermaid using the Sheikh's private jet?'

'I don't care what they think,' he'd ground out. 'I am trying to do what is best.'

Her laugh had been bitter. 'Don't you think it's a little late for that, Kulal?'

She had seen him flinch in response to that particular dig and had tried to enjoy his discomfiture. But it hadn't seemed to work like that. She'd just felt completely wretched. So wretched that she hadn't had the energy to refuse a ride in the limousine that had been waiting on her arrival back in London and had whisked her home in purring luxury. It had felt strange stepping out into the gusty chill of the October evening after her brief exposure to the Zahristan sun, but at once she was back to her small room in the Granchester's staff quarters, she'd finally felt able to rest. She had lain down and slept for a solid twelve hours and had woken with a feeling of resolve before demolishing an enormous breakfast.

She'd convinced herself it was best to keep her dreadful trip to Zahristan quiet, but force of habit had made her text Tamsyn to tell her she was back and when her sister had come rushing round, Hannah had found herself blurting everything out. Because they'd always told each other everything…and because she'd felt as if she would burst if she didn't tell *someone*.

'So how did you leave it with the cold-hearted bastard?' Tamsyn was saying as she sipped the peppermint tea which Hannah had just handed her.

You never entirely relinquished the role of elder sister, Hannah thought as she fixed her sister with another expression of mild reproof. 'Please don't say that. His name is Kulal and I refuse to get into name-calling.'

'But he's—'

'He's probably still reeling from the shock of discovering I'm pregnant—and shock makes people react in all kinds of weird ways.'

'Hannah, why do you always have to be so *kind*?'

'I am not being *kind*,' said Hannah, twisting a strand of her long hair round and round one finger. 'I am trying to be practical. Kulal is the father of my child and even if he never wants to see either of us again, I am not going to bring this baby up to hate him.'

'So you'll lie to your child?' accused Tamsyn bitterly. 'Just like you lied to me?'

Hannah's lips flattened. How the past came back to haunt you when you least expected it! Or when you were least equipped to deal with it. 'I never lied to you, Tamsyn. I just tried to present reality in its least painful form,' she said. 'Just like I'm going to do with this baby. When the subject arises, I will just say that I was swept off my feet by a dashing man—which is true.'

'But words won't pay the bills. How the hell are you going to *manage*, Hannah? Do you really think you can live life as a single mother on a chambermaid's wages?'

'Other women manage.'

'And aren't you forgetting something else? I thought Granchester employees weren't allowed to sleep with the guests. What if somebody finds out?'

Hannah winced at her sister's candour. 'Nobody's going to find out, are they?' she said with a confidence she didn't quite feel as she picked up her mug and sipped from it. But the loud ringing of her phone suddenly broke into the uneasy silence and her heart gave a sudden clench as she glanced down at the number before accepting the call. With a rapidly escalating heartbeat, she listened to the voice at the other end and when she'd cut the connection, she looked into Tamsyn's eyes and tried to keep the tremble of fear from her voice. 'That was HR,' she said unsteadily. 'And they want to see me immediately.'

* * *

Kulal knocked on a door which was exactly the same as all the others on both sides of the narrow corridor, unprepared for the tiny redheaded figure who flew at him when it was opened.

'You bastard!' she declared, curling her hands into small fists. 'How dare you?'

He honestly thought she might be about to hit him and was wondering whether to summon the female bodyguard he'd had the presence of mind to bring and who was standing just along the corridor, when he saw Hannah appear behind the redhead.

'Tamsyn,' she said, her voice sounding unnaturally calm. 'That kind of talk isn't going to help.'

The redhead didn't budge. 'Says who?'

'I do. And now I'd like you to go home because I need to talk to Kulal.'

'You think I'm leaving you alone? With *him*?'

For the first time, Kulal spoke, realising who the little spitfire must be. 'And if I give you my word that I have your sister's welfare at heart?'

The redhead tilted her chin to fix him with a spitting emerald gaze which was so unlike the cool blue of Hannah's eyes. 'I wouldn't trust your word just as far as I could throw it and I'm not going anywhere!' she declared.

But several minutes later, after repeated assurances from Hannah that she would ring her once 'he' had gone, Tamsyn Wilson departed with another furious shake of her red curls and Kulal was left alone with Hannah.

He looked at her. Her face was pale and her eyes were angry, but there was a dignity about her, too. Something almost *noble* about her demeanour, which had the peculiar effect of making Kulal want to take her in his arms and cradle her, but instinct told him not to dare. She didn't look particularly surprised to see him—her expression was one of resignation. But there was certainly no pleasure or delight on her face and he wasn't used to being given such a lukewarm reception.

'Hello, Hannah,' he said.

Hannah took her time before answering him.

How strange to see the Sheikh of Zahristan standing on the doorstep of her humble staff quarters despite the fact that today he wasn't dressed in the flowing robes and headdress which had made him look so imperious on their last meeting. His immaculate suit was unashamedly cosmopolitan and only the hard planes of his face and distinctive hawk-like features spoke of his particular royal heritage. Her heart was pounding and although she tried to tell herself that the rapid beat was caused by apprehension, she knew that wasn't entirely true. Because her breasts were tingling and there was a tug, low in her belly, which spoke of feelings which were a long way from anger. How was it possible to feel attracted to someone, when they were trying to treat you like an inconvenient object who needed to be moved out of the way as quickly as possible?

Well, he might be a king and she might be a chambermaid, but he would only walk all over her if she let him. So don't let him. She tilted her chin. 'Why are you here, Kulal?'

His gaze was steady. 'Don't you think we have some business to discuss?'

'I thought we'd said everything which needed saying.'

'Please, Hannah.'

Was it hearing him say a word she suspected he didn't use very often which made her relent? 'You'd better come in,' she said ungraciously, turning her back on him and retreating into the small room.

'Thanks,' he said and followed her inside.

'Please don't thank me, Kulal. It's not something I particularly want to do,' she said, watching as he closed the door. 'I just didn't want to have a difficult confrontation in the corridor, with the other staff listening. Though of course I'm no longer a member of staff,' she added. 'Since I've just been sacked—for which apparently I have *you* to thank.' Some of her coolness began to evaporate. 'Couldn't you accept the fact I'd refused your insulting offer to buy my baby?' she demanded, her voice rising as she thought of her blameless work record besmirched by an arrogant piece of manoeuvring by the Sheikh. 'Did the King decide he had to try to get his own way, no matter what? Was that why you got straight on the phone to the owner of the Granchester, just because he happens to be a *mate of yours*? I can't believe you actually rang Zac Constantinides to tell him you'd had sex with me—the woman in Human Resources was practically shaking with rage!'

'I saw no alternative,' Kulal answered calmly. 'You made it clear your intention to continue working as a chambermaid and there was no way I could allow that to happen.'

'Why not?'

'Why not?' Kulal glanced around the small room with a look of genuine consternation, taking in the cramped dimensions and the institutional red-and-white sign which pointed to the fire escape. 'Because you are carrying my child! A child who will be a prince or princess of Zahristan. What were you thinking was going to happen, Hannah? That you would carry on making beds and cleaning up after guests until you became too cumbersome to continue? And then what? Perhaps you were planning to bring the royal heir back here and place him or her in a crib while you continued to service the rooms?'

She was grinding her teeth together like a little animal. 'I would have managed,' she said fiercely. 'I have always managed in the past.'

In any other circumstances, Kulal might have coldly drawn her attention to the fact that she was only *just about* managing, but once again instinct told him to tread carefully because he could see the flicker of fear in her eyes, which she was desperately trying to hide. 'When is the baby due?' he questioned, trying to remember the word which Zac's wife, Emma, had used. A word Kulal had said many times before, of course—but never in this particular context. 'Are you…*showing* yet?'

This question seemed to annoy her. 'Not yet. I'm only just over twelve weeks and I could have managed to keep it secret for a few weeks more, if you hadn't blurted it out and…' She stared at him and an exasperated sigh escaped her lips. 'Why have you come here today, Kulal? To gloat?'

'Of course it's not to gloat,' he said impatiently. 'I am here because I want to help you.'

'Funny way you have of showing it. I've already told you I'm not interested in your insulting offer and even if you've come here today to increase your price—*my baby is not for sale!*'

'I haven't. In fact, I've given the matter more deliberation. Perhaps I was a little hasty before.'

Her voice was bitter. 'You don't say?'

'I should have considered all the options before I spoke.' Kulal drew in a deep breath, knowing that what he was about to do was the right thing. The only thing he could do, no matter that it went against everything he'd ever wanted. He tried to smile, but his face felt like a piece of concrete, against which the movement of his mouth barely made an impression. He looked at the tiny woman with the belligerent expression. 'I have decided I will marry you after all,' he said heavily. 'It will be a marriage of duty and of sacrifice on both our parts—for the sake of our baby.'

She was staring at him like someone waiting for the punchline. She narrowed her eyes. 'Is this some kind of joke?'

'Why would I joke about something as serious as offering to make you my Queen?'

'I thought we'd already had this conversation. We both agreed that marriage between two people who don't even like each other is a bad idea.'

It was not the reaction he was expecting and Kulal couldn't quite believe it. He searched her face, wondering if it was a feigned response designed to make him push his case more strongly, but her consternation seemed genuine. Surely she was not opposed to a proposition which most women would have leapt at? He studied her more closely. The sharp pallor which had been in evidence when she had flown to Zahristan had given way to a healthy glow, against which her eyes sparkled like pale blue stars. The pregnancy had made her dark hair even more lustrous than before and it hung in gleaming waves around her shoulders. Perhaps it was time to take charge. To show her he had strength enough for both of them. And wouldn't action be more effective than words—reminding her that they had a rare chemistry between them?

Closing the small space between them, he reached out and pulled her into his arms, recognising from her instinctive shiver of pleasure that sometimes a woman could crave a man's touch, even if she didn't want to. He ran his thumb down the side of her cheek, giving her time to move away, because no way would he be accused of coercion. But she didn't move. She stayed right where she was and her mouth was trembling with unspoken invitation as he lowered his head towards hers.

Their lips collided—first hard, then soft.

A meeting and then a slow exploration.

He heard her moan and the sound was enough to fuel his rising need. Barely a whisper of breath passed from her mouth into his—but it contained a hunger which mirrored his own. His arms tightened and he could feel her breasts pressing into him, her nipples hardening like tiny bullets against his chest. And Kulal found himself driven on by an urgent hunger because never had a kiss tasted as sweet as this. As sweet as any battle victory, he thought longingly, as his tongue laced with hers. Was it because she was pregnant with his child, or because she was the only woman who had ever opposed him and that in itself was a huge turn-on?

'Hannah,' he husked out, aware of the rocky hardness between his thighs and longing to lose himself deep inside her. 'Be my bride.'

Afterwards, he would curse himself for having spoken because his words shattered the erotic interlude—

more than that, his momentary sexual hunger had given *her* all the power. Suddenly, the spell was broken and she pulled away from him, her eyes blazing. She swayed a little and automatically, he put out his hand to steady her, but she waved him away.

'Are you out of your mind?' she demanded, untidy locks of hair tumbling around her flushed cheeks. 'Coming onto me like that when we're supposed to be having a discussion about our baby?'

'Are you trying to deny that you wanted me?' he mocked.

She shook her head. 'No. I can't deny that, but it was…inappropriate. Just like your proposal of marriage was inappropriate.'

'Why?' he demanded hotly.

'Do you think I'm a fool, Kulal? That just because I make beds and clean rooms for a living, I'm incapable of understanding what's staring me in the face?'

Momentarily wrong-footed by such a mercurial switch of mood, Kulal narrowed his eyes. 'I make no such judgment of your character.'

'Are you sure? Did your advisors tell you to marry me after your initial aversion to the idea? Did they suggest that if I wasn't prepared to sell you my baby, then a king's ring on my finger would mean you could get hold of your child by legal means instead?'

'You think that I would take such advice from my *advisors*?' he thundered. 'They would not dare presume to tell me how to live my life!' He drew in a deep breath. 'The decision is mine and mine alone—and besides, marriage to me would protect you, not weaken you.'

She shook her head. 'No, it wouldn't. It would simply make me your possession. We both know that.'

Frustratedly, Kulal turned away from her, staring out of the tiny window which overlooked a courtyard, in which plastic bins were lined up like sentries. Rain had begun to slant down in a thin grey curtain. Everything looked so grey, he thought, and as he tried to imagine his child growing up in such an environment, a feeling of powerlessness washed over him. Once, he had vowed never to allow himself to feel that way again, but suddenly he recognised that you couldn't always dictate events. That sometimes life took you along a path you hadn't intended, and having a royal status made no difference to that journey. He had grown up with all the riches in the world, but that hadn't made a bit of difference to the fact that he and his brother had been at the mercy of a manipulative mother who had wanted only one thing. And it hadn't been them.

His mouth hardened. His mistrust of the opposite sex was rooted deep in his psyche and Hannah Wilson was reinforcing all his worst prejudices. He knew only too well how unpredictable women could be and here was a prime example of someone who manifested that dangerous, innate quality. It hadn't taken long for the humble chambermaid to morph into a self-possessed creature who was airily rejecting a king's marriage proposal, had it? She was far less of a pushover than she should have been, given her status. Did the knowledge that his flesh grew inside her give her the confidence to address him as if he were any other man?

He was tempted to tell her that she would obey him because his wishes were always acceded to. Yet he recognised it wasn't that simple. He couldn't *force* this Englishwoman to marry him, but maybe he could persuade her.

Once again, he allowed his gaze to linger on the cramped dimensions of the tiny staff room. 'So where are you planning to live, once you leave your job?'

Hannah had thought about this. A lot. She hated the fact that economically, she and Kulal were poles apart, but there wasn't a lot she could do about it. She thought longingly about money she'd saved. Money which had taken so long to accumulate and which was nearly enough for the deposit on a tiny apartment. It didn't look as if that little dream of independence was going to happen now, but sometimes you had to let your dreams go. 'I have savings I can live on.'

'How long do you think they're going to last?'

She shrugged. 'Long enough. And when they run out, I can find myself a job as a housekeeper—somewhere which will provide a roof over my head for me and my baby.'

'A housekeeper?' he exclaimed in horror. 'You think I would ever allow you to bring up the future prince or princess of Zahristan as the child of a *housekeeper*?'

'But you can't…' Her fingers moved to her neck, spreading wide as if to disguise the flickering pulse there. 'You can't stop me.'

'You don't think so?' He gave a cynical laugh. 'I can certainly try. I can assign bodyguards and have you watched twenty-four-seven. Every move you make will be reported back to me and analysed.' His eyes were dark. Dark as the coal at the bottom of a bunker which had never seen daylight. 'And before you protest that such a move would be invasive—let's just say I am protecting what is mine.'

'The courts will ask you to pay maintenance.' There was raw appeal in her voice now. 'And I'm not too stupid or too proud to turn it down. Surely that's enough to reassure you that the baby and I won't be living in poverty.'

'Yes, I will pay maintenance,' he affirmed coldly. 'I don't need a court of law to make me honour my obligations. But my child will not have the life it is owed by royal blood. By turning down my offer of marriage, you are condemning he or she to a life of illegitimacy. Is that really what you want, Hannah?'

Hannah flinched as Kulal's words pierced through her armour at last. Having worked his way through all other arguments, had he saved the most powerful for last? Oh, *why* had she told him about her sordid past? Had she really been naïve enough to think he wouldn't store up that information and use it against her if needed? Because her illegitimacy—and Tamsyn's—had always been the dull pain which had eaten away inside her. The shame which had provided the backdrop to their young lives. It had emphasised Hannah's feelings of insecurity and although she'd pretended not to care about being born out of wedlock, she *had* cared. Things were different these days and nobody seemed to care very much whether a man and a woman went through a marriage ceremony before having a child, but it hadn't always been that way.

And she was not carrying any child.

This was a *royal child*.

The flat of her hand drifted down to touch her belly, like someone touching wood for luck—but somehow Hannah sensed that there was no *luck* to be found. 'I could run away and you could never find me,' she breathed.

'I would find you,' he said.

He was beating down her arguments, one by one, and Hannah's head was spinning as she tried to imagine what marriage to such a man would mean. A few minutes ago, he had taken her in his arms and kissed her and she had let him. She had done much more than let him—and he was experienced enough to realise how much she wanted him. She might have had the presence of mind to pull away, but what if he approached her during one of those vulnerable moments which seemed to be on the increase? What then?

Did she really imagine that a man like Kulal would be content to live a celibate life with his new bride?

Lifting her gaze to his, she tried to keep her voice matter-of-fact, but she could feel colour creeping into her cheeks as she asked the all-important question. 'If I were to agree to this…*marriage.*' She drew in a deep breath. 'Do you mean a marriage in…in every sense of the word?'

He seemed to find her discomfiture amusing. 'There's no need to look so terrified, Hannah—I won't be chaining you to the bed and demanding my conjugal rights. Unless that's your secret fantasy, of course.' He gave the ghost of a smile. 'The purpose of marriage is procreation and since we've achieved that without really trying, that just leaves sex. And we're both adults. We both need that release. In fact, I think the sex could work very well between us, since neither of us are blinded by emotion.'

'I can't…' She shook her head, shocked by the matter-of-fact way he had just come out and spoken about *release.* As if they were nothing but a pair of rutting animals. 'I can't think about that right now. It's all such a lot to take in.'

'Indeed it is. For both of us.' His gaze grew thoughtful. 'And you still haven't given me your answer.'

Hannah stared at him, knowing there was only one answer she could give him. Because she didn't have the energy or the inclination to spend her life fighting all that royal power and might, not when she suspected that, ultimately, Kulal would win. 'I will marry you, yes—to make our baby legitimate.'

'Good.'

'And if we find living together intolerable—what then?'

'If we agree from the outset not to make unrealistic demands on each other, then I see no reason why we should find it intolerable.'

'What kind of...unrealistic demands are you talking about?'

His face darkened, his hawk-like features tautening into a forbidding mask. 'I'm talking about love,' he said harshly. 'I don't ever want your *love*, Hannah. Do you understand?'

He said the word as if he had just sworn. As if it were a curse. And Hannah couldn't decide whether to commend him for his honesty or chastise him for his arrogance. Did he just assume that every woman would end up falling in love with him, no matter how badly he treated them? 'I don't think there's any danger of that, Kulal,' she said. 'But if we can't make it work...' she met the gleam of his eyes and said what needed to be said '...then I want your word that you will grant me my freedom and let me return to England.'

Kulal felt a wave of pity as she looked at him, but he didn't comment. Did she *really* think he would ever allow her to take his child out of the country? That he would meekly grant her the divorce she would no doubt demand? Shoving his hands deep into the pockets of his trousers, he clenched his fists. He had never imagined he could feel this way about something which didn't even exist, but when he thought about his unborn baby, something fierce licked at the solid ice which had always surrounded his heart. Fatherhood had been thrust upon him without warning and his response to it had taken him by surprise. Because he wanted this child, he realised. Wanted it with a fervour he had never known before.

And this woman would not stand in his way.

'We don't have to think about that right now,' he said silkily. 'Let's just get through the wedding, shall we?'

CHAPTER EIGHT

THE IMAGE WHICH stared back at her was strange and Hannah had never seen anything quite like it before. A woman clad entirely in a golden gown, the soft gleam emphasising the four-month curve of her fecund belly. The metallic shimmer looked more like armour than satin and her floaty veil of golden thread was held in place by a coronet of bright diamonds, which were fashioned to look like flowers.

This is me, thought Hannah—except it doesn't look like me.

This was the last time she would stand in front of a mirror as a single woman. A last glimpse of the old Hannah, before she was taken into the vast throne room where Kulal and the rest of the wedding party were waiting for her so the ceremony could begin. And *what* a wedding party. A nervous shiver ran down her spine because the size of the congregation was daunting—more than that, all the guests seemed to be billionaires or royalty.

Hannah reminded herself that she'd worked for these kinds of people ever since she'd been a rookie sixteen-year-old starting at the Granchester, and they were only flesh and blood—just like her. Even so, she didn't usually *socialise* with political leaders and sultans or academics and sports stars. The only person she'd met before was Salvatore Di Luca, who had arrived at the palace the previous evening and greeted her with a warmth which felt manufactured. She wondered if he remembered her as the last-minute guest Kulal had taken to his fancy party and whether he secretly disapproved of their unlikely union.

At least Zac Constantinides and his wife, Emma, had been unable to attend, and Hannah had felt nothing but relief when they'd cited a prior engagement in Zac's native Greece. Imagine how embarrassing *that* would have been—saying her vows in front of the ex-boss who'd been forced to fire her. It was just unfortunate that his cousin Xan was present and that he and Tamsyn seemed to have had some kind of run-in during the rehearsal last night.

She pleated her lips together as she made a final unnecessary adjustment to her veil, terrified Tamsyn was going to cause some kind of scene today. Because her little sister was on the rampage and making no attempt to hide her displeasure. Had Tamsyn guessed she was being railroaded into this marriage, despite her repeated assurances to the contrary? And was she determined to fight Hannah's corner for her, as her big sister had done for her so many times in the past?

But in the end, the choice Hannah had been forced to make had been a no-brainer.

Marriage which would confer legitimacy on her unborn child.

Or life as a struggling singleton, with the ever-present fear that Kulal might use his power and his influence to snatch her offspring away from her.

The soft voice of one of the servants interrupted

Hannah's reverie with a gentle question. 'You are ready, mistress?'

Hannah nodded as she picked up the heavy spray of white hyacinth interwoven with juniper berries—both national flowers of Zahristan. Briefly, she lifted the blooms to her nostrils, closing her eyes as she inhaled the heady scent—and then the ornate double doors were opened and she walked into the crowded throne room.

Hannah was aware of all eyes turning in her direction, but her self-consciousness dissolved the moment Kulal stepped towards her. Was it the fact that his eyes gleamed with what looked like approval, or was it the touch of his warm flesh as he brushed his hand over her cold fingers? Because in that moment, everyone else in the high-ceilinged chamber seemed to fade away as she focused her gaze on the man who would soon be her husband.

Beneath her wedding dress, she felt the tight squeeze of her heart—for this was Kulal as she'd never seen him before, wearing the richly embellished robes he'd told her were traditional for a marrying sheikh. He looked so tall and formidable, his raven hair covered by a shimmering headdress and his hawk-like features set and tense. Against the olive gleam of his skin, his eyes were like black diamonds, but as she studied him more closely, Hannah wondered if she had imagined the pain which had briefly shadowed their depths.

Was this ceremony bringing back memories she suspected he kept locked away? He'd told her that all Zahristan kings married within the walls of this ornate room, which meant that his parents must have made their vows here. Was he thinking of them now? Wishing they'd been here to witness the occasion? She'd asked him about his family last night, but his answers had been spare and unwilling, imparting only the most basic of facts. His parents were both dead, and he hadn't seen his twin brother for many years. She'd started to ask why, but he had shut down her queries, telling her that the rehearsal was about to begin.

As she stepped towards the velvet-covered kneeling stool, Hannah was aware of how little she knew about her future husband, but perhaps it was better this way. If she knew the answers, mightn't she get freaked out by the enormity of what she was about to do?

'You are ready?' he said softly.

She nodded, wondering how many more people were going to ask her that. Were they giving her a final opportunity to change her mind? To take her chances and go at it alone? But the time for that had passed. There was no point looking back and thinking about all the 'might have beens'. Didn't matter what had brought them to this moment—what mattered was how they dealt with it. She should be grateful that her child would never have to go hungry, as she had done. Or have to lie in bed at night, fearing eviction because the rent hadn't been paid. Glad, too, that they would bear the name of their father.

Hannah had always made the best of whatever situation she'd been in, so why not continue doing that now? Kulal had warned her not to love him, but there were plenty of workable alternatives to love. Couldn't she learn to respect and to care for him, so that they could be decent parents to their child and something approaching friends to each other? Looking up into the glitter of the Sheikh's eyes, she nodded.

'I'm ready,' she said and smiled.

Kulal tensed as the look she slanted him made his heart kick. Today she seemed receptive, whereas last night at the rehearsal, she had seemed anxious. Glancing around and asking him questions he'd felt unable to deal with, when he was trying to organise one of the most spectacular weddings this desert region had seen in a decade. He could have opted for a more intimate service—some pared-down celebration which could be followed by a lavish party. But something inside him had baulked at that. He didn't want something *hushed up*. Something which would carry echoes of the secrets and senselessness of the past.

Was that the reason why he had evaded Hannah's guileless queries about his late parents? Why he had mentioned his twin brother only in passing? Because what was the point in her knowing stuff—dark stuff— which might affect the way she viewed life here at the palace?

But his heart still clenched as he acknowledged the empty space where his brother should have stood, on the opposite side of the gilded throne room. The runaway twin who had left his desert home at the earliest opportunity, never to return. His no-show today had come as no real surprise, though Kulal couldn't deny the dull beat of disappointment. Had Haydar been shocked at his twin's sudden decision to take a bride—a move which had been made clear when Kulal had confided that Hannah was pregnant? He had wondered whether the baby news would take some of the pressure off his brother, would make him forget about the unbearable reality of their own upbringing. Yet he had not succeeded and it seemed Haydar was determined to continue with his self-imposed exile from his homeland.

But Kulal would not think of that today. He would think only of a duty which had been forced upon him and which he must now make the best of.

He stared down at the top of Hannah's head and the fine golden mesh which covered her shiny hair. In England, she had hinted that theirs might be a marriage in name only—but that was something he refused to countenance. Their union *would* be consummated, he decided grimly, because a satisfied woman was a compliant woman. He would keep her sweet until their child was born.

And after that, she could do whatever the hell she wanted.

He spoke his vows without emotion, hearing Hannah repeat hers through the English interpreter which had been provided by her embassy. He felt her hand tremble as he slid the gold and ruby ring on her finger and turned her huge aquamarine eyes to his.

'You are now my wife,' he said, and as the interpreter translated his words into English the entire international congregation broke into spontaneous applause. He saw the way her teeth slid into her bottom lip, in that way women sometimes had of expressing pleasure. Was she revelling in the fact that she now wore a priceless wedding band and people were bowing and curtseying to her? Was this marriage what she had wanted all along—and all that hesitation false? 'Happy?' he questioned, aware of people around them listening and feeling it his duty to echo the usual sentiments of the bridegroom.

Looking up into Kulal's black eyes, Hannah didn't want to answer. She suspected he hadn't forgotten the bright assertion she'd made that happiness was over-rated—just as she suspected he had only asked the question because there were lots of people milling around them. But then he lifted her fingers to his lips and kissed them, his gaze not leaving her face, and in that moment the truth became blurred. She felt a familiar warmth rush through her veins and, beneath the heavy gold dress, her nipples tightened. And suddenly it was easier to focus on the cravings of her body rather than the emptiness in her heart. If she concentrated on desire, which was starting to lick over her skin like a low-grade fever, rather than the fact that Kulal didn't care for her, wasn't it almost possible to feel the thing she didn't really believe in?

'Very happy,' she said.

His hawk-like features hardened and his eyes darkened. He moved his hand to her waist, his thumb softly stroking at the metallic indentation before propelling her towards a gilded anteroom, where silent servants were circulating with trays of drinks. 'Then let's do what we need to do,' he said roughly. 'Let's play out this pantomime to the full until I can get you alone.'

Hannah's throat was dry with sudden nerves as she was introduced to guest after stellar guest, but it wasn't social unease which was making her feel jittery. It was the unmistakable message of sexual intent which glittered from Kulal's black eyes whenever he looked at her—which was a *lot*. Had she really been naïve enough to think that theirs might be a marriage in name only? She found herself wondering if it was obvious to everyone else that the desert King was looking on his new bride with unashamed lust.

And that she was feeling exactly the same way about him.

The wedding feast took place in an enormous dining gallery, with musicians playing a kind of dreamy music she'd never heard before. One elaborate course followed another—so many that Hannah lost count. But she only picked at the delicious fare, because her weighty golden gown didn't exactly provide a lot of room for expansion. Nobody had actually *mentioned* her pregnancy—she supposed nobody would dare— but it must have been obvious to anyone, especially to the Zahristan dressmaker who had been dispatched to London to make her wedding gown.

Following a fulsome speech from the country's Prime Minister and then a few heavily edited anecdotes from Salvatore, she and Kulal stood up to raise their jewel-encrusted goblets in a toast, before entwining arms so that they could drink from each other's cup. Afterwards, Kulal clasped her fingers in his and led her onto the dance floor. But this was nothing like the private dance they'd shared in Sardinia when they'd been watched by nothing but the silver moon. Now she felt like an exhibit in the zoo as all the guests circled to watch their shimmering movements. Were they observing her bulky silhouette? She was just sixteen weeks pregnant, but her tiny stature made her look much further ahead in her pregnancy than she really was.

And all the longing which had been building up inside her began to evaporate beneath the spotlight of the spectators' stares. Perhaps they were thinking that Kulal had fallen for the oldest trick in the book—though they'd probably be even more appalled if they realised that theirs had been a one-night relationship. Looking around in vain for the encouraging smile of her sister, Hannah felt like a mannequin in her new husband's arms. She was relieved when finally he led her from the vaulted gallery, past the bowing servants who lined the corridors as they made their way towards Kulal's private rooms. Hers, too, from now on, she reminded herself grimly.

But for how long?

As he gestured her inside, Hannah looked around. She'd only been in the palace for a week—which had been spent in her own lavish quarters on the other side of the palace. She had been more than comfortable there, close to the palace's vast central courtyard, where peacocks wandered amid orange trees and the air was fragrant with the heady perfume of gardenia. Kulal had given her a guided tour of all the state rooms, as well as the dimly lit library with all its ancient books, and she remembered her momentary burst of pleasure as she'd realised that here were all the tools to continue her learning. He had shown her the throne room and the crown jewels—to which she would have unfettered access as his new bride. After that, he had taken her to the state-of-the-art stables, as well as the garage complex with a fleet of cars which could have graced any international Grand Prix circuit.

But nothing could compete with the splendour of the King's private residence with its soaring pillars and gilded rooms which each flowed seamlessly into the next. Low velvet divans were scattered with brocade cushions and faded silk rugs were strewn over the floors. Intricate silver lanterns hung from the vaulted gleam of the golden ceiling and the air was richly scented with incense.

'You look subdued, Hannah,' Kulal observed softly as the massive doors clanged shut behind them, leaving them alone at last. 'Does the thought of your wedding night fill you with trepidation?'

She met his ebony gaze and remembered what it had been like when she'd used to clean for him in Sardinia, when her days had seemed impossibly simple and free from care compared to now. When he'd shown her his country on the map and talked about mountains and rivers and the rare, pink-tinted Zahristan deer which drank at the crystal streams, and which you could sometimes observe if you were very quiet. Sometimes he would actually ask her opinion about something and his eyes used to gleam with humour when she told it the way it really was. When she'd talked to him as if he were just a normal man, rather than a royal potentate. Couldn't she do that now?

'I'm scared I'm going to get lost among all these marble corridors,' she admitted.

A brief smile played on his lips but, visibly, he seemed to relax. 'And that's all?'

No, of course it wasn't all. She was terrified of the wedding night which lay ahead, despite the desire which was never far from the surface. Terrified that her newly bulky shape would kill his passion for her stone-dead. And there were other fears, too—nebulous things she didn't dare acknowledge, especially not in these nervous moments before the Sheikh claimed her as she knew he would.

But she had vowed to try to make this marriage work, hadn't she? To give it her best shot—and she wouldn't be able to do that if she behaved like a chambermaid. She could only succeed in her role as his desert

Queen if she adopted a new confidence—if she started believing in herself and her ability to make this work, as she had done so many times before.

Sucking in a deep breath, she lifted the diamond coronet and the golden veil from her head and carefully set them down on a nearby table and began to walk towards him. Each step felt as if it were covering an infinite amount of space during a short journey which seemed to take for ever. And then she was standing before him, her eyes fixed firmly on his, praying that he would be the master of what happened next because, although she was trying like mad to believe in herself, she didn't think she was up to seducing the Sheikh in such intimidating surroundings.

'Not quite all,' she admitted in a rush. 'I feel nervous about the night ahead even though I have no right to. I mean, it's not like I'm a virgin any more, and—'

He silenced her, not with his kiss but with a forefinger placed over her lips. 'You have every right to feel nervous,' he said gravely. 'For although you are no longer a virgin, you are still relatively inexperienced and today must have been very difficult for you in many ways.'

She nodded, warmed enough by his consideration to confide her biggest fear. 'It was pretty daunting,' she confessed. 'And it wasn't helped by wondering where Tamsyn had got to.'

'Or Xan Constantinides,' he offered drily. 'He left the ballroom soon after her. Didn't you see them go?'

'No, I didn't.' Hannah bit her lip. 'Isn't he supposed to be a terrible womaniser?'

'I'm afraid so.'

'Do you think she's okay?'

'I'm sure she's physically safe, if that's what you mean—though it's probably inadvisable to sleep with Xan Constantinides unless she's prepared to get her heart broken.'

'That's the last thing she needs right now!' said Hannah urgently. 'Kulal, we've got to find her!'

He raised his eyebrows. 'What do you want me to do—spend my wedding night ordering my guards to extricate Constantinides from her clutches?'

'Or her from his!' she declared loyally.

Kulal frowned. 'Tamsyn is an adult, Hannah—just like you. I'm sure you were the exemplary big sister to her when you were growing up, but don't you think it's time you cut the apron strings?'

She'd thought that plenty of times, but habit was one of the hardest things to break. 'I don't think it's a good idea if she starts associating with people who are way out of her league,' she said, meeting the sudden mockery in Kulal's eyes.

'Like you did, you mean?'

She was trying to think of a suitable response when suddenly the Sheikh seemed to lose patience with the conversation because he picked her up.

'What are you doing?'

'What do you think I'm doing? I'm taking you to bed. I've had enough talking, particularly about your sister.'

He began to carry her towards a beautiful carved arch at the far end of the room and Hannah kicked her legs a little like a toddler learning to swim.

'Please put me down, Kulal. I'm much too heavy.'

'You weigh nothing,' he said, carelessly discounting her protest. 'Nothing at all.'

And perhaps he decided that kisses *were* better than words—for kisses took you down one path and words another. Perhaps he was bored with talking altogether, for he set her down beside the biggest bed she'd ever seen and pulled her into his arms.

CHAPTER NINE

'So,' said KULAL, his voice unsteady. 'Time to seduce my new wife. But first, I need to get you out of this infernal wedding dress.'

Hannah's heart was hammering as the Sheikh turned her round to begin unhooking her decorative gown. It seemed to take him ages, but that might have had something to do with the fact that he kept brushing his mouth over each inch of newly exposed flesh, so that by the time he had laid her trembling and naked beneath the embroidered bedcover, all her nerves had dissolved beneath a feeling of mounting anticipation. Just *enjoy* this, she told herself fiercely as he pulled the ceremonial robes from his darkly muscular body and slid naked into bed beside her. Because this is your wedding night and it will lay the foundations of your whole life together.

'I've never had sex with a pregnant woman before,' he murmured as he grazed his mouth over hers.

Brushing the back of her hand across her forehead, Hannah mimed relief. 'Thank goodness for that.'

He paused, lifting his head away from hers so that their gazes collided. 'I don't want to hurt you, Hannah.'

'I'm tough,' she said truthfully, though she was talking physically, not emotionally. Because when he looked at her in that seeking way, she felt almost boneless with a deep longing which was alien to her. But surely she was permitted to experience it on her wedding night… Surely just this once she could hint at all the passion lying deep inside her, waiting to be unlocked. 'Just hold me, Kulal.' Her voice trembled a little. 'Touch me.'

His features hardened as he stared at her and she wondered if she'd sounded needy. But suddenly, his mouth was on hers and he was kissing her with a hunger which seemed to echo her own and she felt a great whoosh of excitement flooding through her. And although Hannah wasn't—in Kulal's own words—very experienced, somehow that didn't seem to matter. Not to her and not to him. Not now, when she was his wife. When she was at liberty to touch him without inhibition. And why be shy when his baby was in her belly? Wasn't their flesh combined in more than one way?

'Oh,' she said breathlessly as he began to drift his fingertips over her skin.

'Your breasts are magnificent,' he said throatily.

'You don't think they're too…big?'

He gave a strangled kind of laugh. 'What kind of a question is that?'

Now wasn't the time to admit that the fashion magazines which Tamsyn had always passed on to her to read had always made Hannah feel like an over-curvy freak. Not when he was bending his head to suck hotly on each aroused nipple. She shivered as his fingertips skated over the curve of her belly, lingering there for just a moment. She waited for him to say something about the baby, but he didn't and she told herself it was stupid to feel disappointed. To think that if this were a *normal* honeymoon, then he might have mentioned the unborn life within her.

But why think about the things he wasn't saying when his seeking fingers were delving in between her parted thighs and beginning to stroke her. He was tantalising her as he rubbed his fingers against her slick, wet heat until she moved restlessly—her hunger beginning to mount.

She knew she couldn't just lie there passively. During her solitary nights last week on the other side of the palace, she'd furtively read a book on sexual satisfaction within marriage, which she planned to put to good use. But when she summoned up the courage to slide her palm over the enormous erection which was nudging hard against her belly, Kulal dragged his mouth away from hers and gave a decisive shake of his head, before moving her hand away.

'No,' he said sternly.

'Why not?'

'Because I'm too close to coming and I want to do that when I'm inside you.' His voice was almost gentle as she sank her hot face into the sanctuary of his neck. 'And I don't really think that now is the time for blushes, Hannah. Do you?'

She remembered that once he'd told her he liked her blushes, but that had been way back when—when he'd thought she would be in and out of his life in a few short hours. If he had been able to look into the future—if he'd known that their single night in Sardinia would have ended with her as his new Queen in this amazing golden palace—would he still have gone ahead and had sex with her?

Of course he wouldn't.

Would she?

But the crazy thing was that Hannah couldn't find herself regretting that night—and not just because Kulal had introduced her to a physical pleasure she was discovering hadn't been a one-off. It was more than that. Because already she felt a fierce love for the new life growing inside her—so how could she possibly have regrets?

'Hannah,' he said sternly, as if he'd guessed she was miles away. 'Pay attention.'

With a shy smile, she opened her mouth to his and that was when sensation took over, obliterating all thought and replacing it with feeling. She swallowed as his moist tip nudged against her and gasped as he eased himself inside her molten heat.

'No protection,' he exclaimed as he stilled inside her and gave an exultant sigh. 'Just you and me, with nothing in between us.'

She knew his words were supposed to be erotic, but Hannah felt deeply emotional as he filled her with his hard length and began to move. She'd wondered if making love while she was pregnant would feel any different, but the blissful truth was that it felt amazing. Maybe even better than that blissful night in Sardinia. It certainly felt more *intimate*. Almost *too* intimate. She clung to him as his thrusts deepened and she felt the tantalising build of orgasm, but she was so intent on kissing him that it seemed to creep up on her by stealth, so that when pleasure came, she cried out his name in a way she hadn't planned, the gasped word echoing around the vast bedchamber so that it sounded like some sort of *prayer*. Was she imagining the sudden tension in his body before his movements resumed and he shuddered out his own release?

Afterwards, she waited for him to say something, because she had no idea about post-sex protocol, especially between a man and a woman who'd been forced to marry. Did they act as if today had been no big deal? Did she try to explain that the curiously vulnerable way she'd called out his name hadn't actually *meant* anything? She waited for some sort of reassuring hug, but instead he rolled away from her, his hot black gaze briefly roving over her rounded curves, before lying on his back, his breathing still ragged.

'So...' She cleared her throat. 'All in all, I thought today went off quite well, didn't you?'

He could hear the faltering delivery of her words and a battery of responses ran through Kulal's mind, but he took his time before selecting one. Should he tell her he'd felt nothing but duty as he had exchanged those meaningless vows? Yet the truth was that he'd been almost *comfortable* with that, because he was familiar with detachment and he enjoyed the barrier it created between him and the rest of the world. That part had all gone according to plan and afterwards, at the reception, he had acknowledged the congratulations offered by the Sheikhs and Sultans of adjoining regions, knowing that his royal line would be continued. Again, so far, so expected.

But when he had brought his new wife to bed...

He swallowed.

When he had stripped away her constricting bridal gown to reveal the cushioned flesh which had burgeoned so much since last time he'd seen it and which had welcomed him so eagerly, he hadn't felt quite so detached then, had he? He told himself it was because he'd never had unprotected sex with a woman before and that was the reason why it had felt so...

He stared at the dappled rose light which flickered across the ceiling.

So what?

As if he'd never been that close to a woman before—which in one sense was true, because he'd never had sex without the obligatory thin layer of latex. Was that the reason why he had felt so alive and so *vital*? Why his heart was still pounding fit to burst in his chest? It had been the most incredible sexual experience of his life, yet he couldn't deny that his response had the potential to add complications to his life. Especially if Hannah got the wrong idea. He didn't want his new bride to think his rapturous reaction meant anything more than an amazing orgasm.

Because that was all it had been.

All it ever could be.

Kulal stifled a sigh. Once he had found out about her pregnancy, he'd been determined to keep his baby and known it would make more sense if Hannah was around, too. It would certainly make it easier. But while he was prepared to be *reasonable* to get her to stay, he would not lie to her. Because lies could seep into people's lives like poison. They could darken everything they touched. And the first lie was always the most dangerous. The gentle tap which would send the whole line of dominoes tumbling down...

'Not as bad as I expected,' he said, turning his head to look at her. 'I think it served its purpose, don't you?'

'Oh.'

Her voice sounded muffled and he didn't have to see her face crumple to sense her disappointment. That much was evident from the sudden slump of her shoulders and the way she'd started chewing her lip. Was she secretly longing for him to adorn the day with romantic embellishments which didn't exist? Or was she trying to guilt-trip him—even though she'd known the score from the very start?

'What did you want me to say, Hannah?' he demanded. 'That it was the most wonderful day of my life?'

'No, of course not.'

He saw the confusion which had clouded her eyes and fury at being hit by another wave of guilt prompted his next words. 'To go through a marriage I didn't particularly want—you think that gives me pleasure?'

His words were harsh but honest, and he thought she might turn away from him. To lie there trembling with silent resentment. And wasn't that what he wanted her to do? To draw a line in the sand between them that she would never dare cross again. But she just kept staring at him, those aquamarine eyes so wide and dark in the rosy tint of the lamplight, as if she was summoning up the courage to say something he wouldn't want to hear.

She cleared her throat. 'So are you against marriage generally?'

Kulal's mouth hardened. Too right he didn't want to hear it—the question he'd been asked a million times, usually by women on the make. One he always slapped down as coldly and as finally as possible. But Hannah was not one of those women; she was his wife. She had succeeded where so many had failed and he couldn't slap her down, not completely.

'A man in my position is always expected to marry,' he said. 'But I saw no urgency to do so. For someone who doesn't believe in love, it was always going to be an academic exercise of settling down to produce a family at the optimum time.'

'And what would you consider to be the *optimum time*?' she echoed cautiously.

'Never?' he questioned sarcastically.

'Kulal, I'm serious.'

He shrugged. 'In perhaps a decade and a half, when I had reached fifty years and sown every last wild oat.'

'So this early and unwanted marriage has prevented you from having hundreds of different relationships? All those wild oats which will remain unsown.'

'I am not totally indiscriminate, Hannah,' he said gravely.

'But all that...all that unexplored opportunity,' she breathed. 'Won't it make you resentful?'

Kulal frowned, feeling momentarily wrong-footed. Surely *she* was the one who was supposed to be feeling resentful—not turning it around so that she was coolly interrogating *him*. 'I have no intention of straying, if that's what you're getting at. Infidelity is something I am vehemently opposed to—despite many of my royal peers feeling it their right to keep a mistress.'

He saw the surprise on her face as she brushed a heavy swathe of hair away from her forehead and blinked at him.

'I have the feeling I shouldn't be grateful just because you've told me you won't break our wedding vows, but the fact is that I am,' she said. 'And a little curious, too.'

Her instinctive intelligence was enough to make him prolong the conversation, even though he sensed he was venturing onto precarious territory. 'About what in particular?' he questioned.

'Well, you've told me you don't want love.'

'I don't.'

The rumpled white sheet barely covered the creamy swell of her breasts and her eyes suddenly seemed very bright. 'So why would you care about breaking your wedding vows, if another woman should suddenly take your fancy?'

He was on the verge of telling her that she looked so entrancing at that moment, that he couldn't imagine another woman holding a flame to her.

Until he remembered.

He tried not to remember, but sometimes it came out of nowhere and hit you like a vicious blow. He felt the pain course through him like a black tide and his body tensed. 'If you had grown up with parents like mine,' he said, a trace of savage bitterness creeping into his voice, 'you would understand.'

There was a pause before she spoke. 'But how can I understand if you won't tell me, Kulal?' she whispered. 'And if I understood, then maybe I could help you. Maybe you've forgotten that I grew up in a dysfunctional foster home which wasn't in any way loving, so I don't think anything you can tell me would shock me.'

He could see the eagerness on her face—a desire to help, which tugged at something deep inside him, but successfully he pushed the feeling away. Did she think it was that simple? That telling her would free him from the demons which had lived in his heart for so long? From his secret torture and sense of powerlessness? He felt a new resolve creep through his veins, for he would not give her that power. He would not give it to anyone. Hadn't he promised his brother that?

'And besides—' her voice had softened hopefully

as she fixed him with that same wide-eyed stare '—we're married now. Aren't we supposed to share those kinds of things?'

There was a split-second pause before Kulal was galvanised into action. 'No, we're not,' he grated as he pushed the sheets from his naked body. 'I don't want that kind of marriage. I told you that from the start. Weren't you listening, Hannah? Or did you think you could change my mind just as soon as my ring was on your finger? Did you believe, as so many women mistakenly do, that it was just a matter of time and proximity before you could get me to backtrack on my words? In which case, I fear you may be a little premature, as well as misguided.' His voice hardened even more. 'In my culture, we don't spill out our innermost thoughts and feelings, as if life was just one long therapy session!'

'I didn't mean to pry,' she said, in a small voice. 'I was just trying to…help.'

'Well, don't because it's a waste of time—yours *and* mine. The past is none of your business, Hannah. You'd better accept that now or this isn't going to work. I will give you my fidelity and my support for our child. And I am prepared to make this marriage work within the framework we've laid out.'

'*You've* laid out, you mean.'

He shrugged. 'I'm the King. Sorry, but that's the way it works around here. I am not an unreasonable man and anything you require will be yours, within reason. But please don't ever ask me that again.'

There was a silence as she studied him, like someone hoping for a sudden miraculous change of heart, and Kulal saw the exact moment when resignation entered her eyes. When she realised that he meant every word he said.

'And that's the end of the discussion, is it?' she questioned flatly.

He nodded as he slid from the bed. 'Yes. And now I think it's time you got some sleep.'

'But…' She sat up and the white sheet fell to her waist, showing the luscious thrust of her breasts. 'Where are you going?'

He saw the alarm in her eyes, but years of practice meant he was able to steel his heart against it, even though he wasn't managing to remain quite so indifferent to the sight of her rose-pink nipples. Did she really think he was going to lie there night after night, while she fired her questions at him, shattering those sleepy moments of post-coital intimacy and ruining them? Should he tell her the reasons why he didn't want love and why he never would?

No.

Not on their wedding night. His mouth hardened. Perhaps not ever.

'I'm going to sleep next door. It's better that way.'

'Better?'

'Once again, I will draw your attention to royal protocol,' he said softly. 'It is quite normal for the Sheikh and his Sheikha to sleep separately—a pattern which was set many centuries ago. We can still be intimate.' He reached for his discarded robe. 'But you need your rest, Hannah. And I'm going to make sure you get it.'

CHAPTER TEN

THERE WERE TWO different ways of dealing with a problem. Hannah knew that better than anyone. Stepping from her bath, she bent forwards a little as the servant wrapped a fluffy towel around her damp shoulders. You could either accept the problem and learn to live with it, or you could try to solve it. And hadn't she spent her life trying to do the latter?

She watched rose petals swirling round and round as water drained away from the golden bathtub. When she and Tamsyn had been hungry as children, she'd found food, hadn't she? And when her schooling had suffered as a result of her having to keep house, she'd tried to teach herself. Even when her lack of formal qualifications had led to what some people might have considered the non-aspirational job of chambermaid, she had worked hard and earned herself promotions. Necessity had made her one of life's fixers and that was the way she operated.

So couldn't she apply the same criteria to her marriage—to find a way to elevate it from its current state of stalemate? To make it into something more meaningful, despite Kulal's determination that it should exist only on the most superficial of levels? She swallowed.

Because she was finding that what she had was not enough.

Not nearly enough.

She had a husband who was physically present but emotionally distant. A man who occupied himself by day—and sometimes evenings, too—with the many demands placed on him. Oh, occasionally he made a space for her in his diary, when for a brief time she felt as if she was actually sharing his life rather than living on the periphery of it. Times when she would accompany him to a state banquet, or the opening of some new medical centre, or perhaps they would eat dinner together—but that was the exception, rather than the rule. The only time she really had Kulal to herself was in bed at night.

Patting her skin dry, she sighed, because that wasn't quite true. Even being in bed with him was time-limited. Once they had satisfied their mutual desire several times over, he would slip away to sleep in his own room, rising at five to saddle his horse and pound the desert sands until his hard body was sheened with sweat and little tendrils of black hair clung to his face. She knew this because once, long after he'd left her bed, she'd heard a noise and, on getting up to investigate, had found him stripping off in one of the anterooms of their vast suite. He had pulled the damp shirt from his body and had been in the process of unzipping his jodhpurs when Hannah had walked in and he had frozen.

So had she. Because the sight of Kulal undressing was overwhelming enough to make her heart race erratically. Oh, she got to see his naked body at night—every night, as it happened—but at times that felt almost stage-managed and this totally unexpected half-clothed version of him was unbelievably erotic. She hadn't meant to be provocative when her tongue had slid out to slowly moisten her lips, but the increased tension in Kulal's muscular torso had suggested that he'd found it so.

As she stood in her long, diaphanous nightgown, her rounded shape must have been very apparent with the lamplight shining through the folds of silk-chiffon, and she'd seen her husband's black eyes roving greedily over her body before he deliberately lifted his gaze to hers.

'You are not ill?' he demanded.

She'd shaken her head. 'I heard a noise, that's all. It woke me up.'

He'd lifted his broad shoulders in apology, pointing to the discarded riding crop which had lain beside one leather-booted foot, which had been tapping at the marble floor with impatience. 'I must have thrown that down with more force than I intended.'

She'd wanted to ask him why. Just as she'd wanted to ask him whether he might break his cast-iron rule and take her into his arms and kiss her. Now. Here. No matter how damp and sweaty he was. She had held her breath for one long moment when such a scenario had seemed possible—if the darkening of his eyes and the hungry hardening of his lips had been anything to go by—before he'd given her a dismissive smile.

'Forgive me for waking you.'

'I don't mind.'

'You should. A pregnant woman needs her sleep.' There had been a pause. 'Go back to bed, Hannah.'

The memory retreated as Hannah bent down to dry her toes, then pulled a silky robe over her head. Was that what happened in relationships? Were you always seeking something more, no matter how much you had? And wasn't the danger that she could jeopardise what they *did* have, if she allowed these restless longings to take over?

So she tried to count her blessings and to pray that some of Kulal's icy reserve might melt a little. One morning, he had flown her to the north-eastern side of Zahristan, to his royal beach house, where they had sat beneath a shaded canopy and watched the glitter of the sun on the Murjaan Sea as they'd sipped fire-berry cordial. Their small contingent of protection officers had been entirely female, giving Hannah the opportunity to swim in the enormous pool which was surrounded by palm trees. The silken waters had rippled deliciously over her skin and she'd seen Kulal smile when she'd given a little squeal of delight.

'Come and join me?' she had questioned shyly.

Uncharacteristically, he had hesitated before telling her he needed to make a conference call to New York, and that brief pause had been enough to make a flicker of hope enter her body. Because in that moment, hadn't he been tempted by an intimacy which wasn't just about sex?

And the trouble with hope was that it was like a weed—it grew wildly with the slightest bit of encouragement. Hannah wondered if it was all in her imagination, or whether Kulal's nocturnal visits were getting longer. Last night, it had been almost dawn before he had left the rumpled sheets to retreat to his own bedroom. Her eyelids had fluttered briefly open as she had watched him dressing in the dim light, longing for the time when he might spend an entire night with her. But she didn't dare ask him outright. Not after the humiliation of their wedding night. Not when she suspected such an appeal would prompt the proud desert King into doing the very opposite.

In the meantime, her pregnancy was progressing with textbook perfection. Each day her bump grew bigger, ticking off every developmental milestone along the way. The palace doctor declared herself delighted with Hannah's progress during their regular consultations, though the Sheikh had been absent from all of these.

'It would be inappropriate for the King to be present during such an intimate examination,' Kulal had said in reply to her tentative query about whether he might one day accompany her.

It was an old-fashioned point of view, but in many ways he was an old-fashioned man despite his western business dealings and cosmopolitan lifestyle prior to his marriage. He didn't seem to mind that royal law decreed that the sex of their unborn child should be known only to the attending doctor, even though Hannah was longing to find out if she was having a boy or a girl. Sometimes she reflected on how different Zahristan was from the world she had grown up in.

But somehow, despite all the odds, she liked it and found a peace there she'd never known before. She liked the quiet and beauty of walking in the palace gardens, or drinking her tea in the vast courtyard, with its cobalt-blue mosaic floor and the mingled scent of orange blossom and gardenia filling the air. She liked it when she was appointed a female aide and two female protection officers so that she was able to explore the ancient museums and artefacts in the nearby city of Ashkhazar, though she preferred to make these visits unannounced, so that there wouldn't be too much fuss. And she loved the huge library in the palace itself because, for the first time in her life, she actually had the time and the opportunity to read.

It felt magical to have endless rows of beautifully bound leather books at her fingertips and she began to read up more about Zahristan history, partly because she wanted to take her role as Sheikha seriously and partly because she wanted to understand Kulal's land and, by definition, him. She read that he was from a long line of Zahristan kings from his father's side and that his mother had been a princess from the neighbouring land of Tardistan. But there seemed to be gaps in the various accounts of his family history, even in the more modern publications—and it was only on a neglected shelf in a hidden alcove that she discovered a short biography about Kulal himself.

Her eyes scanned the pages eagerly, her eyes drinking in the portraits of his hawk-like features and flashing black eyes. There were descriptions of his exemplary school record and his daring exploits when he'd run away as a teenager to fight in the fierce border battle with Quzabar. There was an account of his father's lying-in-state and the political turmoil before Kulal's subsequent accession to the throne, but practically nothing about his mother's early death, other than the fact it was 'tragic'. And if Kulal was the younger of twin brothers, as was stated, it didn't explain why he had taken the throne instead of his older brother, Haydar. Hannah wanted to know, but instinct told her not to pry. That the answers she sought would only come about if she and Kulal grew closer as a couple—and wasn't she attempting to help that process along, by increasing the amount of time they spent together?

She'd quickly realised that Kulal working late into the evening before he came to bed was an evasive tactic. She realised that he preferred her to be waiting and ready for sex—she guessed because that ruled out the need for conversation other than the 'do you like it when I do that?' variety. She remembered those far-away days when she'd cleaned his suite in Sardinia when they used to chat about *stuff.* When once in a while he'd even teased her. Couldn't they get back to easy conversations like that—and the sort of intimacy which didn't involve her gasping out her pleasure as he drove into her eager body?

She told herself that the only reason she'd decided to start waiting until Kulal returned to their suite before retiring for the night was so they could chat. But deep down she knew that wasn't the whole truth. Deep down she realised she had started to care for her husband in a way he had emphatically warned her against. A way which felt frighteningly close to love, even though she told herself that wasn't possible.

But something had changed.

She wasn't sure how or when it had happened, because it wasn't the obvious things which had made her feel so differently about him. Not the muscular body which transported her to heaven and back every night. Or the ruler in all his finery with people bowing before him. It was the man with the occasional flicker of vulnerability in his eyes before the shutters came crashing down—that was the Kulal who had captured Hannah's imagination and then her heart. Was it so wrong to wonder if she could ever forge a tiny place for herself in *his* heart?

Her silken robes whispered as she walked over to the desk where she'd left her book open and the dull thud of the outer doors of their suite told her that Kulal had returned. Instantly, she felt her heart begin to thunder.

'Hannah?'

The sound of his voice was enough to send desire rippling down her spine and Hannah struggled to keep the hungry tremble from her voice. 'I'm in here!'

He walked into the bedroom, appearing startled to see her sitting at the desk, a halo of golden lamplight surrounding her. 'You're not in bed?' he questioned.

'As you see,' she said, with a smile. 'I thought I'd wait for you and do a spot of reading.' She put a bookmark in her book and closed it. 'How did your meeting with the Sultan of Marazad go?'

Kulal felt momentarily disorientated because he hadn't been expecting to see her waiting up for him. He swallowed. The sight of her alluring body was making him want to ravish her with a hunger which never seemed to wane, no matter how many times he took his fill of her. And it had never happened to him before—not like this. Every night since their wedding had been spent in her arms and not once had he grown bored. Unusually, he'd found himself cancelling trips to Europe and the States—feeling it wasn't really fair to abandon his pregnant wife in a strange new country, even though no such complaint had come from her. Despite the huge leap of being catapulted from chambermaid to queen, she hadn't been in the least bit clingy or dependent. She had been...

He swallowed.

She had been irresistible.

Beguiling him little by little—her shy sexual confidence had increased daily until he wondered which of them was the tutor and which the pupil. But it wasn't just sex she excelled at. It was other stuff, too. She seemed to instantly grasp what was important to him and what was not. She didn't say unnecessary things or do that glazed-eye thing women did when they were *pretending* to be interested in your job. Her interest in his work seemed genuine. His gaze distracted by the hard points of her nipples, which were thrusting against her pink gown, he dragged his mind back to the question she'd just asked him. Something about a meeting...

'It was good,' he said vaguely, even though this particular meeting had been months in the planning. 'Malik was unusually compliant.'

'So you think he's eager to embrace solar power at last?'

Kulal frowned. He didn't remember discussing that either, but he supposed he must have done. And why the hell was he getting into a discussion about renewable energy when he'd come here specifically to make love to her? 'Not nearly as eager as I am to embrace *you*,' he murmured, walking over to the desk and switching off the lamp, before pulling her to her feet. 'You should be in bed.'

Those amazing eyes widened. 'I've been reading.'

'It's late.'

'So what? I'm pregnant, Kulal—and I'm getting plenty of sleep. The doctor says I'm in peak health and right now I feel wide awake.'

'That's good. Because so do I.' He slid his hand

down over one undulating hip and instantly heard a long breath escape from her lips.

'Kulal.' He heard her swallow. 'I... I wanted to ask you some more about the solar power initiative and... and...*oh*!'

Her words faded away as his lips brushed hungrily over her neck. 'Which is the very last thing I want to talk about, Hannah. I'd rather concentrate on...*this*...' He started rucking up the gauzy gown to explore the silken territory of her thighs, his fingers finding her moist heat as he explored further. 'Wouldn't you?' he said unsteadily.

'Well...' She tipped her head to one side as if she was giving the question careful consideration, but he saw her eyes become opaque as his finger found her sweet spot and began to drum softly against it.

'You were saying?' he prompted softly.

'I don't...remember,' she moaned.

And neither did he. She felt so good and tasted so good that he could wait no longer. With a low groan, he picked her up and carried her over to the bed, ignoring her habitual protestations, because although she was almost six months pregnant with his child, he could still lift her with ease. She was wearing her nightgown, but Kulal was too hungry to care. In fact, he couldn't even wait to remove his own robes. But silk and satin could be pushed aside enough for him to gain all the access he needed and before too long she was breathlessly urging him to enter her. Kulal needed no second bidding as he filled her with an erection that had never felt quite so hard. Each thrust seemed to take him deeper. He felt as if he wanted to explode. As if nothing else in the world existed outside this room and this bed. He teetered on the brink of pleasure until at last she gave a strangled cry and almost immediately he let go with a harsh and breathless shout of his own.

Kulal didn't know how long he lay there before withdrawing from her, but her face was flushed and her eyes dark as they gazed at each other in the lamplight. 'That was a very welcome homecoming,' he said eventually.

'I'm glad,' she said demurely.

'Where the hell did you learn to be so...*responsive*?' He gave a wry smile. 'Or are you just one of life's natural seductresses?'

'I've read some stuff,' she admitted a little shyly. 'I figured that an inexperienced wife might drive you into the arms of someone else if I wasn't careful.'

The unexpected candour and humility of her response made Kulal's heart punch painfully in his chest. 'But I promised you my fidelity,' he growled.

'I know you did, but I...'

She seemed about to say something else when he saw a shadow cross over her face, and instead she shrugged.

'What?' he probed.

'It doesn't matter. Honestly.' She fastened her arms around his neck and planted a lingering kiss on his lips. 'What matters is that you should enjoy your coming home at night as much as I do.'

'I certainly enjoy coming,' he mused.

'Kulal!'

He gave a low laugh. 'I don't really think you're in any position to be shocked by my words, Hannah— not when you seem pretty unshocked by some of the things we do together. Now...' his voice dipped '...

why don't we rid you of this nightgown—beautiful as it is—which, in my haste to be inside you, I neglected to remove?'

He helped her slide out of her nightdress, but took his time while undressing himself, deliberately making himself step back from the easy intimacy which seemed to have developed between them. Because sometimes, didn't disquiet whisper over his skin—as warm and as insidious as the slow trickle of blood? Instinctively, his fingertips went to the ridged scar which ran all the way from nipple to belly. At the time, he hadn't felt the knife enter his body because he had been on a rush of adrenalin, and sometimes he felt the same way now, when he was in bed with his wife.

He had warned Hannah what he would and wouldn't tolerate within their marriage yet he hadn't expected her to be quite so *accepting* of his demands. Hadn't he anticipated rebellion once she realised he would not bend the stringent rules he had imposed on their union? But she had confounded all his expectations. She hadn't sulked, or bargained, or pleaded for him to spend the whole night with her. She hadn't drummed her fingernails on the table and told him what *she* wanted. She had just seemed to slot into palace life as if she'd been born to it. According to his aides, she spent her days quietly, either in the gardens or in the library, with the occasional trip into the city as she prepared for the birth of their child.

'Kulal.' Her voice sounded soft—like a harp playing on a spring evening.

'What is it?' Yanking off his robe, he slid into bed beside her.

'I want…'

'What do you want, Hannah?' he questioned indulgently.

'To…to kiss you.'

It was such an innocent request—how could he refuse? Why would he even *want* to refuse? Was it because he detected a trace of some indefinable emotion in the melodic caress of her words? Or because kissing represented an intimacy which sometimes felt as if it was mushrooming out of his control? As he bent to brush his lips over hers, he told himself it was only a kiss, but within seconds they were having sex again. If she hadn't been pregnant he might have been a little rougher with her—made her ride him like a cowboy riding a bucking bronco, to demonstrate that this was nothing more than physical.

But if she hadn't been pregnant, she wouldn't be here, he reminded himself as his orgasm hit him like a muffled burst of stars. And that was his last coherent thought before he fell into a deep sleep.

His dreams were fitful and he awoke to an unfamiliar smell, forcing open his eyelids to see Hannah on the other side of the bedroom, tipping strong coffee into two tiny glimmering cups. Sitting up in bed, he raked his fingers back through his tousled hair—scowling in confusion as he noticed slats of bright sunlight slanting through the shutters.

'What time is it?' he demanded.

She was undulating towards him, her silken gown flowing around her like a waterfall as she carried one of the tiny golden cups.

'Almost nine,' she replied, putting the coffee down beside him. 'You slept right through.'

Was he imagining the hint of triumph in her voice

and the look of satisfaction on her face? 'Why didn't you wake me?' he questioned, pushing aside the sex-scented sheets and watching her aquamarine gaze automatically flicker towards the hardness at his groin, before she lifted her eyes to his face. 'You know I like to exercise my stallion before dawn.'

'I know you do. But you looked so peaceful lying there that I couldn't bring myself to wake you. And I assumed one of the servants would take your horse out in your absence.'

His mouth thinned. 'How quickly you have become used to having servants, Hannah,' he commented drily. 'But I think we're both aware that nobody gives Baasif a ride quite as hard as I do.'

He saw colour creep into her skin and knew that she wasn't thinking about horse-riding. The throb at his groin intensified. Neither was he. But she needed to understand that this wasn't going to become like a regular marriage, with them spending every constricting moment in each other's company. Did she think he would give up his morning ride and become sedentary and fat? To lie in bed with her, drinking coffee and eating pastries? He scowled as he reached for his robe.

'Why don't you drink your coffee, Kulal?' she said calmly and her words suddenly felt like the domestic kiss of death.

'I don't want any coffee,' he snarled.

He pulled the garment over his head and saw the disappointment on her face. But he would be tolerant with her. He wouldn't berate her for forcing him into something he had told her he didn't want—not when it was his own fault for falling asleep like that. But it would not happen again, he thought grimly. Never again would he waken to some commonplace scene of domesticity, with her giving him that doe-eyed look which was suddenly making him feel so *trapped*.

He thought she might be about to do the sensible thing and just let him leave, but she didn't. She crossed the room and stood in front of him, reaching up to cup his jaw and to run a questing thumb over it—as if testing for herself how rough his new growth of beard was first thing in the morning. It was as much as Kulal could do not to flinch, but somehow he stopped himself in time. And then she started to speak.

'Kulal?'

He stepped away from her touch. 'I hope this is urgent, Hannah,' he said warningly.

She drew in a deep breath as if she hadn't heard him. 'Must you leave my bed every night, as though I am your mistress instead of your wife?'

He raised his eyebrows, trying to keep it light. 'You don't think that such behaviour adds a piquant spice to our relationship?' he drawled.

'You're all the spice I need, Kulal,' she said almost shyly and then did something she hadn't done for many weeks.

She blushed.

She blushed and Kulal felt the whisper of danger.

'Haven't we already had this discussion?'

'Yes, but I wondered whether we might review things.'

'*Review* things?' he echoed. 'Like what?'

She shrugged. 'I like waking up beside you,' she said shyly. 'Just as I like you holding me tightly all night long.'

He frowned. 'Was I holding you all night long?'

'You don't remember? You certainly were. You were

murmuring things to me in Zahristanian in the middle of the night.' She smiled, and the blush deepened. 'I didn't have a clue what the words meant, but they sounded...'

His head jerked up. 'Sounded *what*?'

Nervously, she ran the tip of her pink tongue in a moist and curving path over her lips as if she had suddenly recognised that this line of conversation was unwise. 'Nothing,' she said quickly.

But it was too late because just then, Kulal *did* remember. Something she'd whispered in his ear in the deepest point of the night when he was deep inside her.

Kulal, I love you.

Kulal, I love you so much.

Had that been her response to his own words of appreciation, which had probably been nothing more than murmured praise for her ability to make him orgasm so often? Had she misinterpreted them—seen her opportunity to strike, by professing for him what he had *emphatically told her he didn't want*? He felt the icy clench of rage around his heart as he studied her. Did she think everything had suddenly changed just because they were sexually compatible and could spend the occasional evening eating dinner without having a row? Did she think she could disregard his wishes in order to pursue her own? 'What's this all about, Hannah?' he questioned.

She paced around the suite a bit, moving her shoulders restlessly like someone eager to get a whole load of stuff off their chest. 'I've read various things about your childhood,' she said at last. 'Although the information available was quite patchy.'

'And?' he questioned, though she appeared not to notice the warning in his voice.

'And I can see you probably had to learn to be independent because your mother died when you were so young and your father was away a lot. But I can understand that independence, because I had to grow up fast, too.'

'That's enough!'

'Please, Kulal.' Her words started to falter when she saw his expression, but she forged on. 'Let me just say this.'

'I would strongly advise against saying anything else, since I need to shower and get dressed and go to see my advisors,' he said, but she carried on as if he hadn't spoken and fleetingly Kulal thought how audacious it was that the one-time chambermaid should so openly disregard the wishes of the King.

'I'm not asking for the impossible,' she said, still in that same soft voice. 'Just that you relax and let what happens happen. That you stop leaving my bed straight after we've had sex.' She cleared her throat and slanted him a hopeful smile. 'I've never seen you looking so contented as when you were asleep this morning.'

It might have worked if he hadn't remembered her words and Kulal realised it would be easier to pretend he hadn't heard them. But he knew women well and once that phrase was out there, she would say it again. Oh, it might not be for a week—maybe even a month—but there would be some vulnerable point when she mistook passion or kindness for something more. She would say them again and expect him to start saying them back. And that was never going to happen.

'Have you fallen in love with me, Hannah?' he questioned softly and as she drew in a sharp intake of breath, he could see the flicker of hope in her pale eyes.

'Yes,' she breathed. 'I've tried so hard not to but it's happened almost without me realising it. I love you, Kulal. I love you so much.'

Kulal stared at the woman before him, her eyes bright with passion and her cheeks flushed with emotion.

His wife.

His wife who had just told him she loved him.

His lips curved as he felt anger course through his veins. 'What do you want me to say, Hannah?' he snarled. 'That I love you, too? Because, believe me—that is never going to happen.'

CHAPTER ELEVEN

HANNAH MET KULAL'S icy gaze and desperately wished she could rewind the clock. To take back the words which had stumbled out of her mouth almost before she'd realised she was saying them. Why on earth had she done that? Indulged herself with a declaration of love when she knew for a fact that Kulal didn't want it?

Because she had been unable to hold it back any longer. She'd blurted it out last night when he'd been making love to her and that was almost understandable, because she had been in the middle of an orgasm at the time. But there had been no such excuse just a few moments ago, had there? Yet she had been unable to hold it back any longer. It had been like a dam building up inside her, before bursting free and washing away all reservations in its path.

'My words were unconditional, Kulal,' she amended quickly. 'I wasn't expecting anything in return. Honestly. We can just carry on like before and forget I ever said it.'

Kulal shook his head, his cynicism obvious from the hardening of his lips. 'But life isn't like that, Hannah. You must realise that. You've changed everything. It can't possibly go back to how it was before. How could it? Our relationship will grow increasingly one-sided and you'll want more.' He paused. 'More than I can ever give you.'

'Kulal—'

'No!' The word shot from his lips as he glared at her. 'Perhaps it's time you heard the whole story and then you might understand. Do you want to know why the information about my childhood is so "patchy", Hannah? Do you?'

Something in his tone was frightening her. Warning her that she might have done something from which there was no coming back. Hannah clenched her fists. 'Not…not if you don't want to tell me.'

'Of course I don't want to tell you! I'd rather not have to think of it even at the end of my days,' he iced out. 'But you've forced me into a corner, haven't you? Because that's what women do best. They push and push until there's nowhere left to go.' His face grew dark, almost savage. 'So maybe it's time you heard the facts about my childhood.'

Hannah forced herself to sit down on one of the chairs, but its soft seat did little to ease her rigid posture as she folded her hands in her lap and looked at him. 'Okay,' she breathed.

There was silence for a few seconds, a silence so profound that she wondered if he'd changed his mind and didn't part of her wish he had? But then he began to speak and his voice was as cold as a winter wind whistling through the rooms of an empty house.

'It was a match like so many royal marriages in this region,' he said. 'A traditional marriage intended to unify two great dynasties from neighbouring countries. After the birth of his sons, my father kept mistresses, but he was always discreet about them. And yes, you can widen your eyes in horror, but that was the way things were in those days, Hannah. Once more, I ask you to look no further than your own royal family to see that kings and princes have always broken the fundamental rules of relationships. The difference was that my mother refused to accept it. She didn't want that kind of marriage. She wanted a modern *romantic* marriage—and that had never been on the cards.'

'So what…happened?' she questioned as a long silence followed this pronouncement.

His mouth twisted. 'The love she professed to feel for him became an obsession. She tried everything in her power to command his attention. She was his constant shadow. Wherever he turned, she was there. I remember she used to spend hours in front of the mirror, refining and redefining her appearance to try to become the woman she thought he wanted. Once, she even sought out one of his mistresses and attacked her—flaying her fingernails down the woman's face. It took a lot of money to hush that up.' He his face grew even darker as he continued. 'And the irony was that, not only was her neediness driving my father further away, it blinded her to everything else around her. In the midst of her quest to win his heart, she neglected the needs of her young family.'

'You mean you?'

He nodded. 'Yes, me, but especially my twin brother, Haydar. I had run away to fight in the border battles with Quzabar—I think I used the war as an excuse to escape from the toxic atmosphere within the palace.' His voice grew bitter. 'Now I berate myself for my cowardice.'

'Cowardice?' she echoed. 'A teenager who was hon-

oured for his bravery during that war? Whose body is still scarred from the aftermath?'

'Yes,' he hissed. 'Because Haydar was still here. He was the one who bore the brunt of her increasingly bizarre behaviour.'

'She sounds like she was depressed.'

'Of course she was depressed!'

As his words faded away, Hannah took the opportunity to ask another question. 'And did she ever…did she ever see a doctor?'

'Yes.' Distractedly, he began to pace around the vast room, but when he stopped and turned back to face her, a terrible look had distorted his features into a bleak mask. 'But people can only be helped if they want to be helped, and she didn't.'

'So what happened?' she whispered.

He picked up a small box inlaid with jewels as if to study it, but Hannah suspected he didn't really see it. Putting it carefully back down on the gilded table, he looked up. 'It's not uncommon for families to normalise bizarre behaviour and that's exactly what we did. Everyone lived with it the best they could, and time passed. I only heard second-hand what happened next. Things had been bad. Worse than usual. She refused to leave her room, no matter what the inducement. By this stage, my father had renounced all his other women and was trying to make amends, but it was too late. Haydar went to show her a piece of wood he'd carved for her in the shape of one of the rainbow birds which fly in the palace gardens and that's when he found her…'

His voice had faltered, its grim tone warning Hannah that something unspeakable must have happened. 'Kulal?' she said softly.

'She was dead.'

Hannah saw the blanching of his olive skin and wondered if perhaps she'd asked enough questions but by now she couldn't stop. Because didn't she get the feeling that Kulal had spent his whole life bottling this stuff up, so that it had fermented inside him like a slow poison? Couldn't this disclosure—no matter how painful—help liberate him from some of those locked-away demons, even if it darkened their own relationship as a result? 'How did she die?' she questioned clearly.

His eyes were bleak as they met hers. They looked empty. As if all the light had left them, never to return. 'She slashed her wrists,' he said eventually, not pausing when he heard Hannah's shocked cry, emotion shaking his voice so that it sounded like rock shattering. 'Then daubed our father's name in blood on the walls. And that was how Haydar found her.'

A terrible silence descended on them. Hannah slapped her fingers over her trembling lips and it was minutes before she could bring herself to respond. 'Oh, Kulal,' she whispered. 'I'm so sorry.'

'Of course you're sorry,' he iced back. 'We were all sorry. My father went half mad with guilt, and it nearly broke my brother. It's what made him leave Zahristan as soon as he reached eighteen. Why he renounced the throne so that I was forced to take his place as monarch, even though I am the younger twin and never wanted to rule. Why he has never returned to this country for almost seventeen years,' he finished bitterly. 'That's why the information about my mother's death is so *patchy*, as you defined it—because somehow, I'm still not sure how, the palace managed to hush it all up. But press coverage was also very different at that time. We had more control over the media. Now do you understand what made me the man I am, Hannah?'

She was nodding her head. 'Y-yes,' she said, trying to stop her voice from trembling.

'Why I have no desire for the demands of love?' he continued, still in that same harsh tone. 'It's a word I equate with selfishness and ego. A word which often contradicts itself because people use it as a justification for behaviour which is in no way *loving*. Now, if you can accept that, then maybe we can continue as we are. If you can accept that I can never give you love and that I have no desire to be loved by you, then I am prepared to make the best of this marriage of ours.' He paused and, briefly, his mouth softened. 'A marriage which has been surprisingly tolerable, given its mismatched nature.'

Hannah told herself he wasn't trying to be insulting as she absorbed his words. 'And if I can't?'

He met her eyes, all that softness having left lips which were now hard and unsmiling. 'Then we're in trouble.'

Hannah thought they were in trouble now. Deep trouble. Her instinct after hearing such a terrible story would have been to have taken her husband in her arms and held him close. To have stroked the raven darkness of his hair with fingers intended to comfort, because comfort was something she was good at—she'd comforted Tamsyn time and time again when her little sister had sobbed into her neck during their neglected childhood. But Kulal mistrusted closeness. He didn't want affection unless it involved sex—and suddenly Hannah realised that his revelation had the power to change everything. Would it make her feel ridiculously self-conscious around him? If she was extra-tender towards him in bed would he think she was developing a love for him which might one day border on the obsessive, like his mother's? Was she going to have to walk on eggshells whenever she was in his company, terrified he would misinterpret the simplest of gestures? And all that in addition to being in the inevitable spotlight of royal life…

Could she bear it?

Turning away from him, she walked over to the shutters, pulling them open to let in the bright light which flooded into the room. It should have been a symbolic lightening, but the atmosphere remained dark and heavy as Hannah stared outside. Their bedroom overlooked the rose garden, where a beautiful fountain was sending sprays of water arcing through the air in a shimmer of rainbows, but today the simple beauty of the scene made her feel unbearably sad. Often she would sit in the shade of the veranda outside, just enjoying her book in the peace of the afternoon. But somehow she could never imagine doing that again, because her newfound knowledge had changed everything. Her eyes had been opened and she could no longer pretend.

And that was the problem. Before, she could allow herself to daydream about her husband and hope they would get closer. Actually, what she'd secretly wanted was for them to fall in love. But that was never going to happen. Kulal would never *allow* it to happen—but at least now he'd given her a reason. Why *wouldn't* he run screaming from love, when his mother hadn't shown him or his brother any? When she'd made a mockery of the word by sacrificing herself on the altar of her broken dreams.

'I don't know,' she said huskily and saw his black eyes narrow. 'I don't know whether I can live like that, Kulal.'

He inclined his head. 'Thank you for your honesty, at least.'

'And if I can't, what then?'

His frown deepened as her words tailed off. 'You'll have to be a little more specific than that.'

She supposed she should be grateful that they were discussing the flaws in their marriage so openly, but it was cold comfort indeed. She looked him straight in the eyes and dared voice the fear which had been nagging at her from the very start. 'If I decided I couldn't endure this life, would you try to stop me from bringing up our baby as a single mother?'

Clenching and unclenching fists hidden by the silken folds of his robes, Kulal glowered. If she'd asked him this question even a few weeks ago, the answer would have been an emphatic yes. He would have told her that such a proposition was out of the question. He would have used his wealth and his power to cut Hannah out of their child's life as much as possible. To sideline her and ensure their baby could be brought up as a Zahristan citizen, rather than as a westerner. But that was before he had grown to know her better. Before he'd realised that the pain of her own past had made her into the person she was. She would be a good mother, he recognised instinctively, and it would be wrong to wrench her from her child.

Yet the alternative was something he couldn't bear to contemplate. Surely she didn't imagine he would allow her to bring his son or daughter up in England, thus denying his child its royal roots and all that went with that?

'I don't know,' he said savagely, which was as close to the truth as he dared go. 'Obviously, the best solution would be for you to remain here. I have pledged to you my fidelity and now you will understand why I would never go back on that promise. If you can settle for friendship and respect, as well as the rare chemistry which exists between us—I think we could have a very satisfactory life together.'

He wasn't offering the moon and the stars, but at least he was being honest—and couldn't that be enough? Hannah licked her lips. She didn't know. But if she couldn't accept the limitations of their relationship, then she was going to be very unhappy. And she couldn't afford to be unhappy. Not for their baby's sake. Not for Kulal's, either. How could she bear to put him through any more pain when he'd already suffered so much already? The unwilling King who had made a success of the role which had been forced upon him.

But making promises she might not be able to keep was dangerous and what he was asking was too important to fire off an answer without thinking it through. Even though she had told him her love was unconditional and she wanted nothing in return, what if she couldn't stick to that? What if she found herself yearning for more than Kulal was ever capable of giving her? Wouldn't that drive a terrible wedge between them?

'I don't know,' she said. 'I… I need time to think.'

'How much time?'

She met his searing black gaze and for the first time since she'd known him, Hannah felt like his equal. It was as if all that had happened had given her the strength to finally shake off the insecurities which had helped define her for so long. Proudly, she tilted her chin. 'As long as it takes.'

He shook his head. 'That's not good enough, Hannah,' he clipped out. 'You're pregnant. We need some sort of timescale.'

'Is a week reasonable?'

'That depends,' he growled. 'You must know that I'm reluctant to let you return to England.'

'Scared I won't come back?'

'You think I'd let you run away?' he challenged softly.

But the crazy thing was that Hannah had no desire to go back home to work this out. It wasn't as if she had any sanctuary there—just a stubborn little sister who seemed to have slipped entirely off the radar since the night of the wedding. She didn't even have a home of her own any more. She didn't want England, with all its associations and familiarities, clogging up her head as she tried to work out what was best for everyone.

'No,' she said. 'I want peace and quiet. I'd like to go to your beach house.'

'On your own?'

'Isn't that the whole point?'

He looked at her for a long moment before he nodded. 'Very well,' he said, at last.

She supposed it was a victory of sorts but somehow it felt hollow. His words sounded so *distant* as they matched that cool new expression on his face. Almost as if he was already beginning to detach himself from her. As if he was practising for a different kind of ending. Maybe he would be the one to make the decision for both of them. What if time spent apart made him realise he didn't want a wife, after all? There was nothing to prevent him from using his mighty power to gain custody of their baby and returning to his life of a single man. Hannah bit her lip. And wouldn't she have facilitated that, with her insistence of demanding time away in order to think?

But it was too late to change her mind. Too late to do anything other than watch as Kulal headed towards the double doors, his lips unsmiling as he slammed his way out of the room without a backward glance.

CHAPTER TWELVE

IT WAS VERY peaceful by the Murjaan Sea. The sunlit air had an almost luminous quality about it and the sound of the waves lapping gently against the sandy shore was hypnotic. Each morning, Hannah pulled back the floaty white curtains and opened the shutters so that she could gaze out at the azure glitter of the water. And for a moment, she would just stand there, taking in the elemental beauty while breathing in the clean desert air.

Accompanied by a team of three female protection officers, a qualified midwife and doctor, Hannah had taken just two extra servants with her to the Sheikh's beachside retreat. Kulal had wanted to send a much bigger contingent of staff including a chef—but on this, Hannah had stood firm. She'd told him she didn't want all the accoutrements of the palace or to set up *court* there. She wanted a place which felt as close to ordinary as possible. To be able to go around unbothered by protocol, without the weight of expectation. Because she hadn't come here to play at being queen. She was here to decide how she wanted to spend her future and the choice was stark.

To live with a man who could never love her.

Or merely to exist without him.

She tried to imagine what it would be like if she went back to England—yet already it was hard to remember her life there. It felt like a country she'd visited a long time ago which was slowly fading from her memory. Much more dominant was the vivid nature of this desert land, which she found herself embracing despite her worries about the future.

Each morning, she swam in the infinity pool and, during the cool of the evening, explored the sprawling tropical gardens which Kulal had created there. But Hannah couldn't shake off the feeling of being under some kind of giant microscope. Sometimes it felt almost as if she was being *watched*—even though her security detail kept a safe but respectful distance. She told herself that she was being paranoid. Because who on earth would be able to get through the fortress-like security which surrounded the Sheikh's sprawling estate?

Her mind was like a butterfly, unable to rest on anything for long. She kept thinking about Kulal's hawk-like features and fathomless black eyes. Eyes which could blaze with passion or harden with a flintiness which made them resemble stone. Which was kind of fitting when she forced herself to think how emotionally cold he was. But, always a stickler for fairness, Hannah forced herself to think about other sides of his character, too. His strength and his determination to do the right thing, even if it wasn't what he really wanted. His honesty—and his courage. Sometimes you just had to go with instinct, and something in her heart told her he would be a loving father even if he could never be a loving husband.

Was that enough?

Wouldn't it have to be enough?

And meanwhile, she was finding it difficult to sleep. Despite the cool sea breezes which blew through the palace every evening, Hannah tossed and turned as she lay in bed, missing her husband more than she had thought possible. Because it was at night-time that the memories became difficult to ignore. The way it felt when he took her in his arms and kissed her. The way she trembled when he was deep inside her. Sometimes she would press her hands to her breasts and wish they were Kulal's hands, before guiltily snatching them away.

On the fifth night, she awoke from a troubled dream in the early hours, sitting bolt upright in bed, her skin bathed in sweat. Running the back of her hand over her damp brow, she looked around, her heart thudding. She had left the shutters open and through the floaty white curtains she could see the almost imperceptible lightening of the dawn. Her breath caught in her throat as she thought she heard a faint sound, her narrowed eyes making out the dark shape of a shadow moving outside the window, but it was gone so quickly she was certain she had imagined it. Brushing a damp lock of hair away from her heated cheek, she returned to the constant soundtrack which was playing inside her head. Could she go back to how she'd been before and manage to *stop* loving Kulal, or was that too much to ask?

For the first time in her life, she had found a problem with no real solution and the frustration of realising this made it impossible for Hannah to get back to sleep. The minutes ticked by and in the end, she gave up and got out of bed, splashing her face with cool water and slipping on some clothes. Through the window, she could see dawn lightening the horizon with a soft blaze of colour and she felt the stir of an idea. Why not witness the sun rising over the desert and see for herself how that stark place came to life? Hadn't Kulal told her often enough it was the best time—the time when he loved to ride his stallion, the heavy pound of Baasif's hooves the only sound apart from the occasional hiss of a circling vulture?

Scribbling a hasty note saying where she was going, Hannah shoved it under the door of her security detail who were sleeping nearby, then tiptoed through the silence of the dawn palace. She felt a sense of freedom as she let herself out and began to walk towards the desert, a light sea breeze lifting her sticky hair from the back of her neck. The fireworks of first light were beginning to explode all around her, and the pink sky was shot with yellow and gold and vivid streaks of purple. It was so beautiful, she thought wistfully—and if she hadn't woken up, she might have missed it.

She was careful to take a straight line from the gardens and not to venture far, because only a fool would risk getting lost in such an inhospitable place as this. But maybe her head was too busy for her to pay proper attention, because after a little while Hannah realised she couldn't see the outline of the palace any more.

Her heart began to race.

Don't panic, she told herself calmly. All she needed do was to retrace her footsteps in the sand. She glanced at her watch and frowned. Surely she hadn't been out here *that* long? With a touch of urgency now quickening her walk, she began to follow the sandy imprints back the way she'd come. But maybe the sea breeze was stronger than she'd thought because after a while, the footsteps grew fainter before eventually disappearing.

A coating of fine dust had covered her path, and it was as if she had never been there.

She blinked as she tried to remember the basic rules of survival, cursing herself when she realised that she hadn't even brought water with her.

Because she hadn't been planning to stay.

Her heart began to race. Weren't you supposed to stay still in circumstances like these? Weren't some people clever enough to be able to tell where they were by the movement of the sun? She looked up at the vast dome of the sky and wondered if she had imagined the dark circling of a vulture overhead. It was already getting warmer, but Hannah shivered because in that moment, she felt very small and very alone. She was just wondering what to do next when suddenly the silence was broken by the loud thunder of hooves and she looked up to see the growing shape of an approaching horseman. A huge black horse was pounding across the desert, clouds of dust billowing as it moved with the fluidity of black oil pouring across the sand towards her.

She recognised the rider instantly. How could she not? That proud posture and uncovered raven hair was too unique to belong to anyone else other than the Sheikh. But as the horse drew closer, with a slowing of hooves and a snorting of flared nostrils, the only thing Hannah could see was the naked fury on her husband's face. With a thunderous expression, he leapt from the saddle, his hands reaching out to grasp her wrists as if he was afraid she might suddenly fall to the ground. Narrowed ebony eyes searched her face as he levered her closer so that she could smell the sweat and sandalwood of his heated body.

'I hope by the rise of the desert moon that you are not hurt,' he gritted out.

She nodded, wondering if he could feel the wild race of her pulse beneath his fingers. 'I'm fine.'

'No. You are not fine,' he bit out. 'I'll tell you exactly what you are. You're a fool, Hannah. What do you think you're doing?'

'I couldn't sleep. I thought I'd get up to watch the sunrise,' she said, aware of how lame it sounded.

'And where the hell were your security detail?' he demanded.

A little shamefacedly, Hannah shrugged. 'Last night, I told them I was going to have a lie-in and didn't want to be disturbed. I left them a note.'

He gave a long, low curse in his native tongue. 'So why were you wandering around the desert on your own?'

'I told you. I wanted to see the sunrise.'

'Don't you know how dangerous it can be out here?'

Shaking herself free from his grasp and whipping her mobile phone from one of the pockets hidden in her silken robe, she held it up so that the silvery rectangle flashed in the sunlight. 'I came prepared,' she said triumphantly. 'I brought my phone with me.'

His lip curled in derision. 'You think *that* could save you from the strike of a rattlesnake or the sting of a scorpion?'

But suddenly, Hannah recognised from his anger that this wasn't about the natural dangers of the desert, but about something else. Her eyes narrowed as suspicion began to form and to grow inside her head until she could no longer contain it. And neither should she. Wasn't it time that she addressed the terrible question she suspected would always hover in the darkness of her husband's mind, if she chose to ignore it? 'Why, Kulal,' she questioned quietly, 'what did you think I was doing?'

Kulal saw from her look of comprehension that she had a very good idea what he was thinking, but he shook his head, unwilling to articulate the fears which had rushed through his veins like poison.

'Nothing,' he grated.

'What? It's not *nothing*, is it?' she said again.

And suddenly Kulal was aware that she was the one doing the accusing and her aquamarine eyes were flashing with unaccustomed fire as she continued.

'Did you think I couldn't cope with the insecure future you were offering me and had decided to take the easy way out?' she demanded. 'Did you think I was going to dramatically wander out into the desert and kill myself? Is that what you thought, Kulal?'

He flinched beneath the cruel clarity of her allegation, but he couldn't deny that it was rooted in truth. Distractedly, he shook his head. 'I didn't know what to think.'

'Oh, yes, you did,' she breathed. 'You thought the worst of me because that's what experience has taught you to do. But I am not your mother, Kulal—and I never will be. I would never harm myself, nor the child I carry—not in a million years. What in heaven's name do I have to do to convince you of that?' She sucked in a breath which was ragged and shook her head. 'I think you need to stop blaming your mother for what happened.' Her voice grew gentle. 'She wasn't bad, you know—she was ill. Very ill. And because it was a different time, things like that just got pushed into a corner. People never used to talk about mental health issues because they were seen as something shameful, but that would never happen now. Your mum would have got the treatment she needed.' She swallowed. 'And maybe she would be here now, awaiting the birth of her first grandchild.'

'Hannah—'

'No. I haven't finished, Kulal.' She shook her head and seemed to take a long time before whispering her next words. 'You have to forgive her. And then let her rest in peace. Because until you do that, you can never find your own peace.'

He looked into her eyes and for once, he didn't turn away from the raw emotion he could read in their aquamarine depths. He could see the pain and the consternation which had all but wiped out the hope which had once flickered there. And suddenly Kulal realised that, in trying to protect himself, he had risked everything. He had offered Hannah a life without feeling and without love. He had arrogantly expected her to accept the meagre crumbs of affection he was prepared to offer. More than that, he had regarded her with a suspicion which had no basis in fact.

Wouldn't any woman in her position decide that she wanted no more of him and his controlling nature?

Was it too late for him to make amends?

Suddenly, he reached out and lifted her up into the saddle, her bewilderment muffling her objections as he jumped up behind her, one hand lying protectively around her belly while the other gripped the reins as he eased the horse forward.

'Kulal!' She seemed to find her voice at last. 'What... what do you...?'

But her words were lost on the desert wind as Kulal

began to canter forward with the skill of a man who had ridden from the moment he could walk. Through the silken folds of her robe, he could feel the warmth of her body and sometimes the breeze tantalised him with the occasional drift of her scented hair. His throat grew dry. He thought of how he'd felt during the last five days without her and suddenly Kulal *did* feel fear.

Fear that it might be too late.

Fear that he might have lost her because of his over-arching arrogance and stubbornly black-and-white view of the world.

He felt her relax as the distinctive shape of a huge tent appeared and the horse's pace slowed to a halt. Jumping down, he lifted her carefully onto the sand, but her expression was belligerent and her eyes unforgiving as she looked at him.

'Where are we?' she questioned stonily.

'In a Bedouin tent. Not far from the palace.'

Her eyes narrowed. *'Why?'*

'Why don't you come inside so we can discuss this away from the heat of the rising sun?'

'Said the spider to the fly!'

'And where I can offer you some cool refreshment?'

Her eyes lit up at this, but her nod was grudging. 'Very well.'

She pushed aside the tent-flaps and went inside, but Kulal had to dip his head to follow her. He took his time pouring fire-berry cordial from the stone flask which had kept it cool, telling himself he wanted her to enjoy her first view of this traditional desert homestead, with its sumptuous hangings, fretwork lanterns and silken rugs. But he was also hoping that allowing a little time to elapse might cool her temper. Already he was justifying his behaviour inside his head—and surely if he started being more accommodating towards her from now on, that would be enough to make her contented?

He was quietly hopeful as he handed her the drink, but could instantly see that his assessment had been poor, because after she'd gulped down most of the liquid and thumped the silver goblet down on a low table, she straightened up to glare at him, her eyes flashing in a way he'd never seen before.

'How did you know where I'd be?' she demanded.

Kulal winced. So. There was to be no gratitude for his masterful rescue of the lost Queen! She'd gone straight for the jugular. 'I've been camped out here all week,' he admitted, and saw from the unrelenting look on her face that it was pointless to do anything other than admit the whole truth. 'I have servants staying in nearby tents who were assigned to keep a watch on you at the beach palace, both day and night. They reported to me on your movements at all times.'

She wrinkled her forehead. 'Could that explain why I thought I saw a shadow creeping past my window a few hours ago?'

'Yes.'

'But I have my own protection officers with me, Kulal.'

'I know you do.' He gave a heavy sigh. 'But these are nomadic men of the desert, who know this territory better than any other. They can see things which the ordinary protection team is capable of missing—even a highly trained security detail.'

Her hands flew to her cheeks and he could see all the colour leeching away from her skin. 'So you sent people to spy on me? Because you didn't trust me?'

'I prefer to think of it as protecting you. And in view of what happened, wasn't I right to do so?'

'Protecting your baby, you mean.'

'And you,' he said simply. 'Protecting you is paramount to me, Hannah, because I love you.'

She shook her head and quickly turned away, not answering him immediately, and when she did, her words sounded strained. 'Don't try to manipulate me with words you don't mean.'

'But I do mean them,' said Kulal as, for the first time in his life, he began to express emotions he'd never even dared to feel before. He had always associated emotion with pain and loss and he didn't ever want to have to live through that again. But he could see now that he had no choice. That if he wanted Hannah to stay, he was going to have to get her to believe that what he felt for her was real. Something so big and new that at first he hadn't even recognised it—and when at last he had, it had scared the hell out of him. 'I've never been so sure about anything. Which is that I love you, Hannah,' he repeated shakily. 'I love you so much.'

'Don't you dare lie to me!'

Nobody had ever said that to Kulal before and with good reason—a fondness for sometimes brutal candour was the more usual accusation thrown at him, particularly by women. But now wasn't the time for a proud defence of his reputation; now he needed the kind of persuasive rhetoric which normally came so easily to him. And never had it seemed quite so far away. 'I've never met a woman like you before.'

'Obviously that's not true either!' she said contemptuously. 'You've spent your life surrounded by servants—and that's all I am.'

He told himself she was lashing out because she was scared, too—because the alternative was too daunting to acknowledge. He swallowed. What if she really *did* feel contempt for him—the kind of contempt which had wiped away all the love she'd once declared?

'I'm not talking about your job. I'm talking about your heart—which is a very big heart. You are the most kind and caring woman I've ever met, Hannah—as well as the most thoughtful.'

'*Sensible*, you mean?' she questioned witheringly, still with her back to him.

He shook his head. 'Your qualities go way beyond that. You are loyal—something you demonstrated when you were determined that I should be the first to hear about impending fatherhood when you could have easily sold the story to the press.' He pulled in a deep breath. 'And you have other characteristics, too—and I'm not talking about your obvious attraction or the way I can't seem to keep my hands off you.'

'Kulal…' she said warningly.

'I've never talked to anyone the way I talk to you,' he continued. 'About mountains and spiders and—'

'Don't you dare try to smooth-talk me with senti-mentality, Kulal Al Diya,' she said, her voice crack-ing a little.

'You did the best thing for our baby by agreeing to marry me and then you tried to be the best wife you possibly could,' he forged on. 'And I threw it all back in your face.'

'Well, yes,' she whispered, turning back to face him, and he was startled by the bright glitter of unshed tears in her eyes. 'You did.'

'Everything you accused me of was correct, but the

one accusation which will not stand is the strength of my feelings for you—and I guess that time is the only thing which will prove that. That is, if you give me the gift of time.' His gaze was very steady as he looked at her. 'Because I would like the chance to prove I can be the kind of husband you deserve. The kind of father I pray I can be. And the kind of lover who never stops making you sigh with pleasure. The chance to show you how very much I love you. Will you give me that chance, Hannah?'

For a moment, Hannah couldn't answer because the emotion which was catching in her throat didn't allow her to. She recognised that this was a moment of real power and she tried to think about all the conditions she could demand of him.

But if she turned it around and thought of this as equality rather than power, it meant that she must do this without condition. To take him at his word. She had to trust him. It was a risk, but one she had to take. Because without trust, you could have nothing. No love and no real future.

Her voice was wobbling and the tears she seemed to have been holding back for so long began to stream down her cheeks like rivers. But that didn't matter. Nothing mattered other than the sure-fire certainty which pumped through her veins as she went into his open arms. 'Yes,' she whispered simply, her voice a little faint as she pressed her lips against his own wet cheek. 'I will give you that chance because I love you, Kulal—and deep down I know I always will.'

EPILOGUE

'I CAN'T BELIEVE you didn't tell me.'

Kulal turned back from the balustrade, where he had been standing watching the fiery sun sink slowly into the Murjaan Sea—a stunning spectacle indeed, but one which did not come close to competing with his wife's natural beauty. He gazed at her in a moment of grateful contemplation. The rose-gold light gilded her hair and cast shadows which emphasised the soft delicacy of her features.

'Tell you what?' he said as he walked over to where Hannah sat on the swinging hammock she had installed on the veranda of their beachside palace. But Kulal already knew the answer to his own question and so did Hannah. Just as he knew she must have a special reason for asking it again, and now.

'That girls were not allowed by law to inherit the Zahristan crown. That in order to accede to the throne, the child must be a boy.'

He smiled as he sat down beside her, taking her hand in his and beginning to massage it. 'And would it have made a difference in your decision to marry me?' he mused. 'If you had known, would you have insisted on waiting until the birth to discover if we were having a boy or a girl?'

Deep in love, Hannah smiled back. 'Of course it wouldn't,' she said. 'But I thought that having an heir was the main reason you wanted me to be your bride.'

'So did I,' he admitted, lifting her hand to his lips and kissing each finger almost reflectively. 'But there was obviously something immensely powerful burning between us, which had been there from the start. I guess I was too much of an emotional coward to admit it at the time—even to myself.'

'Not any more, though?' she questioned, her eyes glinting with mischief.

He met her moonlit gaze and shook his head. 'No, Hannah. Not any more.'

'And you're sure you don't want to have any more children, my darling? To try for a boy? Because I am quite willing to do that.'

So *that* was the reason she had brought it up. Kulal shook his head. 'No, my love. Four children is quite enough.'

'But—'

'But, yes,' he insisted softly, drawing her closer. 'I'm blissfully happy with my four daughters. Fate has not given us a son and I accept that. I am not risking your life in pursuit of a crown.'

Wordlessly, Hannah nodded. It had been an eventful time since they had been married—three glorious years which had been filled with both joy and fear. But life was like that, she realised, and they had faced those fears together and shared their joy until their hearts had felt fit to burst. It had been after the birth of their first daughter that Kulal had told her only a boy child could inherit the Zahristanian throne. They had wanted more children anyway, but Hannah had conceived far more quickly than either of them had anticipated. The birth of girl triplets had thrilled them immeasurably, but Hannah had almost died during the delivery and Kulal had asked her very sternly that for their children's sake—and his—could they now call their family complete?

'But who will inherit the throne?' she'd asked, with the sincerity of someone who felt a deep and enduring loyalty towards their adopted homeland.

Kulal's response had been a shrug which had convinced Hannah that he really didn't care. 'It will pass down to my cousin,' he said. 'Who is a good man. That's if my brother doesn't produce an heir in the meantime, which seems unlikely.'

'You don't care that your offspring will miss out on their inheritance?'

And she had cried when Kulal had smiled and shaken his head. 'The only thing I care about is you and my family, my dearest love.'

Hannah had met Haydar at last. Her husband's non-identical twin had finally returned to Zahristan for the celebrations marking the birth of the triplets. He was a charismatic but very silent man, Hannah remembered thinking—with a stillness about him which reminded her of one of Kulal's desert falcons just before it took flight. She'd wanted to take him in her arms and give him a sisterly hug of welcome, but hadn't dared. She'd thought how closed-off he seemed and had wondered if introducing him to a lovely woman might break down some of that shuttered reserve. But she wouldn't dare do that either. Because you couldn't dictate to your siblings how they should live their lives. And what made her think she knew better than anyone else, when she'd made her own share of mistakes in the past?

She thought about her own sister. She'd stopped trying to run Tamsyn's life for her, too. Kulal had gently told her it really was time to let go and Hannah had listened, even if it had been hard to stand back and let the fiery little redhead blaze her own unpredictable path.

Possibly one of the biggest changes in her husband's life had been his change of attitude towards his mother's death. He'd told Hannah that he'd given her words a great deal of thought and realised she was right. He had given the *Ashkhazar Times* an exclusive interview, talking frankly about his mother's suicide for the first time and the need to be open about mental health issues. The piece had gone viral. International charities had applauded his honesty and his candour, and confronting the issue had somehow allowed Kulal to make his peace with it at last—just as Hannah had predicted.

Turning her head, Hannah saw that the Sheikh was watching her and her heart welled up with love. And longing.

'You were looking very wistful just then,' he observed softly.

'Was I? I was thinking about everything which had brought us to the point we're at now.'

'And your conclusion is?'

Luxuriously, Hannah stretched, and smiled. 'My conclusion is that I've never been so happy and I wouldn't want it any other way.' For a second, the smile left her lips as she contemplated an alternative existence. One which didn't involve the hawk-faced Sheikh who was at the blazing centre of their family life. Which didn't involve four demanding little girls and the charity work for orphans which gave her so much fulfilment, because it was important to give something back. Especially when you had been given so much yourself...

'Sometimes I have to pinch myself,' she admitted on a whisper. 'To convince myself I'm not dreaming.'

'Is that so? I can think of a far more gratifying way of reinforcing reality than pinching,' murmured Kulal, as he gathered her in his arms and brushed his lips over hers. 'Would this do it, do you think?'

'Oh, yes. I think so,' she said.

He kissed her for a long time as some of the heat left the evening air. He kissed her until she began to move restlessly in his arms and then he picked her up and carried her through to their bedroom as the sea breeze billowed the floaty white curtains. He carried on kissing her as, slowly, he undressed her and laid her down on the bed and told her again and again how much he loved her.

'And I love you, too, Kulal,' said Hannah shakily. 'So very much.'

And suddenly they were no longer a king and a queen. They were just a man and a woman making love and speaking love, as the silvery moon rose high over the desert sky.

* * * * *

TYCOON'S FORBIDDEN CINDERELLA

MELANIE MILBURNE

To my dear friend Julie Greenwood.

We have been friends since the seventh grade and I can't imagine how different life would be if I hadn't met you.

I have so many fun memories of us horse riding, and sitting in the mulberry tree at my parents' farm with purple-stained fingers and mouths.

You are one of a kind.

Love always. Xxxx

CHAPTER ONE

AUDREY EYED HER mother's wedding invitation as if it were a cockroach next to her breakfast teacup and toast plate. 'I would do anything to get out of this wedding party and I mean *anything*.'

Rosie, her flatmate, slipped into the seat opposite and pinched a slice of toast off Audrey's plate and began munching. 'Three times a bridesmaid, huh? Go you.'

Audrey sighed. 'Yes, well, being a bridesmaid three times would be bad enough but they're my mother's marriages and all to Harlan Fox. I thought she'd learned her lesson by now.'

'I guess that does complicate things a bit…' Rosie twisted her mouth in a *glad-it's-you-and-not-me* manner.

'I don't know why my mother hasn't learnt from her past two mistakes.' Audrey stirred her tea until it created a whirlpool similar to the one she was feeling in her stomach. 'Who marries the same man *three* times? I can't bear another one of my mother's marriages. I can't bear another one of my mother's divorces. None of them were civilised and private. They were nasty and horribly public.' Her teaspoon fell against the saucer with a clatter. 'That's the problem with having a soap opera star for a parent. Nothing they do ever escapes public attention. Nothing. Good or bad or just plain dead embarrassing, it's all splashed over the gossip magazines and the net for millions to read.'

'Yeah, I kind of figured that after that spread about your mother's affair with one of the young cameramen on set,' Rosie said. 'Amazing she has a daughter of twenty-five and yet she can still pull guys like a barman pulls beers.'

'Yes, well, if that wasn't bad enough, Harlan Fox is even more famous than my mother.' Audrey frowned and pushed her cup and saucer away as if it had mortally offended her. 'What can she possibly see in an aging rock star of a heavy metal band?'

'Maybe it's because Harlan and his band mates are in the process of reforming to go back on the tour?' Rosie had clearly been reading the gossip pages rather avidly.

Audrey rolled her eyes. 'A process somewhat stalled by the fact that two of its members are still in rehab for drug and alcohol issues.'

Rosie licked a droplet of raspberry jam off her finger and asked, 'Is Harlan's hot-looking son Lucien going to be best man again?'

Audrey sprang up from the table as if her chair had suddenly exploded. The mere mention of Lucien Fox's name was enough to make her grind her teeth until her molars rolled over and begged for mercy. She scooped her teacup off the table and poured the contents in the sink, wishing she were throwing it in Lucien's impossibly handsome face. 'Yes.' She spat out the word like a lemon pip.

'Funny how you two have never hit it off,' Rosie said. 'I mean, you'd think you'd have heaps in common. You've both lived in the shadow of a celebrity parent. And you've been step-siblings on and off for the last… how long's it been now?'

Audrey turned from the sink and gripped the back of the chair. 'Six years. But it's not going to happen again. No way. This wedding is *not* going to go ahead.'

Rosie's eyebrows lifted until they met her fringe. 'What? You think you can talk them out of it?'

Audrey released her stranglehold on the chair and picked up her phone from the table and checked for messages. Still no answer from her mother. Damn it. 'I'm going to track Mum and Harlan down and give them a stern talking-to. I'll resort to blackmail if I have to. I have to stop them marrying. I *have* to.'

Rosie frowned. 'Track them down? Why? Have they gone into hiding or something?'

'They've both turned off their phones. Their publicists apparently have no idea where they've gone.'

'But you do?'

She drummed her fingers on the back of her phone. 'No, but I have a hunch and I'm going to start there.'

'Have you asked Lucien where he thinks they might be or are you still not talking since the last divorce? How many years ago was that again?' Rosie asked.

'Three,' Audrey said. 'For the last six years my mother and Harlan have been hooking up, getting hitched and then divorcing in a hate fest that makes headlines around the world. I'm over it. I'm not going to let it happen again. They can hook up if they want to but another marriage is out. O.U.T. Out.'

Rosie shifted her lips from side to side as if observing an unusual creature in captivity. 'Wow. You really have a thing about weddings, don't you? Don't you want to get married one day?'

'No. I do not.' Audrey knew she sounded like a starchy old spinster from a nineteenth-century novel but she was beyond caring. She hated weddings. Capital H hated them. She felt like throwing up when she saw a white dress. Maybe she wouldn't hate weddings so much if she hadn't been dragged to so many of her mother's. Before Harlan Fox, Sibella Merrington had had three husbands and not one of them had been Audrey's father. Audrey had no idea who her father was and apparently neither did her mother, although Sibella had narrowed it down to three men.

What was it with her mother and the number three?

'You didn't answer my question,' Rosie said. 'Are you talking to Lucien again or not?'

'Not.'

'Maybe you should reconsider,' Rosie said. 'You never know, he might prove to be an ally in your mission to stop his dad and your mum getting married.'

Audrey snorted. 'The day I speak again to that arrogant, stuck-up jerk will be the day hell turns into an ice factory.'

'Why do you hate him so much? What's he ever done to you?'

Audrey turned and snatched her coat off the hook

behind the door and shrugged it on, pulling her hair out of the collar. She faced her flatmate. 'I don't want to talk about it. I just hate him, that's all.'

Rosie's brows shot up again like skyrockets and she leaned forward in her chair, eyes sparkling with intrigue. 'Did he try it on with you?'

Audrey's cheeks were suddenly feeling so hot she could have cooked another round of toast on them. No way was she going to confess it was *she* who had done the 'trying it on' and been rejected.

Mortifyingly, embarrassingly, ego-crushingly rejected.

Not once but two times. Once when she was eighteen and again when she was twenty-one, both times at her mother's wedding reception to his father. Another good reason to prevent such a marriage occurring again.

No more wedding receptions.

No more champagne.

No more gauche flirting with Lucien Fox.

Oh, God, why, why, *why* had she tried to kiss him? She had been planning to peck him on the cheek to show how sophisticated and cool she was about their respective parents getting married. But somehow her lips had moved. Or maybe his had moved. What did it matter whose had moved? Their mouths had almost touched. It was the closest a man's mouth had ever been to hers.

But he had jerked away as if she had poison on her lips.

The same thing happened at their parents' next wedding. Audrey had been determined to act as if nothing could faze her. She was going to act as if the previous almost-kiss had never happened. To show him it hadn't had any impact on her at all. But after a few champagnes to give her the courage to get on the dance floor, she'd breezed past Lucien and hadn't been able to stop herself from giving him a spontaneous little air kiss. Her mouth had aimed for the air between his cheek and hers but someone bumped her from behind and she had fallen against him. She'd grabbed at the front of his shirt to stop herself from falling. He'd put his hands on her hips to steady her.

And for a moment…an infinitesimal moment when the noise of the reception faded away and it felt they were completely and utterly alone…she'd thought he was going to kiss her. So she'd…

Oh, God, she hated thinking about it even now…

She'd leaned up on tiptoe, closed her eyes and waited for him to kiss her. And waited. And waited.

But of course he hadn't.

Even though Audrey had been tipsy on both occasions, and a part of her knew Lucien had done the honourable thing by rejecting her clumsy advances, another part of her—the female, insecure part—wondered if any man would ever be attracted to her. Would any man ever want to kiss her, much less make love to her? She was twenty-five and still a virgin. She hadn't been on a date since she was a teenager. Not that she hadn't been asked a few times but she'd always declined because she could never tell if guys wanted to go out with her for the right reason. Her first date at the age of sixteen had been a disaster—an ego-smashing disaster she would do anything to avoid repeating. She'd only been asked out because of who her mother was. It had nothing to do with *her* whether the boy liked her or not. It was about her celebrity mother.

It was *always* about her celebrity mother.

Audrey picked up her keys and the overnight bag she'd packed earlier. 'I'm heading out of town for the weekend.'

Rosie's eyes twinkled like they belonged on a Christmas tree. 'Am I allowed to know where you're going or is it a state secret?'

It wasn't that Audrey didn't trust her flatmate, but even Rosie with her down-to-earth nature could at times be a little star-struck by Audrey's mother. 'Sorry, Rosie. I have to keep the press out of this if I can. With Mum and Harlan in hiding, the first person the paps will come looking for is me.'

Please, God, not again. The press had followed her relentlessly after her mother had gone to ground. At Audrey's flat. She'd stayed for three weeks and had taken three overdoses, not serious enough for hospitalisation but serious enough for Audrey to want to prevent another marriage between her mother and the hard-partying Harlan Fox.

'What about Lucien?'

'What about Lucien?' Even saying his name made Audrey's spine tighten and her scalp prickle as if a thousand ants were tugging on the roots of her hair.

'What if Lucien wants to know where you are?'

'He won't. Anyway, he's got my number.'

Not that he'd ever used it in the last three years. Or the last six. But then, why would he? She was hardly his type. His type was tall and blonde and sophisticated, women who didn't drink too much champagne when they were feeling nervous or insecure and out of their depth.

'Gosh, how lucky are you to be on Lucien Fox's speed dial.' Rosie's expression had gone all dreamy. 'I wish I had his number. I don't suppose you'd—?'

Audrey shook her head. 'It'd be a waste of time if I did. He doesn't date boring homespun girls like us. He only dates size zero supermodels.'

Rosie sighed. 'Yeah, like that one he's been dating now for weeks and weeks—Viviana Prestonward.'

Something slipped in Audrey's stomach. 'H-has he?' Her voice came out scratchy and she cleared her throat. 'I mean, yes, yes, I know.'

'Viviana's amazingly beautiful.' Rosie's expression became one part wistful, three parts envious. 'I saw a picture of them at a charity ball last month. Everyone's saying they're about to become engaged. Some girls have all the luck. They get the best looks and the best guys.'

'I wouldn't call Lucien Fox a prize catch.' Audrey couldn't keep the bitter edge from her tone. 'He might be good-looking and rich but his personality needs a serious makeover. He's so stiff and formal you'd think he'd been potty-trained at gunpoint.'

Rosie tilted her head again in her studying-an-exotic-creature manner. 'Maybe he'll ask you to be the bridesmaid at his wedding too, I mean, since you're going to be step-siblings again.'

Audrey clenched her teeth hard enough to crack a coconut. 'Not if I can help it.'

* * *

Audrey drove out of London and within a couple of hours pulled into the country lane that led to the secluded cottage in the Cotswolds. Her mother had bought the house when she landed her first role on television. It often amazed Audrey that her mother hadn't sold it by now, but somehow the cottage remained even though several husbands and their houses had not.

It was too small to be the sort of place the press would expect to find Sibella and Harlan, so it was the first place on Audrey's list. Her mother had left a hint in the note on her doorstep, along with the invitation:

Gone to smell the daffodils with Harlan.

That could only mean Bramble Cottage. At this time of year the rambling garden was full of daffodils. Along the lane, in the fields, under the trees, along the bank of the stream—the swathes of yellow had always delighted Audrey.

Bramble Cottage was a perfect hideaway as it was on a long country lane lined with hedgerows and lots of overarching trees, creating a leafy tunnel. The lane had a rickety bridge over a trickling stream that occasionally swelled enough with rainwater to be considered a river.

When she came down to the cottage with her mother as a child, Audrey had been fascinated by the trees along the lane because they looked as if they were reaching down to hug her. Going through that shady green tunnel had been like driving into another world, a magical world where it was just her and her mother.

A safe world. A world where there were no strange men coming and going from her mother's bedroom.

No press lurking about for candid shots of Sibella's painfully shy daughter.

Audrey couldn't see any sign of activity at the cottage when she got out of her car but she knew her mother and Harlan would have covered their tracks well. On closer inspection, however, she realised the cottage looked a little neglected. She'd thought there was a caretaker who kept an eye on things. There were often months and months or even a couple of years between her mother's fleeting visits. The garden was overgrown but in a way that was part of the charm of the place. Audrey loved how the plants spilled over the garden beds, their blooms filling the air with the fresh and hopeful fragrance of spring.

Audrey left her car parked in the shade of the biggest oak tree a short distance away so as to keep her car from being seen if any paparazzi happened to do a drive-by. She did a mental high-five when she saw the marks of recent tyre tracks on the pebbled area in front of the cottage. She bent down so she could inspect the tracks a little more closely. A car had come in and gone out again, which meant her mother and Harlan hopefully weren't far away. Probably picking up supplies or something. 'Or something' being copious amounts of alcohol most likely.

She straightened and glanced up at the suddenly darkening sky. That was another thing she loved about this place—watching a spring storm from the cosy shelter of the cottage. The spare key was under the left-hand plant pot but Audrey gave the door a quick knock just in case either her mother or Harlan was still inside. When there was no answer, she unlocked the door just as the rain started to pelt down as if someone had turned on a tap.

She closed the door and looked around the cottage but it didn't look as though anyone had been there in months. Disappointment sat on her chest like an overstuffed sofa. She'd been so certain she would find them here. Had she misread her mother's note?

She glanced at the cobwebs hanging from a lampshade and suppressed an icy shiver. There was a fine layer of dust over the furniture and the air inside the cottage had a musty, unaired smell. So much for the caretaker, then. But Audrey figured this would be a good test of the hideously expensive therapy she'd undergone to rid herself of her spider phobia. She pulled back the curtains to let more light in but the storm clouds had gathered to such an extent the world outside had a yellowish, greenish tinge that intensified with each flash of lightning. She turned on the sitting room light and it cast a homey glow over the deep, cushiony sofas and the wing chair positioned in front of the fireplace.

Audrey was battling with an acute sense of dismay that her mission to track down her mother and Harlan had come to a dead end and a sense of sheer unmitigated joy she had the cottage to herself during a storm. She figured she might as well stay for an hour or two to set the place in order, maybe even stay the night while she thought up a Plan B.

She reassured herself with the possibility that her

mother and Harlan would return at any minute. After all, someone had been here—she'd seen the tyre marks. All she had to do was wait until they got back and sit them down and talk them out of this ridiculous third marriage.

Audrey glanced at the fireplace. Was it cold enough to light a fire? There was kindling and wood in the basket next to the fireplace, and before she could talk herself out of it she got to work setting a fire in the grate. It would come in handy if the power was to go off, which was not uncommon during a storm.

As if by her just thinking of a power cut, the light above her head flickered and a flash of lightning rent the sky outside. A sonic boom of thunder sounded, and it made even an avid storm-lover such as she jump. The light flickered again and then went out. It left the room in a low, ghostly sort of light that reminded her of the setting of a fright flick she'd watched recently. A shiver scuttled over her flesh like a legion of little furry feet.

It's just a storm. You love storms.

For once the self-talk wasn't helping. There was something about this storm that felt different. It was more intense, more ferocious.

Between the sound of the rain lashing against the windows and the crash of thunder, she heard another sound—car tyres spinning over the pebbled driveway.

Yes!

Her hunch had been spot-on. Her mother and Harlan were returning. Audrey jumped up to peep out of the window and her heart gave a carthorse kick against her breastbone.

No. No. No.

Not Lucien Fox. Why was he here?

She hid behind part of the curtain to watch him approach the front door, her breathing as laboured as the pair of antique bellows next to the fireplace. The rain was pelting down on his dark head but he seemed oblivious. Would he see her car parked under the oak tree?

She heard Lucien's firm knock on the door. Why hadn't she thought to lock it when she came into the cottage? The door opened and then closed.

Should she come out or hide here behind the curtain, hoping he wouldn't stay long enough to find her? The *Will I or won't I?* was like a seesaw inside her head.

He came into the sitting room and Audrey's heart kept time with the tread of his feet on the creaky floorboards.

Step-creak-boom-step-creak-boom-step-creak-boom.

'Harlan?' Lucien's deep baritone never failed to make her spine tingle. 'Sibella?'

Audrey knew it was too late to step out from her hiding place. She could only hope he would leave before he discovered her. How long was he going to take? Surely he could see no one had been here for months... *Yikes.* She forgot she had been laying a fire. Her breathing rate accelerated, her pulse pounding as loud as the thunder booming outside. She'd been about to strike the match when the power had gone off and it was now lying along with the box it came from on the floor in front of the fireplace.

Would he see it?

Another floorboard creaked and Audrey held her breath. But then her nose began to twitch from the dust clinging to the curtain. There was one thing she did not have and that was a ladylike sneeze. Her sneezes registered on the Richter scale. Her sneezes could trigger an earthquake in Ecuador. Her sneezes had been known to cause savage guard dogs to yelp and small babies to scream. She could feel it building, building, building... She pressed a finger under her nose as hard as she possibly could, her whole body trembling with the effort to keep the sinus explosion from happening.

A huge lightning flash suddenly zigzagged across the sky and an ear-splitting boom of thunder followed, making Audrey momentarily forget about controlling her sneeze. She clutched the curtain in shock, wondering if she'd been struck by lightning. Would she be found as a little pile of smoking ashes behind this curtain? But clutching the curtain brought the dusty fabric even closer to her nostrils and the urge to sneeze became unbearable.

'Ah... Ah... Choo!'

It was like a bomb going off, propelling her forwards, still partially wrapped in the curtain, bringing the rail down with a clatter.

Even from under the dense and mummy-like shroud, Audrey heard Lucien's short, sharp expletive. Then his hands pulled at the curtain, finally uncovering her dishevelled form. 'What the hell?'

'Hi...' She sat up and gave him a fingertip wave.

He frowned at her. *'You?'*

'Yep, me.' Audrey scrambled to her feet with haste

not grace, wishing she'd worn jeans instead of a dress. But jeans made her thighs look fat, she thought, so a dress it was. She smoothed down the cotton fabric over her thighs and then finger-combed her tousled hair. Was he comparing her with his glamorous girlfriend? No doubt Viviana could stumble out of a musty old curtain and still look perfect. Viviana probably had a tiny ladylike sneeze too. And Viviana probably looked amazing in jeans.

'What are you doing here?' His tone had that edge of disapproval that always annoyed her.

'Looking for my mum and your dad.'

Lucien's ink-black brows developed a mocking arch. 'Behind the curtain?'

Audrey gave him a look that would have withered tumbleweed. 'Funny, ha-ha. So what brings you here?'

He bundled up the curtain as if he needed something to do with his hands, his expression as brooding as the sky outside. 'Like you, I'm looking for my father and your mother.'

'Why did you think they'd come here?'

He put the roughly folded curtain over the back of the wing chair and then picked up the curtain rail, setting it to one side. 'My father sent me a text, mentioning something about a quiet weekend in the country.'

'Did his text say anything about daffodils?'

Lucien looked at her as if she'd mentioned fairies instead of flowers. 'Daffodils?'

Audrey folded her arms across her middle. 'Didn't you notice them outside? This place is Wordsworth's heaven.'

The corner of his mouth twitched into an almost-smile. But then his mouth went back to its firm and flat humourless line. 'I think we've been led on a wild-goose chase—or a wild-daffodil chase.'

This time it was Audrey who was trying not to smile. Who knew he had a sense of humour under that stern schoolmastery thing he had going on? 'I suppose you got the invitation to their wedding?'

His expression reminded her of someone not quite over a stomach bug. 'You too?'

'Me too.' She let out a sigh. 'I can't bear to be a bridesmaid for my mother again. Her taste in brides-maid dresses is nearly as bad as her taste in men.'

If he was annoyed by her veiled slight against his fa-ther he didn't show it. 'We need to stop them from mak-ing another stupid mistake before it's too late.'

'We?'

His dark blue gaze collided with hers. Was it even pos-sible to have eyes that shade of sapphire? And why did he have to have such thick, long eyelashes when she had to resort to lashings of mascara? 'Between us we must be able to narrow down the search. Where does your mother go when she wants to get away from the spotlight?'

Audrey rolled her eyes. 'She never wants to get away from the spotlight. Not now. In the early days she did. But it looks like she hasn't been here in months, pos-sibly a year or more. Maybe even longer.'

Lucien ran a finger over the dusty surface of the nearest bookshelf, inspecting his fingertip like a foren-sics detective. He looked at her again. 'Can you think of anywhere else they might go?'

'Erm… Vegas?'

'I don't think so, not after the last time, remember?'

Audrey dearly wished she could forget. After her clumsy air kiss to Lucien—*as if that hadn't been bad enough*—her mother and his father had been ridiculously drunk at the reception of their second wedding and had got into a playful food fight. Some of the guests joined in and before long the room was trashed and three people were taken to hospital and four others arrested over a scuffle that involved a bowl of margarita punch and an ice bucket.

The gossip magazines ran with it for days and the hotel venue banned Harlan and Sibella from ever going there again. The fact that Audrey's mother had been the first to throw a profiterole meant that Lucien had always blamed Sibella and not his father. 'You're right. Not Vegas. Besides, they want us at the wedding to witness the ceremony. Not that the invitation mentioned where it was being held, just a date and venue to be advised.'

Lucien paced the floor, reminding her of a cougar in a cat carrier. 'Think. Think. Think.'

Audrey wasn't sure if he was speaking to her or to himself. The thing was, she found it difficult to think when he was around. His presence disturbed her too much. She couldn't stop herself studying his brooding features. He was one of the most attractive men she'd ever seen—possibly *the* most.

Tall and broad-shouldered and with a jaw you could land a fighter jet on. His mouth always made her think of long, sense-drugging kisses. Not that she'd had many of those, and certainly none from him, but it didn't stop her fantasising. He had thick, black, wavy hair that was neither long nor short but casually styled with the ends curling against his collar. He was clean-shaven but there was enough regrowth to make her wonder how it would feel to have that sexy stubble rub up against her softer skin.

Lucien stopped pacing and met her gaze and frowned. 'What?'

Audrey blinked. 'What?'

'I asked first.'

She licked her lips, which felt as dry as the dust on the bookshelves. 'I was just thinking. I always stare when I think.'

'What are you thinking?'

How hot you look in those jeans and that close-fitting cashmere sweater.

Audrey knew she was blushing, for she could feel her cheeks roaring enough to make lighting a fire pointless. She could have warmed the whole of England with the radiant heat coming off her face. Possibly half of Europe. 'I think the storm is getting worse.'

It was true. The lightning and thunder were much more intense and the rain had now turned into hail, landing like stones on the slate-tiled roof.

Lucien glanced out of the window and swore. 'We'll have to wait it out before we leave. It's too dangerous to drive down that lane in this weather.'

Audrey folded her arms across her middle again and raised her chin. 'I'm not leaving with you, so you can get that thought out of your head right now.'

His eyes took in her indomitable stance as if he were

staring down at a small, recalcitrant child. 'I want you with me when we finally track them down. We need to show them we are both vehemently against this marriage.'

No way was she going on a tandem search with him. 'Were you listening?' She planted her feet as if she were conducting a body language workshop for mules. 'I said I'm not leaving. I'm going to stay the night and tidy this place up.'

'With no power on?'

Audrey had forgotten about the power cut. But even if she had to rub two sticks together to make a fire she would do it rather than go anywhere with him. 'I'll be fine. The fire will be enough. I'm only staying the one night.'

He continued to look at her as if he thought a white van and a straitjacket might be useful right about now. 'What about your thing with spiders?'

How like him to remind her of her embarrassing childhood phobia. But she had no reason to be ashamed these days. She'd taken control. Ridiculously expensive control. Twenty-eight sessions with a therapist that had cost more than her car. She would have done thirty sessions but she'd run out of money. Her income as a library archivist only went so far. 'I've had therapy. I'm cool with spiders now. Spiders and me, we're like that.' She linked two of her fingers in a tight hug.

His expression looked as though he belonged as keynote speaker at a sceptics' conference. 'Really?'

'Yes. Really. I've had hypnotherapy so I don't get triggered when I see a spider. I can even say the word without breaking out in a sweat. I can look at pictures of them too. I even draw doodles of them.'

'So if you turned and saw that big spider hanging from the picture rail you wouldn't scream and throw yourself into my arms?'

Audrey tried to control the urge to turn around. She used every technique she'd been taught. She could cope with cobwebs. Sure, she could. They were pretty in a weird sort of way. Like lace...or something.

She was *not* going to have a totally embarrassing panic attack.

Not after all that therapy. She was going to smile at Incy-Wincy because that was what sensible people who weren't scared spitless of spiders did, right?

Her heart rate skyrocketed. *Breathe. Breathe. Breathe.* Beads of sweat dripped between her shoulder blades as if she were leaking oil. *Don't panic. Don't panic. Don't panic.* Her breathing stop-started as though a tormenting hand were gripping, then releasing her throat. *Grip. Release. Grip. Release. Grip. Release.*

What if the spider moved? What if this very second it was climbing down from the picture rail and was about to land on her head? Or scuttle down the back of her dress? Audrey shivered and took a step closer to Lucien, figuring it was a step further away from the spider even if it brought her closer to her arch-enemy Number One. 'Y-you're joking, right?'

'Why don't you turn around and see?'

Audrey didn't want to turn around. Didn't want to see the spider. She was quite happy looking at Lucien instead. Maybe her therapist should include 'Looking at

Lucien' in her treatment plan. Diversionary therapy… or something.

This close she could smell his aftershave—a lemony and lime combo with an understory of something fresh and woodsy. It flirted with her senses, drugging them into a stupor like a bee exposed to exotic pollen. She could see the way his stubble was dotted around his mouth in little dark pinpricks. Her fingers itched to glide across the sexy rasp of his male flesh. She drew in a calming breath.

You've got this. You've spent a veritable fortune to get this.

She slowly turned around, and saw a spider dangling inches from her face.

A big one.

A ginormous one.

A genetically engineered one.

A throwback from the dinosaur age.

She gave a high-pitched yelp and turned into the rock-hard wall of Lucien's chest, wrapping her arms around his waist and burying her face in the cashmere of his sweater. She danced up and down on her toes to shake off the sensation of sticky spider feet climbing up her legs. 'Get rid of it!'

Lucien's hands settled on her upper arms, his fingers almost overlapping. 'It won't hurt you. It's probably more frightened of you.'

She huddled closer, squeezing her eyes shut, shuddering all over. 'I don't care if it's frightened of me. Tell it to get some therapy.'

She felt the rumble of his laughter against her cheek

and glanced up to see a smile stretching his mouth. 'Oh. My. God,' she said as if witnessing a life-changing phenomenon. 'You smiled. You actually smiled.'

His smile became lopsided, making his eyes gleam in a way she had never witnessed before. Then his gaze went to her mouth as if pulled there by a force he had no control over. She could feel the weight of his eyes on her mouth. She was as close to him as she had been to any man. Closer. Closer than she had been to him at the last wedding reception. Her entire body tingled as if tuning in to a new radar signal. Her flesh contracting, all her nerves on high alert. She could feel the gentle pressure from each of his fingers against her arms, warm and sensual.

His fingers tensed for a moment, but then he dragged his gaze away from her mouth and unwrapped her arms from his waist as if she had scorched him. 'I'll take care of the spider. Wait in the kitchen.'

Audrey sucked in her lower lip. 'You're not going to kill it…are you?'

'That was the general idea,' he said. 'What else do you want me to do? Take it home with me and hand-feed it flies?'

She stole a glance at the spider and fought back a shudder. 'It's probably got babies. It seems cruel to kill it.'

He shook his head as if he was having a bad dream. 'Okay. So I humanely remove the spider.' He picked up an old greetings card off the bookshelf and a glass tumbler from the drinks cabinet. He glanced at her. 'You sure you want to watch?'

Audrey rubbed at the creepy-crawly sensation running along her arms. 'It'll be good for me. Exposure therapy.'

'Ri-i-ight.' Lucien shrugged and approached the spider with the glass and the card.

Audrey covered her face with her hands but then peeped through the gaps in her splayed fingers. There was only so much exposure she would deal with at any one time.

Lucien slipped the card beneath the spider and then placed the glass over it. 'Voila. One captured spider. Alive.' He walked to the front door of the cottage and then, dashing through the pelting rain, placed the spider under the shelter of the garden shed a small distance away.

He came back, sidestepping puddles and keeping his head down against the driving rain. Audrey grabbed a towel from the downstairs bathroom and handed it to him. He rubbed it roughly over his hair.

She was insanely jealous of the towel. She had towel envy. Who knew such a thing existed? She wanted to run her fingers through that thick, dark, damp hair. She wanted to run her hands across his scalp and pull his head down so his mouth could cover hers. She wanted to see if his firm mouth would soften against hers or grow hard and insistent with passion.

She wanted. Wanted. Wanted the one thing she wasn't supposed to want.

Lucien scrunched up the towel in one hand and pushed back his hair with the other. 'This storm looks like it's not going to end anytime soon.'

Just like the storm of need in her body.

What was it about Lucien that made her feel so turned on? No other man triggered this crazy out-of-character reaction in her. She didn't fantasise about other men. She didn't stare at them and wonder what it would be like to kiss them. She didn't ache to feel their hands on her body. But Lucien Fox had always made her feel this way. It was the bane of her life that *he* was the only man she was attracted to. She couldn't walk past him without wanting to touch him. She couldn't be in the same room—the same country—without wanting him.

What was wrong with her?

She didn't even like him as a person. He was too formal and stiff. He rarely smiled. He thought she was silly and irresponsible like her mother. Not that her two tipsy episodes had helped in that regard, but still. She had always hated her mother's weddings ever since she'd gone to the first one as a four-year-old.

By the time Sibella married Lucien's father for the first time, Audrey was eighteen. A couple of glasses of champagne—well, it might have been three or four, but she couldn't remember—had helped her cope reasonably well with the torture of watching her mother marry yet another unsuitable man. Audrey would be the one to pick up the pieces when it all came to a messy and excruciatingly public end.

Why couldn't she get through a simple wedding reception or two or three without lusting over Lucien?

Another boom of thunder sounded so close by it made the whole cottage shudder. Audrey winced. 'Gosh. That was close.'

Lucien looked down at her. 'You're not scared of storms?'

'No. I love them. I particularly love watching them down here, coming across the fields.'

He twitched one of the curtains aside. 'Where did you park your car? I didn't see it when I drove in.'

'Under the biggest oak tree,' Audrey said. 'I didn't want it to be easy to see in case the press followed me.'

'Did you see anyone following you?'

'No, but there were recent tyre tracks on the driveway—I thought they were Mum and Harlan's.'

'The caretaker's, perhaps?'

Audrey lifted her eyebrows. 'Does this place look like it's been taken care of recently?'

'Good point.'

Another flash of lightning split the sky, closely followed by a boom of thunder and then the unmistakable sound of a tree crashing down and limbs and branches splintering on metal.

'Which tree did you say you parked under?' Lucien asked.

Audrey's stomach lurched like a limousine on loose gravel. 'No. No. No. *Noooooo!*'

CHAPTER TWO

LUCIEN HAD TO stop Audrey from dashing outside to check out the state of her car by restraining her with a firm hand on her forearm. 'No. Don't go out there. It's too dangerous. There are still limbs and branches coming down.'

'But I have to see how much damage there is,' she said, wide-eyed.

'Wait until the storm passes. There could be power lines down or anything out there.'

She pulled at her lower lip with her teeth, her expression so woebegone it made something in his chest shift. He suddenly realised he was still holding her by the arm and removed his hand, surreptitiously opening and closing his fingers to stop the tingling sensation.

He usually avoided touching her.

He avoided her—period.

From the moment he'd met her at his father's first wedding to her mother he'd been keen to keep his distance. Audrey had only been eighteen and a young eighteen at that. Her crush on him had been mildly flattering but unwelcome. He'd shut her down with a stern lecture and hoped she would ignore him on the rare occasions their paths crossed.

He'd felt enormous relief when his father had divorced her mother because he hadn't cared for Sibella's influence on his father. But then three years later they'd remarried and his path intersected with Audrey's again. Then twenty-one and not looking much less like the innocent schoolgirl she'd been three years before, she'd made another advance on him at their parents' second wedding. He'd cut her down with a look and hoped she'd finally get the message…even though a small part of him had been tempted to indulge in a little flirtation with her. He had wanted to kiss her. He'd wanted to hold her luscious body against his and let nature do the rest. Sure he had. He had been damn close to doing it too. Way too close. Dangerously close.

But he'd ruthlessly shut down that part of himself because the last thing he wanted was to get involved with Audrey Merrington. Not just because of who her mother was but because Audrey was the cutesy homespun type who wanted the husband, the house, the hearth, the hound and the happy-ever-after.

He wasn't against marriage but he had in mind a certain type of marriage to a certain type of woman some time in the future. In the distant future. He would never marry for passion the way his father did. He would never marry for any other reason than convenience and companionship. And he would always be in control of his emotions.

Audrey rubbed at her arm as if she too was removing the sensation of his touch. 'I suppose you're going to give me a lecture about the stupidity of parking my car under an old tree. But the storm had barely started when I arrived.'

'It's an easy mistake to make,' Lucien said.

'Not for someone as perfect as you.' She followed up the comment with a scowl.

He was the last person who would describe himself as perfect. If he was so damn perfect then what the hell was he doing glancing at her mouth all the time? But something about Audrey's mouth had always tempted his gaze. It was soft and full and shaped in a perfect Cupid's bow.

He wondered how many men had enjoyed those soft, ripe lips. He wondered how many lovers she'd shared her body with and if that innocent Bambi-eyed thing she had going on was just a front. She wasn't traffic-stoppingly beautiful like her mother but she was pretty in a girl-next-door sort of way. Her figure was curvy rather than slim and she had an old-fashioned air about her that was in stark contrast to her mother's out-there-and-up-for-anything personality.

'Once the storm has passed I'll check the damage to your car,' Lucien said. 'But for now I think we'd better formulate a plan. When was the last time you spoke to your mother?'

'Not for a week or more.' Her tone had a wounded quality—disappointment wrapped around each word as if her relationship with her mother wasn't all that it could be. 'She left the invitation and a note at my flat. I found them when I got home from work yesterday. I got the feeling she was coming here with your dad from her note when she mentioned the daffodils. I'm not sure why she didn't text me instead. I've texted her since but I've heard nothing back and it looks like my messages haven't been read.'

Frustration snapped at his nerves, taut with tension. What if his father had already married Sibella? What if there was a repeat of the last two divorces with the salacious scandal played out in the press for weeks on end? He had to put a stop to it. He *had* to. 'They could be anywhere by now.'

'When did you last speak to your father?'

'About two months ago.'

Audrey's smooth brow wrinkled. 'You don't keep in more regular contact?'

Lucien's top lip curled before he could stop it. 'He's never quite got used to the idea of having a son.'

A look of empathy passed over her features. 'He had you when he was very young, didn't he?'

'Eighteen,' Lucien said. 'I didn't meet him until I was ten years old. My mother thought it was safer to keep me away from him given his hard-partying lifestyle.'

Not as if that had changed much over the years, which was another good reason to keep his father from remarrying Audrey's mother. They encouraged each other's bad habits. His dad would never beat the battle of the booze with Sibella by his side. The battle became a binge with a drinking buddy when Sibella was around. She had no idea of the notion of drinking in moderation. Nothing Sibella Merrington did was in moderation.

'At least you finally met him,' Audrey said, looking away.

'You haven't met yours?'

'No. Even my mum doesn't know who it is.'

Why did that not surprise him? 'Does it bother you?'

She gave a little shrug, still not meeting his gaze. 'Not particularly.'

He could tell it bothered her much more than she let on. He suddenly realised how difficult it must have been for her with only one parent and an incompetent one at that. At least he'd had his mother up until he was seventeen, when she'd died of an aneurysm. How had Audrey navigated all the potholes of childhood and adolescence without a reliable and responsible parent by her side? Sibella was still a relatively young woman, which meant she must have been not much older than Lucien's father when she'd had Audrey.

Why hadn't he asked her how it had been for her before now?

'How old was your mother when she had you?'

'Fifteen.' Her mouth became a little downturned. 'She hates me telling anyone that. I think she'd prefer it if I told everyone I was her younger sister. She won't allow me to call her Mum when anyone else is around. But I guess you've already noticed that.'

'I have, but then, I don't call my father Dad, either.'

'Because he prefers you not to?'

'Because *I* prefer not to.'

She considered him for a long moment, her chocolate-brown gaze slightly puzzled. 'If you're not close to him then why do you care if he remarries my mother or not?'

Good question. 'He's not much of a father but he's the only one I've got,' Lucien said. 'And I can't bear to see him go through another financially crippling divorce.'

Resentment shone in her gaze. 'Are you implying my mother asked for more than she deserved?'

'I'm now his accountant as well as his son,' Lucien said. 'Another divorce would ruin him. I've been propping him up financially for years. It won't just be his money he'll be losing—it will be mine.'

Her eyebrows rose as if the notion of his generosity towards his father surprised her. 'Oh... I didn't realise.' She chewed at her lip a couple of times. 'In spite of my mother's success as a soap star, she never seems to have enough money for bills. She blames her manager and he blames her.'

'Do you help her out?'

'No...not often.'

'How often?'

Her left eye twitched and then she suddenly cocked her head like a little bird. 'Listen. The storm's stopped.'

Lucien pulled back the lace curtain and checked the weather. The storm had moved further down the valley and the rain had all but ceased. 'I'll go and check out the damage. Wait here.'

'Stop ordering me about like I'm a child.' Her voice had a sharp edge that reminded him of a Sunday School teacher he'd had once. 'I'm coming with you. After all, it's my car.'

'Yeah, well, let's hope it's still a car and not a mangled piece of useless metal.'

Audrey looked at the mangled piece of useless metal that used to be her car. There was no way she would be driving anywhere in that anytime soon, if ever. Half the tree had come down on top of it and crushed it like a piece of paper. At least her insurance was up to date...or was it? Her chest seized in panic. Had she paid the bill or left it until she sorted out her mother's more pressing final notice bills?

Lucien whistled through his teeth, his gaze trained on the wreckage. 'Just as well you weren't sitting in there when that limb came down.' He glanced at her. 'Is your insurance up to date?'

Audrey disguised a swallow. 'Yes…'

His gaze narrowed. 'Your left eye is twitching again.'

She blinked. 'No, it's not.'

He came up close and brushed a fingertip below her eye. 'There. You did it again.'

'That's because you're touching me.'

His finger moved down the slope of her cheek to settle beneath her chin, elevating it so her gaze had to meet his. 'There was a time—two times—when you begged me to touch you.'

Audrey's cheeks felt hot enough to dry up all the puddles on the ground. 'I'm not begging you to touch me now.'

His eyes searched between each of hers in a back and forth motion that made her heart pick up its pace. 'Are you not?' His voice was low and deep and caused a shiver to ripple down her spine like a ribbon running away from its spool.

His eyes were so dark a blue she could barely make out the inkblot of his pupils. She could feel his body heat emanating from his fingertip beneath her chin right throughout her body as if he were transferring sexual energy from his body to hers. Pulses of lust contracted deep in her female flesh, making her aware of her body in a way she had never felt before. She moistened her mouth, not because her lips were dry but because they were tingling as if they could already feel the hot press of his mouth.

The need to feel his mouth on hers was so intense it was like an ache spreading to every cell of her body. She could feel a distant throbbing between her legs as if that part of her was waking up from a long slumber, like Sleeping Beauty.

Lucien watched the pathway of her tongue with his midnight-blue gaze and she could sense the battle going on inside him even though he had dropped his hand from her face. The tense jaw, the up and down movement of his Adam's apple, the opening and closing of his hands as if he didn't trust them to reach for her again.

Was he thinking about kissing her? Maybe she hadn't been mistaken at their parents' last wedding. Maybe he'd been tempted then but had stopped himself. It was a shock to know he wanted her. A thrilling shock. Six years ago he hadn't. Three years ago he had but he'd tried to disguise it.

Would he act on it this time?

'Were you thinking about kissing me?' The words were out of her mouth before she could think it was wise or not to say them, her voice husky as if she had been snacking on emery boards.

His gaze became shuttered, his body so still, so composed, as if the slightest movement would sabotage his self-control. 'You're mistaken.'

And you're lying. Audrey relished the feminine power she was feeling. Power she had never experienced in her entire adult life. When had anyone ever wanted to kiss her? Never, that was when.

But Lucien did.

His jaw worked as if he was giving his resolve a firm talking-to and his eyes were almost fixedly trained on hers as if he was worried if they would disobey orders and glance at her mouth again.

'I bet if I put my lips to yours right now you wouldn't be able to help yourself.' *Argh. Why did you say that?* One part of Audrey mentally cringed but another part was secretly impressed. Impressed she had the confidence to stand up to him. To challenge him. To flirt with him.

His eyes became hard as if he was steeling himself from the inside out. 'Try it. I dare you.'

A trickle of something hot and liquid spilled over in her belly. His gravelly delivered dare made the blood rush through her veins and set her heart to pounding as if she had run up a flight of stairs carrying a set of dumb-bells. Two sets. And a weight bench. Before she could stop the impulse, she lifted her hand to his face and outlined his firm mouth with her index finger, the rasp of his stubble catching against her skin like silk on tiny thorns. Even the scratchy sound of it was spine-tinglingly sexy. He held himself as still as a marble statue but she could still sense the war going on in his body as if every drop of his blood was thundering through his veins like rocket fuel. His nostrils flared like a stallion taking in the scent of a potential mate, his eyes still glittering with resolve, but there was something else lurking in the dark blue density of his gaze.

The same something she could feel thrumming deep in her core like an echo: desire.

But Audrey wasn't going to betray herself by kissing him. He had rejected her twice already. She wasn't signing up for a third. And if the gossip surrounding Lucien and Viviana was true, she was not the type of woman to kiss another woman's lover. She didn't want him to think she was so desperate for his attention she couldn't control herself. With or without champagne. She lowered her hand from his face and gave him an on-off smile. 'Lucky for you, I don't respond to dares.'

If he was relieved or disappointed he didn't show it. 'We're wasting valuable time.' He turned and strode back to the cottage and took out his phone. 'Call your mother while I call my father. They might have switched their phones back on.'

Audrey let out a sigh and followed him into the cottage. She'd tried calling her mother's phone fifty-three times already. Even under normal circumstances, her mother would only pick up if *she* wanted to talk to Audrey and even then the conversation would be Sibella-centred and not anything that could be loosely called a mutual exchange. She couldn't remember the time she had last talked to her mother. *Really* talked. Maybe when she was four years old? Her mother wasn't the type to listen to others. Sibella was used to people fawning over her and waiting with bated breath for her to talk to them about her acting career and colourful love life.

Audrey should be so lucky to have a love life...even a black and white one would do.

* * *

Lucien left a curt message on his father's answering service—one of many he'd left in the last twenty-four hours—and put away his phone. He had to get back on the road and away from the temptation of Audrey Merrington. Being anywhere near her was like being on a forty-day fast and suddenly coming across a sumptuous feast. He had damn near kissed her down by her wrecked car. Everything that was male in him ached to haul her into his arms and plunder her soft mouth with his. How easy would it have been to crush his mouth to hers? How easy would it have been to draw those sweet and sexy curves of hers even closer?

Too easy.

Scarily easy.

So easy he had to get a grip because he shouldn't be having such X-rated thoughts around Audrey. He shouldn't be looking at her mouth or her curves or any beautiful part of her. He shouldn't be thinking about making love to her just because she threw herself into his arms over that wretched spider. When she had launched herself at him like that, a rush of desire charged through him like high-voltage electricity. Just as it had at their parents' last wedding. Her curves-in-all-the-right-places body had thrown his senses into a tailspin like a hormone-driven teenager. He could still smell her sweet pea and spring lilac perfume on the front of his shirt where she'd pressed herself against him. He could still feel the softness of her breasts and the tempting cradle of her pelvis.

He could still feel the rapacious need marching through his body. Damn it.

He would have to stop wanting her. He would have to send his resolve to boot camp so it could withstand more of her cheeky *'Were you thinking about kissing me?'* comments. He wasn't just thinking about kissing her. He was dreaming of it, fantasising about it, longing for it. But he had a feeling one kiss of her delectable mouth would be like trying to eat only one French fry. Not possible.

But he could hardly leave her here at the cottage without a car. He would have to take her with him. What else could he do? When he'd first seen her at the cottage he'd decided the best plan was for them to drive in two cars so they could tag-team it until they tracked down their respective parents. He hadn't planned a cosy little one-on-one road trip with her. That would be asking for the sort of trouble he could do without.

Audrey came back into the sitting room from the kitchen and put her phone on the coffee table in front of the sofa with a defeated-sounding sigh. 'No answer. Maybe they're on a flight somewhere.'

He dragged a hand down his face so hard he wondered if his eyebrows and eyelashes would slough off. Could this nightmare get any worse? 'This seemed the most obvious place they'd come to. They used to sneak down here together a lot during their first marriage. My father raved about it—how quaint and quiet it was.'

She perched on the arm of the sofa, a small frown settling between her brows, the fingers of her right hand plucking at the fabric of her dress as if it was helping her to mull over something. 'I know, that's why I came here first. But maybe they *wanted* us to come here.'

'You mean, like giving us a false lead or something?'

She gave him an unreadable look and stopped fiddling with her dress and crossed her arms over her middle. 'Or something.'

'What "or something"?' A faint prickle crawled over his scalp. 'You mean, they wanted us both to come here? But why?'

She gave a lip shrug. 'My mother finds it amusing that you and I hate each other so much.'

Lucien frowned. 'I don't hate you.'

She lifted her neat brows like twin question marks. 'Don't you?'

'No.' He hated the way she made him feel. Hated the way his body had a wicked mind of its own when she was around. Hated how he couldn't stop thinking about kissing her and touching her and seeing if her body was as delectable as it looked under the conservative clothes she always seemed to wear.

But he wasn't a man driven by his hormones. That was his father's way of doing things. Lucien had will power and discipline and he was determined to use them. He would not be reduced to base animal desires just because a pretty, curvy woman got under his skin.

And Audrey Merrington was so far under his skin he could feel his organs shifting inside to make room.

'Good to know, since we're going to be related again,' she said with a deadpan expression.

'Not if I can help it.' Lucien was not going to rest until he'd prevented this third disastrous marriage. His father had almost drunk himself into oblivion the last time. There was no way he was going to stand by and watch that happen again. He was sick of picking up the pieces. Sick of trying to put his father back together again like a puzzle with most of the bits damaged or missing.

He picked up his keys. 'Come on. We'd best get on the road before nightfall. I'll organise someone to collect your car when we get back to London.'

She stood up from the arm of the sofa so quickly her feet thudded against the floor like punctuation marks. 'But I don't want to go with—'

'Will you damn well just do what you're told?' Lucien was having trouble controlling his panic at how much time they were wasting. His father could be halfway through his honeymoon at this rate. Not to mention his bank balance. 'You don't have a car, so therefore you come with me. Understood?'

She pursed her lips for a moment as if deciding whether or not to defy him. But then she stalked over to where she had left her overnight bag and her tote, and, picking them up, threw him a mutinous look that wouldn't have looked out of place on the deck of *The Bounty*. 'You can take me back to my flat in London. I'm not going anywhere else with you.'

'Fine.' He opened the front door of the cottage so she could walk out ahead of him. 'Go and sit in the car while I lock up.'

Audrey went to his car, sat inside and pulled the seat belt into place with a savage click. Why did he have to be so cavemanish about getting her to go with him? She could have had a hire car delivered or got a friend to collect her. Even a taxi would be worth the expense rather than suffering a couple of hours in Lucien's disturbing and far too tempting company. The last thing she wanted to do was to make a fool of herself again. She wasn't eighteen now. She wasn't twenty-one. She was twenty-five and mature enough—she hoped—to put this silly crush to bed once and for all.

Okay, so that wasn't the best choice of words.

She would nix her crush on Lucien. It was just a physical thing. It wasn't a cerebral or emotional thing. It was lust. Good old-fashioned lust and it would burn out sooner or later as long as she didn't feed it. Which meant absolutely no fantasising about his mouth. She wouldn't even look at it. She wouldn't daydream about it coming down on hers and his tongue gliding through the seam of her lips and—

Audrey pinched herself on the arm like someone flicking an elastic band around their wrist to stop themselves from smoking. This was like any other addiction and she had to stop it. She had to stop it *right* now. She would be strong. She would conquer this.

Besides, according to Rosie and her gossip magazine source, Lucien was in a committed relationship. It was weird how edgy it made her feel to think of him in a long-term relationship. Why should she care if he was practically engaged? Was he in love with Viviana Prestonward? Funny, but Audrey couldn't imagine him falling in love. He was nowhere near the playboy his father was between marriages, but neither was he a plaster saint. He dated women for a month or two and then moved on.

She sat in the passenger seat of his top model BMW as he got on with the business of locking up the cottage and putting the key under the left-hand plant pot. It seemed strange that he knew the cottage routine so well. She'd always loved the place because it was something she and her mother had shared before all the crazy celebrity stuff happened. But apparently Sibella had shared it with Harlan and now Lucien.

Audrey waited until he got behind the wheel of his car to ask, 'How many times have you been down here?'

'To the cottage?'

'You knew where to put the spare key. I figured you must have been here before or someone's told you the routine.'

He started the engine and did a neat three-point turn on the driveway. His arm was resting on the back of her seat so close to her neck and shoulders she suppressed a tiny shiver. 'I came down for a weekend once.'

'When?'

'A month or two before their second divorce.' His tone was casual but his hands on the steering wheel tightened. 'They asked me down for the weekend. They asked you too, but you had something else on. A date, your mother said.'

Audrey could remember being invited to spend the weekend with her mother and Harlan but neither of them had mentioned inviting Lucien. She'd declined the invitation, as she hadn't wanted her mother and Harlan to think she sat at home every weekend with nothing better to do than read or watch soppy movies. Which was basically what she did most weekends, but still.

Why had they invited him as well as her? They were well aware of the enmity between her and Lucien. 'Why did you accept the invitation? I can't imagine spending a weekend with them would have been high on your list of priorities.'

He drove along the country lane where leaves and small branches from the trees littered the road and along the roadside after the thrashing of the earlier wind. 'True. But I had nothing better to do that weekend and I wanted to see the cottage for myself. My father had talked about it a few times.'

'So, no hot date with a supermodel that weekend, huh?' Audrey said. 'My heart bleeds.'

He flicked a glance her way. 'How was your date that weekend? Worth the sacrifice of missing out on a weekend with your mother and my father?'

'It was great. Fun. Amazing. The best date ever.' *Stop already.*

'Are you dating the same guy now?'

Audrey laughed. Who said she couldn't act? 'No. I've had dozens since him.'

'So, no one permanent?'

She chanced a glance at him. 'What's with all the questions about my love life?'

He shrugged. 'Just wondering if you've got plans to settle down.'

'Nope. Not me.' She turned back to face the front and crossed one leg over the other and folded her arms. 'I've been to enough of my mother's weddings to last a lifetime. Two lifetimes.' She waited a beat and added with what she hoped sounded like mild interest, 'What about you?'

'What about me?'

Audrey glanced at him again. 'Do you plan to get married one day?'

He continued to look at the road in front, negotiating fallen branches and puddles and potholes. 'Maybe one day.'

'One day soon or one day later?'

Why are you asking that?

'Why the sudden interest in my private life?'

Audrey couldn't explain the strange feeling in her stomach—a dragging sensation, a weight that felt as heavy as a tombstone—at the thought of Lucien getting married one day. 'I could read about it in the gossip pages but I thought I'd ask you directly. Just in case what's in the papers isn't true.'

'What did you read?'

'I didn't read it myself but someone who did told me you're about to get engaged to Viviana Prestonward.'

He made a grunting sound. 'It's not true.'

She turned in her seat to look at him but he suddenly frowned and pushed down hard on the brakes. 'Damn it to hell.'

Audrey turned to look at the road ahead where his gaze was trained. A large tree had fallen across the wooden bridge, bringing down a portion of it and making it impassable. 'Oh, dear. That doesn't look good.'

Lucien thumped the heel of his hand on the steering wheel, then turned to look at her, frowning so heavily his eyebrows were knitted. 'Is there any other way around this stream? Another road? Another bridge?'

Audrey shook her head. 'Nope. One road in. One road out.'

He swore and let out a harsh-sounding breath. 'I don't believe this.'

'Welcome to life in the country.'

He got out of the car and strode over to the broken bridge, standing with his hands on his hips and his feet slightly apart. Audrey came over to stand next to him, conscious of the almost palpable tension in his body.

'Can it be…repaired?' Her voice came out one part hesitant, two parts hopeful. 'I mean, maybe we can call someone from the council to fix it. We could tell them it's an emergency or something.'

He turned away from the bridge with another muttered curse. 'There are far bigger emergencies than a single-lane bridge on a lane in the countryside that only a handful of people use.' He strode towards his car, kicking a fallen branch out of the way with his foot. 'We'll have to stay at the cottage until I can get a helicopter down here to take us out.'

Audrey stopped dead like she had come up against an invisible wall. But in a way she had. The invisible wall of her fear of flying. Flying in helicopters, to be precise. No way was she going in a helicopter. No flipping way. Give her a spider any day. Give her a roomful of them. She would cuddle a colony of spiders but flying in an overgrown egg-beater was not going to happen.

Lucien glanced back at her when he got to his car. 'What's wrong?'

Audrey gave a gulping swallow, her stomach churning so fast she could have made butter. 'I'm not going in a helicopter.'

'Don't worry—I'll clear out the spiders first.'

'Very funny.'

He held the passenger door open for her in a pointed manner. 'Are you coming with me or do you plan to walk back?'

Audrey walked to his car and slipped into the passenger seat, keeping her gaze averted. He closed the door and went around to his side and was soon back behind the wheel and doing one of his masterful three-point turns that, if she were driving, would have taken five or six turns. Possibly more...that was, if she didn't end up with the car in the ditch in the process. She looked at the brooding sky and suppressed a shudder. She had to think of a way back to London that didn't involve propellers.

'I should be able to get a helicopter first thing in the morning,' Lucien said. 'I'd try for one now but I'm not sure the weather is all that favourable.'

Argh! Don't remind me how dangerous it is to fly in one of those things.

'I'm surprised Britain's most successful forensic accountant doesn't have a helicopter or two of his own waiting on stand-by.'

'Yes, well, I'm too much of a bean-counter to throw money away on unnecessary luxuries. I leave that sort of thing to my father.'

CHAPTER THREE

THE SHORT TRIP back to the cottage was mostly silent, mainly because Audrey was trying to control her fear at the thought of having to leave in a helicopter in the morning. Maybe she should have got her therapist to work with her on that issue instead of the arachnophobia. But it wasn't every day she had to face a ride in a helicopter. Surely the road would be cleared in a day or two at the most? It wasn't like she'd be stuck down here for weeks or months on end.

But if the next morning's flight was a worry, there was this evening to get through first. Sharing the cottage with Lucien for one night—for one minute—was not going to help her little fantasy problem. It would be like trying to give up chocolate and spending the night in a chocolate factory.

Big mistake.

When Lucien helped her out of the car, the smell of rain-washed earth was as sweet as the perfume of the flowers in the overgrown garden. She could have got out of the car herself but she kind of liked the way he always got there first. No one had ever opened the door for her before. People always rushed to open her mother's door whenever Audrey had accompanied her to an event but she was always left to fend for herself.

She followed him back to the front door of the cottage, waiting while he got the key from under the pot, doing her best not to feast her eyes on his taut buttocks when he bent down to lift it up. He unlocked the door and swept his arm in front of his body. 'After you.'

Audrey chewed at the inside of her mouth and tried to ignore the prickling shiver moving over her skin. Had that spider had company? As far as she was concerned, there was no such thing as a single spider—they were all married with large families. What if there were dozens inside? Maybe even hundreds? Didn't heavy rain drive them indoors? What if a whole colony of them was setting up camp right now? What if they were crawling up and down the walls and over every surface? What if they were in every cupboard? Every drawer? Every corner? What if they were lurking in the shadows just waiting for her to come in? What if one dropped on her head and tiptoed its sticky legs all over her face? What if—? 'Erm…maybe you should go in first in case the spider has found its way back in.'

If he found her suggestion annoying or silly he didn't show it. 'Wait here.'

Audrey waited until he gave the all clear and stepped over the threshold, but even though it was a few hours away from sundown, the heavy cloud cover outside made the cottage seem gloomy and unwelcoming… sort of like an abandoned house, which was pretty much what it was. 'Gosh, it's getting kind of dark in here. Is the power on again yet?'

Lucien flicked one of the light switches but the light didn't come on. 'It could be hours until it comes back on. A tree has probably brought the line down somewhere.' He moved over to the fireplace where she had started preparing the fire. 'I'll get a fire going. Are there any candles about?'

Audrey went to the kitchen—where, thankfully, there were no spiders—and soon found some scented candles she'd bought her mother. It was kind of typical of her that they hadn't been used. She brought them back to the sitting room and set one on the coffee table in front of the two facing sofas and the other one on the antique sideboard. 'These should do the job.'

'Perfect.' Lucien came over with the box of matches and lit the candles and soon the fragrance of patchouli and honeysuckle wafted through the air.

Audrey couldn't stop staring at his features in the muted glow of the candlelight. His skin was olive-toned and tanned as if he had holidayed in the sun recently. The flickering shadows highlighted the planes and contours of his face: the uncompromising jaw, the strong blade of a nose, the prominent dark eyebrows and those amazing midnight-blue eyes.

But it was his mouth that always lured her gaze like a yo-yo dieter to a cake counter. His mouth was both firm and yet sensual with well-defined vermillion borders that made her wonder what a kiss from him would be like. Would those firm lips soften or harden in passion? Would they crush or cajole? Would they evoke a storm of need in her that so far she had only ever dreamed about experiencing?

'Is something wrong?' Lucien frowned.

Audrey did a rapid blink and rocked back on her heels...well, not heels exactly. She was wearing ballet flats. Although, given that Lucien was so tall, maybe she should have worn stilettos...or maybe a pair of stilts. 'Have you been on holiday recently?'

'I spent Easter in Barbados.'

She gave a little laugh with a grace note of envy. 'Of course.'

His frown deepened. 'Why "of course"?'

Audrey gave an off-hand shrug and bent down to tidy the out-of-date magazines on the coffee table. 'Did you go with Viviana Prestonward?'

'I went to see a client there. Not that it's any of your or anyone's business.'

She straightened from the coffee table and turned back to look at him. 'Just asking. There's no need to be so antsy about it.'

He turned to face the fire, stirring it so savagely with the poker the flames leapt and danced. 'I'm not a rock star like my father. I don't like my private life being splashed over every paper or online forum.' He put the poker back in its stand and turned around to look at her. 'Does it happen to you? The press interest?'

Audrey sat on the edge of the sofa and played with the fringe of the rug with her foot. 'Not much, but then, I'm way too boring. Who wants to know what a library archivist gets up to in her spare time?'

His gaze became thoughtful. 'What do you get up to?'

Audrey sat back on the sofa, and, picking up one of

the scatter cushions, cuddled it against her stomach. 'I read, I watch TV, go to the occasional movie.' She made a rueful twist of her mouth. 'See? Boring.'

'What about boyfriends? Those dozens of lovers you were telling me about earlier.'

Audrey knew if she kept going with this conversation her hot cheeks would be giving the fire in the grate some serious competition. She tossed the cushion to one side and rose from the sofa in one movement that was supposed to be agile and graceful as a supermodel's, but her foot snagged on the rug and she banged her shin on the coffee table. 'Ouch!' She clapped a hand to her leg and did a hopping dance as the pain pulsated through her shinbone. The scented candle flickered from the impact but thankfully remained upright.

Lucien came across and steadied her with his hands on her upper arms. 'Are you okay? Did it break the skin?'

'I'm fine. It's just a bump.'

He bent down in front of her and inspected her shin; his warm, dry hand so gentle on her leg she couldn't decide if it felt like a tickle or a caress—maybe it was a bit of both. The sensation of his fingers on her bare flesh stirred her senses, making her aware of each broad pad of his fingers. She suddenly became aware of the intimacy of his position in front of her. His face was level with her pelvis and her mind raced with a host of erotic images of him kissing her, touching her…*there*.

'You're going to bruise—you're starting to already.' His fingertip traced over the red mark on her shin as softly as a feather on a priceless object.

Audrey held her breath for so long she thought she might faint. Or maybe it was because no man had ever knelt down in front of her and touched her with such gentleness. Or maybe it was because she had never felt so aware of her body before—how each cell seemed to swell and throb with a need for more of his touch. Now that he'd touched her it awakened a feverish desire in her for more. What if he was to run his hands further up her legs…up her thighs? To the very heart of her femininity? What if he was to peel down her knickers and—?

Stop it right there.

There was no way she was going to act on her crush. No more clumsy attempts at flirting. No more making a gauche fool of herself. She would be sensible and mature about this. 'You can get up now.' She injected a hint of wryness into her voice. 'Unless you want to rehearse your proposal to Viviana while you're down there?'

Lucien rose from his kneeling position, his mouth so flat and hard it looked like paper-thin sheets of steel. 'I'm not proposing to anyone. You need to put some ice on that bruise. I'll get some from the kitchen.'

Lucien opened the small freezer compartment of the fridge in the kitchen and considered squeezing himself in there to cool off. Okay, so it was a little crazy to go down on bended knee in front of Audrey. Even crazier to touch her but she'd hurt herself and he'd felt compelled to do the Boy Scout thing. It was what any decent man would do…although nothing about his reaction to touching her was decent. As soon as he touched her he felt it. The little zing of electricity that he'd never felt with anyone else.

There was a simple solution: he had to stop touching her. He would keep his distance.

How hard could it be?

He took some ice cubes out of the tray and wrapped them in a tea towel and went back to the sitting room. 'Here we go.' He handed her the ice pack, taking care not to touch her fingers. See? Easy. No touching.

Audrey pressed the pack to her shin, her small white teeth nibbling at her lower lip like a mouse at wainscoting. After a moment she glanced up at him but her eyes didn't quite connect with his gaze. 'So…what do you love about her?'

Lucien looked at her blankly. 'Pardon?'

This time her gaze was direct. 'Viviana. The woman you've been dating longer than anyone else. What do you love about her?'

He knew whatever answer he gave was going to be the wrong one because he wasn't in a relationship per se with Viviana. He had got to know her after doing some accounting work for her father and they'd struck up a casual friendship. It was a charade he was helping her maintain after being cheated on and then dumped by her boyfriend. He had seen far too many relationships—most of them his father's—start in love and end in hate. If and when it came time for him to settle down, he was going for the middle ground: mutual respect, common interests, compatibility. 'I don't have that type of relationship with her.'

Audrey's eyes widened so far it looked like her eyelids were doing Pilates. 'What? But you've been dating her for weeks and weeks. Everyone assumes she's The One.'

Lucien moved across to the fire and put on another log of wood. He considered telling her he had no such plans to marry Viviana but he realised the protection of a 'relationship' could serve him well when dealing with Audrey. Or at least he hoped it would. 'For the record, I don't consider romantic love to be the most important factor in a marriage. That sort of love never lasts. You only have to look at your mother and my father to see that.'

She put the ice pack on the coffee table, a frown troubling her brow. 'Is she in love with you?'

'We get on well and—'

'You get on well?' Audrey let out a laugh that had a jarring chord of scorn. 'So that's all it takes to have a successful marriage? Silly me for thinking for all these years the couple had to actually fall in love with one another, care for each other and want the best for each other.'

'You might want to save your lecture for your mother,' Lucien said. 'How many times has she fallen in and out of love now?'

Her creamy skin became tinged with pink high on her cheekbones and her generous mouth tightened. 'We're not talking about my mother. We're talking about you. Why are you going to marry someone you're not in love with? I mean, who *does* that?'

Lucien straightened one of the trinkets on the mantelpiece. 'Look, we're clearly never going to agree on this, so why don't we change the subject?'

'I'm not finished discussing it,' Audrey said. 'Why would a beautiful-looking woman like Viviana settle for a man who doesn't love her? Oh, I get it.' She tapped the side of her head as if congratulating her brain for coming up with the answer. 'She's only with you because you're the son of a famous rock star, right?'

'Wrong.' He gave her an on-off movement of his lips that could just scrape in as a smile. 'She didn't know who my father was when we first met.' Which was a certain part—the main part—of Viviana's appeal to him as a friend. He was tired of the groupies and sycophants who only wanted to hang around him because of who his father was. He'd been weeding them out since he was a teenager, trying to decide who was genuinely interested in him or just along for the vicarious brush with celebrity.

Audrey got off the sofa and limped across to the window to check on the weather. 'Well, either way, I think you're both making a big mistake. People who get married should love each other at the very least.'

'But you're never getting married, correct?' Lucien decided it was time to direct the questions back at her to take the heat off him.

Her gaze moved to the left of his. 'No.'

'But what if you fall in love?'

Her teeth did that little lip-chewing thing again that never failed to draw his gaze. 'I can't see that happening anytime soon.'

'But what if a guy falls in love with you and wants to marry you?'

She gave a laugh that wasn't quite a laugh. 'And how

will I know it's me they're in love with or whether they want to meet my mother?'

Lucien frowned. 'Has that actually happened?'

She made a wry sideways movement of her mouth. 'Enough times to be annoying.' She moved back to the sofa and plumped up one of the scatter cushions she'd been hugging earlier. 'But then, I'm hardly in the same league as my mother in the looks department.'

Lucien wondered if her low self-esteem came from having such a glamorous mother. Sibella was absolutely stunning; even he had to admit that. It was no wonder his father kept going back to her like a drug he couldn't resist. Had it been difficult for Audrey growing up in her mother's shadow? Had she been compared to her mother and found lacking? He knew the press could be merciless in how they portrayed celebrities, but even family members often came in for a serve at times. He tried to recall any articles that involved Audrey but, since he generally shied away from reading the gossip pages, he drew a blank. 'You have no need to run yourself down.'

'At least you look like your father.'

Lucien thought about the lifestyle that had wreaked so much havoc on his father's once good-looking features. 'I'm not sure if that's meant to be a compliment or not. And, just for the record, your mother's looks don't do it for me, okay?'

Audrey's smile looked a little forced. 'Good to know.'

There was a strange little silence. Strange because Lucien couldn't stop looking at her girl-next-door features with those big brown eyes and her generous mouth and thinking about how naturally pretty she was. Understated and unadorned but still captivating. She reminded him of a painting he had glanced at once without really seeing, only to revisit it on another occasion and being stunned by its subtle beauty and hidden depths.

She had barely any make-up on and her skin had a healthy peaches and cream glow. Her dark brown hair had chestnut highlights that looked so natural he assumed they probably were. She didn't have the show-stopping beauty of her mother, and in a crowd you would miss her at first glance, but she was one of those women whose looks grew on you the more you looked at her. She had hardly changed since she was eighteen, although her figure had developed a little more. He wouldn't be worthy of his testosterone if he hadn't noticed the way her breasts filled out her clothes.

The sound of a phone ringing broke the silence and Audrey turned and fished for her mobile in her bag on the floor near the sofa. She glanced at the screen and mouthed 'It's my mother' before she answered. 'Mum? Where are you? I've called you a thousand times.'

Lucien couldn't hear the other side of the conversation but he could get the gist of it from Audrey's answers. 'What? How did you know I'm at Bramble Cottage? I… I'm with Lucien.' She turned her back to him and continued in a hushed voice. 'Nothing's going on. How could you think—? Look, will you please just tell me where *you* are?' Her hand was so tight around her phone he could see the whitening of her knuckles. 'I know you want to spend time alone with Harlan but—' She let out an unladylike curse and tossed the phone onto the sofa. She turned around and her shoulders went down on a defeated sigh. 'She wouldn't tell me a thing.'

'Nothing at all?'

She lifted her hands in a helpless gesture. 'She kept dodging the question.' Her forehead creased. 'But I've just had a thought. Remember that chateau they rented during their first marriage for your father's birthday in St Remy in Provence? She told me once it was one of her favourite places. Wasn't it one of his favourites too? What if they've gone there? It's a perfect hideaway. They used to go there quite a lot together.'

Lucien remembered the chateau more than he wanted to. He had attended the party for a short time more out of duty than any desire to celebrate his father's birthday. It was one of those parties where there was a lot of alcohol and loud music and a fair bit of debauchery. He remembered Audrey's mother doing a striptease— her birthday present to his father—and feeling embarrassed for Audrey, who'd left the room with her cheeks flaming. He wished now he'd gone in search of her and offered her some sort of comfort, but he'd been wary of being alone with her since the wedding, where she had made that tipsy pass at him. 'Did your mother give any other clue? What did she actually say?'

'She knew I was at the cottage.'

'How did she know that?'

'Phone app. She's blocked me from finding her but she can find me just by clicking on the app.' Her cheeks became a light shade of pink. 'She thought...well, never mind what she thought.'

'Was she drunk?'

Her eyes flicked away from his, her cheeks darkening. 'No, I don't think so… I got the feeling she and your dad just want to be left on their own for a bit.'

'Unusual since they both love nothing more than an audience.'

'Maybe they've both changed…' Her teeth sank into her lip, her brow still wrinkled as if she was mulling over something deeply puzzling.

Lucien had spent the last twenty-four years of his life hoping his father would change. He'd lost count of the number of times he'd been disappointed by his father's irresponsible and reckless behaviour and things didn't get much more irresponsible and reckless than remarrying Sibella Merrington. Sibella wasn't the person to help his father change. She was the one who kept him from changing. She encouraged every bad habit and, after the last time, Lucien was not going to sign up for another clean-up operation.

After the last divorce, it had taken him months to get his father back on his feet without two daily bottles of vodka on board. Numerous times he had come to his father's house and found him blackout drunk. He'd tried everything to get him into rehab but his father always refused. His doctors had warned his father his drinking had to stop or he would suffer irreparable damage to his already struggling liver. Even if Lucien had to fly to every city and village across Europe he would not stop until he found his father and put a stop to this madness. 'Yeah, well, next time you see a leopard running around without its spots, be sure to let me know.'

CHAPTER FOUR

AUDREY WENT TO the kitchen to see about some food for dinner in the pantry, where basic non-perishable items were stored. She lit another candle for the kitchen table and set to making a meal. Lucien was still in the sitting room, making the arrangements for a helicopter—*gulp*—to pick them up the following morning. She thought back over her brief conversation with her mother. She had teased her about being at the cottage with Lucien, but along with the teasing there had been a veiled warning about how far from his type she was.

As if she needed to be reminded.

Audrey had assembled a plate of crackers and a makeshift pâté of tinned tuna and sweetcorn when Lucien came into the kitchen. 'I'm sorry there isn't a gourmet meal on offer but most of the stuff in the pantry is past its use-by date. This is the best I could do.'

'It's fine. You needn't have bothered.'

'There's wine in the fridge.' Audrey nodded her head in the fridge's direction. 'It's cold even though the power's still off.'

Lucien took out a bottle of white wine and held it aloft. 'Will you join me?'

Audrey would have loved a glass of wine but she was worried she might make a fool of herself again. 'No, thanks. I'll stick to water.' She carried the meal on a platter to the scrubbed pine table and privately marvelled at how cosy it looked in spite of the meagre fare.

Lucien waited until she was seated and then he joined her at the table. He had poured himself a glass of wine but so far hadn't taken a sip. He picked up one of the crackers and took a bite and grimaced.

'Sorry, I know they're a bit stale,' Audrey said. 'I don't think my mother's been here for ages. I don't think anyone's been here, not even the caretaker.' She sighed and picked up a cracker. 'She probably forgot to pay him or something.'

Lucien took a sip of his wine and then put the glass down. 'Why does she keep the place if it's empty most of the time? Wouldn't it be better to sell it?'

Audrey thought about losing the cottage, losing the one place where she had felt close to her mother. Something tightened in her chest like a hand pressing down on her lungs. She knew it made financial sense to sell the cottage. But if it was sold that part of her life with her mother would be lost for ever and there would be no hope of reclaiming it. 'I've always talked her out of it.'

'Why?'

Audrey pushed a crumb on her plate with her fingertip. 'She bought it when she got her first role on television. We used to come down here just about every weekend. I loved the garden after living in a council flat. It was like a secret scented paradise. I'd spend hours making daisy chains with her and flower garlands for our hair.

We even used to cook stuff together. She wasn't a great cook but it was a lot of fun…' She smiled at the memory. 'Messy fun…' She stopped speaking and looked up to see him studying her with a thoughtful expression on his face and her smile fell away. 'Sorry for rambling.'

'Don't apologise.' His voice had a gravelly note to it.

Audrey looked back down at the crumb on her plate rather than meet his gaze. 'She wasn't always so…so over the top. Becoming a celebrity changed her.'

'In what way?'

She glanced at him again and saw something she had never seen in his gaze before—compassion. It made the walls and boundaries she had built around herself shiver against their foundations. 'Well…she didn't always drink so much.'

'Do you worry about her drinking?'

'All the time.' Audrey's shoulders drooped. 'I've suggested rehab but she won't go. She doesn't see that she has a problem. So far it hasn't interfered with her work on the show but how soon before it does? I keep worrying someone will smell it on her breath when she turns up for a shoot. Especially now she's back with your father. Sorry. I don't mean to blame him but—'

'It's fine.' His tight smile was more of a grimace. 'They're a bad influence on each other, which is why we have to do whatever we can to put a stop to them marrying again.'

'But what if we can't stop them? What if they get married and then go through yet another hideous breakup and divorce? What then?'

His features clouded as if he was thinking back to

the previous two divorces. Then his gaze refocused on hers. 'How did your mother handle the break-ups?'

Audrey sighed. 'Badly.'

He frowned. 'But wasn't she the one to end their relationship both times?'

'I guess it doesn't matter who ends it, a break-up is still a break-up,' Audrey said. 'She drank. A lot. She hid from the press at my flat for three weeks last time. I was worried sick about her, especially when she…' She bit off the rest of her sentence. She hadn't told anyone about her mother's overdoses. Her mother had begged her not to tell anyone in case it got leaked out somehow in the press. Why had she kept her promise?

Because inside her there was still that small child who loved being at the cottage with her mum.

'Especially when she…?' Lucien said.

Audrey pushed her chair back and fetched herself a glass of water. 'Would you like some water?' She held up a glass but was annoyed to see her hand wasn't quite steady.

Lucien's frown was so deep it looked like he was aiming for a world record. 'No water.' He rose from the table and came over to where she was standing in front of the sink. 'Talk to me, Audrey.'

She couldn't hold his gaze and looked at his mouth instead. Big mistake. It was set in its customary firm line but his evening shadow surrounded his lips in rich, dark stubble that looked so sexy she ached to touch it with her fingers. With her mouth. To taste his lips and trail her tongue over their firm contours to see if they would…

He put a fingertip to the base of her chin and brought her gaze up to meet his. 'What were you going to say?'

Audrey's chin was on fire where his finger was resting. She could feel the heat spreading to every part of her body in deep, pulsating waves. His eyes tethered hers in a lock that had an undercurrent of intimacy, which made her legs feel boneless. 'Erm… I think I will have that glass of wine, after all.' She stepped away and went back to the table, poured half a glass of wine and took a cautious sip.

Lucien came back to his chair and sat down. It was a moment or two before he spoke. 'My father drank two bottles of vodka every day after the last divorce. I thought he was going to die of alcohol poisoning for sure. I'd go to his house and find him… Thankfully he doesn't remember how many times I changed his clothes and his bed for him.'

Audrey swallowed. 'Oh, Lucien. I'm so sorry. That must have been awful for you to see your father like that. You must've been so worried about him. Have you asked him about rehab or—?'

He gave her a world-weary look. 'Like your mother, he refuses point-blank to go. He's been warned by his doctors that his liver won't cope unless he stops drinking.'

'No wonder you want to stop my mother from marrying him,' Audrey said, feeling deeply ashamed of her mother's influence on his father.

'I realise Sibella isn't pouring the liquor down his throat but he can't seem to help himself when she's with him,' Lucien said. 'It's like they're both hell-bent on self-destruction.'

'Their love for each other is toxic,' Audrey said. 'That's why I'm never going to fall in love with anyone. It's way too dangerous.'

He studied her for a moment with an inscrutable look. 'Never is a long time.'

Audrey picked up her wine and took another sip. 'So far you've managed not to fall in love. Why do you think I won't be able to do the same?'

His gaze flicked to her mouth and then back to her eyes but in that infinitesimal beat of time a different quality entered the atmosphere. A tightening. A tension. A temptation. 'Maybe you've been dating the wrong men.'

She hadn't been dating *any* men.

She was too scared she would be exploited. Too scared she wouldn't be loved for who she was instead of who she was related to. Too scared to be so intimate with someone because what if they slept with her and then cast her aside like so many of her mother's lovers had done? She didn't want to turn into an emotional wreck who turned to alcohol when her heart got broken. It was better not to get her heart broken in the first place.

Audrey took another sip of wine. Two sips. Two very big sips, which technically speaking weren't sips but gulps. 'Maybe you've been dating the wrong women. Safe women. Women you wouldn't possibly fall in love with in case you end up like your father.'

His top lip came up and his eyes glinted with his trademark cynicism. 'Right back at you, sweetheart.'

Audrey put her glass back down with a little clatter. 'Mock me all you like but I would hate to love someone that intensely. Your father is like a drug my mother can't give up. She gets herself clean but then keeps going back to him for another fix. It's crazy. It will kill her in the end.' She gave herself a mental slap for the vocal slip and added, 'I mean figuratively, not literally.'

Lucien's gaze sharpened. 'Has she ever tried to end her life?'

Audrey tried to screen her features but just recalling the memories of those times she'd found her mother with a half-empty bottle of pills was too painful to block. What if she'd taken them all? What if she hadn't found her in time? What if next time she took the whole bottle? She could feel her face twitching and her mouth trembling. 'Why would you think that?'

He continued to hold her gaze like a counsellor would a nervous patient. 'It's better to talk about it, Audrey.'

She compressed her lips, torn between wanting to offload some of the burden but worried about compromising her relationship with her mother. 'We have to stop them getting back together, okay? That's all I care about right now. We have to stop them before it's too late.'

'I couldn't agree more.'

Once they'd cleared away the lean pickings of their dinner, Audrey took one of the candles with her and went upstairs to make up the beds. She put Lucien in the room furthest from hers just to make sure he didn't think she was going to do a midnight wander into his room. When she got into her own bed and pulled the covers up, she looked at the candlelight flickering on the ceiling and thought of the times in her early childhood when she had lain in this wrought-iron bed with her mother sleeping in the room next door. She had never managed to be that happy since. Nor felt that safe. The happy memories should have been enough to settle her to sleep but somehow they weren't.

Or maybe it was because she was conscious of Lucien in the bedroom down the corridor. Would he sleep naked or in his underwear? Her mind raced with images of him lying between the sheets her hands had touched when she'd made the bed earlier. Was he a stomach sleeper or a back sleeper? Did he move a lot or stay still?

Audrey sat up and gave her pillow a reshape and settled back down. Her chest suddenly seized. Was that a spider on the ceiling? No. It was just the candlelight. She licked her dry lips. She was thirsty. The wine had made her mouth as dry as a sandbox and she would never be able to sleep unless she had a glass of water. Why hadn't she thought to bring one with her?

She threw off the covers and smoothed her satin nightgown down over her thighs. She padded out to the corridor to check if Lucien was about but his bedroom door was closed. She tiptoed downstairs as quietly as she could, wincing when she got to one of the creaky floorboards. She froze, her other foot poised in mid-air until she was sure it was safe to continue.

The kitchen was bathed in moonlight now the storm clouds had blown away. Audrey got herself a glass of water and sipped it while she looked out of the window at the moonlit garden and fields and woods beyond. Lucien was right. The cottage should be sold at some point. Her mother had outgrown it and it was sadly falling into ruin without regular visits and proper upkeep.

Wasn't that a bit like her relationship with her mother?

Audrey knew she was too old to be still hankering after her mother's affection but it had been so long since she'd felt loved by her. Sibella loved fame and her fans and had no time for anything or anyone that reminded her of her life before her celebrity star was born. It was like that person had never existed. The teenage mum with her much adored little girl was no more. In her place was Sibella Merrington, successful soap star of numerous shows that were broadcast all over the world.

And where was that once adored little girl?

No one adored Audrey now.

She couldn't be sure if the friends she had actually liked her or the fact she had a celebrity mother. There was always that seed of doubt sprouting in her mind, which made it hard for her to get close to people. She always kept something of herself back just in case the friend had the wrong motives.

She turned from the window and sighed. See? A few sips of wine earlier that evening and now she was a maudlin mess, getting overly emotional and down on herself.

Audrey took another glass of water, went to the sitting room and curled up on the sofa. If the power was back on she would have put on a soppy movie to really get herself going. And if there had been any naughty food in the house she would have eaten a block of chocolate. A family-sized block.

She rested her head against one of the scatter cushions and watched the still glowing embers of the fire in the fireplace until finally, on a sleepy sigh, she closed her eyes…

Lucien was having trouble sleeping. Nothing unusual in that, since he was often working late or in different time zones, but this time it was because he was aware of Audrey in the room down the corridor. Too aware. Skin-tingling and blood-pumping aware. He wasn't sure if it was his imagination but he could smell her perfume on his sheets. And the thought of her leaving her scent on his sheets stirred up a host of wickedly tempting images he knew he shouldn't be allowing inside his head. He could feel her presence like radar frequency in the air. His skin prickled into goosebumps and his normally well-controlled sex drive stirred and stretched like a beast in too cramped a space.

You're spending the night alone with Audrey Merrington.

Lucien shied away from the thought like a horse refusing a jump. They were in separate rooms. It was fine. Nothing was going to happen. He would make sure of that. If she came tiptoeing into his room with seduction on her mind he would be ready for her.

To *refuse* her, that was.

Not that he didn't find the prospect of a quick roll around these sheets with her tempting. He did. Way too tempting. Her luscious curves were enough to make a ninety-year-old monk rethink his celibacy vows.

But Lucien wasn't going to make a bad situation worse by complicating things with a dalliance with Audrey. Even if her mouth was the most kissable he'd seen in a long time.

Damn it. He had to stop thinking about kissing her.

He sat on the bed and sorted through a few more emails but he kept an ear out for her returning upstairs. He'd heard her go down half an hour ago. Why hadn't she come back up? He tossed his phone on the bed and wrestled with himself for a moment. Should he go down to check on her?

No. Better keep your distance.

He picked up his phone again and tapped away at the screen but he couldn't concentrate. He let out a long breath and reached for his trousers. He pulled them on and zipped them up and then shrugged on his shirt but didn't bother with the buttons.

He found her lying on the sofa in front of the smouldering fire, her body curled up like a comma and her cheek pressed into one of the scatter cushions. One of her hands was tucked near her chin and the other was dangling over the edge of the sofa. She was wearing a navy blue satin nightgown that clung to her curves like cling film. A stab of lust hit him in the groin at the shape of her thighs showing where the nightgown had ridden up. It intrigued him that she wore such sexy nightwear when during the day she covered herself with such conservative clothes. He knew he shouldn't be staring at her like a lust-struck teenager but he couldn't seem to tear his eyes away from her. The neckline of the nightgown was low, revealing a delicious glimpse of cleavage. She gave a murmur and shifted against the cushion, her dangling hand coming up to brush something invisible away from her face. Her smooth forehead creased in a frown and she swiped at her face again as if she could feel something crawling over her skin.

Maybe she could feel his gaze.

Lucien waited until she'd settled again before he carefully lifted the throw off the end of the sofa and gently laid it over her sleeping form. He figured it was safer to leave her sleeping down here than disturbing her. He stepped backwards but forgot the coffee table was in the way and the side of his leg banged against it with a thump.

Audrey's eyes flew open and she sat bolt upright. 'Oh, it's you. How long have you been here?'

'Not long,' Lucien said. 'I came downstairs for something and found you lying there. I covered you with the throw.'

She gathered it around her shoulders, using it as a wrap. It made her look like a child bundled up in a garment too big for her. Her brown eyes looked glazed with sleep and she had marks on her left cheek where the piping on the cushion had pressed against her skin. 'What time is it?'

'Four-ish, I think.'

She tugged her hair out of the back of the throw and draped it over her left shoulder. 'I hope I didn't disturb you?'

You disturb me all the time. Lucien kept his expression neutral. 'I wasn't asleep. I was working.'

She rose from the sofa still with the throw wrapped around her shoulders. 'I couldn't sleep and came down for a glass of water. I must have fallen asleep in front of the fire.' She glanced at the fireplace with a wistful look on her face. 'I think you're right though about selling this place.' Her gaze drifted back to his. 'It's a waste for it to be unoccupied for months and months on end.'

'Would you take it over?' Lucien said. 'You could use it as a holiday home, couldn't you?'

She shrugged and shifted her gaze. 'I have a pretty busy social life in town and, anyway, I couldn't afford the maintenance.'

Lucien was starting to wonder just how busy her social life was. He'd never heard her mother or his father mention anyone she was dating by name. 'You haven't thought to bring one of your numerous lovers down here for a cosy weekend?'

Her cheeks developed twin circles of pink. 'I think I'll go back up to bed.' She made to walk past him but he stopped her by placing a hand on her arm. Her eyes met his and her brows lifted ever so slightly like those of a haughty spinster in a Regency novel. 'Did you want something, Lucien?'

He let his hand fall away from her arm before he was tempted to tell her what he wanted. What he *shouldn't* be wanting. What he would damn well *stop* himself from wanting.

'No. Goodnight.'

Audrey came downstairs to the kitchen the following morning to find Lucien already packed and ready to go. 'Forget about breakfast,' he said. 'We're leaving.'

Her stomach pitched as if she were already in the helicopter. In a nosedive. 'What? Now?'

'I've managed to get a local farmer to meet us at the bridge. He's going to get us across on his tractor and then we'll pick up a hire car in the village.'

'So we're not going in the helicopter?' Relief swept through her like a rinse cycle through a load of laundry.

'No.'

'Why did you change your mind about it?'

'I don't want to draw too much attention to ourselves. The fewer people who know we've spent the night here together, the better.'

Audrey's relief collided with her anger that he disliked being seen with her in public so much. Was she so hideous he couldn't bear anyone finding out they'd 'spent the night here together'?

She bet he wouldn't be all cloak and dagger about it if it was Viviana holed up here with him. He'd be hiring the biggest helicopter on offer and parading Viviana on his arm like a trophy. He'd probably announce it on a megaphone: *Hey, look who I spent the night with—Viviana Prestonward, the most beautiful supermodel on the planet.*

It made Audrey want to puke…or to punch something. 'You know, if it pains you that much to be in my company, why then are you insisting on taking me with you? I can find my own way back to London to do my own search and you can do yours.'

'Aren't you forgetting your car is out of action and likely to be for some time?'

'I can hire one.'

A look of grim determination entered his gaze. 'No. We stick to my plan to do this together. It'll add more weight if we show a united front once we find them. I think you might be right about St Remy. My father's been there a few times over the last couple of years, so it's highly likely they've headed there.'

Audrey rubbed her lips together as if she were setting lipstick. Why was he insisting she go with him if he didn't want to draw attention to them? Wasn't taking her with him going to cause all sorts of trouble for him? 'What about Viviana?'

'What about her?'

'What's she going to think of us spending all this time together?'

A flicker of something passed over his face. 'She's not the jealous type.'

Audrey arched a brow. 'Would that be because I'm not slim and beautiful like she is?'

Lucien closed his eyes in a slow God-give-me-strength blink. 'Get your bag. The farmer will be waiting for us by now.'

Lucien drove with Audrey a short time later to the bridge, where the local farmer was waiting on the other side with his tractor. There was a hire car parked on the other side as well, presumably left by the company for them to collect. Audrey had to admire Lucien's organisational skills, but then she realised how determined he was to put a stop to his father's marriage to her mother. He wouldn't let even a broken bridge get in his way.

The farmer gave them a wave and they pulled up on the side of the lane and proceeded to cross the river a metre or so away from where the bridge had come down. The tractor climbed up the other bank with a rumbling roar and came to a stop next to where Audrey and Lucien were standing. She recognised the farmer from previous visits to the village and expressed her thanks for his helping them.

'No problem, Audrey lass,' Jim Gordon said. 'Hold on tight when you get on, now. The water's not deep but the bottom is a little uneven in places.'

Lucien handed Jim Audrey's overnight bag and her tote and then came to stand behind her to help her get on the tractor by putting his hands on her hips. His touch—even through her clothes—made her senses do cartwheels. She put her foot on the metal step and gave a spring that would have got her nowhere if it hadn't been for the gentle nudge of his hands. She wriggled to take her place on the back of the tractor and Lucien jumped up next to her and wrapped a firm arm around her waist to keep her secure. 'Okay?'

Audrey was so breathless from his closeness she could barely get her voice to do much more than squeak. 'Okay.'

Jim set the tractor on its way and soon they were across to the other side of the river. Lucien jumped down and, once he had her bags off and on the ground next to him, he held out his hands for her. She placed her hands on his shoulders and he put his hands on her waist and lifted her down as if she weighed less than a child.

For a moment they stood with his hands on her waist and hers on his shoulders. Audrey's gaze met his and it was as if someone had pressed 'pause' on time. Even the birds in the nearby shrubs seemed to have stopped twittering. The blue of his eyes was mesmerising, the touch of his hands making her aware of how close to him she was standing. His thighs were almost brushing hers. She could feel his body warmth like the glow of a radiator. His gaze lowered to her mouth for a brief moment, his hands tightening on her waist as if he was about to bring her even closer. Her heart gave an extra beat as if she'd had one too many energy drinks. She looked at his mouth and something in her belly fluttered like the pages of a book in a playful breeze. She swallowed and moistened her lips but the moment was broken by the sound of the tractor being placed in gear.

Lucien relaxed his hold and stepped back from her and turned to Jim. 'Thanks again, Jim. Really appreciate your help.'

'The hire-car people left the keys in the ignition when they dropped it off,' Jim said, nodding towards the car parked to one side. 'And I'll get the wheels moving on getting young Audrey's car towed to the workshop as you asked.'

Audrey felt like a helpless female surrounded by big, strong, capable men who were taking care of everything for her. She mentally apologised to her emancipated self and lapped it up. She followed Lucien to the hire car and he held the door open for her and helped her in.

Once he was behind the wheel, she said, 'If you drop me at the nearest train station I'll make my way back to—'

'Have you got your passport in your bag?'

'Yes, but—'

He gave her a glance that made something in her belly turn over. 'St Remy, here we come.'

CHAPTER FIVE

LUCIEN KNEW IT was probably a bad idea to take Audrey with him to the south of France but he needed her there to make sure Sibella and his father understood how vehemently they were against their marriage. It was a bad idea to be anywhere near Audrey. He had to help her on and off the tractor, but did he have to stand there staring at her mouth like a punch-drunk teenager anticipating his first kiss?

He had to get his hands off her and get a grip on himself.

But he would be lying if he said it hadn't felt good holding her close like that. Seeing the way her nutmeg-brown eyes widened and the way her tongue swept over her lips as if preparing for the descent of his mouth.

And he'd been pretty damn close to doing it too.

He'd been lost in a moment of mad lust. Feeling her breasts within inches of his chest, imagining what it would feel like to have them pressed against him skin-to-skin. Feeling her thighs so close to his, imagining them wrapped around his as he entered her velvet warmth. He had always dated super-slim women but something about her womanly figure made everything that was male in him sit up and take notice. He was ashamed of his reaction to her, especially as he was supposed to be 'involved' with Viviana.

But that was no excuse to be lusting over Audrey. He wasn't like his father, who got his head turned by sexy women even when he was involved with someone else. He was too strong-willed to let the ripe and sensuous curves of Audrey's body and her supple and generous mouth unravel his self-control like a ball of string.

Way too strong-willed.

He hoped.

Audrey considered refusing to go with Lucien to France but without a car and no spare cash to hire one she knew her search for her mother and Harlan would grind to a halt. The thought of spending the weekend at her flat with nothing better to do than watch her flatmate, Rosie, get ready to go out with her latest boyfriend was not appealing. Well, not as appealing as a weekend in St Remy. It had nothing to do with going with Lucien Fox. Nothing at all. St Remy was the attraction. She hadn't been to the south of France in ages.

But when they arrived at the airport in London, Audrey was shocked to find a small group of paparazzi waiting for them. 'Oh, no...' she said, glancing at Lucien. 'How on earth did they find us?'

His expression was so grim he could have moonlighted as a gravedigger. 'Who knows? But don't say anything. Leave it to me.'

He helped her out of the car as the press gang came

bustling over. 'Lucien? Audrey? Can we have a quick word? What do you two think about your respective parents Harlan and Sibella remarrying for the third time?'

'No comment.' Lucien's tone was as curt as a prison guard's.

'Audrey?' The journalist aimed his recording device at her instead. 'So, what's going on between you and Lucien Fox?'

'Nothing's going on,' Audrey said, feeling a blush steal over her cheeks like a measles rash.

'Is it true you spent last night alone together down at your mother's cottage in the Cotswolds?'

Audrey mentally gulped. Had someone seen them? Had Jim Gordon said something to someone? She glanced at Lucien but his expression was as closed as a bank vault. She turned back to the journalist. 'No comment.'

'What does Viviana Prestonward think of your cosy relationship with your step-sibling Audrey Merrington, Lucien?' another journalist asked with a *nudge-nudge, wink-wink, say no more* look.

Audrey was sure she heard Lucien's back molars grind together. 'At the risk of repeating myself—no comment,' he said through lips that were so tight you couldn't have squeezed a slip of paper through. He took Audrey by the arm and led her further inside the terminal to the check-in area. 'I told you not to say anything.'

'I didn't say anything—well, nothing you didn't say, that is.'

'You told them nothing's going on.' His hand on her arm tightened to steer her out of the way of an older man pushing an overloaded baggage trolley.

'That's because nothing is going on.'

'You made it sound like there was.'

Audrey pulled out of his hold and rubbed at her arm. 'I did not. What did you expect me to do? Just stand there and let them make those insinuations without defending myself? Anyway, I don't see what's your problem. No one would ever think you'd be interested in someone like me.'

His frown gave him an intimidating air. 'This is your mother's doing.'

A weight dropped in Audrey's stomach. 'You think my mother tipped off the press about us? But why would she do that?'

His mouth was set in a cynical line. 'Because she loves nothing more than a bit of pot-stirring. The more press attention on us, the less on her and my father.'

Could it be true? Had her mother done something so mischievous in order to take the spotlight off her relationship with Lucien's father? But why? Sibella knew how much Audrey disliked Lucien.

But the more she thought about it the more likely it seemed. Her mother had blocked Audrey from finding her on the phone app but her mother could still find her. Her mother could have been following her movements ever since Audrey had left her flat yesterday morning. She and Harlan were probably laughing about it over a bottle or two of wine right this very minute.

Lucien's phone rang soon after they had checked in to their flight. He glanced at the screen and grimaced and, mouthing 'Excuse me', stood a little apart from Audrey to answer. She tried not to listen…well, strictly speaking she didn't really try, but even with the background noise of the terminal it was almost impossible not to get the gist of the conversation from the brooding expression on his face. After the call ended he slipped the phone in his trouser pocket.

'Trouble in paradise?' Audrey gave him an arch look.

He shrugged as if it didn't matter one way or the other. 'Come on. It's nearly time to board.'

Audrey waited until they were seated on the plane before she brought up the topic of Viviana again. 'So, she was the jealous type after all.'

His mouth tightened as though it were being tugged on from inside. 'If you're expecting to see me fall in an emotional heap like my father then you'll be waiting a long time.'

'No. I'm not expecting that.' She clipped on her seat belt and settled back into her seat. 'My theory was right. You would only ever get involved with someone who doesn't threaten your locked-away heart.' She turned and gave him a sugar-sweet smile. 'I'm assuming you actually have one?'

He gave her the side-eye. 'I hope you're not one of those annoying passengers who make banal conversation the whole flight?'

'Nope,' Audrey said. 'I like to read or watch movies.'

'Glad to hear it.' He leaned his head back against the headrest and closed his eyes.

Audrey picked up the in-flight magazine but her gaze kept drifting to his silent form beside her. His arm was resting on the armrest, his long legs stretched out and crossed over at the ankles. They were travelling Business Class; apparently he was too much of an accountant to travel First Class. But secretly that impressed her about him. Her mother always insisted on travelling First Class, even when she couldn't always afford it. It was all about her mother's image, how the public perceived her. It seemed such a shallow existence to Audrey and she wondered what was going to happen to her mother when her celebrity star dimmed, as it inevitably would. She sighed and reached for the remote control and clicked on the movie menu. Her mother's star would dim even more quickly if Audrey didn't talk her out of remarrying Harlan Fox.

And, God forbid, it might even be snuffed out completely.

Lucien opened his eyes some time later to find Audrey sniffing in the seat beside him, her knees drawn up, her feet bare. Chocolate wrappers littered the floor and her seat, including one on his seat. She was dabbing at her streaming eyes with a bunched-up tissue—or was it a napkin from the meal tray? The credits were rolling on a movie on the screen in front of her.

'Sad movie?' he said, handing her his handkerchief.

She gave him a sheepish look, pulled out her headphones and took the handkerchief. 'I've seen it twenty-three times and I still cry buckets.'

Who watched a movie twenty-three times? 'Must be a good movie.' He leaned closer to glance at the credits and caught a whiff of her perfume as well as a stronger one of chocolate. *'Notting Hill.'*

'Have you seen it?'

'Once, years ago.'

Audrey gave a heartfelt sigh. 'It's my favourite movie.'

'What do you love about it?'

'Anna Scott, Julia Roberts's character, is one of the most famous actors in the world, but she's just a normal person underneath the fame and that's who Hugh Grant's character—William Thacker—falls in love with, only he nearly loses her because he's put off by her celebrity status. But then he finally comes to his senses when his quirky flatmate calls him a daft prick for turning her down and—' Her mouth twisted. 'Sorry. I'm probably boring you.' She pretended to zip her lips. 'That's it. No more banal conversation from me.'

'You're not boring me.' He was surprised to find it was true. He could have listened to her rave on and on about that movie for the next hour—for the next week. Her face was so animated when she talked, her eyes bright and shiny with her dark lashes all spiky from tears.

'Anyway, you've seen the movie, so…' Her eyes fell away from his and she began fiddling with the fabric of his handkerchief.

'You have chocolate next to your mouth,' Lucien said.

'Where?' She brushed at her mouth with the handkerchief. 'Gone?'

He took the handkerchief and, holding her chin with one hand, gently removed the smear of chocolate.

You're touching her again.

He ignored his conscience and dabbed at the other

side of her mouth. There wasn't any chocolate there but he couldn't resist the way her big brown eyes reacted when he touched her—they opened and closed in a slow blink like a kitten enjoying a sensuous stroke. Her pupils widened like spreading pools of ink and she gave a tiny swallow, her tongue darting out to wet her lips. Something tightly bound up in his chest loosened like the sudden slip of a knot.

He placed his thumb on her lower lip and moved it back and forth against its pillowy softness, his blood stirring, simmering, smouldering. She made a little whimpering sound—it wasn't much more than the catch of her breath, but it ignited his desire like a taper against dry tinder. He brought his head closer, closer, closer, giving her time to pull back, giving himself time to rethink this madness. His madness.

Stop. Stop. Stop.

The warnings sounded like a distant horn—slightly muffled, muted, making it easy to ignore.

He covered her mouth with his and her softness clung to his dry lips like silk on sandpaper. He pressed on her lips once—a touchdown. A test.

But he wanted more. He ached, he throbbed, he craved more.

He pressed down again on her lips and she opened her mouth on a breathless sigh, her hands slid up his chest, grasped the front of his shirt. His tongue found hers and a hot dart of need speared him. He lost his mind. His self-control. Her mouth tasted of chocolate and milk and something that was uniquely her. Her mouth was like exotic nectar. A potent potion he would die without consuming. His lips were fused to hers, his tongue dancing and flirting and mating with hers like two champion dancers who knew each other's movements as well as their own.

He slid his hands under her hair to cradle her head. A fresh wave of lust consumed him like a wall of flame, whooshing through him with incendiary heat. He wanted her with such fierce desire he could feel it thundering through his groin and tingling his spine. He groaned against her mouth, flicked his tongue in and out against hers in erotic play. He lifted to change position but Audrey pulled away with a dazed look on her face. Her mouth was plump and swollen and her chin reddened from where his stubble had grazed her.

It was a new experience for Lucien to be lost for words.

What the hell just happened?

He cleared his throat and made a show of straightening the front of his creased shirt where her hands had fisted. 'Right, well. That must not happen again.' He knew he sounded stiff and formal. Damn it, he *was* stiff. But he had to break the sensual spell she had cast over him.

Audrey touched her top lip with her fingertip, still looking a little shell-shocked. 'You didn't…enjoy it?'

He'd enjoyed it too darn much. 'Sure. But we're not doing it again. Understood?' He put on his stern schoolmaster face, not wanting to show how undone he was. Seriously undone.

She glanced at his mouth and nodded. 'Probably a good idea… I mean, you were really going for it there. I thought you might start ripping my clothes off and—'

Lucien sliced the air with his hand with such force it bumped his tray table. 'Not going to happen.' But he'd wanted to. Oh, how he'd wanted to. *Still* wanted to. 'You and me getting it on is a crazy idea.'

'Because?' Was that a note of self-doubt in her voice?

'Did you just hear what I said? I said we're *not* doing this, Audrey. No more kissing. No more touching. No more anything.'

She gave him a guileless look. 'Why are you making such a big thing about this? I'm not asking you to sleep with me. Anyway, it was just a kiss.'

Was it just a kiss? Or was it the kiss of a lifetime? A kiss from which all past and future kisses would be measured? His lips were still tingling. He could still taste her. His blood was still hammering.

He needed a cold shower.

He needed his head examined.

He needed to straitjacket and shackle his desire.

Lucien's gaze kept tracking to her mouth like a sniffer dog on a drug bust. 'Listen to me, Audrey.' He took a breath and dragged his eyes back to hers. 'We have to be sensible about this…situation. We're on a mission to stop your mother and my father from making a terrible mistake. Their third terrible mistake. It's not going to help matters if we start making our own mistakes.'

Her eyes drifted and focused on a point below his chin. 'I hear you, okay? There's no need to keep banging on about it. I get that you're not into me even though you kissed me like you were.' She gave him a little stab of a glare. 'You shouldn't send mixed signals—it can give people the wrong idea. Not that I got the wrong idea. I'm just saying you should be more careful in future.'

He sucked in a breath and released it in a quick draft. 'Let's just forget that kiss ever happened, okay?'

She sat back with a little thump against her seat and picked up the remote control. 'What kiss?' She pressed on the remote as if she were switching him off.

Lucien settled in his seat and tried to rebalance himself. Forget about the kiss. *Forget. Forget. Forget.* But every time he swallowed he tasted the sweetness of her, the temptation of her. He would never be able to eat chocolate again without thinking of her. Without remembering that kiss.

For six years he had resisted Audrey. He had been sensible and responsible about her tipsy passes.

But now he'd kissed her.

Not just kissed her but all but feasted off her mouth like it was his last meal. His body was still feeling the dragging ache of unrelieved desire. It pulled and pulsed in his groin, running down his thighs and up again as if every nerve was on fire.

But now he didn't have his 'relationship' with Viviana to hide behind, his self-control had collapsed like a house of cards in a stiff breeze. Damn it, there was that word 'stiff' again. He'd needed that relationship to keep his boundaries secure. He wasn't the sort of guy to kiss another woman when he was in a relationship with someone else, even if that relationship was only a charade.

He had standards. Principles. Morals.

But the irony was Viviana hadn't ended the charade

out of jealousy because of that mischievous tweet of Audrey's mother's but because she had fallen in love with someone on her photo shoot—a cameraman she'd known for years.

Now Lucien was inconveniently free. Inconveniently, because without the protection of a 'relationship' with someone else he was tempted to indulge in a fling with Audrey.

Seriously, dangerously tempted.

Bad idea. Dumb idea. Wicked idea. It didn't matter how many arguments he put up, his mind kept coming back to it like a tongue to a niggling tooth. They were both adults, weren't they? They were clearly attracted to each other. She didn't want marriage, nor did he.

He had always chosen his partners carefully. No strings. No promises. No commitment. He didn't choose women who made him feel out of control. He wasn't averse to a bit of passion. He was a man with all the normal desires and needs. But he'd always been selective in how that passion was expressed.

He had no such control when it came to Audrey. He knew it on a cellular level. She had the potential to undo him. To unravel the self-control he worked so hard to maintain.

But maybe if he got it on with her it would purge her from his system. Get the fantasies of her out of his head once and for all.

Audrey clicked off the remote and turned to look at him. 'You know, for someone who just broke up with the person they were thinking about marrying, you certainly moved on indecently quickly.'

She didn't know how indecent his thoughts were right now. Shockingly indecent. But he figured he might as well tell her the truth about Viviana, otherwise Audrey would never stop banging on about his attitude to love and marriage. 'We were only pretending to be dating. I was doing her a favour.'

Her eyebrows came together. 'Friends with benefits, you mean?'

'No benefits. We just hung out so her cheating ex would get annoyed she moved on so quickly.'

'Oh...' Her teeth pulled at her lip. 'That was...nice of you. But weren't you a little bit tempted to sleep with her? I mean, she's gorgeous and—'

'I'm assuming you're currently between relationships or should I be worried some guy is going to take my kneecaps out with a baseball bat?'

Her lips made a funny little movement—a quirky, wry movement. 'I haven't dated anyone for a while.'

'How long a while?'

Her eyes flicked away from his. 'You wouldn't believe me if I told you.'

'Try me.'

She looked at his mouth, then back to his eyes and he felt a strange little jolt. 'Are you thinking about that kiss?'

'No.' It was such a blatant lie he mentally braced himself for a deity's lightning strike.

'Then why do you keep staring at my mouth?'

Lucien forced his gaze back to hers. 'I'm not.'

'Yes, you are. See? You did it just then. Your eyes flicked down and then up again.'

'I was checking out the stubble rash on your chin.' He brushed his finger over the reddened patch. 'Is it sore?'

She gave a delicate shiver as if his touch had sent a current through her flesh. 'You're touching me again.' Her voice was soft and husky, making his body give an answering shiver.

Lucien dropped his hand and curled his fingers into a fist. 'While we're on the subject, why do you keep staring at my mouth?'

'Do I?'

'You do.'

Her eyes darted to his mouth. 'Maybe it's because no one's ever kissed me like that before.'

Right back at you, sweetheart.

'No one?'

'No one.'

Lucien stroked a finger across her lower lip. She closed her eyes and swayed slightly. He moved his finger under her jaw, applying gentle pressure beneath her chin to raise her gaze back to his. 'Stop that thought right now.'

Her expression was as innocent as a child's. 'What thought?'

He gave a soft grunt of laughter. 'You're thinking what I'm thinking, so don't try and deny it.'

The tip of her tongue passed over her lips and she gave the tiniest of swallows. 'How do you know what I'm thinking? You're not a mind reader.'

Desire throbbed through him, a dull pain in his groin. 'You want me.'

'So? It doesn't mean I'm going to act on it. Anyway, you said no more kissing or touching.' She batted her eyelashes. 'But maybe you only said that for *your* benefit.'

'Don't worry. I can control myself.'

One of her brows lifted and her eyes flashed with a challenge. 'So if I leaned forward and pressed my lips against yours, you wouldn't kiss me back?'

Lucien had to call on every ounce of willpower to stop himself from looking at her lush, ripe mouth. 'Want to try it and see?'

Her smile flickered, then disappeared. 'No.'

No? What did she mean, no? He wanted to prove to her—to prove to himself—that he could resist her. It had nothing to do with how disappointed he felt. He wasn't disappointed. Not one bit. Why should he care if she kissed him or not? He was trying *not* to kiss her, wasn't he?

And he would keep on trying. Harder. Much harder.

He summoned up an easy-going smile. 'Coward.'

Even after the two-hour flight to Marseille, Audrey was still reliving every moment of that kiss. They had picked up a hire car and were driving through a small village on the way to the chateau a few kilometres out of St Remy. She kept touching her lips with her fingers when Lucien wasn't looking, wondering how it could be that all this time later her lips would still feel so…so awakened. So sensitive. So alive. Every time she moistened her lips she tasted him. Every time she looked in a mirror she saw the tiny patch of beard rash on her chin and a frisson would go through her. His kiss had been passionate, thrilling, magical. Their mouths had responded to each other like the flames of two fires meeting—exploding in a maelstrom of heat she could feel even now smouldering in her core. She could feel the restless pulse of unsatisfied desire in her body—an ache that twinged with each breath she took.

Audrey looked out of the car window at the quaint village shops and houses, wishing they had time to stop and explore. The tiny village had once been surrounded by a circular wall and many of the charming medieval buildings dated back to the fourteen-hundreds.

Lucien slowed the car to allow a mother and her two children and little fluffy dog cross the narrow street before he continued. 'Did you know St Remy is the birthplace of Nostradamus, the sixteenth-century author of prophecies?'

'Yes,' Audrey said. 'And the place where Vincent Van Gogh came for treatment for his mental illness. I wish we had time to stop and have a wander around.'

'We're not here to sightsee.'

'I know, but what if Mum and Harlan aren't at the chateau?'

'I've already spoken to the owner. I called before we left London.'

Audrey glanced at him. 'What did he tell you? Did he confirm they were there?'

'No.'

'Then why are we heading there if you don't think—?'

'He was cagey, evasive, which made me suspect he's been sworn to secrecy.'

'But you're Harlan's son, so why wouldn't he tell you? You're family.'

Lucien gave a lip-shrug. 'I don't have that sort of family.'

Neither do I.

Audrey shifted her gaze from his mouth and looked at the view again. She was glad it was Lucien that had started the kiss. It gave her a sense of one-upmanship she badly needed, given their history. His attraction might be reluctant but it was there all the same. She saw it every time he looked at her—the way his gaze kept going to her mouth and the way his eyes darkened and glittered with lust. She felt it in his touch—the way his hands set fire to her skin even through her clothes.

It had surprised her to find out he hadn't been in a real relationship with Viviana. Surprised and secretly delighted. But he'd allowed everyone, including Audrey, to think he was until Viviana had called him, no doubt after seeing her mother's tweet. Did Viviana think he was now involved with Audrey? He hadn't said anything to the contrary on the phone.

But it had always seemed strange to her that Lucien would even want to get married one day in the future if he was trying to avoid love. Even arranged marriages often ended up with the partners falling in love with each other. Or was he so determined his heart would never be touched?

As determined as *she* was?

And Audrey was determined. Steely and determined. No way was she going to fall in love like her mother, losing all sense of dignity and autonomy by becoming hopelessly besotted with a man who would only leave her or disappoint her.

But that didn't mean she didn't want to experience sensuality. To feel a man's touch, to feel a man's rougher skin move against hers. To feel a man's mouth on her lips, on her breasts, his hands on her...

You could have a fling with Lucien.

She allowed the thought some traction...

He was attracted to her. *Tick.* She was attracted to him. *Tick.* They were both currently single. *Tick.*

What harm could it do? They were both consenting adults. He was the *one* person she would consider having a fling with because she knew he wasn't interested in her mother's stardom. She wouldn't have the worry about his motives. His motives would be pure and simple lust.

Just like hers.

Lucien suddenly braked and grabbed her by the arm, and for a startled moment Audrey thought he must have read her mind. 'Look. Is that your mother over there near that market stall?'

Audrey peered in the direction he was pointing. 'Which stall?' It wasn't Wednesday, the main market day, but there were still a lot of stalls full of fruit and vegetables and freshly baked bread and the gorgeous cheeses this region was famous for. Just looking at all that food made her stomach growl. But then she glimpsed a blonde head before it disappeared into the maze of the stalls. 'I'm not sure if that was Mum or not. It looked like her, but—'

'I'll quickly park and we can do a search on foot,' Lucien said. 'They might not be staying at the chateau. They might be staying here in the village. Small as it is, it's easier to blend into the crowd down here.'

CHAPTER SIX

LUCIEN PARKED IN a shady side-street and then they made their way back to the market stalls. In her attempt to keep up with his quick striding pace, Audrey almost stumbled on the cobblestones and he grabbed her hand to steady her. 'Careful. We can't have you breaking a leg.'

'I'm fine.' Audrey tried to pull her hand out of his but he held it securely. 'But wouldn't we be better to split up and search? We could cover twice the ground that way. We can text each other if we spot them.'

His fingers tightened on her hand for a moment before he released her. 'Good idea. I'll cover this side of the market area and you can do that side. I'll text or call you in ten minutes.'

Audrey started searching through the crowd but her eyes kept being drawn by the glorious food. The smell of fresh bread and croissants was nothing short of torture. She was salivating so badly she was going to cause a flash flood on the cobbled street. She saw several blonde women but none of them was her mother. Right now she didn't care a jot about finding her mother.

What she wanted was one of those chocolate croissants.

She glanced up and down the market, looking for Lucien. He was tall enough for her to see over the top of most people…ah, yes, there he was, right at the other end near a vegetable stall. She took out her purse and, recalling her schoolgirl French, bought one of the croissants. The first bite into the sweet flakiness sent a shiver of delight through her body almost the same as when Lucien had kissed her. Almost. The second bite evoked a blissful groan, but just as she was about to take her third bite she saw her mother coming out of a tiny boutique less than a metre away. Or at least a downplayed version of her mother. She was carrying a shopping bag with a paper-wrapped baguette poking out of the top as well as some fresh fruit and vegetables.

'Mumffh?' Audrey's mouthful of pastry didn't make for the best diction and she quickly swallowed and rushed over. 'Mum?'

At first she wondered if she'd made a mistake. The woman in front of her had her mother's eyes and hair colour but the hair wasn't styled and her eyes weren't made up. Her eyelashes weren't false; they weren't even coated with mascara. Her mother's normally glowing skin looked pale and drawn and there were fine lines around her mouth Audrey had never seen before. Even her mother's clothes were different. Instead of a brightly coloured *look-at-me* designer outfit, her mother was wearing faded jeans and a cotton shirt and a man's grey sweater tied around her waist. And she had trainers on her feet. No sky-high heels.

This was taking stars without make-up to a whole new level.

Sibella glanced around nervously. 'Is Lucien with you?'

'Yes.' Audrey pointed further up the market. 'Over there somewhere. He thought he saw you when we were driving past.'

Sibella grasped Audrey's hand with her free hand and tugged her under the awning of the boutique. 'Tell him you didn't see me. Tell him it was someone else who looked like me. Please?'

Audrey was shocked at the urgent tone of her mother's voice and the desperation in her gaze. 'But why?'

'Harlan and I want to be left alone without being lectured by everyone on how bad we are for each other.'

'But you are bad for each other,' Audrey said. 'You bring out the worst in each other and I can't stand by and watch it all fall apart again.'

A middle-aged woman came out of the boutique and walked past them without even glancing at Audrey's mother. Her mother was famous all over the world. Sibella couldn't walk down a deserted country lane without being recognised. What was even more surprising, her mother seemed relieved no one was looking at her and asking for an autograph or to pose for a selfie.

'Please, Audrey.' Her mother gripped Audrey's hand tighter and her eyes took on such a beseeching look it reminded Audrey of a puppy begging for a forbidden treat. 'Please just give me a few days with Harlan. He's...' Her mother choked back a tiny sob and tears shone in her eyes. 'He's not well.'

Audrey knew her mother was a good actor and could sob and cry on demand, but something about her expression told her this was no act. She was genuinely upset. 'Not well? What's wrong with him?'

Sibella's gaze did another nervous dart around the crowded market before she pulled Audrey into a quiet narrow lane. 'He only told me last night.' Her bottom lip quivered. 'He's got cancer.'

Audrey swallowed. 'What sort of cancer? Is it—?'

'A brain tumour,' Sibella said. 'I'm trying to talk him into having an operation and chemo. He refuses to have any treatment because the doctors have told him there's only a small chance of success and he might end up having a stroke or worse. But I want him to try. To give himself the best chance. To give *us* the best chance.'

Audrey was no medical specialist but even she knew of the low rate of survival for brain cancers. Surgery was fraught with danger even when there was a possibility of removing the tumour. It was a daunting prognosis for anyone to face, and for someone like Harlan, who had never been sick other than from a hangover, she could imagine it was hitting him hard. 'Oh, Mum, that's terrible… Is there anything I can do?'

'Yes.' Her mother's eyes took on a determined gleam. 'Keep Lucien away. Don't tell him you've found us.'

'But—'

'We're not staying at the chateau,' her mother said. 'I wanted to but it wasn't available, and anyway, Harlan decided we had to go somewhere different for a change. Somewhere smaller and more intimate.'

'But don't you think Lucien should know his father's so sick?'

Sibella pursed her lips. 'Harlan is going to tell him himself. But not right now. I know what Lucien is like. He'll try and talk Harlan and me out of remarrying. Harlan wants me back in his life…in what's left of his life.' She gave another choked-off sob. 'We're planning to have a private ceremony. No fanfare this time.'

Audrey thought back to the luxury vellum wedding invitation that had been delivered to her flat. 'Then why did you send that invitation if you're not going to have a big showy wedding?'

'That was before Harlan knew he was sick,' Sibella said. 'He found out last week but didn't want to tell me until we went away together. Please, promise me you won't tell Lucien you've seen me. Tell him I called you and told you we were staying somewhere else.'

'But Mum, you know what a hopeless liar I am,' Audrey said. 'Where will I say you've gone?'

'I don't care just as long as it's not here.'

'But why did you come here in the first place? Lucien knows it's one of his father's favourite haunts. Surely Harlan knew he would come here to look for you both?'

Sibella sighed and the lines around her mouth deepened. 'It was a risk he was prepared to take because he knows how much I love this village. We both love it.' She swallowed and swiped at her streaming eyes with the back of her hand. 'I guess he thought it might be the last time we will be on holiday together, so where else would he want to go but here, where we've had some of our happiest…' she gave another tight swallow '…times?'

Audrey's phone buzzed with a text and her heart

jumped. 'That's probably Lucien, looking for me.' She pulled out her phone and read the message:

Where are you?

'Please, sweetie,' Sibella said. 'Please just give Harlan and me three days.'

There was that number three again. But it was the 'sweetie' that did it. Her mother hadn't called her that since Audrey was a little kid. She didn't like the thought of lying to Lucien but what else could she do? It was Harlan's place to tell Lucien he was sick, not hers. Her mother said Harlan planned to tell Lucien himself. It would be wrong of Audrey to deliver the news he should hear from his father first-hand.

The news of Harlan's illness changed everything. What would it hurt if her mother remarried him? He might not have long to live and at least he would die happy. 'Okay, but I can't say I'm happy about—'

'I'll send you a text now and drop a hint about some other place we might be staying so at least you'll have something concrete to show Lucien.' Sibella put her shopping bag down and quickly texted a message and within a couple of seconds Audrey's phoned pinged.

She clicked on the message. 'Okay. Got it. But I still feel really uncomfortable about lying to Lucien.'

'Why? You don't even like him.'

The trouble was Audrey liked him way too much. The longer she spent with him the more she liked him. The more she wanted him with a fierce ache that radiated throughout her body. And that kiss… How would she ever be able to forget it? Would she ever stop wanting it to be repeated? She frowned at her mother. 'That reminds me. What were you thinking, making everyone think he and I were having some sort of…thing?'

Her mother had the grace to look a little ashamed. 'I know it was bit naughty of me but Harlan thought Lucien was going to ask that broomstick model to marry him. He'd dated her longer than anyone else, but Harlan knew Lucien wasn't in love with her. Apparently he doesn't believe in falling in love. He must think it's a weakness of his father's that he's fallen in love with me so many times.' She rolled her eyes in a *can-you-believe-it?* manner.

'Why did you send me to the cottage with that false lead?'

'I've had an agent look at it. I want to sell it. I thought it might be the last time you got to go there. I seem to remember you liked it quite a lot.'

Audrey's phone pinged again with another message from Lucien. 'Look, I'd better meet back up with Lucien or he'll suspect something.' She typed a message back that she was at a public restroom. She put her phone away and looked at her mother again. 'Three days, okay?'

Sibella wrapped her arms around Audrey and gave her a big squishy hug, just like she'd used to do when Audrey was a little girl. 'Thank you, sweetie. This means so much to me.' She eased back with tears shining in her eyes. 'We want to keep Harlan's illness out of the press for as long as we can. And I really want to talk him into having the operation and chemo. But in the meantime, I'm cooking him healthy food and keeping him away from alcohol.'

Audrey glanced at the fresh produce poking out of her mother's shopping bag. Could there be a bottle of wine or cognac hidden in there somewhere? 'Are you—?'

'No,' Sibella said. 'I'm not drinking. I've decided to give it up for a while, at least until Harlan gets better…' Her bottom lip quivered again and she added, 'If he gets better.'

Audrey waited until her mother disappeared out of sight from the other end of the lane before she turned back to re-enter the market area. She saw Lucien almost immediately and her heart came to a juddering halt. The acting gene had escaped her but she hoped she could still give a credible performance.

'Where the hell have you been all this time?' Lucien asked, frowning. 'I was starting to get worried.' His gaze narrowed when he looked down at her mouth. 'Is that chocolate?'

Audrey brushed at her face and her hand came away with a smear of chocolate plus a couple of croissant crumbs. Why hadn't her mother said something? 'Erm… I had a croissant.' She could feel her cheeks blazing hot enough to cook a dozen croissants.

'Was it good?' His expression was unreadable but she got the feeling he was smiling on the inside.

'Heaven.'

'Did you catch sight of your mother?'

Here we go…

Audrey rummaged in her bag for her phone. 'No, but I just got a text. They're not here. They're in Spain.'

His brows snapped together. 'Spain?'

'Yep. See?' She held her phone up so he could read the message:

Having a wonderful time in Barcelona.

Lucien looked back at her. 'My father hates Spain, in particular Barcelona.'

Audrey's stomach lurched. 'He...he does?'

'He had a bad experience with a tour director there early in his career and hasn't been back since. He swore the only way anyone could get him to go back to Barcelona would be in a coffin.'

Audrey smothered a gulp. 'Maybe he's changed his mind. People do.'

Lucien gave a snort. 'Not my father. Not about Spain. No, this is another false lead of your mother's.' He glanced around the market, shielding his eyes with one of his hands. 'I know this is going to sound strange but I can almost sense they're here.'

Audrey's heart was beating so fast she thought she might faint. *Now, there's a thought.* Maybe she could feign a faint. She put a hand to her brow and staged a slight swoon. 'Gosh, it's hot, isn't it? I think I've had too much sun. Do you think we could go back to the car now?'

Lucien took her by the arm and looped it through one of his. 'Are you okay?' He brushed a finger across her cheek. 'You do look a little flushed. There's a café over here. Let's get you something to drink. You're probably dehydrated.'

Audrey sat with him in the café a short time later, her mind whirling on how she was going to get him out of St Remy without him suspecting something. She'd promised her mother and there was no way she was going to break that promise. Three days. That was all she needed to keep him away. Why hadn't she thought to ask where her mother and Harlan were staying? Maybe they were staying in one of those cute medieval houses. They might even be able to see her and Lucien right this minute. She sipped at her mineral water and covertly watched him as he surveyed the street outside the café.

His gaze suddenly swung back to her. 'How are you feeling?'

'Erm…better, I think.' She drained her drink and smiled. 'Time to go?'

He rose from the table and helped her out of her chair. 'Do you feel up to a little walk around if we stick to the shady side of the street?'

Audrey was torn between wanting to explore the village and needing to keep him out of it. 'Why don't we drive out to the chateau? Isn't that where we're supposed to be heading?' At least she knew her mother and Harlan weren't there and she figured once Lucien accepted that he might then agree to fly back to London.

'They're not staying there.'

Audrey was starting to wonder if he was channelling Nostradamus or something. 'How do you know? I mean, apart from my mother's text, that is.'

'I spoke to one of the stallholders,' he said. 'The chateau is undergoing extensive maintenance and repairs. It's not being rented out at present.'

'Then why was the owner so cagey on the phone the other day?'

Lucien shrugged. 'Who knows? Maybe he thought I was a building inspector.'

Lucien led Audrey outside and made sure she was out of direct sunlight as they walked through the village. It was one of his father's favourite places and he had come here for a month to recuperate after the last divorce. He couldn't imagine his father would ever change his mind about Barcelona. In spite of her mother's text message, he couldn't rid himself of the sense his father was here. He would stick around with Audrey in St Remy for the rest of the weekend.

They wandered in and out of some of the shops so Audrey could keep cool, and Lucien couldn't help noticing how taken she was with everything—the medieval architecture, the flowers hanging in baskets or spilling out of tubs, the street cafés and, of course, the food. For someone who claimed to be feeling unwell it certainly hadn't tainted her appetite. He found it rather cute she was such a foodie, sneaking off to eat a chocolate croissant when he wasn't looking. He couldn't remember the last time he'd dated a woman who wasn't on some sort of diet.

But Audrey clearly loved food, which made him wonder if she was just as passionate about other appetites. He had tasted that fiery passion in her kiss. Felt it thrumming in her lips as they clung to his. Was she thinking about that kiss now? Every time he looked at her, her gaze would dart away and she would bite her lip and her brow would furrow.

Was she finding it as hard as he was *not* to think about that kiss?

'We'd better find a place to stay,' Lucien said once they'd come out of a handcrafts boutique.

Audrey's eyes flew to his as if he'd said he'd booked them a room in purgatory. 'Stay? You mean here? Here in St Remy?'

'Of course here,' Lucien said. 'I want to hang around for the rest of the weekend in case—'

'The rest of the weekend?' Her eyes were as big as Christmas baubles. 'But…but why? I mean, I—I need to get back to London. I can't flit around Provence all weekend now we know Mum and Harlan aren't here.'

'It's all right. I'll book us into separate rooms. Your virtue is safe.'

'Of course it is.' Her voice contained a note of something he couldn't identify. Was it cynicism or hurt or both? 'You'd never lower your standards to sleep with someone like me.'

'We really need to do something about that self-esteem of yours, don't we?' Lucien stepped closer to brush a flyaway strand of her hair away from her face. 'Do you really think I'm not attracted to you?' It was a dangerous admission on his part but he was unable to stop himself. He did want her. He wanted her badly. He kept trying to remember the reasons he'd put up against sleeping with her, but now none of them seemed strong enough. Maybe they had never been strong enough and all this time he'd been deluding himself he could withstand the temptation.

But now nothing was strong enough to counter the red-hot desire that moved through his body in fizzing currents and eddies. He had fought his desire for her. Fought with it, wrestled with it, battled with it and yet it had been beyond him, because deep down he knew she was the one woman to unravel his control in a way no one else could.

Her tongue came out and left a glistening sheen over her lips. 'You want to sleep with me? Really? But I thought you said—'

He ran his fingertip over her bottom lip. 'Forget what I said. We're both consenting adults.'

What the heck are you doing?

But right then, Lucien wasn't listening to the faintly ringing warning bell of his conscience. He was going on instinct—primal instinct—and reading the signals from her that told him she wanted him just as much as he wanted her.

Her lip quivered against his finger and her hands came to rest on his chest. 'But you said if we got involved it would only encourage our parents.'

'I'm not proposing marriage,' Lucien said. 'Just a short-term fling to explore this chemistry.'

She glanced at his mouth and swallowed. 'You feel it too?'

He picked up her hand and brought it to his mouth, holding her gaze with his. 'All the time.'

Audrey walked with Lucien into the luxury villa he'd booked for the weekend with her body tingling in anticipation. He wanted her. He was offering her a short-term fling. They were going to spend the weekend together as lovers.

But her mind kept throwing up flags of panic. They were still in St Remy, when she'd promised her mother she would keep him away from the village. What if he ran into his father and her mother? What if her mother thought she'd betrayed them? It was like trying to choose between two favourite desserts. Impossible.

She would have to have both.

She could have the weekend with Lucien but she would keep him off the streets of the village by indulging in heaps of bed-wrecking sex. Not that she knew much about bed-wrecking sex or anything.

But *he* didn't need to know that.

The more she thought about it, the more it seemed the perfect plan. She would have to give her mother the heads-up to avoid any chance encounters. But, since her mother and Harlan wanted time alone and with his health being so poorly, she couldn't imagine they would be out too much anyway…she hoped.

Lucien led her inside the gorgeous villa and Audrey gasped and turned in a full circle, taking it all in. The décor was simple but elegant and perfectly complemented the medieval origins of the villa. Crystal chandeliers with polished brass fittings and soft furnishings in muted tones of white and dove-grey. Persian rugs softened the tiled floors and the furniture was stylish and sophisticated with typical French flair.

She darted over to the windows to look at the view of the maze of the streets outside and the neighbouring ivy-clad villas. Flowers spilled from hanging baskets on iron hooks that looked as if they had been forged centuries ago. Overflowing tubs of vivid red and scarlet pelargoniums lined the cobblestoned street below.

She turned and smiled at Lucien. 'Isn't it fabulous? I could stay here for a month.'

His smouldering gaze and his half-smile made something in her stomach rise and fall like the swell of an ocean wave. 'Come here.'

Audrey shivered at his commanding tone. Should she tell him she was a virgin? No. He might not make love to her then. He might think her a freak or get all old-fashioned and principled about it. 'Do you mind if I have a shower first? I'm all hot and sticky and—'

'Let's have one together.'

Audrey hadn't let anyone see her body naked since she was twelve. Of course, when they made love he would see her naked but at least she could drape herself with the sheet or something. 'Erm... Do you mind if I have one by myself this time?'

Lucien came over to her and stroked a finger down the slope of her burning cheek. 'Are you sure about this, Audrey? Us sleeping together?'

'Of course I'm sure,' Audrey said, disguising a gulp. 'It's just I have some...some body issues and—'

His fingertip moved from her face to glide in a sensual stroke against her collarbone and then down to the shadow of her cleavage. Her skin was so sensitive to his touch she was convinced she could feel every whorl of his fingerprint. Nerves she hadn't known she possessed shook and shivered and shuddered. 'You don't have to be shy with me.' His voice had a husky edge to it as if he'd been gargling with gravel. He stroked his finger over the swell of her breast and even through her clothes she could feel her nipples tightening. 'You're beautiful. Sexy and beautiful and I want you like crazy.'

'I want you too.' Was that her voice? That whispery, soft, breathless sound?

He lowered his head and covered her mouth with his in a searing kiss that made every cell of her body sigh in bliss. His lips moved with heat and passion against hers—a soft, massaging movement that made her mouth open like a flower. His tongue found hers, tangling with it in an erotic dance that made her skin tighten in anticipation. His hands gathered her closer, pulling her against the swelling heat of his body, making her own body weep with intimate moisture. His mouth continued its mesmerising magic on hers and his hands stroked and squeezed her bottom, holding her tight against his growing erection until she was making whimpering and gasping noises.

He lifted his mouth and began to undo the buttons on her top one by one, his eyes holding hers in a sensually charged lock that made her inner core contract with need. The brush of his fingers on her naked skin as he removed her top made her scalp shiver in a rush of pleasure. He slid her shirt from her body and his hands skated over her breasts still encased in her bra. 'So beautiful,' he said, his thumbs moving over her lace-covered nipples in a back and forth motion that sent a tremor of exquisite longing through her body.

Audrey set to work on his shirt buttons, revealing the tanned, sculptured perfection of his chest—the well-defined pectoral muscles, the flat dark nipples, the light dusting of ink-black hair that felt rough and springy and sexy under her fingertips. She brought her mouth to the strong column of his throat, her tongue licking over the bulge of his Adam's apple, his stubble grazing her tongue like sandpaper. The citrus-based scent of his aftershave tantalised her senses as if she were inhaling a psychedelic drug. The hint of male perspiration on his skin was just as intoxicating, making her long to taste him—every inch of him—as she had fantasised about doing for so long.

Lucien reached behind her and unclipped her bra and it fell to the floor. Audrey fought the urge to cover herself and stood and allowed him to feast his eyes on her. He gently cradled her breasts, touching them respectfully, reverently, worshipfully. She had never felt such powerful sensations in her body. No one had ever touched her that way before and the thrill of it snatched her breath away. He bent his head and swept his tongue over each curve—first the right breast, then the left—taking his time until her nerves shivered and danced in a frenzy. He brought his mouth to each of her nipples, sucking on them softly, taking them between his teeth in a gentle bite that made her legs almost go from under her. He circled each nipple with his tongue as if he was marking out a territory, the sexy glide making the base of her spine shiver like fizzing sherbet was trickling down her backbone.

Audrey was so turned on she could barely stand upright. She tugged at his waistband and popped the silver button on his jeans. The flat plane of his abdomen contracted under her touch and it made her emboldened to go lower. His masculine hair tickled her fingers and he sucked in a harsh-sounding breath, his hands gripping her by the waist. He released his breath in a steady stream as if trying to garner some self-control. He undid the button and zip at the back of her skirt and it, too, fell with a whisper of fabric to the floor, leaving her in nothing but her knickers.

'Do you have any idea how much I want you?' He spoke the words against her lips, dazzling her senses all over again.

Audrey licked the seam of his mouth with her tongue, a part of her shocked at her wanton behaviour but another part relishing in the feminine power she felt to be desired so fiercely by him. The potency of his erection pressed against her belly, so near to where her body ached and pulsed with need. 'I can feel it.' She licked his lower lip this time—a slow stroke that made him groan and crush his mouth to hers.

His hands went to her hips, peeling down her knickers, and he walked her backwards to the nearest wall, pinning her hands either side of her head as he feasted off her mouth. His commanding hold of her called out to something primal in her. When he lifted his mouth for air she bit down on his shoulder playfully, tugging at his flesh and then sweeping her tongue over the bite mark.

Lucien gave a low grunt of approval and eased back to step out of his jeans and source a condom from his wallet. His movements were rushed, almost feverish, echoing the storm of urgency she could feel barrelling through her body.

She wanted him *now*.

He slipped the condom in place and Audrey drank in the sight of him, marvelling that it was her who had made him feel so aroused. She stroked him with her hand, going on instinct…well, not quite on instinct alone because she'd read plenty of the sealed sections in women's magazines. But reading about it was nothing compared with doing it in the flesh. Even through the fine membrane of the condom, he felt amazing— like velvet-wrapped steel. He quivered under her touch and made another sound deep at the back of his throat and gently pushed her back against the wall.

He ran one of his hands from her breast to her belly and then below. She sucked in a breath when he came to her folds, sensations spiralling through her when he inserted one finger. 'Oh, God…that feels so good…' She gripped him by the shoulders. 'Make love to me. Please do it. Do it now.'

Lucien hitched one of her legs over his hip and entered her with a deep thrust that made her head bump against the wall. 'Ouch.'

He stopped and looked at her in concern. 'Am I rushing you? You were so wet, I thought—'

Audrey tried to relax her pelvis but the thick presence of him felt strange…as if she was too small for him or something. It wasn't painful now he had stopped but she knew if he moved again it might tug at her tender flesh, which made it even harder for her to relax. 'You didn't rush me at all. It's just you're so…so big…' Could she sound any more clichéd?

Lucien stroked her hair back off her face in a touch

so gentle it felt like the brush of a feather, his dark blue gaze intense and penetrating. 'Are you sure you want to do this?'

'Of course I'm sure.' Audrey could feel a blush stealing over her cheeks. 'I'm just a little out of practice, that's all.'

He brushed his thumb over her lower lip. 'I'll take things a little more slowly. And maybe a bed instead of up against the wall would be better.' He began to withdraw and she couldn't disguise her wince in time. He frowned again. 'I'm hurting you?'

Audrey bit down on her lip. 'Not much…'

Something flickered over his face as if he was shuffling through his thoughts and not liking what his brain produced. 'When was the last time you had sex?'

Audrey swallowed. 'Erm…not…not recently.'

'When?' His gaze was so direct she felt like a suspect in front of a very determined detective.

'Does it matter?' She tried for a casual tone but didn't quite pull it off. Yep, that acting gene certainly hadn't come her way.

Something that looked like horror passed through his gaze and his throat moved up and down over a convulsive swallow. 'Oh, my God…' He moved away from her and she had never felt so naked and exposed in her entire life.

Or so terrifyingly vulnerable.

'You're a…a *virgin*?' He said it like it was an affliction from which there was no known cure.

Audrey made a paltry attempt to cover her breasts.

'Not now I'm not. Although… I'm not sure if what we just did counts.'

He opened and closed his mouth a couple of times but no sound came out other than a strangled noise. He sent one of his hands through his hair, then over his face, rubbing at it as if to erase the last few minutes from his memory. He turned and got rid of the condom and put his jeans back on, his movements as jerky as a string puppet. He turned back to face her and blinked at her like someone exposed to too bright a light. 'Sorry…' He searched around for her clothes but ended up picking up his shirt instead and handing it to her.

Audrey slipped her arms into the sleeves and closed it over her front without doing up the buttons because she knew her fingers wouldn't be up to the task. 'Thanks.'

'Audrey…' His voice sounded as if it had been scraped over concrete. 'Why on earth didn't you tell me?'

'Because I knew if I did you wouldn't want to make love to me. You'd get all preachy and stuffy about it.'

And think I'm a freak.

'Did you not think it might be appropriate to tell me I was about to make love to a virgin? I *hurt* you, damn it.'

'No you didn't.' She couldn't hold his piercing look. 'Well, only a little.'

He let out a muttered curse and paced the floor as if he were intent on thinning the pile of the carpet down a few centimetres. He stopped and came back to stand in front of her and touched her gently on her upper arms. 'I'm sorry. I can't tell you how sorry I am.'

'Don't be,' Audrey said. 'I wanted you to make love

to me. I wouldn't have let things go that far if I hadn't... I just didn't want you to think there's something wrong with me for being twenty-five years old and still a virgin.'

He stroked his hands up and down her arms in a soothing fashion, his gaze tender. 'Do you want to talk about it?'

She exhaled on a sigh. 'Not sure where to start... I was sixteen when I went on my first date with a guy I had a huge crush on. Halfway through the date he asked to meet my mother. Turns out he was a wannabe actor and thought by dating me he might land himself a leg up to the big time of soapy television. He humiliated me. He talked to all his mates about what a disappointment I was in bed and I hadn't even been to bed with him. We had only kissed the once. And he wasn't such a great kisser anyway.' Nothing like Lucien.

Lucien frowned. 'What a jerk. That must have been so upsetting for you. Did you talk to anyone about it? Your mother? A teacher or a friend?'

Audrey made a wry movement of her lips. 'I felt too embarrassed talking to my mother about it. Men fall at her feet if she so much as looks at them. How could I ever compete with that?'

'Oh, sweetheart.' Lucien gave her arms a gentle squeeze. 'You don't have to compete. You're in a league of your own. You have so much going for you. You're funny and smart and so cute I can barely keep my hands off you.'

'Cute.' Audrey sighed. 'Puppies and kittens and little kids are cute.'

He brought up her chin with his finger and meshed his gaze with hers. 'I'm not talking puppy and kitten and kid cute. I'm talking I want to carry you to the nearest bed and make love to you cute.'

She looked into his eyes and something unfurled in her belly. 'Do you mean that?'

Indecision flitted over his features as if he was weighing up the pros and cons. 'Of course I do. But I'm concerned that you might want something different out of a relationship with me. Something permanent. I wouldn't want you to get the wrong idea.'

'But I don't want anything permanent,' Audrey said. 'The last thing I want is to get married. My mother's multiple marriages has turned me off the whole notion of in sickness and in health and till death....erm...and all that.' She stumbled over the phrase 'death do us part', thinking of her mother looking after Harlan as he faced a possibly terminal illness. She'd always thought her mother's 'love' of Harlan was an obsessional type of love, a selfish sort of obsession that was all about Sibella and not much about Harlan. But after witnessing her mother's distress over the prospect of losing him, not through divorce but through death, Audrey realised her mother's love had matured into something to be admired, to be emulated.

To aspire to and want for herself.

Lucien brushed his thumb over her lower lip, his eyes still searching hers. 'Are you sure?'

She wasn't but she wasn't going to admit it. She stretched up on tiptoe and linked her arms around his neck. 'I don't want a wedding ring from you, Lucien. But I do want you to make love to me.'

His hands cupped her bottom and drew her closer to his hard heat. 'A couple of days ago I had a long list of reasons why I thought making love to you would be a really bad idea.'

'And now?'

His eyes glinted and his mouth came down to just above hers. 'Can't think of a single one of them.' And then his mouth covered hers.

CHAPTER SEVEN

AUDREY SIGHED AS his mouth came down and covered hers in a kiss that communicated not just lust and longing but also something else…something she couldn't quite describe. There was passion in his kiss but also gentleness—a slow exploration of her mouth that made her senses sing like they were in a choral symphony. His hands cradled her face, angling it so he could deepen the kiss with strokes and glides of his tongue that made her insides quake and quiver and quicken with need. She made breathless sounds of approval and her fingers delved into the thickness of his hair, wanting him so badly it was like a firestorm rampaging through her flesh. Her breasts prickled and tingled where they were crushed against his chest, her thighs heavy with desire as they rubbed against his.

Lucien dragged his mouth off hers and began to scoop her up in his arms. Audrey tried to stop him. 'No. Wait. I'm too heavy. You'll do yourself an injury.'

'Don't be silly.' He lifted her effortlessly as if she were a feather bolster instead of an adult woman who had a sweet tooth. A whole set of sweet teeth.

He carried her to the master bedroom of the villa, and, lowering her to the floor, he slid her down the length of his body, sending shockwaves of delight through her.

He brushed back her hair from her face and stood with her in the circle of his arms, his pelvis tight and aroused against hers. 'Still sure about this?'

Audrey stroked his jaw from just below his ear to the base of his chin. 'I don't think I've wanted anything more than this.'

He peeled his shirt away from her shoulders and gently cradled her breasts, his thumbs rolling over her tight nipples like a slow-moving metronome. His touch was achingly light, so light the sensations were like exquisite torture. But then his mouth came down and he laved each nipple with his tongue. She'd had no idea her breasts were that sensitive. No idea they would trigger other sensations deeper in her body as the network of her nerves transmitted pulses of pleasure from one place to another. He continued his assault on her senses by taking her nipple into his mouth and gently sucking on it. The warm moisture of his mouth and the slight graze of his stubble against her flesh made her whimper with wanton need. There was a smouldering fire between her legs and a hollow ache spreading across her thighs and belly.

Lucien laid her down on the bed and stepped back, and for a stomach-dropping moment Audrey wondered if he was going to call a stop to their lovemaking. 'What's wrong?' she said, instinctively drawing her knees up and covering her breasts.

He leaned down and placed his hands either side of her head and pressed a hot kiss to her mouth. 'Wait for me. I need to get another condom.'

Relief coursed through her. 'Oh… I thought you might have changed your mind.'

He gently stroked her cheek with the tip of his finger. 'If I was a better man then maybe I would.'

'You are a good man, Lucien.' Audrey's voice came out husky. 'I wouldn't allow you to make love to me if you weren't.'

He gave her one more kiss and left the room to get the condom. She couldn't keep her eyes off his aroused male form as he came back in and her body gave a tremor of anticipation. He joined her on the bed and sent his hand down the side of her body in a slow stroke that made every nerve pirouette. He kissed his way down from her breasts to her stomach, dipping his tongue into the shallow cave of her belly button before going lower.

Audrey tensed and clutched his arms. 'I'm not sure I—'

'Relax, sweetheart,' he said. 'This is the best way for me to give you pleasure without hurting you.'

'But don't you want to—?'

He placed a hand just above her pubic bone. 'I want to pleasure you and I want you to be comfortable. That's my priority right now.' He paused for a moment and added, 'As long as you're okay with me touching you like this?'

Audrey couldn't imagine ever wanting anyone else to touch her so intimately. Her body was feverishly excited about his touch, so excited she could feel the intense moisture gathering. 'I'm okay with it.'

'I'll make it good for you but you have to tell me if anything I do isn't working for you,' he said. 'Promise?'

'Promise.'

He stroked his fingers down over the seam of her body, his touch so gentle it was almost a tickle. He parted her folds and stroked her again, his touch feather-light, allowing her time to get used to it. She quivered under the caress, shocked at how wonderful it felt to be touched by someone other than herself. He continued exploring her, moving his fingers at varying speeds, and the pleasure grew—tight pleasure, straining pleasure, pleasure that needed just a little more of a push.

He brought his mouth down to her and stroked her with his tongue, the action so shockingly intimate, so thrillingly pleasurable she drew in a staggered breath and whimpered. He continued caressing her, building the pace and the pressure until she lifted off into a dazzling world where thoughts were blocked out and only physical ecstasy remained. Waves and pulses of pleasure rippled and flowed through her lower body, spiralling out from the tightly budded heart of her. She gasped and cried and clutched at the bedcovers to anchor herself but the orgasm wasn't finished with her. Lucien wasn't finished with her. He kept caressing her, leading her into another release that was stronger and even more powerful than the first.

He waited until she settled with a huge sigh and he smiled and glided his hand up and down the flank of her thigh. 'I hope that was as good as it sounded?'

'Better.' Audrey touched his face in a state of wonderment. 'I can't believe that just happened. I've never felt anything like that before when I've...' Her cheeks grew hot and she lowered her gaze.

He pushed up her chin with his finger. 'Hey. Why are you embarrassed about touching yourself? It's perfectly natural and sensible because it helps you learn how your body works.'

'I know, but there's still a double standard when it comes to sex,' Audrey said. 'It's still hard for women to own and celebrate their sexual desire. To not feel guilty about wanting to give and receive pleasure.'

Lucien circled her left nipple with a lazy finger. 'Tell me what you want now.'

She cupped his face in her hands. 'I want you to make love to me. I want you inside me.'

A frown flickered across his brow. 'What if I hurt you again?'

'I'm sure it won't hurt now that I'm more relaxed,' Audrey said. 'I want to feel you. I want to give you pleasure as well as receive it.'

He kissed her on the mouth—a deep, lingering kiss that made her desire for him move through her body in a rush of heat. His tongue played with hers, calling it into a dance that was thrillingly erotic. He left her mouth to work his way down her body, pressing tingling kisses to her breasts, her ribcage, her hips and stomach and back again to her mouth.

He applied the condom he'd collected earlier and gently parted her, pausing at her entrance, uncertainty shadowing his eyes. 'Are you sure you're ready for this?'

Audrey grabbed at his shoulders. 'You've made me so ready for you.'

Doubt flickered over his features but then he smiled and lowered his mouth back to hers in a mind-drugging kiss. After a moment, he slowly began to enter her, pausing every step of the way until he was sure she was accommodating him without pain. It was uncomfortable at first, not painfully so but just a tightness that eased the more he progressed. Her body wrapped around him and, while it wasn't as intense as him touching her with his fingers, the sensation eased that hollow, achy feeling. And then when he slowly began to move the sensations increased in intensity and she felt a growing urge, a growing restlessness within her flesh for more contact, more direct friction.

She moved underneath him, searching for the point of contact that would get her over the edge, soft, breathless sounds coming from her throat. Just when she thought she could stand it no longer, he brought his hand down between their bodies and stroked her until she broke free into an orgasm that lifted every hair on her scalp and sent her spinning into a vortex of feeling unlike anything she had felt before.

He waited until the last ripples passed through her before he took his own pleasure. She held him as he thrust and thrust and then he tensed and spilled in a series of pumps that made her own skin lift in a pepper of goosebumps as waves of vicarious pleasure pulsed through her body.

Audrey lay in a blissful stupor, the sensations slowly petering out inside her like the quietening of ocean waves after a storm had blown past. Never had she thought her body capable of such mind-blowing pleasure. It felt reborn, awakened, stimulated into life and she knew nothing would ever be or feel the same.

Lucien raised himself up on one elbow and played with a tendril of her hair. 'No regrets?'

'Not one.' Audrey outlined his mouth with her fingertip. 'It was amazing. You were amazing and so gentle.'

'You're the one who was amazing.' He brushed her lips with his. 'And if you weren't so new to this, I'd suggest a replay but I don't want to make you sore.'

She was touched by his concern for her but another part of her was disappointed she couldn't experience another round of his earth-shattering lovemaking right now when her body was already stirring for more of his touch. He gave her one last kiss and rolled away to sit on the edge of the bed to dispose of the condom. She stroked a hand down his back and then traced around each of his vertebrae in slow-moving circles. 'Do you think that's why my mother and your father keep going back to each other? Because of sex?'

He turned his head to look at her and gave a shrug. 'Maybe. But a marriage needs to be based on more than good sex to last the distance.' He got off the bed and held out a hand to her with a glinting look. 'Didn't you mention something about a shower earlier?'

Audrey took his hand and he helped her to her feet and she gave him a coy smile. 'I had no idea you were so into water conservation.'

He smiled and drew her closer. 'Right now I'm into you.'

* * *

Even as Lucien led Audrey into the shower his conscience kept pinging at him. He'd thought they were indulging in a bit of itch-relieving sex, only to find out she was a virgin. To say he was shocked was an understatement, especially finding out the way he had. He wanted to be angry with her for not telling him but deep down he understood why she hadn't. He wouldn't have made love to her if she'd told him up front. He had never slept with a virgin before. One or two of his lovers had only had sex a couple of times before but no one had ever shared their first time with him. He wasn't sure how it made him feel. How was it supposed to make him feel? Wasn't it a little outdated to hold a woman's virginity up as some sort of male prize to claim? But something about the experience touched him in a way no one had done before. Her confidence that he would take care of her needs made him feel as if she had given him a precious gift.

Not just her virginity but also her trust.

He turned on the water and waited until it was the right temperature before leading her under the spray. He was already hard from being so close to her luscious body. How had he refrained from making love to her before now? Her shyness about her body made him determined to show her how much her curves delighted him. They more than delighted him—they ignited him. Firing up his lust until he was almost mad with it. He always prided himself on his self-control. He wasn't a man driven by his sexual appetite. He dealt with his primal needs in such a way as never to exploit or hurt a partner and if there wasn't a partner available he wasn't averse to relieving himself, or distracting himself with work. But with Audrey standing in the shower with him he could feel the throb and pound of his blood swelling him as he drank in the shape of her breasts and the womanly curve of her hips.

He brought his mouth down to hers and kissed her as the shower sprayed over their faces, adding another level of sensuality. Her hands came up around his neck, her breasts and nipples poking sexily at his chest. He slid his hands down her back to cup her bottom, holding her against the throbbing ache of his flesh. Her hips moved against him in a circular motion that threatened his hold on his self-control. He knew he should be out on the streets of the village searching for his father and Sibella, but here he was in the shower with Audrey and all he wanted was to sink into her tight, wet warmth and experience again the head-spinning rush of release.

But there was her likely tenderness to consider and there was no way he was going to put his needs ahead of hers. This wasn't like any other relationship he'd had, which was faintly disturbing…but in a nice way. This wasn't a simple hook-up or casual short-term relationship. By allowing him to share her first time, Audrey had stepped outside the boundaries he normally set on his relationships.

He was in completely new territory and for the first time in his life, he wasn't sure how to handle it. Audrey wasn't a woman he probably would never see again. Even if his father and her mother went through another marriage and yet another divorce, it still left a connection between Lucien and Audrey—a connection not so easily eradicated.

'Lucien?' Audrey pulled him out of his reverie by trailing a wet hand down his abdomen and he drew in a breath when her fingers wrapped around his erection. 'I want to pleasure you the way you did—'

'You don't have to feel obliged,' Lucien said. 'I want this to be about you, not me.'

Weird how altruistic he was becoming.

'But I want to.' She slithered down in front of him and took matters into her own hands, so to speak. 'Tell me if I'm doing it wrong.'

Lucien couldn't speak. Couldn't think. All he could do was feel the tentative sweep and glide of her tongue over the head of his erection, and then the way her mouth opened over him and drew on him softly at first, and then with greater suction. Again and again she drew on him, her mouth wet from the shower and her own warm saliva, and his self-control didn't stand a chance. He staggered under the force of his orgasm, the pulses of pleasure taking him to a place he had never been before with a partner. Was it the absence of a condom? Was it the more-than-just-a-hook-up nature of their relationship?

Or was it something else?

Something he didn't want to examine too closely. He didn't do close relationships. He didn't believe true love existed except between the title and credit roll of a Hollywood movie. Sure, some relationships survived the distance but most didn't. The only way he could see himself marrying one day would be to make sure his emotions were not fully engaged.

Audrey came back up to link her arms around his neck, her eyes shining with newfound confidence. 'How did I do for a beginner?'

Lucien wondered how could she not feel confident. He could still sense the aftershocks running down the backs of his legs. He cupped her face in his hands and pressed a kiss to her mouth. 'You were perfect.'

Her smile became crooked. 'No one's ever called me that before…'

He stroked his thumb over her cheek. 'Then maybe it's about time someone did.' And he brought his mouth back down to hers.

Audrey couldn't remember a time when she'd enjoyed a shower more. Pleasuring Lucien had felt so…so right somehow. She had never thought she would want to do something so intimate with a partner, especially if she was pressured into it. But he hadn't pressured her. He hadn't expressed any sense of entitlement. He had allowed her the choice and she had made it and relished in it.

But now the shower was over and they were dressed and Lucien was talking about going out to dinner. Even though Audrey was hungry she knew their meal out would not be simply about food or even companionship, let alone romance.

It would be about tracking down Harlan and her mother.

That was Lucien's mission, not a romantic dinner for two to celebrate their recent lovemaking.

'Why don't we order Room Service?' Audrey said.

Lucien straightened the cuffs of his shirt. 'What would be the point of that? You know how much my father and your mother love to eat out.' He frowned in concentration. 'What was the name of that restaurant they used to like? They used to go there every night because they enjoyed the food so much.'

There was no way Audrey was going to tell him, even though she remembered it well. Her mother had raved about the food and the service and the chef who had asked for their autographs and numerous photos with her and Harlan. 'I don't know... I'm hopeless at remembering French names.'

He picked up the hotel room key card and slipped it in his pocket. 'Come on. We'll have a wander around and see if we can find it. I'm sure it wasn't far from here.'

Audrey needed to text her mother to make sure she and Harlan weren't out. It wasn't likely, given Harlan was unwell, but what if they had decided to go out? Her mother was a disaster chef not a master chef. 'Erm... can you give me a second? I just want to fix my hair.'

'Your hair looks great.'

'And... I need the bathroom.' She gave him a winning smile. 'I'll be five seconds.'

Audrey dashed into the bathroom and quickly typed a text to her mother. She waited thirty seconds for her to read the text but the message icon showed the text had been delivered but not read. She turned on one of the taps and with the cover of the running water called Sibella, but the message said the phone was either switched off or not in a mobile phone reception area.

Damn. Double damn.

How was she supposed to warn her mother if she didn't turn on her phone?

There was a knock at the bathroom door. 'Are you okay in there?' Lucien said.

Audrey jumped off the closed toilet seat where she'd been sitting and pressed the flush button. She washed her hands because they were clammy with panic at the thought of her and Lucien running into her mother and Harlan. 'I'm coming.'

She opened the door with a bright smile in place. 'Sorry.'

Lucien's gaze searched hers. 'What's wrong?'

'Nothing's wrong.'

He glided a finger down her cheek where she could feel a fire burning. 'Are you sure you're not sore?'

Audrey knew if she said she was there would be no more lovemaking tonight. He was too considerate a man to put his needs ahead of hers. But how else could she stop him from taking her out to dinner? 'No, I'm not sore at all… I'm just not really very hungry.' Just then her stomach gave the biggest growl, which sounded like a gurgling drain.

His gaze narrowed slightly. 'Okay. But if you don't mind, I'll go out for a bit and have a look around for an hour or so. If you feel hungry later then just order something to the room.'

Panic was a giant claw tearing at Audrey's stomach, even worse than the pain of her hunger. She couldn't let him go out without her. She couldn't risk it. 'Erm…

I've changed my mind. I am a bit hungry…and the fresh air will be nice.'

He held out his hand and she slipped hers into it. 'Good. For a moment there you had me worried.'

'Why? Because I turned down a meal?'

He studied her for a long moment, a small frown pulling at his brow. 'Are you being completely honest with me, Audrey?'

Audrey tried to disguise a swallow but it felt as if she were swallowing a feather pillow. 'Honest about what?'

His eyes were like searchlights and every pulsing second they held hers she felt her heart trip and flip. 'You seem a little agitated.'

'No, I'm not.' She answered too quickly for it to be convincing.

He took both of her hands in his, holding them loosely but securely. 'What's troubling you, sweetheart? Is it being seen out in public with me now that we've made love? Is that it? You feel embarrassed?'

It was just the lifeline she needed. 'What are we going to tell people about us? I mean, I know my mother already led the press to believe something is going on between us, but now that something is going on…well, what *is* going on? How will we describe it? A fling sounds a bit… I don't know…a bit tacky…'

Lucien's mouth firmed as if coming to a decision in his mind. 'We'll tell everyone we're dating exclusively.'

Audrey mentally breathed a sigh of relief. She didn't want to be grouped with all the other women Lucien had had flings with in the past. She didn't want to be just another name, just another face, just another body to show up in the press on his arm.

She wanted to be special.

She wanted to be special because he made her feel special. His touch made her feel she was the only woman he wanted to make love to. She couldn't imagine making love with anyone else now she had made love with him. He knew her body better than she knew it herself. He had drawn from it responses she hadn't thought she was capable of experiencing. Her body was in love with him even if her mind refused to go there.

Was it pathetic of her to hope his body was a little bit in love with hers too?

The air was cool outside but not as cold as if the mistral wind St Remy was famous for were blowing. Lucien's arm was around Audrey's waist as they walked out of the hotel and, while one part of her was thrilled at being in his company, the other part was dreading the prospect of running into his father and her mother. She had checked her phone for any texts back from her mother but her text still appeared unread. She tried to relax because she could feel Lucien's contemplative gaze on her from time to time.

There were several restaurants along the street their hotel was on and Audrey knew the one he was thinking of—the one her mother and Harlan frequented—was only a couple of streets away. She stopped in front of a quaint restaurant that had a sandwich board on the footpath with a menu of specials written on it. 'This one looks good.' She pointed to the sign. 'Even with my shocking schoolgirl French I can see it has my favourite dessert.'

'There are more restaurants further along this street. Don't you want to check them out first before we make a decision?'

'But I'm now starving and it will take ages to check out all the other restaurants.'

Lucien shook his head as if dealing with a small child whom he couldn't resist indulging. 'All right. Here it is.'

He led her inside and with perfect French he asked for a table for two. The waiter asked if they would prefer a table near the window or in a more private corner.

'Window,' Lucien said.

'What if I wanted to sit in the private corner?' Audrey said once they were seated with wine and mineral water and two bread rolls fresh from the oven in front of them. Well, one bread roll was left because she had already eaten hers.

His gaze met hers. 'You're not convinced Sibella and my father are in the village, are you?'

Audrey was glad the lighting in the restaurant was low because it would at least hide the way her cheeks were glowing. 'They could be anywhere by now.'

'Have you heard anything since that last text?'

She had to think for a minute which text he meant. 'No. Nothing.' She waited a beat before adding, 'What makes you so convinced they're here?'

He picked up the single glass of red wine he'd ordered and took a measured sip. He put the glass back down with a sigh. 'My father came here for a month after their last break-up. After I got him back on his feet, that is. I think it was what saved him, actually—a month just pottering about the village being a normal person instead of a rock star. He came back looking refreshed and tanned and the healthiest I'd seen him in ages.'

Audrey pushed a crumb around her side plate with her finger. 'My mother really struggled after that last divorce too.' She stopped pushing the crumb and glanced at him. 'I mean, *really* struggled.'

Concern entered his gaze. 'What do you mean?'

She let out her breath on a long exhalation. Why shouldn't she tell Lucien what she had gone through with her mother? He'd told her about the dramas he'd been through with his father. 'She took a couple of overdoses when she was hiding out at my place. Not enough to require hospitalisation but enough to terrify the heck out of me.'

His expression communicated compassion as well as concern. 'What a shock it must have been for you to find her like that. But why didn't you insist on her going to hospital?'

'I begged her to let me call an ambulance or even to drive her there myself, but she got all hysterical and weepy about her fans finding out so I relented,' Audrey said. 'I managed to get her to agree to let me call her doctor, who checked her out at home. He said she had only taken enough to be a bit sleepy and wobbly on her feet.'

His frown was so heavy it closed the distance between his eyes. 'That was a big risk to take. What if she had taken more than she'd said?'

'I know it was risky, but her doctor assessed the situation. And then I stayed home from work for the next few days until I was sure she was safe.'

'You said she took a couple of overdoses,' he said. 'When did she take the other one?'

'Actually, she took three in total,' Audrey said. 'One a week for three weeks.'

'And you or the doctor still didn't insist on her going into hospital?'

Audrey didn't care for the note of criticism in his voice. 'Look, I did my best, okay? Her doctor thought she would be worse off in hospital with fans trying to get in to see her. He thought it best for her to have some quiet supervision at home out of the spotlight. I didn't want to break her trust, which I might add I've just done by telling you. She's the only mother I've got—the only parent—and I didn't want to damage our relationship by acting against her wishes. The overdoses were a cry for help so I gave that help and I continued to give it until she didn't need it any more.'

'I'm sorry, I didn't mean to criticise—'

'Did I criticise you for not getting your father into rehab? No. I realise how hard it is with a difficult parent to get them to do what you think is best for them. But have you ever considered that maybe what we think is best for them isn't always best for them?'

He looked at her for a moment with a quizzical look on his face. 'What are you saying?'

Audrey wished she'd kept her mouth shut. 'I don't know… I guess if we can't stop them remarrying then maybe we should just accept it. Who knows? If we stop

criticising from the sidelines, this time their relationship might actually work.'

'You can't be serious?'

She forced herself to meet his incredulous gaze.
'Have you ever said anything nice about my mother to
your father? Something positive instead of negative?'

Lucien frowned as if mentally sorting through his
compliments folder in his head. 'Not that I can recall.'

'Exactly my point, because I can't think of a positive
thing I've said about your father to my mother, either,'
Audrey said. 'They're not bad people, Lucien. They just
make bad choices. And the more we fight their being
together then the more they'll want to prove us wrong.'

His forehead was creased in lines like isobars on a
weather map. 'So you're saying we call off the hunt?
Just let them get on with it and hope for the best? I can't
do it. I'm sorry but I'm not going to let your mother destroy him a third time.'

'But what if she doesn't destroy him?' Audrey said.
'What if she's the best thing for him right now?'

Lucien's expression went from frowning to suspicious.
'What's brought about this change of heart? You can't
stand my father any more than I can stand your mother.'

'That's not true,' Audrey said. 'I can think of heaps
of positive things to say about your father.'

'Go on.'

She chewed at her lip. 'Well…he's a fabulous musi-
cian for one thing.'

'And?'

'And he's good-looking, or at least he was when he
was younger.'

'And?'

Audrey sighed. 'Okay, so it's a little hard to think of stuff, but I haven't spent a lot of time with him. And I certainly haven't made an effort to get to know him. I've always felt a little bit intimidated by him, to be perfectly honest.'

'By his fame, you mean?'

'That and because I always feel as if he's comparing me to my mother.' She gave another sigh. 'The first time I met him he asked if I was adopted.'

Lucien reached for her hand across the table. 'I'm sorry he hurt your feelings. He can be a bit of a jerk at times. Most of the time, actually.' His fingers stroked hers. 'I've lost count of the number of times I've felt hurt or let down by him.'

'Why do you keep trying to have a relationship with him if you don't even like him?'

He gave a soft laugh. 'Yeah, well, that's the thing, isn't it? I don't like him much as a person but I love him because he's my father. Doesn't make sense, does it?'

Audrey squeezed his fingers. 'It makes perfect sense. My mother drives me nuts but I still love her and would do anything for her. I guess because before all the fame stuff happened she was a pretty good mum. Much better than her own mum because her mother kicked her out of home when she got pregnant with me.'

'Are they still estranged?'

'Permanently because now my grandmother is dead,' Audrey said. 'She was killed in a car crash before my mother could repair the relationship. I think it's one of the reasons she drinks so much when she goes through a break-up or a disappointment of some kind. It triggers all those feelings of rejection. It's also why she draws unnecessary attention to herself in order to be noticed.'

She couldn't believe how much she had told him about her mother. About her feelings about her mother. There were so few people she could talk to. Really talk to. She was always conscious of 'tainting her mother's brand' or afraid she wouldn't be believed. But now it felt as if a weight had come off her shoulders, as if she were shrugging off a heavy overcoat.

Lucien had a thoughtful expression on his face. 'That's sad. I guess I didn't consider the circumstances that had contributed to your mother's personality. I took an instant dislike to her because she seemed to bring out my father's reckless and irresponsible streak. But then, he probably brings out hers.'

Audrey gave a wry smile. 'I heard once that people who fall in love at first sight are actually falling in love with each other's emotional wounds. Their relationship doesn't usually last unless they address and heal those wounds.'

He gave a *that-makes-sense* lip-shrug. 'Interesting.'

'What's yours?'

He frowned. 'What's my what?'

'Your wound.'

His half-smile didn't reach his eyes. 'Whoa, this is starting to get heavy. Let's see… I guess I'm a little wary of investing too much of myself in a relationship because I've been let down so many times.'

'By your father?'

'Not just my father,' Lucien said, with a flicker of

pain in his gaze. 'My mother died when I was in my final year of school. Of course, it wasn't her fault or anything. She had a brain aneurysm, so it wasn't as if she could give me any warning. One day she was alive, the next she wasn't.'

'I'm so sorry,' Audrey said, thinking of the secret she was keeping about his father's health and how it might hurt him to be excluded from it. 'What did you do? Did you go and live with your father after that?'

He made a sound that was part laugh, part snort. 'No. He gave me a heap of money instead to set myself up in a flat so I could finish my year at school. He didn't even come to her funeral. He was doing a show in Europe that he didn't want to cancel. After I finished school, I went to university and lived on campus.'

Audrey hadn't realised he'd had to be so self-sufficient…but then, hadn't she too had to fend for herself more times than she could count? 'It's funny how people on the outside see us as lucky to have famous parents but they don't realise it comes with a cost. A cost no amount of money can fix.'

'So what's your wound?' Lucien asked.

Audrey wished now she hadn't started this heart-to-heart. It made her feel exposed and needy when she'd spent years trying to give him the opposite impression. 'I guess it's what we talked about the other day. I have trouble believing people want to be with me because of me or because of who my mother is.'

His eyes held her with a tender beat of understanding that made something tight in her chest soften. 'So how will you heal it? Your wound, I mean.'

Audrey couldn't hold his gaze and looked at her mineral water instead, pretending to be fascinated by the tiny stems of bubbles in the glass. 'I guess one day I might be lucky enough to meet someone who loves me for me.'

There was a strange silence…like the collectively held breath of an audience before a crucial scene in a play.

Lucien was the first to break it but his voice sounded distinctly husky. 'I'm sure you will, Audrey.'

But it won't be you…

CHAPTER EIGHT

LUCIEN DIDN'T ALLOW his thoughts to run to what sort of man would fall in love with Audrey. Not because he didn't want her to find happiness but because he didn't want to examine too closely the strange sense of discomfort he felt at the thought of her with someone else.

Someone other than him.

Which was quite frankly ridiculous of him because he wasn't in the market for a long-term relationship. None that involved emotions like love. Never had been, never would be. Too many complications when things turned sour, as they nearly always did. He was still cleaning up the financial messes from every time his father had fallen in 'love'.

He liked his life the way it was. Dating didn't have to be complicated when you were clear about your terms. And he was always clear. Although, he had to admit, this thing he had going with Audrey was a little blurry around the edges. He couldn't just have a weekend fling and set her free. Not after sharing her first time. She was still finding her way sexually and it would be cruel to cut it short. Cruel to her and cruel to him because he had never had such intimate sex before. Sex that was intensely physical but with an added element of emotional depth he hadn't expected.

She hadn't just shared her body with him. They had both shared confidences they hadn't shared with anyone else. He'd told her more than he'd told anyone about his father—even stuff about his mother. They had talked as intimately as they had made love. No holds barred, no screens or barriers up.

No secrets.

He was surprised by her change of heart over her mother's marriage to his father. What had brought that about? Or was she tired of traipsing around the country looking for people who didn't want to be found? He was a little tired of it himself but he was sure his father was here. He couldn't explain it. He wasn't normally one for relying on gut feelings. He was a numbers and data man. But ever since he'd driven with Audrey into St Remy he'd sensed his father's presence and he wasn't going to leave until he knew one way or the other.

Lucien watched Audrey eat her chocolate *religieuse*, somehow without getting any traces of chocolate on her mouth, which was a pity because he could think of nothing better than kissing it off. And not just kissing her mouth, but every inch of her body. He was getting hard just thinking about it. Uncomfortably hard. *I-want-you-now* hard.

She suddenly looked up from her dessert and caught him watching her. She picked up her napkin and dabbed it around her mouth, her expression a little sheepish. 'I think you can see now why I don't have my mother's figure.'

He smiled. 'I like your figure just the way it is. In fact, I'm having wicked fantasies about your figure right now.'

Her cheeks gave a delicate blush and her toffee-brown eyes twinkled like fairy lights. 'Didn't you want to go for a walk after dinner?'

It was scary how easily she could distract him from his mission, and if it hadn't been for her inexperience, he would have taken her straight back to the hotel and made love to her again and again and again.

But it wasn't just about pacing her. He had to pace himself. He was acting like a lovestruck teenager, all raging hormones and out-of-control feelings. Feelings he wouldn't allow any purchase because he wasn't going to be a fool like his father and fall in and out of love and leave a trail of despair and destruction behind. 'Walk first, bed later,' he said, softening his words with another smile.

A flicker of disappointment flashed over her features. 'Do we have to walk now? We've been on the go all day and—'

He took her hand and brought it up to his mouth, kissing her bent fingers. 'Just a short walk, okay? That's what we're here for, remember?'

Her eyes skittered away from his. 'How could I forget? It's not like you really want to be here with me. I'm a convenient bonus bit of entertainment while you get on with your mission of breaking up your father's relationship with my mother.'

Lucien frowned at her tone and brought her gaze back to his with a finger beneath her chin. 'That was your mission too, up until today. And I'm here with you because I want to be here with you.'

Because right now I can't imagine being with anyone else.

Audrey gave him one of her cute pouts that made him want to kiss her so badly he had to glue his butt to his chair. 'Do you mean that?' Her voice came out whispery soft.

He stroked her cheek with his thumb. 'It kind of scares me how much I mean it.' It scared him even more to have admitted it out loud.

Her eyes went all shimmery as if she was close to tears but she blinked rapidly a couple of times and gave him a tight smile. 'Sorry. I know this is just a fling and I promise I won't get all clingy and start dragging my feet past jewellery shops or anything, but I just want for once in my life to be special to someone, even if it's for a short time.'

Lucien brought her hand back up to his mouth, holding her bent knuckles against his lips. 'You are special, sweetheart.' So special he was having trouble recalling his reasons for keeping his relationship with her sensibly short. 'You're amazingly special.'

'I think you're pretty special too.' She gave him a wry smile and, pulling away from him, added, 'Not special enough for me to fall in love with but special all the same.'

He didn't want her to fall in love with him, so why did her throwaway comment sting like a dart? In the past, things always got a little messy when any of his lovers had said those three little words, and these days he carefully extricated himself from the relationship well before it could happen.

But now he felt a strange sense of emptiness…a hole inside him that opened up like a painful fissure at the thought of Audrey saying those words to another man. He had never said them to anyone apart from his mother and even then he hadn't said them enough times. It was one of his biggest regrets that he hadn't told his mother how much he loved and appreciated her for all the sacrifices she had made for him. He couldn't even remember the last time he'd told her, which was even more distressing.

Audrey did her lip-chewing thing. 'I'm sorry. Have I offended you?'

Lucien quickly rearranged his frowning features into an easy-going smile. 'Why would I be offended?'

'I don't know…you were frowning so heavily, I thought I must have upset you.'

'I was thinking about my mother, actually,' Lucien said. 'I can't remember the last time I told her I loved her before she died. It's niggled at me for years.'

'I'm sure she knew it without your having to say it,' Audrey said. 'You probably showed it in heaps of ways.'

He gave her a crooked smile. 'Maybe.'

There was a little silence.

'Have you told your father you love him?' Audrey asked.

'No.' He had never felt comfortable enough within his relationship with his father to say it. He had only realised he cared about his father in the last few years, especially seeing him go through the last break-up with Sibella. It had made Lucien realise how much he cared about him when he thought he was going to lose him.

And yet he hadn't told him he loved him.

Was it anger that held him back? Anger at the reckless way his father had always lived his life? Anger at the way he had left Lucien's mother to struggle on her own as a single mum with no support? Anger that even now, when his father should be acting responsibly and sensibly, he was doing the opposite?

Audrey winced as if she found the thought of him not saying it to his father painful. 'Maybe you should…you know, before it's too late…or something…'

He let out a long sigh. 'Yeah, maybe I should.' He drummed his fingers on the table for a moment, then pushed back his chair to stand. 'Come on, little lady. Time for some fresh air before bed.'

'Can I use the bathroom first?'

'Sure. I'll settle the bill and wait for you at the front.'

Audrey dashed into the bathroom and checked her phone. The message still hadn't been read by her mother, which meant Sibella had her phone switched off. Normally her mother never switched her phone off in case her agent wanted to call her. It used to drive Audrey crazy whenever she spent time with her because her mother would always be checking her phone instead of listening to her. Why hadn't she thought to ask exactly where her mother and Harlan were staying?

She went back out to where Lucien was waiting for her at the front of the restaurant and when he smiled her heart gave a little kick. They had talked like a real couple over dinner, sharing hurts and disappointments about their lives that she—and she suspected he—had never shared with anyone else.

But they weren't a real couple. Not in the sense that this relationship—this fling—could go any significant distance. Which would have been perfectly fine even a couple of days ago because back then she hadn't seen herself wanting any relationship to go the distance, especially the distance towards marriage and happy-ever-after.

But after running into her mother and seeing the heartfelt love and distress on her face at the thought of permanently losing the love of her life Audrey had undergone a change—a change that both surprised and terrified her. She had promised not to fall in love with Lucien. She had told him it wasn't going to happen.

But hadn't it already happened?

Hadn't she already opened her heart to him both literally and figuratively? By sharing her body with him, by allowing him to be her first lover, it had made it darn near impossible not to fall in love with him. He'd been so gentle and considerate. He insisted on putting her needs ahead of his. He made her feel special. Damn it, he even told her she *was* special. He'd sounded pretty damn convincing.

Was it too much of a pipe dream to hope he might love her?

Lucien led her outside with her arm looped through one of his. The night had cooled down considerably but there were still plenty of people out and about. Audrey hoped none of them would be Harlan or her mother, but who knew what they might want to do, since this might be Harlan's last few months or even weeks of life? They might risk the threat of exposure by the press to enjoy a romantic dinner out, or a leisurely walk through the quaint village at night, when it was less easy to be recognised.

Within a block they came to the restaurant Harlan and Audrey's mother had frequented in the past. 'That's it,' Lucien said. 'It's had a name change but that's the building.' He looked through the window for any sign of his father and Sibella while Audrey's heart began a bumpy ride to her throat.

After a moment, he sighed and turned away from the window. 'No sign of them in there.'

'That's because they're in Barcelona.' Audrey hated lying to him. She felt tainted, soiled by the secret her mother had begged her to keep.

For the first time she saw a tiny flicker of doubt pass across his features. 'Maybe, maybe not.' He gave her arm a gentle pat. 'It's getting late anyway.'

They walked back to their hotel in silence. Audrey felt torn at the way she was keeping her knowledge about his father's illness from him, especially when he'd told her how gutted he'd felt when his mother died. What if something happened and he never got to say those words to his father? She opened her mouth a couple of times on the way back to the hotel but then closed it again. She had made a promise to her mother. And it was Harlan's place to deliver the news to Lucien, not hers. Not only that, but she also knew how determined Lucien was to end Harlan and Sibella's relationship. She had been just as determined a matter of days ago. What would a couple more days do? Her mother had asked—*begged*—for three days to be left alone with Harlan. One of those days was almost over. Two more to go.

'You're very quiet,' Lucien said when they got back to their room.

Audrey forced a smile to her lips. 'Just tired, I guess.'

He gathered her close, brushing her hair back from her face with a touch so gentle it made her heart contract. His eyes searched hers for a pulsing moment before they went to her mouth. 'I told myself I wasn't going to kiss you when we got back here tonight.'

A tiny ping of hurt bruised her chest. 'Why not?'

'Because I can't seem to stop at a kiss any more.' His fingertip moved over her lips like the slow sweep of a sable brush. 'You have done some serious damage to my self-control.'

Audrey leaned closer, her hips pressing against his and her arms going around his waist. 'Yeah, well, mine's not in such good shape, either.'

'That's why I didn't kiss you at the wedding three years ago.'

Audrey blinked. 'You were going to kiss me? Really?'

'Yes. But I knew if I did I might not be able to stop.' He smiled and bent down to brush her mouth with his. 'There. I'll ration myself. One kiss.'

She lifted herself up on tiptoe and pressed a soft kiss to his mouth. 'That's one apiece. Dare you to go two apiece.'

His hands moved so they were cupping her bottom and he drew her closer so she could feel the ridge of his arousal. 'Mmm...not sure that's wise.'

'Go on,' Audrey said. 'You're not going to back down from a dare, are you?'

His eyes glinted. 'You're playing with a fire that is already burning out of control.'

She moved against him and shuddered with the same longing she could feel in his body. 'I don't want you to be in control. I want you to make love to me.'

Regret tightened his expression. 'It's too soon. You need time to—'

'I need you, Lucien,' Audrey said, holding his face in her hands. 'I need you now.'

He lowered his mouth to hers in a long, sensual kiss that made every cell in her body ache for his possession. His tongue entered her mouth in a sexy glide that mimicked the intimate entry of his body, tangling with hers in an erotic combat that made her inner core clench with need. He groaned against her mouth and his hands on her bottom gripped her even tighter against the swollen heat of his erection. 'I want you so damn much it hurts,' he said.

'I want you too,' Audrey said, planting kisses on his mouth one after the other. 'Want, want, want you.'

He led her to the bedroom, stopping every couple of steps to place another kiss on her lips. Once they were in the bedroom, Audrey kicked off her shoes and slipped out of her clothes, her gaze feasting on him as he did the same. They came back together naked, skin-on-skin, and she sighed with delight. 'If anyone had told me a couple of days ago I'd be stripping off my clothes in front of you without flinching in embarrassment I would have said they were certifiably crazy.'

Lucien gave her a teasing smile. 'Does that mean you're not going to blush any more?'

'Urgh. I hate how I blush.'

He stroked a lazy finger down the slope of her cheek. 'I think it's cute. I only have to look at you a certain way and off you go. There. You're doing it now.'

Audrey grimaced. 'That's because you're looking at me like you're going to eat me.'

His eyes glittered and he guided her towards the bed, drawing her down beside him. 'That's exactly what I'm going to do.'

Audrey shivered when his hand came down on her belly, her legs trembling at the thought of the pleasure and raw intimacy to come. He parted her first with his fingers as gently as if she were a precious hothouse orchid that needed careful handling. Then he brought his mouth to her, using his tongue to trace her, sending her senses haywire like a sudden power surge. Electric sensations flickered through her pelvis and down her thighs in little pulses and currents. He continued the sensual torture until she was tipped over the edge of a precipice, falling, falling, falling into an abyss of sublime pleasure that ricocheted through her body, making even the arches of her feet contract. 'Oh. My. God…'

Lucien moved back up her body, planting kisses on her flesh along the way: her hips, her belly, her ribcage and then her breasts, finally making it to her mouth. Tasting her essence on his mouth was so intensely erotic and it made another barrier around her heart come down like paint peeling off a wall. 'You're so sexy when you come,' he said.

Sexy. Now, that was a word she had never used to describe herself. But she felt it when she was with Lucien. She felt sexy and beautiful and…and special. She smiled and traced his mouth with her finger. 'Sexy, huh?'

He captured her finger and sucked on it deeply, releasing it to say, 'Extremely sexy.'

Audrey slipped her hand down to caress him. 'I think you're pretty sexy too.'

He drew in a deep, shuddery breath as her hand moved up and down his shaft. 'You can keep touching me like that if you like.'

'What? And not have you inside me where I want you?'

He placed a gentle hand on her belly once more, his gaze full of concern. 'The last thing I want to do is hurt you again.'

Audrey brought his head down so his mouth was within a breath of hers. 'You worry too much. You won't hurt me.'

For a moment she thought he was going to pull away but then he gave her a lopsided smile. 'See how dangerous you are? You're making me shift all my boundaries.'

Not quite all of them.

It would be foolish to hope he would unlock his heart for her, but who said she wasn't foolish? She'd been foolish from the first moment she'd met him. But that schoolgirl crush had morphed into something far more dangerous. Dangerous because she was never going to be happy with a simple, no-strings fling. How could she have thought she would be? She wasn't built that way. She was more like her mother than she realised. She wanted marriage. She needed the security of a formal commitment.

She needed to be loved, not just lusted over.

Lucien kissed the side of her neck, his evening stubble tickling her skin and making her forget all about her reservations over their current relationship. This was what they had now—this mad lust for each other that made everything else fade into the background.

His mouth came back to hers in a deep kiss that rocked her senses like an earthquake in a glass factory. She shivered as his tongue played with hers, calling it into a seductive dance that made her toes curl with pleasure. He moved down her body, kissing and caressing her breasts, teasing the nipples into hard peaks.

He left her momentarily to reach for a condom, coming back to position himself above her, his legs in a sexy tangle with hers. 'Tell me if I'm going too fast for you.'

'You're not going fast enough,' Audrey said, lifting her hips to receive him, sighing with sheer delight when he entered her with a smooth, slick but gentle thrust. She could feel her body wrap around him, triggering pleasurable sensations in her intimate muscles.

He moved within her body, slowly at first, making sure she was comfortable until increasing his pace. If she hadn't been in love with him before, his lovemaking would have surely tipped her over. She could feel his restraint, the way he was gauging every gasp and whimper of hers, treating her with the utmost care and respect while tantalising her senses into a frenzy of delight. He stroked her intimately to give her that extra bit of friction she needed to finally fly. The orgasm swept her up in a whirlpool that made her thoughts fade to the background until she was only aware of the ripples and waves of ecstasy that were consuming her entire body. His release came soon after hers and she felt it shudder through him. He pressed against her, totally spent, his breathing heavy and uneven against her neck.

Audrey stroked his back and shoulders, content to hold him close in the blissful aftermath. But her thoughts kept drifting to the future…the future he wasn't promising to share with her. Who else would she love other than him? Who else would she want to make love with and lie like this with her body still tingling from his touch? She couldn't imagine a future without him and yet there was no future with him. Not unless he changed his mind. Not unless he fell in love with her as deeply as she had fallen in love with him.

Lucien lifted his head and gave a long, deep sigh, not quite meeting her gaze. 'I guess this was always going to feel a little different with you.' He picked up a strand of her hair and tucked it behind her ear. His eyes meshed with hers for a beat before he looked back at her mouth. 'A nice different, of course.'

'Because we already had a relationship of sorts?' Audrey screwed up her mouth and added, 'Well, hardly a relationship. An acquaintance maybe?'

He gave a wry smile and found another stray hair to tuck away. 'I guess I hadn't realised how much in common we had with our parents, acting like out-of-control teenagers all the time. Plus, I've been fighting this attraction for longer than I care to admit.'

'You're good at hiding what you're feeling. I thought you hated me.'

His crooked smile returned. 'Hate is a strong word. I guess what I hated was the way you made me feel.'

'What did I make you feel?' The question was begging to be asked, so she asked it, even though she was worried she might be disappointed with his answer. But before he could answer there was the sound of her phone ringing from inside her bag in the other room.

'Do you want to get that?' he said.

'Whoever it is can leave a message.'

He frowned. 'What if it's your mother?'

Audrey sighed. 'You're right.' He moved aside so she could get off the bed but before she could get to the bedroom door the phone had stopped. She slipped on a bathrobe, tied the ends loosely and padded out to where her bag was. She took the phone out and saw the missed call was from her mother. She was about to press 'redial' when it started to ring again. There was no way of hiding the call from Lucien because he had followed her out of the bedroom and was standing near by. She took a breath and answered the phone. 'Hello?'

Her mother was a television star but right then her voice sounded as if it were theatre-trained. It projected out of the phone as if she were trying to reach the back row of a five-thousand-seat auditorium. 'Oh, thank God you answered. Harlan's collapsed. He had a seizure and I can't bring him round. Help me. Please help me. I don't know what to do!'

Audrey glanced at Lucien's shocked face and before she could answer he took the phone from her. 'Sibella, it's me, Lucien. Have you called an ambulance?' His brow was so tightly furrowed it looked as if it would split the bones of his skull. 'Where are you?'

Audrey swallowed a triple knot of panic. Panic for Harlan. Panic for her mother. Panic for Lucien. She listened as her mother said they were in St Remy in a farmhouse a short drive away.

'Okay, listen to me,' Lucien's voice was calm and authoritative. 'Give me the address. I'll call an ambulance. You stay with him and check his breathing and pulse. Do you know how to do CPR? Good. Try and stay calm and we'll be there as quickly as we can.'

He ended the call and used Audrey's phone to call an ambulance. She listened to him give the information in that enviably calm voice and wondered how he was ever going to forgive her if his father didn't regain consciousness.

'Get dressed,' he said as soon as he ended the call with the emergency services.

Audrey got dressed and later wondered how she'd managed to do it without putting something on back to front or inside out. Her heart was beating in her throat like a pigeon stuck in a pipe and her palms were sweaty and her legs trembling so much she could barely get them to transport her to Lucien's car.

He drove like a rally driver, only managing to remain within the designated speed limits because he wasn't the sort of man to put others' lives at risk. 'Damn it. I knew they were here,' he said, his hands gripping the steering wheel so tightly she could see the whitened bulge of his knuckles.

Should she tell him she'd known it too? She was ashamed for thinking he might not have to find out. Her mother hadn't said anything to betray her part in the secrecy. There hadn't been time with all the panic that was going on. Maybe nothing would be said. Maybe her part in the cover-up wouldn't be exposed. 'Lucien…' She moistened her bone-dry lips and tried to get her voice to cooperate past that scratchy whisper of sound.

'I *knew* she would do this to him.' He banged one of his hands on the steering wheel with such force she thought it would snap off the steering column. 'I knew she would kill him in the end. They've probably been drinking for days and God knows what else.'

She wanted to express her hurt at his misjudgement of her mother but knew it would be pointless. She sat in a miserable silence, not even able to access the words of comfort she knew she should be giving him at such a harrowing time.

He flicked her a quick glance. 'Sorry. I know she's your mother but if I find out she's played any role in making him unwell…' He didn't finish the sentence but his jaw locked so tightly she could see a muscle working overtime.

'It's okay…'

The ambulance had already arrived by the time they found the farmhouse. Lucien rushed inside with Audrey just as they were loading his still unconscious father onto the stretcher. He went to his father's side and grasped one of his limp hands. 'Dad?'

It nearly tore Audrey's heart out of her chest to hear him say that word. She had never heard him refer to his father as anything but 'Harlan' or 'my father'.

Audrey's mother stood wringing her hands and sobbing uncontrollably. Audrey went to her and gathered her close, trying her best to comfort her but knowing it would never be enough. 'Try not to panic, Mum. They'll take good care of him. The sooner he's in hospital the better.'

Sibella pulled out of Audrey's hold. 'I need to go in the ambulance with him.'

'No,' Lucien said, stepping in the way.

Sibella straightened like a flagpole defying a hurricane. 'You can't stop me, Lucien. You're not his next of kin. I am. I'm his wife. We got married yesterday.'

CHAPTER NINE

AUDREY HAD NEVER seen anyone look more furious than Lucien at that point. But somehow he managed to control himself enough to step aside to let her mother get into the back of the ambulance. His eyes flashed like lightning when he took Audrey's hand to lead her back to his car, the grip of his hand around hers painfully tight. 'No doubt they've been celebrating ever since they tied the knot. He's probably got alcohol poisoning or something. Excessive alcohol can cause swelling on the brain. It can set off seizures.'

She closed her eyes for a brief moment, wishing she could open them again and find this was all a bad dream. 'Lucien…there's something I—'

'You know what really gets to me?' he said before she could complete her sentence. 'The way she crowed about their marriage. What was that about next of kin? I'm his only child. *I'm* his next of kin. She's just another one of the wives he's loved and who's left him.'

Audrey drew in a breath that clawed at her throat like a fishhook. 'She *is* his legal next of kin, Lucien. That's the whole point of marrying someone you love—so they can be with you at all the important stages of your life. He wanted to marry her and he did. You shouldn't be questioning it. You have to accept it. They love each other and want to spend any time that's remaining with each other.'

She felt his glance like the thrust of a dagger. The silence building in tension, stretching, stretching, stretching like an elastic band pulled too tight.

'You knew they were here.' He thumped the steering wheel again, his breath leaving his mouth in a rush. 'You knew they were here, didn't you?'

Audrey couldn't look at him and looked instead at her hands in her lap. 'I've been trying to tell you—'

'When did you find out?' His voice was so hard she was surprised it didn't shatter the window on her side of the car.

'Today.'

'Today?' She could almost hear the cogs of his brain ticking over. 'Before or after we had sex?'

Audrey put a hand to her forehead. 'Don't do this, Lucien. Please. Isn't everyone upset enough without—?'

'You've taken prostitution to a whole new level.' The words were as savage as lethal arrows. 'You saw your mother at the market, didn't you? You saw her and then lied to me. You lied to me and then offered yourself like some sort of boudoir distraction to stop me from continuing the search.'

She swallowed without speaking, unable to look at him, unable to witness the caustic loathing and hatred she could hear in his words.

'Answer me, damn it!'

Audrey flinched and fought back tears. 'I made a promise—'

'A promise?' Scorn dripped from his tone like corrosive acid.

'I ran into my mother at the market and she begged me not to tell you that your father was unwell with a brain tumour,' Audrey said. 'She wanted to talk him into having surgery. He was refusing all treatment and she was trying to talk him round. She loves him, Lucien, and he loves her. They want to be together with whatever time is remaining. They were both worried you would try and talk them out of being together. I agreed to keep their location a secret because...because I wish someone loved me like that.'

Her words dropped into a cavernous silence.

'Let me get this straight...you've known since earlier today that my father was critically unwell and you didn't see it as a priority to inform me of that fact?'

How could she explain her motivations when he put it like that? How could she tell Lucien his father hadn't wanted him to know about his illness until after he was married to her mother? It seemed too cruel to dump that on him now when he was already so upset. 'I made a promise to my—'

'I don't care what promise you made to your mother,' he said. 'This is about my father, not your mother. I had the right to know he was unwell.'

'I know... I'm sorry. I should have told you but I didn't want to hurt her. She trusted me and I wanted to honour that trust.'

'And what about the trust that had developed between us?' His eyes bored into hers, as determined as a drill through steel. 'Didn't that count for something?'

'We're having a fling, Lucien. It's not the same as a committed or formal relationship.'

He pulled into the hospital entrance with a squeal of brakes. He parked the car before he spoke, his hand still gripping the steering wheel with white-knuckled force. He didn't turn to look at her but stared fixedly straight ahead. 'Would you have entered into a fling with me if you hadn't run into your mother today?' His voice was so cold it made her skin shiver.

'Yes. Yes, I would.'

His glance was so pointed she felt as if she'd been jabbed with a pin. 'Sorry but I don't believe you. You offered yourself to me because you knew it would be enough of a distraction to stop me trawling the streets of the village.'

She took a breath and continued. 'That's not true. I wanted to make love with you. I settled for a fling but I think we could have more than that, Lucien. I think you know that too. We're good together—you said it yourself. You said how different it was between us than your other—'

'Oh, you thought this was going to *go* somewhere?' The derision in his tone was as savage as a switchblade. 'So you lied to me about that too. You told me you never wanted to get married. But all the time you've been hanging out for the fairy tale. Well, guess what? It's over. I'm ending it right here, right now. I should have trusted my instincts and left you well alone.'

Audrey had been preparing herself for this moment

but now that it had come it was even more devastating than she'd thought. He was upset, of course he was, and he had every right to be. She would be too if the situation was reversed. He needed time to come to terms with the shock of his father's illness. Maybe he would change his mind once he talked to his father...her stomach swooped...*if* he ever got the chance to talk to his father. 'Can we talk about this later, when you've had time to—?'

'Did you hear me?' His voice contained an edge of steel that made every hair on her head shiver at the roots. 'I said it's over.'

Audrey couldn't look at him and quietly gathered her bag from the floor. 'I'm just going to see my mother and then I'll get a cab back to the hotel to collect my things. I'll stay with her until the...the crisis is over with your father.'

'Fine.'

Fine? Was that all he could say after what they'd shared? Nothing was fine about this. Audrey's heart felt like it was jammed between two solid, splinter-ridden planks, every breath she took increasing the pressure. Her eyes stung with tears but she refused to cry in front of him. She couldn't bear the humiliation of him witnessing her heartbreak.

She followed him into the hospital but he barely gave her a glance. He went straight to the desk to ask where his father had been taken and Audrey peeled away to find her mother.

She was in the waiting room outside the emergency room and Audrey went straight to her and enveloped her in a hug. 'Oh, Mum, I'm so sorry. Is there any news?'

Sibella lifted her tear-stained face off Audrey's shoulder, her bottom lip trembling. 'They're going to do a CAT scan to see what's going on. They think he's having some sort of intracranial bleed from the tumour. They're going to fly him to Paris for surgery because they don't have the facilities here. I can't bear the thought of losing him. Not now that I've finally got him back.'

'I know, it's so sad,' Audrey said, blinking back her own tears. 'But you've been with him for the last few days and made him as happy as you could. Hold on to that.'

'We had such a lovely wedding ceremony,' Sibella said, taking the tissue Audrey handed her and mopping at her eyes. 'So intimate and private at the farmhouse in the garden. I'm sorry I didn't invite you and Lucien but Harlan wanted it to be just us this time. No fanfare. No fuss. Just us.'

'I think you did the right thing,' Audrey said. 'I'm glad you two got married again. I couldn't be happier for you. Well, I could if Harlan wasn't so unwell.'

Her mother looked at her with reddened eyes. 'You really mean that, don't you?'

Audrey smiled. 'Perhaps you and Harlan do belong together. You're lucky to have experienced such passionate love not once but three times. I hope and pray he gets through this so you can prove all the doubters wrong.'

'Speaking of doubters,' Sibella said, glancing past

Audrey for any sign of Lucien, 'I hope I haven't made things difficult between you and Lucien.'

Audrey wasn't going to burden her mother with her own heartbreak at this point, if ever. Sibella had enough emotion to deal with without Audrey dumping more on her. 'No, it's fine. He's upset about his father, of course. It's been a terrible shock for him.'

Her mother's gaze searched hers. 'You're not in love with him or anything, are you?'

'In love?' Audrey made an attempt at a laugh but it sounded more like a choke. 'We had a bit of a fling but we've called time on it. It was never going to work. I'm not his type and he's not mine.'

Sibella chewed at her lower lip for a moment, her brow creased in a tiny frown. 'It's not always about being the right type of person, sweetie. It's about the right type of love you feel for each other. It took me three times to find that love with Harlan but now I've found it I'm going to hold on to it no matter what.'

'Lucien doesn't love me, Mum,' Audrey said in a quiet voice. 'I don't think he's capable of loving anyone like that.'

'Mrs Fox?' A doctor with an English accent came towards them and stopped in front of Sibella. 'The air patient transfer has been arranged so we're taking your husband soon. He's not conscious but if you'd like to spend a couple of minutes with him before the flight to Paris that would be okay.'

'Oh, thank you,' Sibella said and followed the doctor away to where Harlan was being held.

Audrey sighed and went back to the waiting room to

wait for her mother to return, wondering if it would have been wiser to leave now before there was any chance of running into Lucien. Had he had a chance to spend time with his father?

Lucien walked out of the hospital after speaking to his father's doctor and stood for a moment trying to get his emotions under control. His father had cancer. A brain tumour. It was operable but the risks of permanent damage were huge. His fun-loving, irresponsible and reckless father might turn into a comatose body on a ventilator. He couldn't understand why his father hadn't told him he was ill. He handled all his father's financial affairs, fixed up every mess and monitored every detail of his father's life and yet his father had shut him out of this health crisis. What sort of father did that to his only son? Didn't his father realise how much he cared about him?

But it was Audrey's role in the cover-up that was eating at him the most. She had only slept with him to distract him from finding out where his father and Sibella were. He'd thought…he'd thought… Damn it. He wasn't going to think about it now. He wasn't going to think their relationship was different from anything he'd experienced before because it wasn't different. It was just a fling that had turned sour. But it had only turned sour because she'd deceived him. Openly lied to his face, making him believe…

No. No. No. Don't go there.

He had to stop thinking she might have been The One. The one person—the only person—he could see himself building a future with that involved trust and openness and, yes, even love. But it was all a bald-faced lie. Their relationship had sprung up out of her desperation to keep him from the truth about his father's and her mother's whereabouts.

Had she been working against him from the start?

He mentally backtracked through the last couple of days, wondering how he could have been so stupid to be hoodwinked by lust. That was all it was, of course. Lust. He refused to consider it as anything else. He'd lusted after her and she'd seen it as an opportunity to manipulate him. Now his father was dying and his next of kin was that attention-seeking, wine-swilling witch Sibella, who gloated over his father's unconscious body about her brand-new status as his wife.

For the third freaking time.

Lucien dragged in a lungful of cool night air, trying to loosen the tight feeling in his chest. It might be hours before his father came out of surgery in Paris. It might be hours, days even, before there was news, either good or bad. He didn't want to see Audrey. He never wanted to see her again. Seeing her would remind him of every cunning and clever lie she'd told him and how he'd foolishly fallen for it.

Fallen for her.

No. Damn it. No. He'd fallen in lust. He wasn't going to name it as anything else. What was the point in admitting she had done what no other woman had done? What he had allowed no other woman to do. He had lost his head over her. Lost everything he had worked so hard to maintain. Her betrayal had stung him, more than stung him, but it was the fact she had got into his heart that hurt the most. He should never have allowed it to happen. He should have taken greater care. He should have resisted her.

Lust, not love. Lust, not love. Lust, not love. If he had to say it like a mantra until he believed it then that was what he would damn well do.

Lust was all it was and now it was over.

CHAPTER TEN

AUDREY HADN'T BOTHERED collecting her things from the hotel and had flown with her mother to Paris as soon as she could organise a flight. By the time they arrived at the large and busy Paris hospital, Harlan was still on a ventilator but the bleed had been controlled and a large section of the tumour had been removed. The neurosurgeon had expressed cautious optimism that Harlan would regain consciousness in a few days when the swelling had receded.

Audrey had been terrified of running into Lucien when she and her mother came to the hospital, but, given the size of the place, somehow she had managed to miss him and hadn't seen him since the night they'd followed the ambulance to the smaller hospital in St Remy.

The time spent supporting her mother was just the distraction she needed to take her mind off her own heartache. But in spite of the warm and loving chats with her mother, the visits to the hospital and the day-to-day duties she assigned herself at the small Airbnb they were staying in, Audrey still had plenty of time to feel the stinging pain of Lucien's rejection. How different would this time be if he'd allowed her to support him as well as her mother?

How different would it be if he loved her as she loved him?

Audrey wanted what her mother had with Harlan this third time around. The right type of love. A mature and lasting love. A love that wanted the best for the other partner—a love that gave sacrificially instead of selfishly taking.

But Lucien had locked his heart away and built an impenetrable fortress around it. It pained her to think he thought so badly of her after all they'd shared. But he had refused to listen to her explanation and had cut her coldly and clinically and cruelly from his life.

On day five Harlan woke when his doctors removed him from the ventilator. The first person he asked for was Sibella and Audrey sat outside ICU while her mother was taken in to see him. She couldn't help thinking how special it must be to be the first person a desperately ill patient asked for when they woke from a coma. Would she ever be that special person to someone? Would anyone love her the way Harlan loved her mother? Or would she always be lonely like this? Sitting alone in the waiting room of life.

When her mother came out a short time later she was crying but with happy tears. 'Oh, sweetie, he's awake and even managed to make a joke. He's still not out of danger but the doctors think he might be well enough for chemo in a week or two, if we can convince him to go through it.'

Audrey hugged her mother so tightly she worried she might snap a rib. 'I'm so glad he's made it this far. So very glad.'

Sibella pulled back from the hug but still held on to Audrey's arms. 'He's asking for Lucien. Do you think you could call him? I'm not sure he'll take a call from me.'

Or from me.

Audrey took out her phone and pulled up his number. Even seeing his name there on her screen made her heart clench and her stomach sink. She pressed 'dial' and held the phone to her ear but it went straight to his message service. She tried to think of something to say but her mouth wouldn't cooperate. In the end she hung up the phone and sighed and faced her mother. 'No answer.'

'I suppose the hospital will call him,' Sibella said and scraped a hand through her blonde tresses. 'I could do with a drink.' She grinned cheekily at Audrey's frown. 'Coffee, okay? Harlan and I are booked in to do couple's rehab. I reckon we'll have more chance of kicking the habit better together than doing it alone.'

Audrey smiled and linked her arm through her mother's. 'Coffee sounds great.'

Lucien sat by his father's bedside in ICU later that day when he'd flown back in from London. He'd had some work to see to for a client awaiting his report for court so he hadn't had any choice but to fly back to London and sort it out. His father had been sleeping on and off but had woken a couple of times to speak to him. It was strange having that time with his father. Alone time, if you could call it that when you were surrounded by machines and monitors and multiple medical staff milling about as they attended to their duties.

Whenever he'd spent time with his father in the past there were always managers or publicists or other band members about. When he'd met his father for the first time when he was ten years old there'd been twenty other people in the room.

But now it felt as if it was just the two of them. A father and his son just…hanging out.

Harlan opened his eyes again and gave Lucien a lop-sided smile. 'I thought you'd have something better to do than hang around here.'

'Nowhere I'd rather be right now.'

Harlan's eyes watered. 'I haven't been a good father to you, Lucien. Thing is… I didn't know how to be a dad. Mine was a mean, sadistic bastard who beat my mother up and sold our belongings to feed his gambling habit. Beat me up too. Heaps of times.' His fingers gripped the sheet under his hand as if he was remembering each and every blow of his father's fists. 'It made me worried I might do the same…you know…if I got too close to you.'

Lucien had never heard his father mention his own father. He'd had no idea his dad's childhood had been so grim. Was that why his dad drank and partied to cover up his pain at how he'd been treated? He took his dad's hand, suddenly realising it was the first time he had ever touched him in such an affectionate way. 'You're a better father than I am a son. I've been too critical of you, too judgemental. I haven't taken the time to see the man behind the fame.'

Harlan squeezed Lucien's hand. 'I know you don't care for Sibella but I love her and want to spend whatever time I have left with her. We've been bad for each other in the past but we've made some changes. Good changes. Tough changes. I hope one day you get to feel the same sort of love for someone. Don't settle for anything less. Promise me that.'

Lucien was finding it hard to find his voice. He had already found that sort of love. What he felt for Audrey was so much more than lust. If it had been simply lust then why was he still feeling so empty? Why was he feeling like his heart had been severed from his chest? He'd been pushing his feelings from his mind. Shoving them back like a shirt in his wardrobe he couldn't bring himself to look at for the memories it triggered. He hadn't been able to stop thinking about her. Torn between dreading running into her at the hospital and yet feeling bitterly, achingly disappointed when he didn't. Tempted to call her so much he'd turned off his phone. He'd pushed her away because he'd believed she had disappointed him, betrayed him. Lied to him.

But who was the bigger liar?

He was. He'd been lying to himself for years. Six years. It had started when Audrey flirted with him at his dad's first wedding to her mother. And he'd continued lying to himself when Audrey approached him the second time, smiling up at him with those big brown eyes of hers.

And what had he done? Each time he'd pushed her

away. Cruelly rejected her. She'd given herself to him. He was her first and only lover. Didn't that mean something?

His gut clenched, his heart gave a spasm and regret tasted like bile in his mouth.

It meant he'd made a terrible mistake.

Lucien brought himself back to his conversation with his father with an effort. 'Why didn't you tell me you were ill? I could have organised the best medical—'

'I made Sibella promise not to tell you,' Harlan said. 'I wanted her to know first, and then, when we got the wedding out of the way, we were going to tell you and Audrey. I didn't want either of you to try and talk us out of it. You know what you two are like. Fricking fun police, the pair of you.'

Lucien swallowed again. 'So when did Audrey find out you were ill?'

'When she ran into Sibella the other day,' Harlan said. 'She made Audrey promise not to tell you because that's what I wanted. I insisted on telling you in person but only when I was ready to. She was only acting on my wishes, Lucien. Please don't be too offended I didn't tell you first. But you have to understand Sibella's my go-to person now. The person I want to tell everything to, the good stuff and the bad stuff. It doesn't mean I don't love you. I do in my own inept and clumsy way.'

Lucien put his other hand on top of his father's and somehow managed a smile. 'I love you, too... Dad.'

Harlan blinked away tears but he was still wearing his bad-boy rock star smile. 'If you tell anyone I've been bawling like a teething baby I'll have to kill you, okay?'

* * *

Lucien walked out of ICU a short time later in a daze.
What had he done? He'd destroyed his only chance at
happiness with Audrey. He'd ruthlessly, cruelly cut her
from his life. He hadn't given her time to explain anything. If only he'd listened. If only he'd realised his
feelings for her weren't a bad thing. She was the best
thing that had ever happened to him. Just like Sibella
was for his father. The love Sibella and his father shared
had matured into something that could withstand illness, even death.

It was exactly the sort of love he felt for Audrey. He
had fought so hard not to fall for her. He had fought
so hard not to lose control. But she had been too much
for his willpower. She had always been too much for
his willpower, which was why he'd held her aloft for
so long.

His chest cramped as if someone had kicked him
square in the heart. What if he'd lost her? Was it too
late to tell her? Was it too late to hope she might forgive her? Sweat prickled his back and shoulders. A
sick feeling churned in his stomach. He couldn't lose
her. Not now. Not now he'd finally realised he'd been
waiting for this sort of love for most of his adult life.

He couldn't lose her.

Oh, God. If he lost her…

Audrey left her mother chatting to some fans in the
hospital cafeteria. The press had been around when
they'd first arrived at the hospital but she had managed
to avoid them. Sibella had issued a press release about

Harlan's condition and asked for privacy and, thankfully, that was mostly what they'd had. Now that Harlan was a little better, Audrey knew it would soon be time for her to go back to London. She knew she should have already made arrangements well before now but hadn't been able to let go of a gossamer thread of hope Lucien might seek her out and tell her he'd changed his mind.

She was walking along the wide corridor when she saw him walking towards her. She considered darting into one of the storage rooms out of sight, but his stride length increased and so did his speed. Before she could make up her mind which door to choose he was within arm's reach. 'Audrey?' The way he said her name made her heart skip. Was that a note of...of desperation in his voice?

She kept her face blank and turned with her spine so rigid and straight it looked as if she'd just graduated as star pupil from deportment school. 'Yes?'

His expression was hard to read but she thought she could see a flicker of worry in his eyes. 'I need to talk to you.'

'I think you've said all that needs to be—'

He held her by the upper arms, his voice gruff and with that same note of desperation she'd heard before. 'Please, sweetheart. Just hear me out. I know I don't deserve it after the way I cut you from my life the other day. I was wrong to blame you for not telling me about my father's illness. You were acting on his wishes and I would've done exactly the same if the tables were turned.'

Audrey wasn't ready to forgive him. Why should

she when he'd treated her so cruelly? He could apologise all he liked but it wasn't an apology she wanted from him. She wanted his love and that was unlikely to be why he was standing in front of her now. He was too proud a man to grovel. He was probably clearing his conscience after his cosy little chat with his father. 'Oh, so now you're apologising because he's told you he was the one who insisted you not be told? How terribly gallant of you, Lucien.'

He gave a slow blink as if her words pained him like a vicious stab but he still maintained his hold on her arms. 'I'd already realised I loved you before my father told me he'd insisted I not be told.' His hands slid down her arms to grasp her hands, holding them gently. 'I love you, Audrey. I think I've been in love with you ever since you hit on me at our parents' first wedding.'

Audrey couldn't find her voice. She opened and closed her mouth and blinked a couple of times to make sure she wasn't imagining this conversation. 'You…you love me? Really and truly love me?'

He smiled a wide smile that made his dark blue eyes shine. 'Really and truly and desperately love you. I've been such a fool for denying it all this time. I don't know why I did. It's so obvious you're the only one for me. You're the other half of my heart. I feel so empty without you. Will you marry me, sweetheart?'

Audrey beamed up at him and threw her arms around his neck. 'You're the only person I want to marry. I love you. I don't want anyone else but you. I think that's why I never dated all these years because I've been secretly waiting for you.'

'The wait is over, my darling,' Lucien said, holding her close. 'We belong together. I can't imagine how miserable my life would be without you in it.'

'I was so sad when you ended our fling—'

'Don't call it that ever again.' He grimaced as if in pain. 'It was never a fling. It was never just about lust, even though I kept telling myself it was. It was always about love. How could I have been so deluded as to convince myself otherwise?'

'I did it too,' Audrey said, holding on to him to keep herself from falling over out of sheer relief and joy. 'I pretended I hated you. I couldn't even hear your name mentioned without wanting to grind my teeth to powder. But I was always a bit in love with you.'

He grimaced again. 'I can't bear to think we might have missed out on being together. I've been such an idiot. Forgive me? Please?'

'Of course I forgive you. I love you.'

He brushed her hair back from her face. 'I want to build a life together. Do you want children? God, I can't believe I'm even asking that in a hospital corridor.'

'Do you want them?'

'I asked first.'

Audrey gazed into his twinkling eyes. 'I only want them if they're yours.'

He smiled and brought his mouth down to hers. 'I'll see what I can do.'

EPILOGUE

Ten months later...

LUCIEN SAT NEXT to Audrey at the dining table at Bramble Cottage. She reached for his hand under the table and, smiling at him, gave it a squeeze. His heart gave a leap just as it always did when her beautiful brown eyes looked at him like that. He smiled back and winked at her and, yes, she still blushed.

'Hey, you two, the honeymoon should be well and truly over by now,' Harlan said, from the other side of the table. His hair hadn't grown back yet from the gruelling chemo but his cranial scar was fading and his specialists were happy with his progress so far. So far. No promises were being made about a complete recovery but Lucien was determined that, no matter what awaited them in the weeks and months ahead, his father's happiness would be a top priority.

And no one made his dad happier than Sibella.

'Like you can talk,' Lucien said, smiling at the way his father's arm was around Sibella's shoulders and how she was beaming at Harlan with such love in her eyes it made him feel ashamed of how he had misjudged her in the past. His father and Sibella weren't perfect, but he had come to a place where he accepted them as they were and didn't expect them to change to suit him.

'Mum, Dad, we have something to tell you,' Audrey said, looking like she was about to burst with the secret she'd been keeping for the last couple of weeks until they hit the twelve-week mark in their pregnancy.

It just about made Lucien's heart explode with emotion every time she called his father 'Dad'. It spoke of the deep affection she had for his father, and her care and concern and nursing abilities over the last few months had made Lucien, and of course his father, love her all the more.

And now Lucien was to become a father. In the not so distant future a little person would look up at him and call him Dad.

'Will you tell them or will I?' Audrey said, smiling at him.

He took her hand and brought it up to his mouth. 'Let's do it together.'

And so they did.

* * * * *

COMING SOON!

We really hope you enjoyed reading this book. If you're looking for more romance, be sure to head to the shops when new books are available on

Thursday
12th July

To see which titles are coming soon, please visit
millsandboon.co.uk

MILLS & BOON

MILLS & BOON

Coming next month

MARRIAGE MADE IN BLACKMAIL
Michelle Smart

'You want me to move?'

'Yes.'

A gleam pulsed in his eyes. 'Make me.'

Instead of closing her hand into a fist and aiming it at his nose as he deserved, Chloe placed it flat on his cheek.

An unwitting sigh escaped from her lips as she drank in the ruggedly handsome features she had dreamed about for so long. The texture of his skin was so different from her own, smooth but with the bristles of his stubble breaking through...had he not shaved? She had never seen him anything other than clean-shaven.

His face was close enough for her to catch the faint trace of coffee and the more potent scent of his cologne.

Luis was the cause of all this chaos rampaging through her. She hated him so much but the feelings she'd carried for him for all these years were still there, refusing to die, making her doubt herself and what she'd believed to be the truth.

Her lips tingled, yearning to feel his mouth on hers again, all her senses springing to life and waving surrender flags at her.

Just kiss him...

Closing her eyes tightly, Chloe gathered all her wits about her, wriggled out from under him and sat up.

Her lungs didn't want to work properly and she had to force air into them.

She shifted to the side, needing physical distance, suddenly terrified of what would happen if she were to brush against him or touch him in any form again.

Fighting to clear her head of the fog clouding it, she blinked rapidly and said, 'Do I have your word that your feud with Benjamin ends with our marriage?'

Things had gone far enough. It was time to put an end to it.

'*Sí.* Marry me and it ends.'

Continue reading
MARRIAGE MADE IN BLACKMAIL
Michelle Smart

Available next month
www.millsandboon.co.uk

LET'S TALK
Romance

For exclusive extracts, competitions
and special offers, find us online:

f facebook.com/millsandboon

◎ @millsandboonuk

🐦 @millsandboon

Or get in touch on 0844 844 1351*

For all the latest titles coming soon, visit
millsandboon.co.uk/nextmonth

*Calls cost 7p per minute plus your phone company's price per minute access charge